GODDESS OF LIGHT

UNDERWORLD GODS

BOOK FOUR

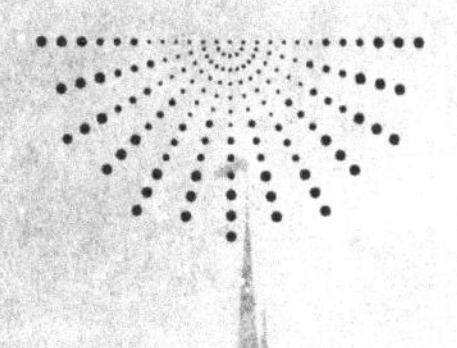

KARINA HALLE

Cover: Hang Le

Editing: The Fiction Fix

Proofing: Laura Helseth

Art of Hanna by: Joanna Hadzhieva

All other images: Adobe Stock

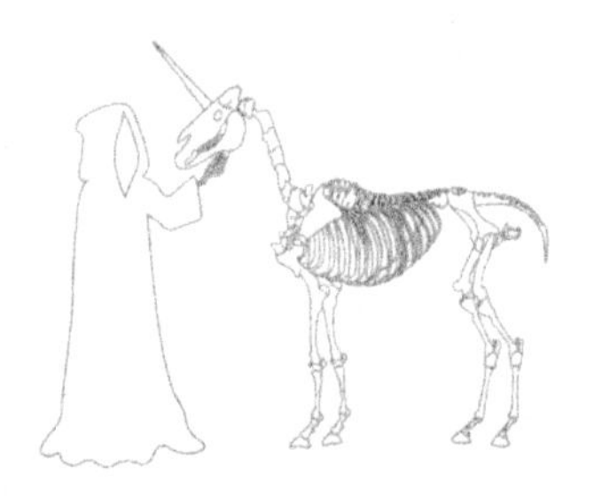

GODDESS OF LIGHT

To those who are soft; your humanity isn't your weakness, it's your superpower

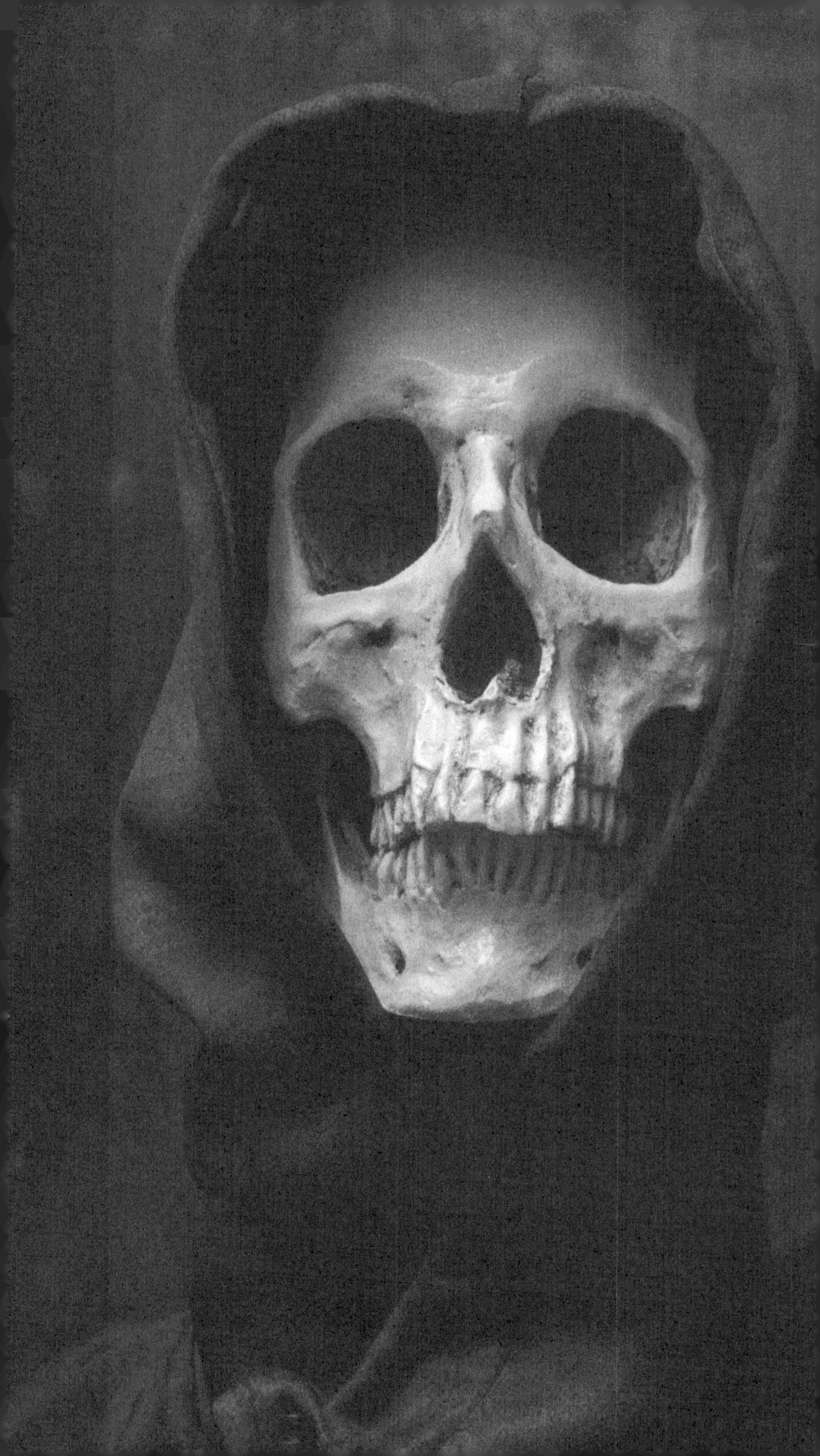

GODDESS OF LIGHT

The battle for the Underworld has begun...

When Hanna Heikkinen sacrificed herself to the God of Death to save her father, she never imagined she'd fall in love with the grumpy God—or thrive as Queen of Tuonela. Nor did she expect to uncover the truth of her divine lineage, a secret tied to powers far beyond her understanding.

But when the Old Gods rise and Louhi's dark forces plunge the Land of the Dead into *Kaaos,* threatening to destroy the balance of life and death, Hanna must fight for more than just her realm.

With Tuonela unraveling and the souls of the dead at risk of eternal Oblivion, Hanna and Tuoni face impossible odds as love and duty collide.

Can Hanna save Tuonela before it's lost to the void, or will her greatest sacrifice come at the cost of the one she loves most?

Goddess of Light **is the conclusion to Underworld Gods, a romantasy series based on Finnish mythology. Reading order:** ***River of Shadows, Crown of Crimson, City of Darkness, Goddess of Light.***

Tuonela
Realm of the Dead
Death's Landing
The Frozen Void
Ice River
Great
Inland
Sea
Castle Syntri
Star Swamp
The Shaman Way
River of Shadows
The Hiisi Forest
Pile of Decay
Gorge of Despair
The Leikkio Plains
Mountain Lair
Iron Mountains
City of Death
The Grotto

Mountains of Vipunen
Death's Passage
Crystal caves
Evernight Point
Shadow's End

GLOSSARY & PRONOUNCIATION

Tuonela (too-oh-nella)

Realm or Land of the Dead. It is a large island that floats between worlds, with varied geography and terrain. The recently deceased travel via the River of Shadows to the City of Death, where they are divided into factions (Amaranthus, the Golden Mean, and Inmost) and admitted into the after-life. Outside the City of Death, Gods, Goddesses, spirits, shamans, and the dead who have escaped the city can be found.

Tuoni (too-oh-nee)

The God of Death, otherwise called Death, and King of Tuonela, who rules over the realm from his castle at Shadow's End.

Louhi (low-hee)

Ex-wife of Death, former Goddess, half-demon daughter of Rangaista.

Loviatar (low-vee-ah-tar)

The Lesser Goddess of Death and Death's daughter. Her job is to ferry the dead down the River of Shadows to the City of Death, a role she shares with her brother Tuonen.

Tuonen (too-oh-nen)

The Lesser God of Death and Death's Son. He shares ferrying duties with his sister, Loviatar. Tuonen is also a lord in the City of Death and helps oversee things in the afterlife.

Sarvi (sar-vih)

Short for Yksisarvinen, Sarvi is a relic from the times of the Old Gods and originally from another world. Sarvi is a unicorn with bat-like wings who died a long time ago and is composed of skin and bone. Sentient, Sarvi is able to communicate telepathically. While he is a loyal and refined servant to Death, he is also vicious, violent, and bloodthirsty by nature, as all unicorns are.

Ilmarinen (ill-mar-ee-nen)

Louhi's consort, the demigod shaman she left Death for. He lives with Louhi in their castle by the Star Swamps.

Eero (ay-ro)

A powerful shaman from Northern Finland.

Väinämöinen (vah-ee-nah-moy-nen)
Death's past adversary and legendary shaman, who became a Finnish folk-hero.

Ukko (oo-koh)
A supreme God and the father of Tuoni, Ahto, and Ilmatar. Husband to Akka.

Akka (ah-ka)
A supreme Goddess, wife to Ukko, and the mother of Tuoni, Ahto, and Ilmatar.

Ilmatar (ill-mah-tar)
Goddess of the Air, sister to Tuoni and Ahto.

Vellamo (vell-ah-mo)
Goddess of the Deep, wife of Ahto. Protector of mermaids. Vellamo can be found in the Great Inland Sea.

Ahto (ah-to)
God of the Oceans and Seas, husband of Vellamo, brother of Tuoni and Ilmatar.

Kuutar (koo-tar)
Goddess of the Moon, Mother of Stars, protector of sea creatures.

Päivätär (pah-ee-vah-tar)
Goddess of the Sun, protector of birds.

Kalma (kahl-ma)
God of Graves and Tuoni's right-hand man and advisor.

Surma (soor-mah)

A relic from the days of the Old Gods and the personification of killing.

Raila (ray-lah)
Hanna's personal Deadmaiden.

Pyry (pee-ree)
Deadmaiden. Head cook and gardener of Shadow's End.

Harma (har-mah)
Deadmaiden. Head of the Shadow's End servants.

Tapio (tah-pee-oh)
God of the Forest.

Tellervo (tell-air-voh)
Lesser Goddess of the Forest and daughter of Tapio.

Mielikki (mi-eh-li-kee)
Goddess of the Forest, Tapio's wife

Nyyrikki (nye-rick-ee)
Lesser God of the Forest, brother to Tellervo

Hiisi (hee-si)
Demons and goblins of Tuonela, spawns of Rangaista.

Rangaista (ran-gais-tah)
A powerful demon and Old God, father of Louhi.

Liekkiö (lehk-kio)
The spirits of murdered children who haunt the Leikkio Plains. They are made of bones and burn eternally.

Vipunen (vee-pooh-nen)

An unseen giant who lives in the Caves of Vipunen near Shadow's End. The most ancient and wise being in Tuonela from before the time of the Old Gods.

Keskelli (kes-kell-ee)

Friendly trolls that live in the Frozen Void

PLAYLIST

"The Prophecy" – Taylor Swift

"I am not a woman, I'm a god" – Halsey

"Don't Say You Love Me" – Depeche Mode

"And Nothing is Forever" – The Cure

"The Night Does Not Belong to God" – Sleep Token

"Help Me I Am in Hell" – NIN

"Dark Signs" – Sleep Token

"Who's Afraid of Little Old Me?" – Taylor Swift

"Into the Void" – NIN

"God Games" – The Kills

"Combat" – Deftones

"The Great Destroyer" – NIN (Modwheelmod version)

"God Given" – NIN (Stephen Morris and Gillian Gilbert version)

"Risk" – Deftones

"Gods" – Sleep Token

"March of the Pigs" – NIN

"Kingdome Come" – The Kills

"Always You" – Depeche Mode

"Going to Heaven" – The Kills

"Warsong" – The Cure
"I Let Love In" – Nick Cave and the Bad Seeds
"Hole in the Earth" – Deftones
"Last Rites" – +++ (Crosses)
"Castle" – Halsey
"Everything in its Right Place" – Radiohead
"The Epilogue" – +++ (Crosses)
"Endsong" – The Cure

CHAPTER ONE

HANNA

When I was young, maybe eight years old, I visited my father in Finland during the height of summer. I remember the days were long and warm, and the woods held so much life, every day was an adventure to me. My father was happy to let me play by myself or with the kids who lived on the other side of the lake but, sometimes, he would take me on nature walks for hours at a time.

One day, the two of us had walked deep into the woods behind our house, where the pines grew so tall, they blocked out the sky. It was dark, strangely so, like I was seeing everything through a black veil. I remember being a little afraid, but my father held my hand and told me the woods were always looking out for me.

Eventually, he led me to a small clearing with a ring of moss-covered stones in the middle. There was a quiet stillness that suddenly fell around us, something so deep, it felt as if even the wind dared not enter the circle.

My father knelt, reaching into his pockets and spreading wild herbs across the stones, murmuring words in Finnish, words I should have understood but didn't. I had always found his voice comforting, almost jolly, yet here, it carried a weight that made my chest tighten, as if his words had a power of their own. I felt something stir within myself, a feeling I couldn't quite place—like a memory or a dream. Something old, maybe even something that didn't belong to me.

"Close your eyes, Hanna," he'd whispered, his voice reverent. "Feel the earth beneath you."

I remember dropping to my knees beside him and pressing my small hands to the stones. I expected it to feel cool, but instead, it was slowly warming, like sunlight breaking through clouds. There was a pulse beneath my palms, as if energy was being pushed back into my skin, enough that I had to pull my hands away. When I opened my eyes, my father looked at me with an expression I didn't understand—something like pride, sadness, and knowing all at once.

I never understood that moment, never understood what it meant. It had always stayed dormant in the back of my head, like a dream you forget upon waking.

But now, I know. I don't remember anything else—if he said something, if he ever explained what the stones meant and why we were there, but it doesn't matter. He was trying to see if I was a pure mortal or something more. He was trying to see how much of my mother—my real mother—I had in me.

The mother I'm staring at right now.

"Hanna, your mother is here," the Goddess of the Sea says, but I know this without Vellamo's announcement. I know it from the bone-warming heat, from the radiant light that fills the forest where we're hunkering down for the night. I know it from this strange feeling of deep affection, something both beautiful and sad, a longing for something I never knew.

Something I had lost then found.

At first, my mother is just light. It's like staring into the sun, but it doesn't hurt your eyes, doesn't make you squint. It's powerful and gentle all at once.

Divine.

Then, the light begins to fade, and her outline slowly comes into view. It's hard to focus on it clearly; her form keeps shifting, like rays of the sun bending shadows. She's just like Ilmatar, Goddess of the Air, in that you see more of her when you view her in your peripheral.

"Hanna," a voice says. It is rich yet feminine, primordial. It doesn't seem to come from the light but from all around me, like it's embedded in the air.

I can only stare dumbly at the glow as she slowly comes into focus, until, finally, I can see her clearly.

She's so beautiful, it makes my chest ache.

My mother is at least a foot taller than me, close to seven feet, with long limbs and skin that hums a subtle golden hue, as if kissed by shimmering sunlight. Her hair cascades in waves of molten gold, streaked with fiery reds and soft, glowing ambers, constantly shifting as though alive with the sun's flames. When she moves, her hair seems to emit a soft halo of light, casting a warm glow around her. Flowing robes of radiant silk envelop her body, the fabric almost weightless, moving like ripples of heat. Golden embroidery depicting solar flares and constellations adorns the edges.

Most striking are her eyes. They shift between molten amber and deep copper, burning with intensity. Looking into them feels like staring into the heart of the sun itself, an unstoppable force of life.

She is very much a God, her power and presence rendering me speechless. I can't imagine there's any way I could have possibly come from such a being. Maybe everyone was wrong about her being my mother. I mean, *me*?

A girl from North Hollywood who drank boba tea and worried about never owning a house?

We are *not* the same.

"You have nothing to say to me?" she says, her voice light and melodic now. "Because I have much I would like to say to you."

"I—I'm sorry, I just...I never expected to..." My voice trails off as I struggle to find the words that could possibly convey the overwhelming mix of emotions swirling inside me. "It's nice to finally meet you?" I finish dumbly.

There's no way I'm about to start calling her mom.

Her gaze softens as she reaches out, fingers glowing softly with a warm light as she beckons me closer. Without a second thought, I step toward her, feeling a surge of warmth enveloping me. It's like being wrapped in sunlight itself, full of life and power, something that sings a song deep inside my veins.

"My dear Hanna," she whispers, her voice resonating within my soul, bringing with it an aching sense of familiarity. "You may feel small now, but you carry within you the spark of my divine essence. It slumbers, waiting for the right moment to awaken and illuminate the world. This is that moment, my child."

Tears prickle at the corners of my eyes as I look up at her, overwhelmed by a sense of belonging I never knew was missing. All my life I felt like I didn't fit in. I thought it was because I was the product of divorced parents, my love being split across two countries, never really belonging to either, but now I know that wasn't it. I felt different because I *was* different and others knew it before I even did.

And now, with my real mother in front of me, I feel a deep sense of *yes, this is it. This is who you are and who you were meant to be.*

Fucking hell, I need to get a grip. I don't even know her or what any of this means.

"You are destined for greatness," she continues, her eyes alight with pride and a distant sort of affection. "But first, you must come with me to my realm on the sun. It is only there I can help you unlock the full extent of your powers and guide you on your path to embracing your true heritage."

Right. Her realm.

On the fucking *sun*.

Vellamo clears her throat behind me, pulling me out of the trance my mother seems to have wrapped me in.

"You're going to take her to the sun?" Vellamo asks in a stern voice.

I turn around to look at the Sea Goddess standing beside the fire. Even next to my mother, she still looks regal and formidable, her damp body glowing in the light, though the sadness in her eyes runs deep.

"Are you sure that's wise?" Vellamo adds, raising her chin. "The world has dissolved into Kaaos, in case you haven't noticed. My husband, Ahto, is dead. There are God-killers on the loose. This world will be lost to Oblivion in no time, and you think it's best to take the Queen of Tuonela to your world to, what? Hide?"

My mother's gaze flickers at Vellamo with a fierce determination, the light in her eyes blazing brighter.

"This is not about hiding, Vellamo," she says. "This is about preparing my daughter for the challenges that lie ahead. The forces of Kaaos may be strong, but Hanna carries within her the legacy of the sun and the strength to face whatever darkness threatens our realms. She is key to all of this—she is the prophecy."

"You know about the prophecy?" I ask her.

"Of course I do," she says patiently. "I'm the one who ensured it would come to light. You were no accident, my child. Only light can fight darkness. I knew that the chances of you fulfilling the prophecy were high. Your father knew that too."

My mouth drops. "My father knew?"

What the actual fuck? He's the one who acted like he didn't believe me when I told him I was the prophecy. It took Tuoni holding my bare hand to prove it.

"Your father knew you *could* become the prophecy," my mother clarifies, clearly reading my thoughts. Not intrusive, or anything. "Doesn't mean he believed it until you revealed the truth." She gives me a small smile, her lips glittering like golden dust. "He had hopes, though. We both did. What if the blood of the sun was mixed with that of a mortal? Not just any mortal, but a descendant of a powerful shaman, one who wields magic? What if it produced a being who was the best of both worlds, tied to humanity, to the cycle of life and death, given the powers of a God and the restraint to use them?"

I blink at her, trying to wrap my head around all of this. It's nice to know my existence wasn't a *whoops someone got pregnant out of wedlock* scenario, but to know my birth was actually planned as some feeble attempt to save the Underworld one day is kind of a mind fuck.

I'm no longer the Chosen One. I'm the Planned One. No wonder my father went to such lengths to smuggle me into the real world and create Salainen as a decoy.

My dad is going to get a fucking earful when I see him again.

"Don't be so hard on your father." She answers my silent words. "He didn't have much say in the matter."

I raise my hand. "I'm gonna stop you right there," I tell her. The last thing I need to hear is that my father was coerced into having me.

She nods. "I understand. We can speak more later. But the

sooner we leave this realm, the faster your powers will evolve and the better it is for everyone."

I look back at Vellamo for her input. Right now, I trust her more than my mother.

Vellamo narrows her eyes, wearing an expression of skepticism mixed with concern. "What if she is not ready?" Vellamo asks. "What if the power within her proves to be too much?" She pauses. "Or not enough."

A flicker of uncertainty crosses my mother's face before she squares her shoulders, regaining her composure. "Hanna has a strength and courage that surpasses even my expectations," she says firmly. "I have seen my fair share of it. There isn't much in this land my rays don't touch. She will rise to meet the challenges ahead, guided by the light that burns within her."

Vellamo grumbles something inaudible under her breath, something my mother ignores.

"Are you ready, my child?" my mother asks, her gaze searching mine for any sign of doubt.

And yet, all I have is doubt.

I look back at Vellamo, unsure of what to do.

Vellamo holds my gaze for a moment before she slowly nods.

"Very well," Vellamo says stiffly. "I am not your mother, Hanna, merely a friend and advisor. I can't prevent you from going if that's what you wish. And if your mother says that's where your powers will come to fruition, if that's what we need to save us from Kaaos, then I can't be the one to stand in your way. Who am I to stop the one who might save us all?"

I gulp. No pressure or anything.

"Can't I just somehow get my powers down here?" I ask. They showed up before when Tuoni died while we were stuck in Inmost. Isn't there some way my mother can teach me the ropes, much like Vipunen did?

"I can't stay here for long," my mother says in a low voice. "The longer I'm here, the more I lose my strength, and the more mortal I become. You gather your strength from the sun, just as I do."

"Yeah, but the sun..." I say warily. "Like the actual sun? Isn't it a ball of gas? Won't I just, you know, die?"

"It's not what you think," she says.

Uh huh. Very helpful.

"I will come back, won't I?" I ask her.

"You will," she assures me.

"You must," Vellamo chimes in. "Otherwise, you might as well stay here."

"She will be back," my mother says sharply, her hair briefly turning into curling flames that rise like solar flares. "I will make sure she doesn't forget."

I frown. "Why would I forget?"

My mother's gaze slides to mine, and she stares at me in such a way that I have a little Galadrial and Frodo moment. I would hate to see her angry.

Suddenly, I'm flooded with fear. I know she's my mother and all, I know there's so much I don't understand and that there's a fuckload of questions that need answering, but I really don't know her at all. It's not like she's remotely personable. She even talks differently than the gods down here, as if she's saying words she thinks are something a human would say.

I don't even know if I should trust her.

What if Louhi has already gotten to her? The thought terrorizes me. What if this is a trap to take me out of the equation?

"You know what?" I say uneasily. "On second thought, maybe it's better I stay here and help fight as I am. Vellamo and I just have to find the other Gods, the real ones, and Lovia and Tuonen, and then regroup. Tuoni and my father must be making their way through a portal somewhere, and honestly, I feel I should discuss this with him first before I—"

But before I can finish my sentence, my mother reaches out and grabs my arm, plunging my world into blinding light and an electrifying hum that makes my ears feel as if they're about to explode.

And then suddenly...darkness.

CHAPTER TWO

LOVIA

"You have no idea what my mother will do to you when she finds out what you've done," Rasmus says like a sniveling little weasel we've trapped.

I yank at the mycelia cord wrapped around him, causing him to stumble behind me over a tree root.

"*Our* mother," I sneer as I glare at him over my shoulder. "Don't pretend we aren't related."

He regains his balance at the last minute, his red hair falling across his brow, his eyes full of hate. I know enough about the kind of hate that's programmed into you; I've seen it in my voyages to the Upper World. It's the kind that's passed down through generations, coddled by society until it blooms into something wretched. I have to remind myself that Rasmus was just a mortal boy living in that world until my mother decided to use him for her own gain. The hate that burns in his eyes was put there by *her*, ignited under controlled circumstances.

Careful, a voice reminds me. *Don't make excuses for him. He'll kill you the first chance he gets, and then it won't matter who taught him how to hate.*

I glance over at the Magician. He meets my eyes with two swirling galaxies amidst the black void of his face that's sheltered beneath his hood. While we've walked through the beginning of the Hiisi Forest, the roots high, the trees thickening the further we go, we haven't said much to each other. Rasmus has blathered on and on about how fucked we are, that we're on the losing side, that we'll regret this, but we've been more or less silent. A lot of thinking, a lot of planning.

And while I'm unsure how much capacity the Magician has for worrying, I'm doing enough for the both of us.

Still, I'm glad he's here. When I thought he died, I felt the ground collapse under me. The thought of having to do all this alone was terrifying when it shouldn't be. I should be stronger than that. I know how to fight, I know I've proven myself time and time again, and yet…with the Underworld as I know it, my land, my home, slipping through my fingers, I couldn't bear facing the end of it alone.

I'm glad you're here, I think, hoping he can maybe hear me.

The galaxies in his face swirl into a cosmos of pink and purple before turning into shooting stars. I don't know if that means he heard me or not, but it comforts me regardless. Actually, it more than comforts me. It causes my heart to skip a few beats, for my blood to run hot and my skin to grow tight.

Or that could be an infection setting in, given that I still have an arrow sticking out of the back of my leg. The Magician was able to lop off the end of it with my sword, but still, it's there, making me feel painfully mortal with each and every step.

I growl and look back at Rasmus, rage kindled in my belly. "You know, since you stuck an arrow in me, it's only fair I stick something in you."

I pass his leash to the Magician and then brandish my

sword, the metal glistening even in the dim light of the forest.

Rasmus raises his chin. “Go ahead,” he says. “You’re just as petty as your father.”

I snort. “My father would have run the blade into your eye already and been done with you.”

“Like I said, petty,” Rasmus glowers. “Too bad your father isn’t here now to show you the ropes.” His face contorts with mock concern. “You don’t think he could be dead, do you? Maybe that’s why all of this is happening.”

His voice is dripping with sarcasm, and yet the gleam in his eyes holds knowledge full of malicious intent.

I swallow hard, my palms starting to feel clammy, enough so that I nearly drop the sword.

“Don’t listen to him,” the Magician says. “Your father isn’t dead.”

“That’s funny,” Rasmus says. “Because I could have sworn he was killed alongside Hanna when they were taken prisoner by my mother and Salainen at the bone match. At least, that’s what they told me. Makes sense, considering they were disguised as the beloved king and queen. How else could they use shadow magic and Sala’s likeness to fool everyone at Shadow’s End if they hadn’t been removed from the picture?”

What he’s saying sounds too real and complicated to be a lie. My grip on the sword tightens.

“They are not dead, Loviatar,” the Magician says again, sternly this time. “I promise you this.”

“Then where are they?” I cry out in frustration. “Why is this happening? How could my mother have gotten control of Tuonela like this? How could it crumble so easily?”

The Magician goes silent. A moon waxes and wanes as it rotates across his face.

"Your father is not in this world," he eventually says, his voice sounding airy and far away.

"Because he's floating in Oblivion forever," Rasmus finishes for him.

I react without thinking, drawing the sword across his throat, nearly breaking the skin. "Shut the fuck up, or you'll be the one in the endless void, and mommy won't be able to save you then," I snarl into his ear.

"Tuoni is in the Upper World," the Magician tells me quickly, trying to calm me down. "He is with Rasmus and Hanna's father. The shaman, Torben."

Rasmus goes still, his eyes widening. Ah. So this he fears more than the blade at his throat. Torben. His own father.

"Are you sure?" I ask, my heart stuttering between my ribs, too afraid to hope.

"I am," the Magician says. "They will be finding a portal to come back."

"And Hanna?"

"She is not dead," the Magician says. "But I don't know where she is. She is beyond where I can see."

"What does that even mean?"

"It means to have faith and stay on course," the Magician says as he walks over to me and curls his fingers around my forearms in a powerful grip that burns my skin. I can't help but stare into his galaxy face, and I find myself lowering the sword, as if not in control anymore.

Is he hypnotizing me?

A shooting star curls up where his mouth should be.

Oh, he's smirking.

Again, a strange sensation rushes over my limbs, creating goosebumps in its wake. A dangerous feeling. I force myself to ignore it.

He then turns his attention to Rasmus. The wound the

Magician had caused earlier has reopened thanks to my sword, a drop of blood spilling down his neck.

"Your voice has worn out its welcome," the Magician says. He raises his hand and does a quick, graceful dance with his fingers. The mycelia that wraps around Rasmus like rope suddenly move and shoot up like sprouts, covering his mouth like a gag.

Rasmus yells against the fungi, but it comes out muffled, his eyes going wide with rage and panic.

"Come on," the Magician says to me. "The sooner we get through this forest and to Tapio and the other Gods, the sooner we can make use of him and get your leg looked at."

The Magician tugs at the rope of mycelia, and Rasmus stumbles forward. We start walking again, stepping over the roots, winding around the ferns, the trees getting wider and taller the deeper into the forest we go. It gets darker too, quieter. I haven't spent a lot of time in these parts of the world, other than when I've had to deliver a message to the Forest Gods, and it unnerves me. One would think being the Goddess of Death means I would never be creeped out, but here? I'm thoroughly disturbed.

It's probably because this forest is the birthplace of Rangaista, Louhi's father, the Devil as an Old God, a place where other demons and goblins have spawned. It has always existed in an uneasy middle ground under my father's watchful eye, but now that the world has started to crumble, it feels even more precarious than usual.

"How much longer until we reach the Gods?" the Magician asks me, his voice low, as if he thinks the forest is listening.

"How should I know? I rarely come here."

He glances at me, his head cocked slightly. "I would keep your voice down if I were you," he says. "We're not alone."

Of course we're not alone; we've got this asshole trailing behind us, I want to say, but he's right. The birds are no longer singing, the animals no longer rustling in the bushes. The stillness that blankets us doesn't feel natural.

It feels insidious and suffocating.

Alien.

The Magician stops and slowly raises his hand, motioning for me to be quiet. Thank the gods he had the foresight to gag Rasmus; otherwise, I'm sure he'd be making a raucous and calling for help. I have to wonder what other foresight the Magician has. He had said he knows things he can't even begin to explain.

Does he know how all of this will end?

"Listen," the Magician whispers, his head craned up to the thick canopy of ironwood above us.

I hold my breath, my ears straining.

At first, there's nothing at all, just that thickening silence that makes the blood whoosh loudly in my head.

Then, I hear it.

A low rumbling, one that steadily gets louder, as if the sound is coming toward us like a freight train.

"What is that?" I squeak just as the ground starts to tremble.

All around us, the trees start to sway back and forth. I look over at Rasmus, wondering if this is somehow his doing as a shaman, but he's frowning. He doesn't look scared, just concerned enough to make me think he's surprised.

"Get your sword ready," the Magician says in a steely voice.

I adjust my grip, lowering into a fighting stance. The rumbling is so loud now, it makes my bones tremble, and the ground starts to shift beneath me.

Up ahead, in the depths of the forest, the trees start to lift, their roots thrusting toward the sky. They land with a smash, huge trunks crashing into the ground so hard, the shock-waves nearly knock me off balance.

"*Yggthra*," the Magician says, "an Old God who manifests as a root system, an ancient parasite that drains the life force of anything it entangles." He looks over at me. "Yggthra's roots burrow into the soil and bodies alike, sapping strength and corrupting souls in mindless thralls."

"Is this your doing?" I sneer at Rasmus.

He shakes his head, but there's something in his eyes, a calmness that defies the situation. He isn't as worried as he should be.

"It doesn't matter," the Magician says. "Even if he could control it, even if he called it forth, he's powerless to stop it. In the end, this Old God is here because of Louhi, and it won't stop until it stops us."

I tighten my grip on my sword, feeling the weight of it in my hand. Yggthra's roots start to emerge from the ground, writhing and twisting towards us like gnarled, monstrous snakes. They burst forward, throwing soil into the air before plunging back down again.

This isn't a crocodile monster I can stab in the skull. I have a feeling if I cut off one root, another will quickly pop up in its place.

The Magician quickly assessed the situation, his face scanning the thick forest for any possible path or escape.

"We need to move," the Magician says urgently, grabbing my arm and pulling me back as another wave of roots erupts from the ground.

I don't hesitate—we start running, dragging Rasmus with us. Part of me wants to cut him loose, but I think that's exactly what my mother wants. Yggthra isn't just about destroying me and the Magician; it's also a rescue operation for Rasmus.

The Hiisi Forest grows darker and thicker as we run

deeper, the roots becoming tangled around us. Every so often, Rasmus grunts in pain as he struggles to keep up with us.

"Can you stop that thing?" I ask the Magician.

The Magician glances at me for a moment before looking back at Rasmus. "Not without help."

"Can *I* stop that thing?" I add as we burst through a copse of white-and-red mistberry brambles that leave long scratches on my arms and legs.

He gives his head a small shake. It makes me want to prove him wrong, but there's probably something he's not telling me.

"Yggthra wants Rasmus," he says, confirming my suspicions. "Maybe we should give it what it wants," he adds.

I come to a stop and give the Magician a bewildered look just as Yggthra crashes through the forest not far behind—much too close for comfort.

"You said we had to keep him because he might serve a purpose," I quickly remind him.

"And what if this is that purpose?" he says.

Then, he drops the mycelia cord.

Rasmus stares down at it in shock.

"He can't run away," I point out. "He's completely bound."

The Magician shrugs. "That isn't our problem, it's Louhi's. Come on."

I blink for a moment, both happy to be free of Rasmus and yet feeling conflicted about it all the same. We captured him and brought him all this way just to let him go now?

But the forest erupts in chaos as Yggthra bursts through the ground again, yards away, its gnarled roots twisting and snapping like monstrous tentacles, and with a yelp, I start running again, the Magician by my side. The ground beneath us ripples and cracks, the air thick with the scent of deep soil and decay.

We run further, and I nearly lose my balance before the Magician pulls me behind a wall of ten-foot-tall ferns.

"Why are we stopping?" I ask him, peering breathlessly between the leaves. I spot Rasmus in the middle of the forest, facing the Old God as it comes for him.

"Yggthra," the Magician says, his voice low and tense, "is confined to the forest. As long as we're in here, it will find us, and we're in deep. Running is futile until I know how Rasmus is involved."

As if he can hear us, Rasmus, still gagged by the mycelia cords, turns to look back with wide, panicked eyes. His chest heaves as he struggles against his restraints, but Yggthra's roots seem to reach for him with deliberate intent, weaving through the dirt toward his feet like a knot of snakes.

Rasmus looks back to the giant roots rising from the soil and lets out a muffled yell. For a moment, hesitation flickers in my chest—just a moment—but I harden my resolve and force myself to watch.

Yggthra's massive trunk groans as it rises from the soil, its form like a skeletal tree made of blackened wood and shifting shadows. It looms over Rasmus, the roots coiling around his legs, his waist, and, finally, his chest. They tighten around his body, pulling him off the ground, but his expression isn't one of relief or triumph—it's terror.

"He can't control it," I say to the Magician. "Look. He's afraid."

Yggthra pulls Rasmus closer, roots tightening like a noose. At first, I think it's just restraining him, examining him, figuring out if he's friend or foe.

But then, it begins to crush him.

Rasmus screams against the gag, a sound so raw, it slices through me. "This isn't Louhi's pet," I comment, panic swirling in my chest. "Yggthra doesn't serve her. It serves itself."

"Or it does serve Louhi and she's cast her son aside already," the Magician notes.

We both fall silent, watching as the roots squeeze around Rasmus' chest, his feet dangling above the ground. There's a sick cracking sound, and I don't know if it's a root or Rasmus' bones.

"Damn it," I growl. Without thinking, I burst through the ferns and sprint back toward the monster.

"Lovia, what are you doing!?" the Magician shouts from behind me, but I'm already there, slashing my sword at the nearest root. Sparks fly as the blade bites into the ancient wood, and Yggthra recoils with a deafening screech. Rasmus drops to the ground with a deep gasp.

The Magician appears beside me in an instant, his hands weaving sigils in the air. Tendrils of glowing energy spiral from his fingers then shoot down into the ground. Through the churned soil, between where the Old God's roots emerge, thousands of white mycelia rise and wrap around them.

Yggthra thrashes, roots whipping through the air and slamming back down, breaking the mycelia's grip in places.

"It's not going down easily," the Magician says.

"Then we don't stop fighting," I reply, dodging a root as it lashes out at me. My blade finds its mark again, cutting deep into the trunk. The forest trembles with Yggthra's pain, its groaning wail echoing through the trees.

A new root shoots from the soil, coming right for Rasmus, who is trying to get to his knees. I slice my sword through it before it can reach him, severing it, then go to Rasmus and pull him up.

"I just saved your fucking life two times already," I snarl at him. "Give me a good reason to do it again."

Rasmus nods, and I glance over my shoulder at the Magician, who is trying to coax more mycelia from the underground.

"Hold still," I tell Rasmus and bring the tip of my sword down over the mycelium gag, managing to split it in half without breaking his skin.

Rasmus gasps for breath, his eyes widening at something behind me.

I whirl around to see the Magician floating a few feet above the ground, the black void of his hands stretched, creating rivers that pour down to the forest floor, the force pushing his body up into the air.

Suddenly, the black starry rivers sprout up from the ground, burying the mycelia and flowing over the trunk of Yggthra. They wrap around it, spreading over the writhing roots like a black stain until everything is completely covered.

For a moment, Yggthra just shakes violently, as if trying to escape the void. Then, a bright eruption rips through the air, like an exploding sun, and Yggthra's form begins to collapse in on itself, its roots retreating like wounded snakes.

With one final screech, the Old God crumbles, its blackened wood splintering and dissolving into ash. The forest falls eerily silent, the only sound our ragged breathing.

The Magician lowers himself back to the ground, the black universe coming back to his hands until they look human-ish again.

"That was…impressive," I tell him. I mean, I know he's the universe and all, but until now, I was starting to forget he was as powerful and mysterious as he is. It makes my heart skip a beat.

The Magician doesn't say anything. He walks over and stands beside me, staring down at Rasmus. A powerful energy seems to envelop his robes, making him glow slightly, as if the power he used to defeat Yggthra still clings to him.

Rasmus coughs, staring up at us. His face is pale, his eyes wild.

I keep my sword drawn where he can see it.

"Why?" Rasmus croaks, his voice barely audible. "Why did you save me?"

I glare down at him, gripping the hilt tighter. "Because no one gets to kill you but me."

"Now that you've found out your mother thinks you're expendable, perhaps you might want to strike a bargain with us," the Magician says to Rasmus, his voice calm but cold. "A real one. Your chance to be on the right side of things for once."

Rasmus rubs his lips together for a moment. "Release the rest of me."

I can't see it, but I can feel the Magician smiling.

"Always an opportunist," the Magician comments. "No, I think we'll keep you bound just like this. You're still our prisoner, after all. Only this time, we're the ones with the cards that mean something. We'll draw yours later."

Rasmus doesn't say anything as we haul him to his feet. My legs ache, the arrow wound on my calf burns, and my heart is still racing, but as we stumble away from the wreckage of Yggthra, I can't help but glance back at the pile of ash and shattered roots.

One Old God down, too many left to go.

CHAPTER THREE

DEATH

I'M SURROUNDED BY IDIOTS.

It's not their fault, of course. They are but mere mortals. Still, I expected more from soldiers, though I suppose the fact that I have gently coerced them into following my orders has taken away a bit of their resolve and gumption. I have to remind myself that when I'm inside their minds and controlling them by the power of suggestion, their overall intelligence takes a hit. Their brains have to decrease in power in order for me to mold them.

Torben and I have taken over the northernmost barracks in Finland, the Jaeger Brigade. Here, there are over a thousand men, and a few voluntary women, trained to handle the raw and desolate terrain of Lapland and the surrounding area. I guess the threat of an invasion from Russia is always on their mind.

Originally, I wanted to take military from all bases across the country, but Torben attempted to use his human logic to illustrate the risks. Apparently, if we had the whole Finnish army under my control, people would notice, and it would cause widespread panic, not just here, but around the world. He then went on to tell me that even though I was an all-powerful God—which was nice of him to finally recognize—I couldn't possibly control the brains of the entire world.

He had a point. I have my limits, as much as I hate to admit it. Even coercing the soldiers here is draining my energy, fast. I'll feel better once I get back to Tuonela and I'm back in my own realm.

Of course, that can't happen until Torben does his job.

We're all waiting on him.

"Well?" I ask him. "Have you figured it out yet?"

The old man glances up at me from the stack of books he has been pouring over, a grey brow raised. "The answers won't appear out of your impatience," he says.

We're sitting in the command room of the barracks. The generals in charge of the troops loiter near us in a perpetually half-dazed state, ready to do our bidding, except we don't know yet what that is, other than getting them to tend to my every whim.

Torben and I are by the wood stove, the sound of the crackling flames filling the room while the generals exist in silence. I've tried a few times to read the spellbooks Torben has procured from his cabin, but the magic seems foreign to me. Even his Book of Spells that he depends on the most doesn't strike a chord.

Then again, it's not really striking a chord with him either. None of his books have a list of portals to the Underworld. All they have, as he has told me ad nauseum, are spells to conjure up the portals, and none of them seem to be working. We've been here for days now, and every second that ticks by, I fear I'm losing my connection to Tuonela, that I'm losing precious time. The only thing that calms me is the fact that time here passes so much quicker.

I sigh loudly, voicing my displeasure, and then snap my

fingers at the general closest to me. "You there. What's your name?"

"General Anton Pekka," he says, snapping to attention.

"General Anton Pekka," I repeat, "bring me more cardamon buns and coffee. Black. None of that oat milk shit."

The general salutes me and scurries out the door and down the hall.

"You really shouldn't boss them around like that," Torben says in a tired voice as he licks his thumb and flicks to the next page.

"Why not? They won't remember any of this." At least, I assume they won't. I never did put this to the test.

"Because it's not right," he says. "Morally speaking."

I scoff. "And suddenly you're a better judge of morality? No one is a better judge of morals than the God of Death."

He gives me a pointed look. "You may be able to judge the morals of others, but have you ever taken that gaze inward and judged yourself?"

I wave my hand at him. "Bah. You should speak, Torben Heikkinen. I know what you did. I know what everyone has done. Humans are fallible."

"And so are the Gods."

Well, I suppose he's not wrong about that. Right now, the entire Underworld is crumbling because of some fallible gods who should have stayed buried eons ago. I've been trying not to think about it, lest I lose my temper, or worse, my hope. I know Hanna has made her way back over—I have to believe that—but I have no way of keeping tabs on her from here. Even our connection was severed the moment that cave collapsed and we became stranded in the Upper World. She remains as unreachable to me as the rest of my family.

I have no idea what I'll be heading back to once we find the portal. I don't know if having an army of a thousand soldiers will make any difference if there is no Underworld to fight for. And if there are still vestiges of the Tuonela I know and love, I don't know if these mortals can actually make a dent against Louhi's army.

But this sort of thinking does me no good. I must coerce my own thoughts into something positive. If I took to heart all the possibilities of what might be happening over there, of what might be lost, there's a chance I could give up.

"The longer I stay here, the less I become," I whisper to myself.

Torben pauses and looks at me. "Not that you need any compliments," he says gruffly, "but you are not becoming less of anything." He looks me up and down. "If anything, I say you're taking up more and more space."

I have to admit, that makes me sit up straighter.

Soon, General Pekka comes back with the sweet cardamom buns and coffee, which I quickly polish off. It distracts me and alleviates a bit of my impatience.

The general hovers in the background, clearly waiting to take my dishes away, but I don't want his servitude at the moment. I want his intel.

"General," I say to him, "you understand what I'm trying to do with your troops, don't you?"

The man nods. He's got a sharp chin and an even sharper nose, high cheekbones and small blue eyes. He looks young, too young to do this sort of thing, but his blond hair is going grey at the temples, which I suppose means he's old enough. Hard to tell with these mortals and their flimsy little life spans.

"Say we were to find a portal not too far from here," I continue. "How would you propose we get everyone where they need to be and do so without causing alarm?"

The general blinks at me for a moment, and I have to reach into my power, scaling back on my influence inside his mind, letting him accept the situation as nothing unusual while letting analysis and agency come back into play.

Finally, clarity comes into his eyes. "We can mobilize using our trucks," he says. "They are off-road and can go anywhere. If there is an obstacle and the trucks cannot travel any further, we are prepared to travel on foot. No one would bat an eye, as this is typical for our training."

"And what weapons do you have at your disposal?"

"Rifles, of course."

I mull that over. While Torben has been lost in the spell-books, I've been trying to imagine how a mortal army could possibly stack up against the skeleton army comprised of my former subjects, Bone Stragglers, and the Inmost Dwellers who have escaped from the city, not to mention any Old Gods Louhi may have raised. Bullets might be able to blast off someone's head, but the skeletons will need to be completely disabled limb from limb in order to send them to Oblivion.

"What about bombs?" I ask.

The general frowns. "We have some…"

"Then we will need those. How skilled are your troops with swords or bow and arrow?"

His frown deepens. "Most have minimal knowledge of either. They aren't usually a requirement for the army these days."

"But if they were given swords, they could figure it out?"

"If they had to."

"They might have to. I take it you don't have any on base?"

"No, sir," he says.

Fools. To put all their stock into impersonal guns and bullets, not once thinking about ever entering a war that might require hand-to-hand combat…

But it will have to do.

I clear my throat and hand my mug and plate to the general. "Very well. As soon as we can take on some of the army on the other side, we'll gain access to their weapons. I just want your troops to know what they're up against. Can you call a strategy meeting with your top people? The sooner we get this underway with a plan, the better. At the moment, it seems we have more than enough time to start training."

"Except we don't," Torben says in an odd voice.

I glance at him, and he breaks into a broad smile.

"Because I found the spell," he says. "The spell that will bring us to the portal."

CHAPTER FOUR

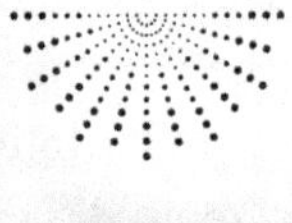

TUONEN

"Sarvi," I whisper. "Sarvi, can you hear me?"

Just like every time I've asked before, which is maybe twice, or maybe a couple of hundred times, for I have no idea how long I've been in this dungeon, there's no response. In the distance, something drips, a steady beat that has been driving me slowly insane. Someone—or something—cries out in pain from another cell. Bonemice squeak and scurry in the shadows, occasionally venturing into the light of the candles, whose wax drips into small white mountains on the stone floor.

The only reason I know Sarvi is even alive is because I can hear the unicorn's labored breathing and the occasional rustling, as if Sarvi is adjusting. It's a very specific sound of hooves against rock and seems like it's coming from the next cell over from mine. It hadn't been clear where Sarvi went after their horn was sawed off, but it would make sense for Louhi to jail the unicorn as well.

More than that, I feel it in my marrow, the energy and presence of a soul that has been my father's confidant since the day I was born. Sarvi is not dead, but I fear for their life anyway. I'm not sure how much life essence is in the unicorn's horn, but to see them crumble like I did, Oblivion could be lurking around the corner. Sarvi would become one more good soul lost to the eternal void.

I reach up and gingerly touch my own horns. The ends where my mother sliced them off still throb with pain. Even worse, I can't make the horns disappear back inside my skull. They're permanently out now, cumbersome to wield when there's no relief on my neck and shoulders. One would think that being a God, even a lesser God of Death, would mean not dealing with mortal-like pain, but I fear that my mother did more than just gain magic from the ends of my horns. I fear she took whatever immortality I had.

I feel weaker than I should, like death—real death—is waiting for me around the corner. Sometimes, I fall asleep, and when I wake up, I swear I'm being watched outside the cell by a wretched beast biding its time before it kills me. Other times, I can barely move, just lying propped up against the cold stone wall, wondering if it's even possible to take my last breath.

Sometimes, I nearly ask for that last breath to come.

But it doesn't. And somewhere deep inside, I have resolve. There's not a lot, but it's there. Driven by anger, spite, and humiliation, I let it fuel me, enough to keep breathing, to try and plan my escape.

I want to be able to talk to Sarvi. The unicorn has so much intimate knowledge of Shadow's End, far more than I do. They would know exactly how to get out of here. Once we're out of the castle, then perhaps we can find help. There has to be someone left out there that hasn't fallen under Louhi's influence.

And Rangaista, I remind myself. Fucking Devil, it makes me feel sick knowing I'm related to him. I don't know if he's still in the castle or if he ventured out, but whoever comes across the demon won't last damn minute.

I sigh and close my eyes, trying to think. Down here, there is no natural light, so I have no idea how many days or nights have passed. I don't even know what time it is right now. There hasn't been any food or water, which is affecting my mind and body. Part of me thinks there might be some residual power in me, because if I was completely mortal, I'm not sure I'd even be alive.

But what power have I always had anyway? Thinking back to the before times, my life before I ended up in here, is like slogging through mud. I can barely remember. I know that I have a connection to every soul in Tuonela, helpful when you spend half your days as the ferryman. It's not as strong as my father's, but still, it's there. It's that connection I've tried to use in order to reach Sarvi in my head when talking out loud hasn't worked.

But perhaps I need to use the connection on someone else, someone who can help. Ideally, it would be a God, someone with the power to actually get us out of here, but I fear if there are any good Gods left, they are too far away for me to reach them.

My best shot is someone in this castle, which means I have to be strategic. If I reach the wrong person, someone under Louhi's control, then I'll only alert her to what I'm trying to do. And yet, I can't think of who could still be on my side. Kalma is officially out. The Deadmaidens will do Louhi's bidding, especially under the guise of my father.

I stare out through the bars of the cell at the dripping candle wax and try to think, but it feels hopeless, and I keep coming up empty.

Another bonemouse comes teetering out of the shadows, raising its nose into the air, the candlelight gleaming off its black fur and smooth white bones. It looks at me with empty sockets, whiskers moving up and down, one torn ear rotating. Perhaps I could communicate with the mouse, but what good would that do? A mouse can't save me.

No. A mouse can't, but another creature could.

Rauta.

My father's iron dog.

Normally, he's up in the Library of the Veils, guarding the Book of Runes. Of course, there's a chance Louhi has already been up there and come across him in her search for all the magic she can muster. If so, she'd have no problem sending him to Oblivion. She always hated that dog.

I sigh, succumbing to the certainty of it. I doubt there is much she hasn't already destroyed.

The bonemouse emits a squeak and sits back on its haunches as it continues to stare at me.

"What?" I whisper to it. "How are you going to help me?"

The mouse gets down on all fours and starts wagging its stringy tail back and forth.

Like a dog.

Are you trying to tell me something? I project silently. *Can you hear my thoughts?*

The mouse squeaks again and nods.

Is Rauta alive?

The mouse squeaks once more, then looks down the corridor and quickly scampers off into the shadows. The sound of heavy boots and rattling chains fills the air, and my body tenses as someone steps into view.

It's a guard dressed in heavy armor and carrying a sword, his skull visible under a metal helmet. The eye sockets stare at me for a moment before he keeps walking down the corridor. The guards usually patrol past every so often; it will at least grant me some time.

Once the guard is gone and the footsteps have faded, I close my eyes and try to reach Rauta. I picture my father's library and how when you first enter, the dog is lying there at the base of the Book of Runes. I focus on the smell of the room, the dusty scent of old pages, the rich, earthy loam of the various burning candles, incense, and dried herbs used for spells. I narrow in on Rauta, the dog's coat made of patches of black fur, bones, and iron welded here and there. Rauta's eyes glow red in the black metal sockets, an iron tongue hanging out of its mouth.

Rauta, I whisper inside my mind, feeling energy stir up inside me, floating like sediment in water. *Rauta, you good boy, can you hear me?*

The energy stirs faster, becoming a vortex, and it's as if I can feel it spreading through the bars, up to the ceiling, and then into the rest of the castle. I keep concentrating, not letting my attention waver.

Then, suddenly, there's something there, like something is pushing itself through an invisible layer into me. At first, I don't know what it is, but then I can feel it. It's like I'm being…licked inside my soul, in a very comforting, yet slightly disturbing way.

Rauta! I exclaim. *Good boy! You came.*

A low whine sounds from my head, and it's like the dog has formed itself inside me, iron body, red eyes, and all.

Listen, I go on, feeling the dog's heavy tail wagging. *I need your help. Sarvi and I are trapped in the dungeon, and I need you to free us somehow. But you can't trust Tuoni or Hanna. Neither of them are who they say they are, but I guess you already sense that, don't you?*

Rauta whines again, agreeing. Of course, dogs would be able to sniff out that Louhi is impersonating my father. Animals can sense hate and are better judges of character than even the Gods.

Please hurry, I add. *I don't think we have much time left. You can come with us as we try to find my father. He's out there somewhere. Only then can we make things right.*

Rauta lets out a loud bark, and then suddenly, the sensation is over, and I feel alone in my body.

I exhale and lean back against the wall, my breath shaking.

Sarvi? I think, trying to do the same to the unicorn, but, as usual, there is no sign.

So, I sit and I wait and I try not to worry, try not to let my mind race.

It's unavoidable, though. What if Rauta doesn't make it? What if he can't help? He's just a dog, after all. What if he's caught? What if *we're* caught? What if I'm the cause of his death?

Or worse?

When my mother threw me in this cell, she never explained what she had planned for me, just a vague threat about meeting my grandfather—Rangaista—some other day, but neither of them have come by. No doubt I've been forgotten, and that might be for the best.

If I were a betting God, one who bet on anything other than bone matches, I'd say my mother means to leave me here until she has taken over the entire realm and destroyed everyone who opposes her. Then, she'll come back and give me an ultimatum—join her or else.

I just don't know what that else would be. Would she sentence me to die? Actually end my life and send me to Oblivion? Could she do that to her own flesh and blood? Or would she keep me locked up here forever as a prisoner of war for never bowing to her or recognizing her as a queen?

Because I will never recognize her as a queen.

Only as a monster.

I sit there for a good while, my ears attuned to the slightest noise. I still feel nothing from Sarvi. Even the bonemouse seems to have stopped scurrying to and fro, as if it already served its purpose. In the distance, water drips, lulling me off into a daze.

Then, I hear a soft padding sound approaching from the right, as if something is coming down the stairs. I immediately go tense, not knowing what it is. Rauta's paws are metal, aren't they? They would make a distinct noise.

A shadow appears on the stone floor, looming closer and closer as it comes down the corridor toward my cell.

Rangaista.

CHAPTER FIVE

HANNA

Gold.

My entire world goes from black to gold, all while it feels like I'm hurtling headfirst toward…something.

Nothing.

Everything.

There is no up or down, left or right. I'm just moving so fast, the space around me dissolves, like the world doesn't exist and there's only me.

For a moment, I don't even feel the presence of the Goddess, my mother. She has either turned into gold herself or has disappeared completely. There's just me, flying through what feels like all of time and space and the reality I'd been born into.

And then, just as quickly as it started, it stops.

I feel something solid beneath my feet before the gold of my vision starts to fade, and shapes and shadows come into view. Yet, there is no darkness here. The shadows are somehow bright and glistening, and I have that same sense I had when I first stared at my mother: that I can't quite see what I'm looking at until I look at it from another angle.

I close my eyes, even though it gives no relief from the light. I'm about to teeter over, the ground suddenly feeling unstable, when a hand reaches out and grabs my arm to steady me. The touch is searing hot, as if I leaned on a burning stove, but it doesn't hurt.

"It will take you time to acclimatize," my mother says. "Take a moment. Find your balance and your footing before opening your eyes to this world. There might not be any oxygen, but I advise you to breathe deep anyway."

No oxygen?!

My eyes fly open, lungs seizing in panic, and I immediately start to sway from the intensity, from the enormity of what I'm looking at. My mother keeps her grip on me, tsking under her breath, but all I can do is stare.

Before me is a radiant, utterly mythical landscape that looks like it was created in a fever dream. There are fields of glowing plants with shimmering petals that cast rainbows instead of shadows. Weaving between these iridescent fields are what look like vast deserts of fine golden sand sparkling intermittently. Every now and then, something blooms from the sand, cacti-like flora with luminescent leaves that open and close with the warm breeze.

Beyond are rivers of molten gold flowing through shimmering mesas and valleys. There, crystalline mountains and amber-colored forests stretch toward the sky, with tree leaves that glint like stained glass, absorbing the light and refracting it in a spectrum that fills the air like a soft aura. They stretch toward what feels like an endless horizon bathed in hues of gold, orange, and soft pinks, the light constantly shifting between a living sunrise and sunset.

"This is the sun," I whisper. "How is this possible?"

Everything is illuminated by warm, golden light, including my own body, which, to my surprise, is no longer dressed in the damp clothes I left the Upper World in.

Instead, I'm in a silk-like dress that drapes over my body like gossamer, the threads sparkling as if they've come alive.

It's all the most beautiful thing I've ever seen, enough that my eyes burn like I'm about to cry.

"Hold your tears, Hanna," my mother says, a hint of disapproval in her voice. "If you want to gain access to the powers of a God, you have to start acting less like a mortal."

I nod, even though I don't know how that's possible, not here, where I feel so insignificant, like every inch of my mortality, of my humanity, has been amplified.

But despite feeling dwarfed by the grandeur of this realm, I straighten my spine and take a deep breath. Though she said there is no oxygen, air still fills my lungs, giving me strength. The atmosphere is warm and rich, carrying scents of exotic flowers and something akin to cinnamon. As I exhale, a sense of empowerment surges through me, as if the very breath I release is filled with latent magic waiting to be unleashed. Something inside my core fizzes like champagne, floating and sparkling in buoyant song.

It feels like my body is coming alive.

"There," my mother says with a satisfied nod as she looks me over. "This is all part of the becoming. Let your inner self recognize this place. Let your divine heritage seep into your bones. This is the first part of the process."

I close my eyes and let the radiant feeling wash over me, sinking in deep.

"What's the second part?" I ask before opening my eyes.

She lets go of my arm and gestures for me to follow her as she walks along a path that lies in front of us, glossy and faintly yellow, as if made of shimmering citrine. I walk carefully, the gravity here making me feel buoyant. Each step we take resonates with a melodious chime, music that follows us.

As we walk, ethereal beings flit among the towering

amber trees flanking the side of the path, their forms translucent and ever-shifting like dancing flames. They pay us no heed, consumed by their own mysterious activities as they weave patterns in the air with trails of light. I reach out to touch a luminescent thread, and it wraps around my fingers before dissipating into a shower of golden sparks.

I laugh, and even that sound is melodic. This is like one hell of a mushroom trip, except without any of the I'm-going-to-die anxiety. It's ironic, because you'd think being on the fucking *sun*, of all places, might fill one with dread, but now that I'm here, I only feel wonder and belonging.

We continue along the path as it skirts the edge of the forest, taking us under towering crystal peaks that shine from the inside, until we come across a ridge of golden quartz, the interior sparkling with metallic lines. As we get closer, I see an archway in the ridged surface, carved from a single enormous opal, its surface reflecting the hues of the landscape in a mesmerizing display.

"Just through here," my mother says as she disappears beneath it. I quickly follow, entering a vast chamber where the walls seem to pulsate with an inner light, casting intricate shadows that twist and writhe like living things.

At the center of the chamber stands a pool of liquid fire, its surface undulating with molten energy that beckons me closer. My mother gazes at me expectantly, her eyes ablaze with a mixture of pride and something more inscrutable. I can feel the power thrumming beneath my skin, a primal energy that seems to resonate with the very fabric of this surreal world and vice versa.

"This is the Crucible of Awakening," my mother's voice rings with authority, cutting through the ambient hum. "Here, you will undergo a cleansing to claim your birthright as a Goddess."

I step closer to the pool of liquid fire, the heat radiating from it gently blowing back my hair. As I peer into its depths, I see visions swirling atop the molten surface—visions of my past, present, and potential futures all converging in a kaleidoscopic dance of light and shadow. I try to pick out each one, but they move so fast, I'm only left with the essence of the memory, something slippery and transparent.

"You must embrace your true self, Hanna," she says, her words echoing against the chamber walls. "Only by facing your life and confronting your deepest fears and desires, of what it truly means to be human, will you unlock the full extent of your powers."

I take a deep breath, steeling myself for what is to come. With a sense of determination burning in my chest, I raise my hands towards the pool. The surface ripples and distorts, as if responding to my touch, and I feel a surge of energy coursing through me, culminating in my fingertips.

In that moment, I let go of everything holding me back—my doubts, my insecurities, my mortal limitations. I surrender myself to the flames, and in doing so, they rise from the pool, reaching for my fingers.

For a second, I'm filled with the deepest fear of all: the fear of dying, an acute sense of my mortality that has me about to pull away and run as far as I can.

But the fire leaps onto my hands, as if sentient, as if sensing my fear, and climbs up my arms. I open my mouth to scream, to move, but something equally as fiery rises inside me, overpowering the human instinct to avoid death.

Instead, I allow the fire to consume me, to transform me into something new, something ancient and powerful. Then, as the flames envelop me, I feel a searing pain unlike anything I have ever experienced. It is as if every atom of my being is being torn apart and reassembled in a violent cacophony of light and sound. I scream, though whether in agony or ecstasy, I can't tell. The world blurs and distorts around me, shifting and twisting in ways that defy comprehension. I am no longer sure where my body ends and the fire begins, the boundaries between us merging and melding into a single entity.

And then, just as suddenly as it began, the pain subsides, leaving me gasping for breath as I collapse to my knees beside the now-calm pool of liquid fire. My entire being feels as if it is vibrating with a newfound power, a raw energy that pulses beneath my skin like there's some other being living inside me.

What the hell just happened to me?

"Get up, Hanna." My mother's voice rings through the throbbing sound in my head. "You're all right. You're better than all right."

I exhale and slowly rise to my feet, feeling taller and stronger than I have ever been. The world around me seems sharper, more vivid, as if a veil has been lifted from my eyes. I look down at my hands and find they are no longer mine; no, they are adorned with intricate patterns of glowing runes that seem to writhe and shift of their own accord, much like the dress I'm wearing.

My mother stands before me, her eyes alight with pride. "You have done it," she says softly. "You have embraced your true self—your divine self—and unlocked the Goddess within you."

That was easy, I can't help but think, but even the joke quickly slips away, a sense of gravity replacing it.

I look at her, feeling a surge of gratitude and love welling up within me. "Thank you, Mother," I whisper, though the words feel inadequate to express the depth of what I'm feeling. It's as if she saved me from a different future, one that was heading toward certain doom.

In fact, in this moment, I feel as if I've split away from my former self.

She smiles warmly at me before gesturing towards the archway we entered through. "It is time for you to return to Tuonela, my daughter of the sun. You have a destiny to fulfill and a world that needs you."

I frown, unsure of what she's saying. "What do you mean, return to Tuonela?"

Her posture stiffens as her gaze cools. "Your destiny, Hanna. You can't have forgotten already. You haven't been here long enough."

I still don't understand. Tuonela? I shake my head. It sounds familiar but the more I try to think about the word and what it means, the more the meaning slips away from me. It's like trying to remember a dream. All I know is that all is right and I'm exactly where I'm supposed to be.

"My destiny is here, Mother, to become one with the sun, with the power of the universe, just like you."

"*Tuonela*," she says that word again, her voice hard, as if I'm supposed to know what that means. Her eyes blaze with fire now, and I don't know why she's so angry. "The Underworld. You have to reunite with Tuoni. He's on his way. You must join with him and defeat Louhi, or the realm of the dead will be lost forever. You know this, Hanna. You saw everything you were and are and will be in the pool."

I swallow uneasily as fragments come back, like fossils barely visible beneath the sand. "Right," I say slowly. Now, the visions and memories come back, like ghosts. I remember Tuoni. The God of Death. My husband. Which makes me the Goddess of Death. But how can I be that when I am the Goddess of the Sun? How can I worry about what happens in a world that's buried so far beneath this one?

My mother looks away, grumbling under her breath. "This is not supposed to happen this way. Your father was here for ages before he started to lose his connection to the earth."

"What are you talking about? My father?" But I picture him, grey hair and a beard, and my heart pinches with sadness. I realize I have lost him a few times over, but the moment I stop thinking about him, the pain goes away.

It's so much easier to stop thinking.

She grabs my hand and leads me out of the cave, back into the gold light. I can't help but laugh as fiery butterflies land on my arms and in my hair, singing softly to me.

"Perhaps you weren't ready," my mother says, more to herself. "Maybe Vellamo was right. But what choice did I have? Leave you in Tuonela? You had no hope of defeating Louhi otherwise. Rangaista and the Old Gods would see to that."

"You seem troubled," I say, watching as a butterfly crawls to the ends of my hair, which flow around me like molten copper.

She exhales before giving her head a shake. "It doesn't matter what I seem. I need to get you back to the Underworld in time. I didn't think the power here would affect you so quickly, but the longer you're here, the more trouble you'll have connecting to your previous life. Gaining the powers of a God means gaining distance from your humanity, but you were wanted and chosen because of your humanity, Hanna. Your mortality is your morality, your connection to Earth and those you love. That's supposed to temper your powers. We are frightening, terrible beings without morality to rein us in."

"But you're not human," I tell her. "And you don't seem frightening or terrible. You say you to want to help others, right?"

"I do so out of a sense of duty but I don't have a heart, Hanna," she says. "I am too distant out here to feel deeply for beings beneath me. I am used to only being the observer. The most I can get involved is through you. I know what must be done and that you're the only one who can do it. But if you're already starting to forget who and what you are, that's going to be a problem."

"So you're sending me away from this wonderful place, from my home, so I can fight for someone else?"

Why would she do that when I only just got here?

"So you can fight for everyone you love and hold dear. So you can fight for the world itself. Life and death have always been in perfect balance, and with Louhi rewriting what it means to die, turning it into a place of perpetual hell, life will no longer have the meaning it should. Life will not be worth living if the afterlife is worse than dying."

The words are starting to sink in. I feel their weight, even though I have to fight the urge to shrug them off.

Tuoni.

My father.

Lovia.

I remember them.

I just don't...*feel* them.

"What should I do?" I ask.

"You must hold onto their memories," she says. "And the memories will hold onto you. But you must find a balance. The more you hold on, the more your powers might wane. Hopefully, when we get you back, you'll be able to do some damage to Louhi without losing your connection to the others."

"And if that doesn't happen?" I ask. "What's more important? Do I sacrifice my humanity to save the Underworld? Or is holding on to love worth the loss?"

She gives me a grim smile. "That will be your choice to

make, Hanna. I can't make that choice for you. But we will have to get you back before that opportunity is taken away entirely."

My mother quickly leads me through the golden realm, across drifting fields of shimmering blossoms and spectral vines that sway in the warm breeze. The sky seems to shift between dawn and dusk with each step we take, creating a dizzying pattern of halos and glimmers, as if the world itself is breathing in light. The edges of my vision pulse, and I have to focus, to anchor my thoughts. Each time I try to recall Tuoni—his handsome face, his rough voice, the touch of his bare hands—I feel it slip farther away, as if I'm trying to clutch smoke.

"I can't feel them," I say, voice tight, as we approach a formation of opalescent stones arranged in a crescent. "I remember them, but it's hollow. I'm trying to hold on, but it's like...unwrapping a present to find an empty box."

My mother stops in front of a great cleft in the ground from which fire whirls upward, bright tongues of flame twisting into a luminous archway. Within the blaze, I see flickers of distant shapes—crooked silhouettes, faint outlines of twisting roots and darkened halls that shimmer and fade. It must be Tuonela beckoning me, reminding me I have something to fight for.

"Your humanity is both your weakness and your strength," my mother says, turning to me, her eyes glinting like molten gold. "You must decide what matters more: the power you've gained here, or the love and compassion that forged you into who you are."

I can barely hear her over the roar of the flames. Heat presses against my skin, prickling like hot needles. My new powers thrum inside me, anxious, as if eager to test themselves in battle. But what's the point of power if it isolates me, if I cannot feel what drives me to protect those I love?

I step forward, the soles of my bare feet warm against the shimmering ground. The air feels thinner now, charged with strange energy. The butterflies that followed us earlier now keep their distance, hovering at the edges of the glowing meadow, their wings refracting light into delicate prisms.

"Once you cross this threshold," my mother says, lifting her chin, "you will find yourself in your old realm. You will face Louhi's corruption, the unraveling of Tuonela. You must remember why you fight, Hanna. You must remember who you are. The longer you hesitate, the less of your mortal self you will retain."

I tighten my jaw, heart fluttering in my chest. I think of Lovia, of her fierce grin. I think of my father, the warmth of his laughter. I think of Tuoni, how he once anchored me to a world I thought I understood. The man I love. Their faces flicker behind my eyelids, distant stars threatening to wink out. Still, I refuse to let them vanish entirely.

"It's time," my mother says, no softness in her tone. She steps aside, and I face the fiery portal alone. It roars hungrily, an elemental maw ready to devour me, transform me, or both. The heat from it makes my eyes water, blurring the dreamlike landscape. I take a breath, and the essence of this place fills my lungs with something vibrant and alive. Magic, perhaps, or eternity condensed. It may not be oxygen, but it fuels me with strength just the same.

I lift my hand and place it into the flames, expecting pain. Instead, the fire swirls around my wrist like silk, and my heart clenches. In a few steps, I'll be gone from this radiant world, returning to what must now feel like shadow and ash. Will I lose this sense of limitless potential?

Can I carry it with me?

My mother watches, silent and stern. The sky above shifts from gold to bronze, as if the world itself is urging me onward. I inhale one last time, trying to memorize the scent of cinnamon and flowers and the strange, comforting hum of this realm.

I step forward. The flames part. My vision flares bright.

And I move into the fire.

CHAPTER SIX

LOVIA

The forest seems to sigh as we leave the ash behind, Yggthra's final shriek still echoing faintly in my ears. The silence that follows is heavy, an invisible weight pressing down on our shoulders. The Magician walks ahead, guiding us through the maze of twisted trunks and arching roots. I keep my sword ready, my eye firmly on Rasmus to keep him in check. The further we go, the deeper the hush grows, until we move through a world of muffled footsteps, rustling leaves, and water that drips down mossy rock faces.

We tread carefully, and I'm half-expecting another ambush, or for Rasmus to try some trick, even though he's still bound and the Magician gagged him with mycelia again. Thankfully, though, nothing disturbs our journey—no sign of Louhi's henchmen, no flash of monstrous eyes between the trees. There's only an uneasy calm that leaves my nerves taut as a wire.

My leg throbs and burns, and I grit my teeth, determined not to slow us down. Ahead, the Magician's hooded form glides almost soundlessly between towering trunks, as if he's a ghost. Rasmus shuffles behind me, his breathing shallow and irregular. I'm starting to think Yggthra might have cracked a rib or two of his, and I warn myself not to feel sorry for him.

We press on and, before long, shapes begin to loom in the twilight of the forest. More than just trees now—structures, perhaps, wooden huts half-buried in leaves and vines, overgrown platforms winding around colossal trunks. The scent of moss and rich soil intensifies, and an odd warmth blows through the damp air.

Something stirs beyond the ferns, and we freeze, my sword half-raised, my heart pounding.

A sudden whisper runs through the trees, like leaves brushing against bark, and then, they appear. At first, I don't recognize them. They look too rooted in this place, as much a part of the forest as the trees themselves.

Tapio emerges from behind a massive cedar, his beard a wilderness of twisted branches and tangled moss. A squirrel peeks from within his leafy tangle, their eyes curious and afraid. When the Forest God recognizes us, he lifts a hand in greeting, leaves falling from his sleeves like dust motes.

Behind him stands his daughter, Tellervo, her wild red hair tangled over her shoulders. Two small antlers curl from her head, adorned with ribbons of vine and flowers. She peers at us through narrowed green eyes, posture guarded, brow furrowed in mistrust, even though we have met many times before. I guess I can't really blame her; I probably shouldn't be trusting them either, especially with Louhi's black magic permeating these woods.

They are not alone. More shapes flit behind them—lesser forest spirits, perhaps—staying to the shadows, chittering and whispering anxiously. I have never seen them like this before: hiding, uncertain, on edge, as if they fear their own home. It's enough to get me to lower my defenses.

Tapio's voice crackles softly through the silence. "Lovia?

What news do you bring?" He rakes his eyes over me and the Magician, lingering on Rasmus with clear disdain. The squirrel darts back into his beard, as if to emphasize his agitation.

Tellervo steps forward, head tilted, antlers catching a stray beam of dim forest light. She eyes Rasmus first, lip curling. "You dare come here with him?" she demands, her voice sharper than thorns at the edge of the thicket. "He stinks of Louhi's foul magic."

At the mention of Louhi, the lesser spirits hiss quietly from the greenery, and a hush falls so thick, I can almost taste the tension.

The Magician raises a hand, galaxies swirling faintly in the dark void beneath his hood. "We mean no harm, Tapio, Tellervo," he says smoothly, voice resonating between the trunks. "We seek your help. Shadow's End has been taken over. Tuoni and Hanna have been disposed of, Louhi is controlling Death's double, and Salainen is pretending to be Hanna."

Tapio's eyes narrow as he strokes his beard, dislodging a sparrow that flutters out nervously. "I knew it. I knew something was wrong. That's why we left Shadow's End in a hurry after the bone match. Where is Tuonen? I tried to warn him, but I'm not sure he understood."

At the mention of my brother's name, my heart sinks. "You haven't seen him?"

The Magician had said he felt my brother was still alive, but other than that, I have no idea where he could be.

Tapio shakes his head. "Only at Shadow's End. We escaped in the night. I had a feeling in my gut that I wasn't dealing with either Tuoni or Hanna. I knew it was Louhi's influence."

Fuck. That means Tuonen might still be with her. I can only hope that when he realizes the truth—he's bound to sooner or later—that he at least fakes it with her. If she knows he's wise to her, I don't know what she'll do. Once upon a time, I could never imagine my mother hurting either of us, but now that I know what she'd do to take over the world and unleash Kaaos, I fear he won't be spared.

"Where have you come from?" Tellervo asks us, still glaring at Rasmus. "And why is he here?"

"I had been ferrying the boat when the Old Gods began to rise," I explain, trying to give her the simplest version of events. "I battled them before I ran into the Magician. The City of Death has collapsed, with Inmost breaking free. There is no more Golden Mean or Amaranthus. There is only depravity."

"I was there when it crumbled," the Magician adds. "Luckily, I ran into Lovia. We headed here to find you, to find our allies. Along the way, Rasmus came to stop us. Then, an Old God tried to do the same."

"You didn't see Nyyrikki or Mielikki, did you?" Tapio asks, his voice heavy with worry, to which I shake my head. "When we returned to the forest, we sensed something evil had already permeated the soil here. We immediately started looking for Nyyrikki, who had stayed in the forest and never made it to the bone match. But while we were searching, we became separated from Mielikki. I can't explain it. One minute, she was here, the next, she wasn't. We have been searching the forest ever since and still we cannot find either of them."

"We hear them," Tellervo says, her eyes darting around the trees nervously. "The Old Gods. They have awakened in the deep groves outside of our wards, but we don't know how much longer they can hold. It's as if our own magic is weakening, like the forest is turning on us. Nothing is as it should be."

"And so why is he still alive?" Tapio says, nodding at

Rasmus. "He's Louhi's son, is he not? Why didn't you kill him the first chance you got?"

"Because Yggthra, the Old God that tried to stop us, was about to kill him," I explain.

"So you got soft?" Tapio says gruffly, in a way that reminds me of my father.

"I didn't get *soft*," I say, struggling to keep my voice calm. "I just realized that if Louhi was willing to kill him, then he's no longer under her command—not blindly, anyway. He is our prisoner. He may be dangerous, but we need him alive. If he is not useful as leverage, then he may be helpful with intel."

Tellervo snorts, unimpressed, but Tapio's gaze seems to search my face, as if looking for truth etched amid the pain and grime in my features.

"The only intel we need is where to find my wife and son," Tapio says slowly. "We need to find them before we can make any other plans."

The Magician dips his head. "That is why we seek you. Time is short, and we need all the allies we can get, including your wife and son. We will help you find them if you promise us to help find others—Ahto, Vellamo, Ilmatar. Especially Tuoni, as I know he'll be back in this world before long."

"Don't forget Hanna," Tellervo says.

"And Hanna, of course," he affirms. "She has a part to play here too, maybe the biggest part of all. But we can't fight against Louhi unless we are united. It is only then we have a fighting chance."

Tellervo takes in his words, her gaze lingering on Rasmus, distrust shining in her eyes. I tighten my hold on the mycelium rope, feeling the hostility radiating from the gods.

"Your prisoner," Tapio says, raising his chin, "carries the stain of Louhi. He does not belong in this forest."

Tellervo steps forward and tilts her head at Rasmus, wild

red hair shifting over her shoulders like a living vine. "Louhi's spawn," she repeats, her tone flat but vibrating with disgust. "If we let him live, we risk more corruption taking root here. None of us can trust him. How can we even start searching for my brother and mother when we'll be looking over our shoulder, waiting for him to make his move? What if his very presence here is enough to break the wards protecting us?"

The Magician's hands make a prayer gesture. "It will be our task to watch him. We ask only for your patience," he says gently. "I feel the part he has to play will be revealed before long."

"Why wait?" I ask. "Let him speak for himself. We've kept him gagged for our own safety, not to mention how fucking annoying he is, but perhaps he should decide his fate. If he's truly beyond saving, he can prove it with his own words."

Tellervo's eyes narrow at the idea, and the forest hushes, as if holding its breath.

"You would set him free?" Tapio asks, tone suspicious as he strokes his beard.

"I didn't say that," I say firmly. "But let him talk. Let him state his allegiance. If he speaks about treachery, let alone attempts it..." I shrug, letting the gleam of my sword say the rest. "We have shown him we can kill Old Gods. He might be a shaman, but he is mortal."

Rasmus's eyes dart from side to side. The Magician steps forward and, with a careful flick of his hand, the mycelia retract slightly from Rasmus' mouth, unveiling his lips but keeping his arms and legs bound.

Rasmus coughs once, finding his voice. When he speaks, it's hoarse but clearer than before. "You think I'm a pawn," he says, glaring at each of us in turn. "You think I have no choice, but I do."

We all stare at him expectantly, the Magician's hands raised, ready to shut him up if needed.

Rasmus tries to stand straighter, though the bonds pull him taut. He wets his cracked lips. "Louhi may be my mother," he begins, "but she left me to die. She sent Yggthra to finish the job, didn't she?" He glances at me and the Magician, fear and hatred mingling in his stare. "I'm aware you saved me—Gods know you keep reminding me—but you have things the other way around. You don't trust me, but I have no reason to trust you either.

"But I don't want to die," he goes on after a deep breath, his voice steadier now. "Not for Louhi, not for any of you. If I must choose, I will choose survival, my own skin." He grits his teeth, anger making his eyes gleam. "If helping you fight back means I get to live another day, then I'll do it. If betraying you later means a better bargain, then maybe I'll do that too."

Well, I certainly didn't expect him to admit that.

A hush falls. Tapio's beard ripples with quiet disapproval, the squirrel chattering uneasily. Tellervo's nostrils flare. The Magician remains silent, galaxies swirling, unreadable.

"So you're a selfish bastard, that's what you're saying?" I ask.

Rasmus juts out his chin. "I'm an honest bastard, more honest than you'll ever get from a cornered animal. Let me go, and I'll help you because it's in my interest. I can't return to Shadow's End now, and being alone here means certain death." He looks at the Magician's voided face. "Or keep me leashed; it guarantees I won't be able to help any of you, including myself."

Tapio's shoulders sag slightly. "This is what mortals have become," he says with disappointment. "Rootless and faithless, serving only themselves."

I step forward, sword lowered. "Then we let him live," I

say. "For now. We will see if his self-interest keeps him useful. Otherwise..."

"So you'll free me?" Rasmus asks.

I give him a grim smile. "Don't get ahead of yourself. We'll see when the time is right."

"Very well," Tapio says. "This forest is no place for traitors or turncoats, but if you vouch for his momentary worth, we won't interfere. We have greater fears at the moment." He gestures to the sky slowly growing dark beyond the trees. "The longer we stand here talking about this, the further we get from finding my wife and son. We must set off again before darkness falls."

Rasmus exhales, and I can feel his relief. His honesty probably saved his life, but I'll be damned if I let my guard down around him. I know he can't help us if he's bound, but if or when his help is needed, then I'll reassess the situation. Until then, that boy is still our prisoner.

Tellervo's eyes flicker toward my leg. I know I'm still limping, that the arrowhead is still lodged in my calf, causing a constant, throbbing ache I've done my best to ignore.

"Your leg," she says, voice softer now, the brusqueness fading. "It weakens you, and we have little time for weakness." Her tone is blunt but not cruel. "How did it happen?" Her gaze shifts to Rasmus before I even get the chance to tell her.

To his credit, he looks away, seeming ashamed.

"Sit," she instructs me as she glares at him. A mossy rock beside me glows faintly, and I reluctantly lower myself on it, my legs straining from the effort.

Tapio shifts, and I sense the forest around us humming with a subtle energy. The Magician watches from a short distance, galaxies swirling quietly under his hood. Rasmus, still bound, keeps silent, perhaps realizing that making a sound right now would be unwise.

Tellervo kneels gracefully and studies the torn flesh. She nods once, and without a word, she places her hands on either side of the wound. Her fingers are warm but not hot, as if infused with gentle sunlight filtered through leaves.

I brace myself for pain, but what I feel is something else—a slow, radiating warmth that seeps into the muscle and bone. I gasp softly as I sense the arrowhead shifting. There's a moment of pressure, then a sudden relief as the shard of metal slides free. I look down to see green shoots coming from the ground, carrying the broken part away.

Chartreuse light swirls around Tellervo's hands, filtering into the wound. I watch, stunned, as the torn edges of flesh knit themselves back together. The raw agony dulls to a faint throb before it vanishes entirely. Within moments, my skin is smooth, unbroken, save for a faint, shimmering scar.

Tellervo sits back on her heels, brushing her palms together. "There. Take care not to get shot again. Your body keeps score when it comes to my magic. It can only take so much before it won't work at all."

Good to know.

I test my leg, putting weight on it, astonished at how easily I rise. "Thank you," I manage to say. The pain that has dogged me feels like a memory, and with it, some of my uncertainty lifts. I feel stronger—more myself again. You don't realize what a hold pain has over you until it's gone.

Tapio's deep eyes shift between us, lingering on Rasmus then returning to me and the Magician. "I hate to seem insensitive, but we really should get going."

"We'll find them, don't worry," I tell him. "And once we do, I know just where to go. Louhi has spread her influence wide. Her servants, her allies—they're in the open. They've taken over Tuonela. We need somewhere to gather and hide far away from her, somewhere she would never suspect us to go."

The Magician tilts his head. "You have something in mind?"

From the tone of his voice, I think he already knows what I'm about to say.

I nod. "Castle Syntri. Louhi's palace by the Star Swamp."

Rasmus makes a muffled sound of protest—he knows the place. Everyone does. The Star Swamp is a realm of luminous bogs, of twisted spirits, of dangerous illusions. The swamp itself isn't made of water but of Oblivion; falling in means a fate worse than death. After Louhi left my father, it became her own seat of power in the north, one she shared with her shaman consort, Ilmarinen. It's the last place she'd think we'd go, a place no sane creature willingly ventures, let alone us.

"Her palace?" Tellervo asks, her antlered head tilting in disbelief. The animals in Tapio's beard grow silent, as if stunned. "You want to march right into her old domain? When everything that surrounds it is Oblivion?"

"Not march," I say. "We sneak and we hide. We plan. She won't be expecting us there, not if she believes we're searching for her in our usual haunts. We find Nyyrikki and Mielikki and we head straight there. If we can do it undiscovered, then we might be able to gather enough allies and make a good enough plan. It's shelter. We can turn it into a fortress."

The Magician's galaxies flare in a silent show of agreement. Tapio's forehead creases with concern as he nods gravely, while Tellervo stares at me for a moment before she finally gives me a wry smile.

"You're mad," she says softly, "but I think we might need to be in order to survive."

She gets it. I look over at Rasmus. "Well? If you know something or have anything to say about this plan, now is the time to speak up."

He gnaws on his lip for a moment. "Ilmarinen is still there. Louhi left him behind."

"And? He is mortal, is he not? I'm sure we can take care of him."

"He is still a shaman, no matter how much magic Louhi has drained from him," he says. "Remember, it's his power that helped her gain so much. It would be a mistake to discount him."

"But she's been torturing that man for years," Tapio says. "How could he still be on her side?"

The look in Rasmus' eyes darkens. "Because that's what abuse looks like. That's what brainwashing looks like. Your loyalty is ingrained in you through pain," he adds quietly. "Until it becomes all you know."

I have to admit, I'm starting to feel a little sorry for Rasmus. I know I shouldn't; I know he's probably trying to manipulate me after I saved his life, after he saw my compassion, my weakness. My father never would have made such a mistake—neither would my mother, for that matter. Where I get this bleeding heart from, I don't know, but I sure as hell don't like it.

My eyes meet the Magician's face, and I feel strength in those spinning stars. It gives me my resolve back.

"Then we'll be ready for him and whatever magic he might wield," I say as I nod at Tapio to lead us through the forest.

CHAPTER SEVEN

TUONEN

RANGAISTA, I THINK, MY HEART SINKING LIKE A STONE AS THE figure comes down the steps into the dungeon.

The demon has returned to pay its grandson a visit after all.

But as it approaches, the shadow gets smaller and smaller until a dog made of metal, fur, and bone appears, sitting back on his haunches, his iron tail scraping against the ground as it wags.

"Rauta!" I whisper. "You came!"

Rauta lifts a paw as if to wave at me, and I notice the soft padding under the metal, enabling him to sneak around quietly.

"Good boy," I tell him, moving to the bars and crouching down to his level. His head tilts, and he looks at me as if to say, *now what?*

"See if you can find something to break me out of here," I whisper. "Are there any keys hanging on the wall somewhere?"

It's unlikely, but Rauta understands and starts sniffing around, nose to the ground and tail wagging. I'm not surprised when he comes back shaking his head.

"Well, fuck," I mumble.

Rauta pads forward and pushes his soft nose against one of the cell bars, opening his mouth and slowly running its iron tongue along the metal. Then, he bares his metallic teeth, sharp and strong, as thick and long as my thumb.

I move back cautiously, unsure what he has planned.

The dog bites down on the bar, and sparks fly, the sound so grating, I have to cover my ears. He starts to tug at it as if it's a meager chew toy, and I watch, wincing, as Rauta pulls the bar out, widening the gap. He moves on to the next bar, pulling it in the opposite direction until there's just enough room for me to squeeze through.

Fuck. That dog is a lot stronger than I thought.

I quickly get up and squeeze through the bars, stepping out into the dimly lit corridor.

"You did it," I whisper, leaning down and scratching behind his ears. "Good boy, good boy. Now, let's get Sarvi. We have no time to lose."

We hurry to the next cell over, the place I expected Sarvi to be, only to find it empty.

I stare at it for a moment, dumbfounded. I could have sworn I heard the unicorn in here. Then again, I have been in and out of consciousness for a while, and Sarvi never once communicated back. Perhaps it was someone or something else. Perhaps it was nothing at all.

Panicked, I go to the next cell and the next, but I'm the only prisoner here.

And I'm running out of time.

"Okay, Rauta," I say to the dog, "looks like it's just you and me, boy. Do you know the way out to the Crystal Caves?"

The dog nods and then starts trotting down the corridor, already disappearing around a corner.

I hurry after him, trying not to think about what could

have possibly happened to Sarvi. I have to believe my mother spared them, welcomed them into the fold, that Sarvi is smart enough to play along and pledge allegiance, even if it's a lie. I have to believe Sarvi made it out of here alive. The alternative is too bitter of a pill to swallow, not when it feels like I keep losing everyone by the minute.

I round the corner, going past one of the statues outside of the crypt that hasn't turned into a living saint and walked away like the rest of them. It has one sword implanted in its hand, and I use all my strength to try and pry it off the marble. In the end, I headbutt it with my horns. They're strong enough to shatter the hand into pieces, freeing the sword into my grasp. It's old and slightly rusty in places, but it will have to do. I can't depend on an iron-jawed dog to save me if we run up against any of the guards—or anything else.

But as Rauta leads me to the underground water system where my father often launches his boats, we don't come across anyone. Still, I know our luck won't last if we don't move fast.

I look to the right, to where the water passes through the gate and empties out into the sea. Part of me thinks that would be an easier way of escape, but the moment we enter the open water, we'd be sitting ducks for the guards patrolling the castle above.

So, we climb into the small boat, with me at the oars, my new sword at the ready, and Rauta at the front. I start rowing toward the darkness, which should eventually lead us to the sparkling spectacle that is the Crystal Caves.

The boat creaks as I set the oars into motion, the faint echo of water lapping against stone walls following each stroke. Rauta sits at the bow, his iron jaw parted slightly, as if tasting the air. Darkness surrounds us like a heavy blanket, with only faint phosphorence high on the cave ceiling, and with my ability to see in the dark now lacking, I have to strain my eyes to see where I'm going.

I keep my new sword balanced across my knees, trying not to think about what it will be like if we run into trouble here. I can't expect anything friendly in these depths. I think the two of us could handle a couple of guards, but anything more than that, and we might be outmatched.

Still, I find myself whispering into the gloom. "We just have to reach the Crystal Caves. There's a route there that leads deeper underground—maybe we can slip away, find allies, or just hide until...until what?" The question drifts unanswered. I shake my head, refocusing on the sound of the oars, the splash and pull of water.

Rauta's tail scrapes softly against the wooden boards, a subtle rhythm that keeps my nerves from unraveling completely—he must sense my tension. He's the only ally I have left right now, and I'm grateful for his steady presence. There's no fear, no doubt, just silent loyalty.

The air down here is damp and stale, heavy with the scent of algae and rot. The occasional drip from above makes me flinch, and I can't help but imagine threats lurking in every shadow, but nothing attacks us yet. The tunnel widens gradually, the ceiling arching higher, the silence growing more profound. If we can get to the Crystal Caves, I remind myself, we'll have a chance to navigate beyond Louhi's grasp and disappear into the rest of Tuonela. I must believe that.

When it feels like I've been rowing forever, the darkness starts to recede. Ahead, I see a soft, eerie glow—phosphorescent moss or lichen clinging to the cavern's walls. As we approach, the waterway broadens into an underground lake that bends around corners. Amethyst stalactites drip overhead, and strange crystal formations loom like sentinels. I slow the oars, letting the boat drift.

"Rauta," I whisper. The dog's head lifts, ears tilting as he listens. "We must be getting close." The hound offers no reply, only a faint scraping of claws on wood, but I imagine he approves.

I dip the oars again and begin to steer the boat around the perimeter. The glow intensifies in patches where clusters of fungus and moss thrive. My father once mentioned that these waterways wind through a series of interconnected caves, some filled with crystals as bright as the sun. I hope that once we reach them, their brilliance might help us find a safe path.

Just as I relax into a rhythm, a subtle ripple disturbs the surface of the lake. I freeze, lifting the oars. The water settles, and then another ripple appears, radiating outward from a point somewhere to my left. Rauta stands, iron joints creaking softly, and lowers his head, a low growl escaping his throat. My heart hammers.

Something is here.

A scent hits me—stale brine, decaying fish, a hint of sulfur. I pick up the sword and grip it tight, trying to pinpoint the direction of the disturbance. Then, I see it: a shadow beneath the water, sliding beneath the boat. I lean over instinctively, squinting, and regret it instantly when the shadow rises.

With a roar, a monstrous form heaves itself partially out of the water on the other side of the boat, enough for me to glimpse a cluster of eyes, bulbous and shining, set into a grotesque amalgamation of bone and shell that serves as a face. Tendrils of kelp hang from its scaled hide, and barnacle-like growths pockmark its body. It has to be an Old God—its presence is both ancient and unmistakably predatory.

And, frankly, disgusting.

"Rauta!" I shout, but the hound is already moving. He leaps onto the skinny prow, iron jaws snapping. The Old God's eyes blink in eerie syncopation as a sinuous tentacle-like limb lashes out of the water. It slams into the boat's side with a crack, sending it rocking violently. I yelp, nearly losing the sword overboard, and scramble for balance.

The creature's mouth opens—not a normal mouth, but a vertical slit rimmed with serrated edges. It emits a sound that vibrates through my bones, and I grit my teeth, forcing myself not to freeze. We have to fight back, or else we'll die here.

Rauta lunges, jaws clamping down on something that might be an appendage or a protruding spine. There's a sick crunching sound as metal grinds bone. The Old God thrashes, whipping the water into a frenzy. Waves splash into the boat, soaking my trousers. I raise the sword, a determined growl escaping my throat.

I swing the blade down toward the creature's closest limb, slicing through a fleshy tendril. The Old God shrieks, retracting into the water but not retreating. Instead, it circles beneath us, the boat spinning in its wake. My knuckles ache from gripping the sword, my body pathetically weak without the tips of my horns, and I hunch low to keep from being tossed overboard.

The hound turns, poised at the front. Without warning, the beast's tail—if that's what it is—breaks the surface behind us, crashing down. The boat lurches upward then slams down. I'm thrown forward, sword clattering against the hull. Pain radiates through my arm, but I scramble upright, heart pounding. Water sloshes around my ankles now, but I can't tell if we're sinking yet.

Then, Rauta decides to leap from the boat into the water.

"No!" I cry out as the dog disappears under the murky surface with a large splash. For one horrible, excruciating second, I think I've lost him.

Then, the Old God rears up, shrieking as bubbles erupt

where Rauta attacks beneath the waves. The beast half-rises, revealing twisted limbs and a ridged carapace.

It's now or never.

I lunge forward, half-submerged in the water quickly filling the boat, swinging the sword with both hands. The blade strikes the Old God's chitinous flank, and chips of shell rain down. The monster's eyes swivel toward me, each one burning with a ghastly inner light. It hisses, whipping a muscular limb toward me. I try to dodge, but it hits my fore-arm, numbing it in an instant.

I cry out, almost dropping the sword. What the fuck?

Is its touch paralyzing?

The boat spins wildly, and I realize we're drifting away from the cavern wall, further into the open lake. If I can just push the Old God back, maybe we can escape around it, but it seems determined to make a meal of our bones.

My breath comes in ragged gasps. The stale air and the stench of the creature's hide threaten to choke me, and I shake out my arm violently until I get some feeling back, the sword now in my other, weaker hand.

Rauta resurfaces on the other side of the Old God, clinging to a ridge of bone with his iron jaws. The monster wails, torn between attacking me and shaking off the hound. Its tail slams down again, missing the boat by inches, sending a spray of foul droplets into my face. I wipe my eyes, fury mounting inside me. We cannot die here, not after escaping that dungeon.

I brace my feet against the boat's edge, summoning my courage. The sword trembles in my grip until I pass it over to my other hand, strength and feeling returning in the nick of time. With a warrior's cry, I thrust it forward into a gap between shell plates. The metal grinds into softer flesh beneath, and black ichor gushes out, coating my hand. The Old God screeches, thrashing violently as Rauta digs deeper, ripping free a piece of cartilage with a grating crunch.

The creature's limbs flail blindly, tearing at stalactites and sending chunks of rock tumbling. One fragment glances off my shoulder, but I ignore the pain. The Old God tries to dive, to slip back into the safety of the lake's depths, but Rauta holds fast. I can see the hound's eyes glinting in the phosphorescent light, no fear, no hesitation.

"Finish it," I grit out. I adjust my angle and slide the sword deeper, twisting it with every ounce of strength I have left. My muscles burn, and I feel the blade meet resistance. I push harder until something gives—a sickening crack—and the Old God's shrieks reach a fever pitch.

Rauta yanks downward, and I see one of the creature's eyes burst into milky fluid. The horror convulses, tentacles slapping helplessly against the boat's hull. I pull the sword free and stab again, this time straight into its gaping maw. Teeth crumble as the blade penetrates deeper. The Old God's cry turns into a ragged, bubbling gasp.

Then, with one last, spasmodic jerk, it collapses, half of it still above the surface. I scramble back as it begins to sink, its weight pulling it down. Rauta leaps free just in time, splashing into the water and dog-paddling back to the boat. I lean over, grabbing his collar with my free hand, and haul him aboard. He shakes his head, spraying me with droplets, then settles onto the damp planks, tail thumping happily, as if that was no big deal at all.

I'm trembling, half in shock. My ears ring and my lungs burn. If I wasn't so terrified and exhausted, I might laugh at how close we came to death. Instead, I slump down, sword still clutched tight, staring at the ripples as the beast slowly sinks beneath the surface. The water, stained with black sludge, slowly settles.

The boat rocks gently, filled with water but still floating.

There's a metaphor there somewhere.

I run a hand over my face, smearing ichor across my cheek, and Rauta nudges my shoulder with a comforting whine. My shoulder aches from where the rocks hit it, but I'm alive. We're both alive.

"Good job, Rauta," I whisper, voice shaking. "Good boy." The words sound absurd after what we just endured. *Good boy*, as if he fetched a stick, not tore apart a monster.

I take a few moments to catch my breath. We must keep moving. The Crystal Caves lie ahead, somewhere through this labyrinth of waterways. I can't stop now. The longer we linger, the more likely we'll attract attention from other horrors.

I retrieve the oars, my hands unsteady. Every muscle protests as I row, guiding us away from the scene of the battle. The damp air rasps in my throat, but I row on, following the faint glow in the distance, one that burns brighter than the phosphoresce on the walls.

Rauta sits at the bow again, iron tail tapping lightly, as if beating a drum to encourage a warrior. The silence that follows is almost peaceful, but I know it's only a lull. Yet, I feel a grim spark of confidence kindle in my chest. We survived an attack from an Old God—not easily, but we made it through. If we can endure that, maybe we can find our way out of this nightmare after all.

I pray it's not wishful thinking.

I row through the darkness, water dripping from stalactites like a strange, slow applause. Rauta's silhouette remains steady, a guardian who knows no fear. I need to borrow some of the dog's courage.

Eventually, the waterways narrow until the light is a bright pinprick at the end of the tunnel, which slowly grows bigger and blinding until we find ourselves in the Crystal Caves.

Like before, there are amethyst stalactites, but it has increased tenfold. There are also formations of citrine, rose quartz, aquamarine, and fire quartz coming from all directions, including up through the water like a forest of shimmering tree trunks.

Even Rauta looks in awe as his eyes take in the cave, everything sparkling and shimmering in millions of pastel shades. It's beautiful and mesmerizing, especially as the crystals seem to emit a faint melodic chime, but even so, I remain on guard. I know I can't take anything for granted here.

Eventually, the boat slides against the shore, against sand made of crushed crystals in shifting colors and fine white moss, the water in the shallows the color of pink milk.

Rauta leaps onto the land as I step out of the boat, my sword gripped firmly. There's a passage ahead of us, the walls made of tourmaline. It leads somewhere, hopefully the way out.

Rauta trots off in that direction, and I start to follow.

"Tuonen, Son of Death," a deep, primordial voice echoes through the caves, causing stalactites of quartz and amethyst to fall from the ceiling and shatter.

Rauta stops and barks, looking at me over his shoulder for guidance.

Vipunen!

I thought we could end up near Vipunen's cave, the all-knowing giant who taught Lovia and I how to fight in our blind masks. But now that alliances have shifted, the cryptic deity might be as compromised as the rest of them.

"Come closer," the giant's voice rumbles, coming from everywhere all at once. "Do you see that light?"

The glow shines in the distance, illuminating the pockets of crystals in the walls, turning everything a shade of lavender.

"Follow the light," he booms.

"How do we know we can trust you?" I ask, wincing at the tremble in my voice, though the sword remains steady in my grip.

"At this point, Tuonen, I don't think you have a choice," he says with a chuckle. "If I meant you any harm, I would have caused it already."

Uh huh.

"And that thing back there wasn't it?"

"Oh, that?" Vipunen booms. "That was just Iku-Turso, an Old God I haven't seen in a very long time. Pain in the ass, if you ask me, but you did a fine job of disposing of it. Better you hurry in case another takes its place. Those tentacles regenerate, you know."

I glance behind me at the water and sigh, exchanging a look with Rauta.

Looks like we don't have a choice.

CHAPTER EIGHT

DEATH

The wind bites at my face as we step out of the barracks into the bleak Finnish winter, the sky a pall of heavy, low clouds that seem to trap the light. It's midday, and yet everything is as dim as twilight. We stand on a tarmac that leads to the fields beyond, where a procession of trucks sits rumbling, idling in place. Soldiers—my soldiers, at least for now—wait in half-dazed silence. Their breath clouds in the air, their gloved hands clenching rifles, their bodies bundled against the cold in white-and-black camo that makes them blend in with the scenery. I've numbed their fear, their reason, their doubts. With me guiding their thoughts, they do as I ask, their minds barely aware of how strange all of this is.

And this is all very fucking strange.

Torben stands beside me, tugging at his scarf, his blue eyes watering as the wind whips against us. He found the spell and cast it, a fine step forward. Now, we just have to get to the place where the portal will be summoned. Thankfully, it's not far—just a few valleys over. Torben explained that the right combination of natural ley lines converge deep in that forest, lending itself to magical manipulation. With ash, salt, and a spark of the Underworld's essence—mine—we can open a doorway back home.

"Is everyone ready?" I ask, voice echoing in the hushed gloom.

General Pekka gives a curt nod before he barks an order in Finnish. The soldiers move, mechanical yet quiet, the snow crunching beneath their boots as they clamber into the back of the trucks. The engines growl. No one questions the strangeness of it all—a God of Death, an old shaman, and a troop of mortal soldiers heading off into the wilderness, simply because there is no one out here in the middle of nowhere to witness it.

Torben and I climb into the truck with General Pekka at the wheel. I lean out the window and raise a hand, and the drivers, as if guided by invisible strings, set the trucks into motion. We head out along a narrow, snow-packed road, the tires grinding over ice. The forest on either side grows taller, darker, going from bare birch to thick pine. Though the heater is on full blast, the wind still finds its way into the truck and cuts through my cloak, chilling me in a way that reminds me of how out of my element I am. I hate how utterly human this world makes me feel. I hate that it makes me feel *period*.

Torben sits hunched over a small wooden box on his lap that he pulled from his satchel. Inside the box are the ingredients for the spell—ash from a birch branch, salt wrapped in a cloth pouch, and a strand of hair he plucked from my head when I wasn't looking. "Relic of the Underworld," he'd said with a shrug. Turns out, I hate being called a relic.

I didn't protest, though I'll be pissed if that hair doesn't grow back. If this works, we have a chance. If not... Well, if it doesn't, I'll have a thousand mortal soldiers under my command and nothing to do with them while I'm trapped in the Upper World, forced to try and find another portal, hopefully one that's already in existence and not conjured by a spell.

But no delays are acceptable at this point. I must return. Hanna, Lovia, Tuonen, my realm, my people—they all need me.

We drive for over an hour. Day darkens into a purple bruise. Snow begins to fall, lazy flakes that glitter in the headlights. Torben says little—occasionally he mutters to himself, running through words of the incantation, checking and re-checking the lines from his spellbook. The general remains quiet, trusting my mental push to keep him docile but invested and unalarmed by this bizarre mission.

At some point, the road narrows until it's barely a path. The trucks lumber through snow-laden pines, their branches sagging overhead like tired shoulders. We slow as the terrain grows wilder, more uneven, until eventually, the trucks can't go on.

Everything comes to a stop.

The general's voice crackles over a radio, but I shut out the words as I step out of the cab to survey our route. I'm focused on the land, the subtle pulse I feel beneath my boots. It's faint, but I recognize the underlying hum of magic. This place is not ordinary. Something old and potent lingers here—perhaps these very hills remember the old faiths, the old ways, when this world and mine were so much closer.

"I feel it," Torben whispers beside me. He crouches near a hollow stump, brushing away snow to reveal something carved in the wood: a spiral, half-erased by time. "A marker left by those who knew the paths between worlds, perhaps Väinämöinen himself," he says softly, his eyes gleaming with both hope and worry. "We're on the right track."

I nod and signal the soldiers. They abandon the trucks now, leaving them behind. The portal, if it opens, will not be made in the middle of a road. I push my influence out, calming any stray doubts in their minds. They follow without question, rifles strapped across their chests, boots crunching through old snow and brittle undergrowth.

We find a glade beyond a ridge of ice-crusted stones. The trees arch high overhead, their trunks pale and ghostly. The ground underfoot is oddly level, and I feel my heart quicken —this must be the spot. Torben runs a hand along the bark of a birch tree and then scans the clearing, nodding to himself.

"This is it," he murmurs. "I can feel it."

"But it's not a cave," I say, looking around.

"It doesn't have to be," he says.

The soldiers line up single file behind me at my silent command as Torben places the wooden box on the ground and kneels. He sprinkles ash in a wide circle, then the salt. The wind dies down, as if holding its breath. My mouth goes dry. Everything hinges on this.

"Give me your hand," Torben says, his voice low. I take off my glove and extend it, and he takes a small knife from his coat pocket, careful to prick my fingertip without touching me. A bead of dark blood wells up and I smear it onto a scrap of cloth with my hair tied inside—the energy of Tuonela, the essence of me, staining the fabric.

He places it at the center of the circle then pulls out the book. The soldiers stand motionless behind us, human statues in the twilight that mimic the trees.

Torben begins to chant. The language sounds old yet strangely familiar, each word strung like beads of sound that hum through my bones. The ash and salt stir in an unseen breeze. The cloth trembles. I feel something crack in the air, like a door creaking on ancient hinges. The soldiers shift uneasily, picking up on changes they can't understand. I exert more pressure on their minds, keeping them calm.

A faint glow appears above the circle. No, not just a glow —a tear, a rip in reality. It shimmers at first, like heat haze, then broadens, revealing murky shapes beyond. Cold air spills through, richer and darker than the night that has fallen around us. I catch a scent: damp soil, faint rot, and something else I can't name but know all too well—Tuonela's fragrance.

Torben's voice rises in intensity, the spell slipping from his tongue. The portal widens, an oval of shimmering darkness. It's not stable, flickering at the edges. I step closer, peering into the void. I can see something large in the distance, like a building that rises from nothing. Are we truly looking into the Underworld, because though the shapes are vague, they don't seem familiar.

Where are we?

I spare a glance at Torben. He's sweating despite the cold, his breath coming in ragged bursts. I know he's giving it everything he has. I'm grateful, though I won't say it out loud, lest it goes to his head.

In a few moments, we will step through that gash in the fabric of worlds and find ourselves back where we belong—or at least where I belong. My heart twists at the thought that I still don't know what awaits us on the other side. But uncertainty is better than stagnation, better than staying in a frozen world with no answers and far too many humans.

I glance at Torben. "Are you certain that if we walk through here, we'll end up in Tuonela?"

"Where else could we possibly end up?" he asks, wriggling his nose.

In other dimensions and universes and timelines, I can't help but think, though of course I don't voice these thoughts. It would look foolish for a God to fear realms he might not be aware of. Besides, Torben has been sneaking into Tuonela for ages, and before that, Shamans such as Väinämöinen had been doing the same.

"Very well," I say.

I can't help but hold my breath as I step through the portal, leading the way.

It immediately feels like I'm passing through a thin membrane of ice-cold water. For a disorienting moment, I'm suspended between worlds, caught in a swirl of dark shapes and flickering lights. There's a pulling sensation, like something has snared me by the chest and yanked me forward. A heartbeat later, I stagger out onto solid ground—if it can be called that—and nearly lose my footing.

All around, the soldiers spill through, stumbling and blinking. I glimpse Torben emerging as well, his worn face twisted with concentration, still chanting under his breath. The portal crackles and wavers at the edges of my vision, staying open as more and more troops pile through.

I've returned to the Underworld, but it's not the one I remember. We stand on a vast, empty plain beneath a sky of smudged ink. Snow drifts lazily from above, but these are not gentle, familiar flakes; they seem to glow faintly before settling onto a land of eerie stillness.

With a vague pang of horror, I realize we're at the fucking Star Swamp of all places. The land is a frozen bog stretching in all directions, its surface dark and half-reflective like black glass. But it's not glass—my boots crunch and then sink slightly as I shift my weight. The swamp beneath us is not water or soil; it's Oblivion itself, cosmic emptiness suffused with specks of starlight. When I peer down at my feet, I can see tiny pinpoints of light scattered in a liquid darkness that seems both impossibly deep and startlingly close. It's as if I'm standing atop a shard of fallen sky. If anyone slips through the surface, they won't find mud or water. No, they'll find nothingness, the endless void where souls float among the stars forever. The very thought of it makes my spine crawl. As the God of Death, this is the place I should be protecting my people from.

I look around and motion for everyone to stay still as the last soldiers come through the portal, fanning out in all directions before the shimmering doorway snaps shut with a thunderclap, leaving no sign of it behind.

"Listen up," I tell them. "It's imperative that you follow my instructions. Whatever you do, do not fall in the swamp, or you will be lost forever."

The soldiers huddle closer, their rifles clinking. They look around with vacant eyes, only faintly aware they should be shocked. My mental influence is still in place, yet I can sense their growing confusion. I need to assert control before panic sets in.

"Steady," I say, projecting my will. They stiffen slightly, their minds docile again. It's harder here, though I can't tell if it's because they're in Tuonela or because I'm in the Star Swamp. This land was Louhi's domain; of course it would not welcome me back easily.

I turn and look over the landscape. Snow is falling, dusting the black swamp with a pale powder before it sinks into the darkness, mirroring my feelings. In the distance, I see the faint silhouette I saw earlier: Castle Syntri, Louhi's palace. She chose a wretched spot to build her seat of power, perched on a rise of jagged stone, its spires dark and icy. I know there are halls inside filled with old weapons, relics, magic tools. If we can reach her palace, we might find what we need—a vantage point, supplies, maybe even secrets to turn the tide. But getting there is another matter. The swamp stretches for miles, and every step is treacherous.

With a sigh, I gesture toward the distant castle. "That's where we must go," I say to Torben. My breath puffs white in the chill. "That's Louhi's old stronghold. If we can get inside, we can gather ourselves, find what we need, and plan."

Torben tugs his scarf tighter and squints at the distant

silhouette. "It looks close, but I know better than to trust my eyes here."

He's right. Distances in the Underworld can be deceiving, especially in a place like the Star Swamp, where perspective is warped by the deadly pools.

I pick a path forward. Torben, the generals, and the soldiers follow behind me, trudging carefully. I warn them again to step lightly, to test each patch of ground, but my warning comes too late for some. There's a sudden splash, followed by a despairing cry that makes my heart stop.

I whip around and watch in horror as a man slips waist-deep, his rifle falling from numb hands. He screams, a raw, panicked sound that sends a shiver through me. I scramble back to him, reaching out, but before I can grasp his hand, he's yanked down into the star-studded darkness below. For an instant, I see his face twisted in terror beneath me, lit by the faint glimmer of cosmic lights. Then, he vanishes, swallowed by Oblivion.

Only silence remains.

My stomach twists. That soldier is gone forever, lost. Not even the realm of death can reclaim him now. He's trapped in that infinite void, drifting among stars that care nothing for souls. The realization that my carelessness cost him his eternity hits me like a hammer. Although I coerced him, he was still under my charge. If I intend to use these mortals to save Tuonela, I owe it to them not to discard their lives so easily.

"Careful!" I shout, voice cracking. The soldiers hesitate, shuffling nervously. Another one steps wrong, the ground giving way beneath her foot. She yelps, grabbing at a comrade's shoulder. They manage to haul her back before she slips under, but the tension is mounting. They can smell danger now, and no amount of mental manipulation will entirely quell it.

Torben kneels, pressing a hand to the surface of the

swamp. "This won't do," he mutters. "We can't cross it, not like this."

"I know," I snap, trying to keep the panic from my voice. "But we must. The palace is our only hope, the only place I can hide this many troops from Louhi's spies."

He glances up at me, annoyance briefly sparking in his eyes. "Do you think I don't know that? Give me a moment." He fumbles in his satchel, producing his spellbook again, the pages rustling in the frigid wind.

"Another spell?" I ask, voice low. I can feel the soldiers watching me, looking for reassurance. I send a calming wave of thought through their minds, telling them to stay still, to not move an inch. In the silence, I can hear Torben's quiet chanting.

He sprinkles a handful of something onto the swamp. Salt? Ash? I can't tell. He closes his eyes, murmuring a string of words I do not understand. The sound of his voice changes, becoming resonant, echoing in this wretched landscape. I'm reminded of how he summoned the portal earlier —only now, we're using magic in a place that already has magic infused in its very bones.

At first, nothing happens. Then, I hear a crackling sound, like ice forming on a pond. The soldiers gasp. I look down and see that the black surface is freezing over with a layer of frost. It spreads outward from Torben's fingertips, radiating across the swamp's surface. Snowflakes settle on the newly forming crust and do not sink. The sparkling darkness below grows dim, veiled by translucent ice. I test it with the toe of my boot, and it holds firm.

"Clever old man," I say, relieved. He stands, shoulders slumping with effort. "You can keep it frozen?"

He nods grimly. "Not indefinitely," he warns, "but long enough for us to cross if we move swiftly."

I don't waste a second. "Forward!" I bark to the soldiers,

filling their minds with encouragement, a gentle push that makes their feet find purpose. They pick their way across the swamp now, careful but quick, each step clicking on the thin film of ice. I keep them in a loose formation, rifles at the ready, though what good bullets will be against Old Gods and horrors of the Underworld, I don't know.

Torben and I fall into step near the center of the group. The cold bites at my cheeks, and I taste iron on the wind. The palace looms larger with every stride, a cluster of dark, jagged towers that look like claws scraping at the white stained sky, a poor man's version of Shadow's End. I remember this place from ages past, its halls lined with strange relics and Louhi's awful decorating. Her sour presence still lingers here, though she's gone—for now.

Oh the irony that the two of us have switched places. If I wasn't in such a mood, I might even laugh.

We press on in tense silence, the only sounds the crunch of boots on ice and the faint whisper of snowfall, the soldiers marching forward, eyes ahead, focused on the task I implanted in their minds: get to Castle Syntri and get there safely.

Torben looks drained, his breath coming in harsh puffs. The ice under us is stable for now, but I see hairline cracks forming as we walk. Oblivion resists being tamed. We must make haste.

Soon, the ground beneath us begins to slope upward. The ice gives way to actual ground—if you can call it that—where skeletal trees cluster, their branches rattling like old bones. I sigh with relief; the swamp is behind us now, a shimmering field of starlit blackness hidden under a thin shell of Torben's magic. I feel a surge of gratitude for the shaman, my mortal father-in-law. Without his spell, we would have lost more troops, maybe even all of them.

The soldiers pause, waiting at the base of a rough, frozen

hill. I nod at them, and they line up, disciplined and quiet. The palace is just ahead, rising from the snow like a gravestone. Once inside, we can take stock, search for what we need—weapons that bite deeper than mortal bullets, armor that can withstand curses and claws, clues as to Louhi's fate and how we might stop her forces.

And I must hope Hanna, Lovia, Tuonen, and the rest of my family hold on, wherever they are. I'm no savior yet, but at least I have a path forward. I have men who will fight for me, even if coerced. I have a shaman who can bend magic to our needs. I have this dreadful land beneath my feet, reminding me that to rule death, one must face it down a thousand times.

With a silent command, I push the soldiers onward, toward Louhi's lair and whatever comes next.

CHAPTER NINE

LOVIA

THE FOREST FEELS DIFFERENT AT NIGHT.

There's a hush in the air, as if the trees lean in to listen to our footsteps. The five of us move through a realm of towering trunks and sweeping canopies, tangled vines and ferns brushing at our ankles. In the lead are Tapio and Tellervo, stepping lightly, the old forest father and his antler-crowned daughter. They move as if they belong here—because they do. The forest is part of them, and they are part of it, like limbs of the same ancient creature.

Rasmus, still bound though no longer gagged, trudges unhappily a short distance behind them. Somehow, he has managed to stay quiet, I guess because he knows how quickly the Forest Gods would turn on him. I watch him stumble, and though he has certainly earned no sympathy from me, I can't help but sense an unease pulsing beneath his bravado. He's rattled. He knows he's alive only because we allow it, and he's right not to trust us.

At the back of the line, I walk beside the Magician. Tellervo occasionally glances our way, ensuring we keep pace, and her father casts a stern eye over his shoulder now and then, as if worried we'll vanish. Their worry and concern over their loved ones is palpable, lending tension to the air.

My leg feels surprisingly good, at least. Tellervo performed a miracle, and that I can walk without limping or feeling any pain is amazing. But still, there's anxiety inside me that can't be healed.

It's because of the Magician. He is right beside me, silent yet not silent. Even when he isn't speaking, the presence of those swirling galaxies under his hood is a language of its own. In the dark, the stars on his face glow, and I know his mood in the subtle shifts of constellations, the way colors bloom and fade. I've never met anyone like him—divine yet not a God, not a human or a creature. Something else entirely.

I can't help but notice how the ferns brush against his robes, how leaves get caught and released, how carefully he avoids stepping on saplings. The forest here respects him as much as they do the Forest Gods, and he respects the forest. There's an ease to his existence here, to everywhere, really.

I clear my throat quietly, choosing my moment. "We've never really talked, have we?" I say, keeping my voice low so it doesn't carry to the others ahead.

The Magician's head tilts slightly, galaxies swirling into a gentle lavender hue. "Not openly," he agrees, his voice that curious blend of distant and intimate, like a whisper in a quiet hall. "You give orders, that's for certain. But you're right—we haven't really talked."

I smile at that as I pick my way over a root snaking across the path, Tapio and Tellervo guiding us deeper into denser forest. "Sorry. I guess I can be a little bossy."

"No need to apologize to me," he says. "I like to be bossed around from time to time." He pauses. "What would you like to talk about?"

"I don't know," I say, feeling silly suddenly. This is not my usual territory. Emotions, confessions…these things come easily when I'm in the Upper World, seducing a mortal for a night or a week. I can play the part of the dark goddess, feed their fantasies, and leave without regret. But this? Sharing something genuine—or what I believe to be genuine—with someone from my own world? It's strange. "Back there, with Yggthra," I say, trying to find a good opening, "thank you for saving my life. Again."

Man, I need to work on my conversational skills, because they are lacking big time right now.

"You saved mine," he replies simply. "It's mutual."

But…do you really have a life to save? You're not mortal, I think.

What are you?

My gaze drifts to the sides of the path, to the twisted trunks and the moss that hangs in curtains from branches. Something about the silence of this forest puts me on edge, but at least we're moving, pressing forward.

"Your powers… Do you know where they come from?" I ask, deciding it's a nicer question than *what are you*? I mean, I know he's "the universe," but even as a Goddess, I just can't wrap my head around what that means.

He's silent for a few steps, considering. "My powers are a tapestry woven from many threads," he says. "Some come from the primordial essence of the Underworld, some from deals made long ago, with forces beyond Gods and mortals. Some come direct from the Creator themself. You've noticed I see things others can't."

"You do more than see," I say. "I think you can manipulate reality, just enough to tilt the odds. That's unusual. Most Gods have direct dominion over something natural—seasons, elements, life, death—but you? You're different."

Really different.

A soft laugh escapes him, a sound like distant bells. "I'm

not a God," he says. "And obviously, I'm no mortal. Think of me as a…traveling scholar of arcane arts. When I say I know things, it's because I've studied countless scrolls, spoken to ancient spirits that existed before even the Old Gods, wandered realms where time folds on itself. The galaxy you see is…a byproduct, a reflection of how I perceive the world. Sometimes, I reflect how you perceive the world."

I stare at him for a moment before laughing, feeling a slight flush on my cheeks. "Now my mind is really blown."

"There's so much more out there that you don't understand, Lovia," he says. "And it's not an insult to your intelligence. It's that even Gods have limits. Even Gods can't comprehend how the universe really works. They aren't meant to."

"Well, I'm definitely not a philosopher," I admit, growing quieter. "Until recently, I don't think I had much interest in anything, really. Definitely nothing in Tuonela. Did you know I've been sneaking out to the Upper World for years now? I even talked to Hanna about maybe leaving my duty here behind and going away for a while."

He's silent for a moment before he nods. "I did know that."

"Oh. No secrets, then."

"You can have your secrets, Lovia," he says. "I don't have to know everything. I can choose not to. But somewhere along the way, you've caught my attention."

My cheeks grow warmer. "Is that so? You mean to tell me, as you've sat outside the City of Death and dealt cards for each incoming mortal, you've managed to find the time to think about little old me?"

I'm half-teasing him, but even so, my heart is starting to pound at the thought. Which, really, is ridiculous. With everything happening around us, the absolute last thing I need is to be flirting with an ancient, mysterious deity like the Magician, the universe itself, whatever that means.

And yet...

Here I am, fumbling through it.

"I haven't sought you out," he says, to which my chest deflates. "Rather, your life has infiltrated my vision from time to time. You more than anyone else."

I swallow hard, daring to ask. "And what do you think that means?"

"I think," he begins, pausing as a comet shoots across his face, lighting up the darkness in front of us, "it means that the two of us have some purpose here. Together."

That idea makes my heart flutter, but it might just be from the anxiety of knowing he knows more than he's letting on.

"Well, I'm glad you're here. I'm not good at relying on others," I admit softly. "Maybe you're here to give me strength."

He turns his head toward me. I can't see his eyes, but I feel them, a gentle pressure. "Maybe it's more than that, Loviatar."

My name on his lips sends a shiver through me. Gods, what is this feeling? It's a straight shot of warmth when all around is damp and gloom.

"I don't know what's happening to me," I admit quietly, feeling like I'm breaking open my ribs, my heart exposed. "This war, this upheaval...I always thought I knew who I was. I'm the daughter of Death. I carry out my duties. I sometimes cross into the Upper World and play with mortals. I never expected to care about anyone from here. It's easier to keep it distant. But now, I think about losing you or my father or even Hanna, and it terrifies me. I'm not used to fear either." I snort softly at my own admission. "Fear, caring, worry—I'm ticking all the boxes of mortal vulnerability."

A quiet hum emanates from him. We walk as he digests my words, the forest path twisting ahead. Up front, Tapio and Tellervo speak in hushed tones, their voices blending with the rustle of ferns as Rasmus stumbles on in silence.

The Magician steps closer. As we navigate a particularly root-choked section, I feel his hand brush against mine. At first, it's incidental, a gentle contact. But then, his fingers curl around mine, and we're holding hands as if it's the most natural thing in the world. He's not leading me somewhere as he has before; he's heading there with me, as if I'm his equal.

My heart skips. I can't remember the last time I held someone's hand in a moment that wasn't about control or seduction. This is different. It's comfort, warmth, solidarity.

Maybe even something more?

I squeeze back, a small, tentative gesture.

"Is this…okay?" I ask, surprised by how vulnerable I sound.

He doesn't release my hand. "I think so," he says quietly. His words carry a gravity that matches the hush of the forest. "You're not alone in being unsettled by all this. Perhaps we can share that burden. As for fear… Fear can be good. It means you have something worth protecting."

I breathe out slowly, letting his words settle in me. Something worth protecting. Maybe that's what I've lacked before. My family had never faced any sort of war or danger, and mortals were never worth protecting. They arrived at the shores and rang the bell, and I brought them to the city to live out their destiny. Now, I'm forced to consider that I do have something to lose.

Everything.

As we walk, the canopy thickens, the moss-laden branches twisting overhead like skeletal arms. Tension and sadness crackle in the air. Mushrooms with iridescent caps blend in with vines that glow faintly in the gloom. The vegetation mutates, the familiar shapes of the Hiisi Forest blending with something more alien. I feel we're close to leaving the known paths behind.

Tapio and Tellervo sense it too. They slow, scanning the underbrush. The old Forest God runs a thick-fingered hand through his leafy beard, sending a glowing moth flitting away. Tellervo's eyes glow softly in the dark, narrowing in suspicion. I can't hear their conversation, but I see worry etched in their posture.

"There's something out there," Rasmus suddenly whispers as he comes to a stop. We do the same as I release the Magician's hand reluctantly, and Tapio motions for silence.

Tellervo jerks her head toward a tangled thicket off to our left.

The Magician murmurs, "Something's wrong."

I step past Rasmus, sword at the ready. Tapio joins me, a hand raised to command the forest to help in whatever way it can. The underbrush rustles, and a foul smell creeps into my nostrils—a scent of decay, but not the natural kind that belongs to the forest cycle of life and death. This is something sour. Foul.

Evil.

Tellervo and the Magician fan out, flanking me, while Rasmus tries to follow, tethered by the mycelia. I push aside a curtain of lichen and step over a low root. My boot sinks into damp soil as I move deeper into the darkness. There's a small clearing here, no more than a dozen paces across, surrounded by leaning trees coated in furry moss, fungus glowing softly at the base of a nearby trunk.

And in the center of the clearing lies something that makes my stomach flip.

Two figures, laid out in the dirt. One is a woman of the forest, her face frozen in terror, her long hair tangled with leaves and twigs. Her attire is simple—woven bark and lichen cloth—though it's shredded now, stained with dark fluid. Her hands are folded over her abdomen, and tiny vines have begun to creep across her limbs, nature's first attempt at reclamation.

Beside her is a young man with a shock of mossy hair around my brother's age, lying as still as death.

It takes me a moment to take in the horror, to see what has been done to them, how their bodies have been opened and insides spilled out, intestines wrapped into bows, binding them to each other. It takes a moment to realize who I'm looking at.

It's Mielikki and her son, Nyyrikki.

Tapio staggers backward, horror etched into the lines his face. "Mielikki..." he chokes out, voice cracking. "Nyyrikki."

Tellervo cries out, a sharp, wounded sound. She rushes forward, dropping to her knees beside the bodies, tears spilling down her cheeks. The Forest Goddess touches her mother's cheek gently, despair woven into every movement.

The Old Gods have struck another cruel blow.

The Magician steps closer to me, though he does not reach for my hand now. This is no moment for comfort—this is a shock that radiates through all of us, at least all of us who can't see the future.

He raises his voided face, galaxies swirling in somber hues. "They must have found each other then been ambushed," he says softly. "The Old Gods are sending a message."

I want to say something, anything, to break the suffocating silence, but there's nothing I could possibly say that would make any of this right, that would make any of this horror and grief vanish. My chest is unbearably tight, and I fight back the tears, my vision blurring. I look to the line of strange marks along Nyyrikki's arm—thin scratches, almost runes.

No, it's script.

A signature.

One that looks suspiciously like Louhi's.

Sour water fills my mouth as I hold back the urge to vomit at the sheer villainy of my mother. I wish I could cut open my veins and drain my body of her blood, severing my link to her.

Tapio crouches over his wife's lifeless, gruesome form, his shoulders trembling. The ancient God's grief is a raw thing that sends ripples through the forest. Leaves rustle and twist overhead, branches creaking, creatures crying out in confusion. I can feel the realm shuddering, responding to his loss. This isn't just a death of two beings; it's a wound in the forest's heart.

They've lost their own mother.

Tellervo's sobbing is soft but gut-wrenching. She leans over her brother's body, smoothing his hair back from his brow. "This isn't supposed to happen," she whispers.

I take a step back, reeling, my sword seeming useless now. I meet the Magician's gaze, and his galaxies shimmer with a sadness I can feel. Rasmus is pale as bone, his bravado drained as he stares at what might have been him if Yggthra got its way.

This death, this brutality, it changes everything. They've broken our fragile sense of hope, shown us that nothing is safe. If the Forest Gods can be slain in their own realm, wards broken, what hope do we have?

My throat closes. I reach out blindly, and the Magician's hand meets mine again. His grip is strong, steady, and for a moment, I wonder how much of this he foresaw, if there was anything that could have been done to prevent this. Something tells me the Magician is a slave to the tide of things as much as I am. He can change outcomes, but he can't be everywhere at once, and this isn't the kind of darkness we can banish easily. It's a darkness that seeps into the roots of Tuonela, twisting beneath our feet.

The forest sighs, a mournful wind passing through the leaves, and I squeeze the Magician's hand, feeling terror and anger swirl together in my chest.

The silence stretches. Tapio's grief is profound, Tellervo's shock numbing. Rasmus stares in quiet disbelief. The Magician stands beside me, and I cling to the warmth of his presence. I see a determination in the swirl of his stars, as if he's already thinking of what comes next, how to strike back or survive. I taste blood in my mouth where I've bitten my tongue. I don't even remember doing it.

Finally, I drag my eyes away from the bodies, away from the broken tree of a family cut down. We must move on, faster now. If the Old Gods and Louhi can penetrate the wards of the Forest Gods, we aren't safe.

We have to keep going toward the Star Swamp, into dangers untold. We have to keep going, even though the Old Gods have proven how ruthless they can be. We will carry their death like a fire in our chests, fueling what comes next.

But right now, all I can think is, this was a message.

We've received it loud and clear.

CHAPTER TEN

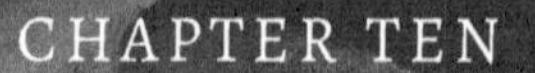

DEATH

The palace looms before us in jagged lines, each spire and parapet silhouetted against the murky sky. From a distance, it looked imposing, but now that I stand at its threshold, it feels like some wretched animal carcass picked clean by vultures—a place devoid of warmth or comfort, Louhi's evil having seeped into the bones.

I order the troops to remain outside in the snow, to dig trenches, fortify positions, set guards. They obey wordlessly, rifles slung over their shoulders, the frost clinging to their eyelashes. The Star Swamp lies not far behind them, a shimmering deathtrap now mercifully iced over, but the air is bitter, the cold unrelenting. It doesn't bother me now that I'm in my realm, but it must bother them. I know they are weary; humans always are. They last so briefly, burn so quickly. Yet, here they stand, mine to command. My coercion holds them to a strange neutrality—no one protests my decisions, no one asks the obvious questions. Without my influence, they would be terrified. I'm doing them a kindness, I think.

At least, that's what I tell myself.

Torben shuffles at my side, his shoulders hunched against the chill. Beyond the towering black gates, the palace beckons, its doors ajar, as if opened in haste long ago and never shut. A layer of grime and frost coats the threshold, old footprints still visible.

For some strange reason, I had hoped that perhaps fate, if there is such a thing, would have brought me straight to Hanna. But of course, that was a foolish thought to begin with. The portal Hanna went through would have dropped her out somewhere else, not here.

I close my eyes and test my connection to her, but it comes up blank.

My heart twinges in response.

It can't mean anything. Perhaps this place dampens my power.

I try to reach Lovia, Tuonen, even Ahto, but again, there is nothing.

"Are you all right?" Torben asks quietly from beside me.

I open my eyes and glance down at him, surprised by his concern.

"I can't feel any of them," I admit in a hush.

He nods solemnly. "Neither can I. It's this place. It's laced with wards and black magic. Don't take it to mean your family isn't out there."

I nod, my jaw clenching. "I'm worried about Hanna."

"You shouldn't be," he says. "I'm not."

I frown at him. "How can that be? You're her father."

"And she's a Goddess," he reminds me. "She's the prophecy. You don't become that for nothing. She's somewhere and she's fine. We'll find her when the time is right."

And now, I feel bested by the shaman. I'm the one who should have such steady, stoic feelings here. I'm the one who is supposed to be an unstoppable, hardhearted God.

That's what you get for having feelings for her, I tell myself, my chest tightening, revealing that my heart has grown so much softer than I'd like.

Hanna—fierce, clever, mortal-born, but with a lineage and a purpose that still mystifies me. She made me feel things I am not supposed to feel—hope and longing, frustration and tenderness, all muddled together. There is something in me —something old, stubborn, and proud—that resists admitting love, but I know I cannot bear to lose her. Not now, not when so much is already lost.

I push these thoughts aside. I have a more immediate goal I need to focus on: Ilmarinen, Louhi's consort, the shaman she left me for. I have never met this mortal—I would have killed him and probably prevented this whole uprising if I had—but rumor has it she was siphoning him for his magic, letting it fuel her own power. Louhi was clever and had a demon's power all her own, but she needed mortal magic, mortal blood, to amplify hers enough to take over my shadow self and raise the Old Gods.

Ilmarinen is supposed to be a sad excuse for a man, like a dog she kicks around, and I have a hard time believing she took him with her if she already gained the power she needed. If he still lives in this forsaken palace, he may have crucial answers. If she has discarded Ilmarinen, that might mean he's still here, drained of power, somewhere in these halls.

I summon a few generals to accompany Torben and me inside. Three of them follow, their minds heavily influenced by my power. They carry rifles and lanterns, spreading a weak golden glow over the black stone walls and warped floors. This palace is a labyrinth of twisted corridors, many caked with frost and something darker—old blood, perhaps. Rusted chains hang from walls, hooks that once held tapestries now covered by dangling cobwebs. An odor of stagnant rot lingers, as if the place itself is decaying already.

"This is pleasant," Torben says dryly, his breath steaming from his lips. His eyes dart around warily. "I'm guessing Louhi never bothered with housekeeping."

"She had servants for that, though it's curious how quickly this place has crumbled." I trace a claw-like fingertip along the wall, where old carvings depict strange scenes—twisted faces, ominous symbols. The place was crafted to unnerve, to impress upon any who entered that they are in the domain of someone powerful and cruel. "If we're lucky, we'll find Ilmarinen quickly. I have no desire to linger here longer than necessary."

Torben nods and gestures to a corridor branching off to the right. "This way feels…heavier," he says. I trust his instinct; he can sense magic resonances. If Ilmarinen is a conduit of power, Torben might feel it.

We move down a spiral staircase carved from volcanic stone. The generals' boots clink softly on the steps, lantern-light striking facets of black crystal embedded in the walls. My nerves feel taut—something is wrong here, some old echo of suffering that puts me on edge. Perhaps it's the knowledge that everything is in jeopardy: my realm, my family, Hanna. It has all slipped out of my control, and I cannot abide that. I am the God of Death. I rule the afterlife. I am supposed to be on top, unchallenged, and yet here I am, sneaking through my ex-wife's palace, praying I can find some half-dead mortal who might help me.

I hate feeling powerless. I hate that without Hanna at my side, without my loyal subjects, I feel hollowed. The desire to see her again is sharp, almost painful. It's not just because she was useful to me, either. She's something else. She touched something deep within me I thought long dead. If I let myself think on it too long, I might lose my composure, and I cannot afford that now.

We reach a broad hallway lit by pale, phosphorescent

fungi growing between cracked stones. A door made of iron bars stands at the end. The generals hesitate, so I prod their minds gently, pushing them forward. We must see what lies beyond.

The door is locked. I run my hand over the iron, feeling the residue of old spells. Louhi's magic lingers like a stale perfume. Torben kneels and studies the lock, muttering softly. After a moment, he presses his palm to it, whispers a few words, and the iron creaks and yields. One of the generals shoulders the door open, and we step into a chamber that reeks of rot.

It's a dungeon of sorts, or a torture chamber, or perhaps both. Chains dangle from the ceiling, old stains mar the floor, and along one wall is a raised platform, half-covered in dusty animal pelts. Lying there is a figure, barely moving, chained at the wrists and ankles, the sound emanating from him a low, wheezing breath. We approach, lanterns held high, illuminating a face as pale as bone, cheeks hollowed, eyes sunken, bearded chin crusted with old blood and saliva.

"Ilmarinen?" I say, more to test the name than anything else. He doesn't respond. I glance at Torben, who tries a gentler approach.

"Ilmarinen," Torben says softly. He steps closer and places a palm on the man's forehead. The shaman flinches but is too weak to pull away. I notice his ribs pressing against his skin, as if he hasn't eaten in weeks. His hair is matted, and scars crisscross his arms, strange marks carved into his flesh.

A flicker of recognition passes over Ilmarinen's dull eyes. He tries to speak, but only a ragged cough comes out. Torben waves a hand, and one of the generals passes a canteen of water. We help Ilmarinen drink, tilting it carefully. After a moment of choking and sputtering, he manages a rasping whisper. "Who…who are you?"

I straighten. "You don't know?" I ask, feeling humbled by his ignorance. "I am Tuoni, the God of Death. The very God Louhi left for you."

His eyes widen slightly. "D-Death...? Why are you here?" He coughs again, voice cracking. "She's...gone. Left me. Needed...my magic. Used me up."

"How did she use you?" Torben asks quietly, wiping some grime from the man's brow. "Tell us."

Ilmarinen licks his cracked lips, and I see now that runes have been etched into his skin. Not just random patterns—they look like siphon marks, sigils that drain a person's essence. "She...took me from the Upper World," he croaks. "Said she needed mortal power. Blood. Soul. She bound me, carved these runes so my magic would bleed into her. She... consumed it, every day, growing stronger until...she had enough."

My fists clench. Louhi's cruelty never surprises me, but I feel a fresh surge of disgust. She weaponized this mortal, stole his energy and twisted it into fuel for her conquests. "Where is she now?" I demand, voice colder than the ice outside.

Ilmarinen's head lolls. His eyes focus somewhere past me, on the chains rattling in a faint draft. "Don't know," he murmurs. "She left. Said she had what she needed. Something about...Hanna and power awakening."

His words strike me like a hammer.

I lean over Ilmarinen, letting him see my eyes, letting him feel a fraction of my influence. "What else do you know?" I say, this time softer, cajoling. "What are her plans? How can I stop her?"

The chained shaman shudders and tries to lift his head. "She...she said the Underworld would be hers," he wheezes. "She wants to rewrite death...turn it into something monstrous. A place of eternal suffering. No rest, no peace. And Hanna…she fears Hanna. Or…needs her. I don't remember." His voice breaks, tears leaking from the corners of his eyes. "My mind…fuzzy. She took so much. I can't remember everything."

I swallow thickly. The idea that Louhi wants to change the nature of death itself enrages me. Death should be a release, a transition, not endless torment. That's not how I designed Tuonela. I might be arrogant, might delight in reminding mortals of their mortality, but I am not cruel for cruelty's sake. Death must have order, purpose. Louhi is destroying that order. She is usurping my domain and the one mercy we've allowed humans after they die.

I realize I'm trembling, fury coursing through my veins. I glance at Torben, his mouth set into a hard line. The generals stand mute, not understanding what any of this means but ready all the same.

"Ilmarinen," I say, voice steady now. "We will free you, but you must tell us how we can fight her."

His gaze flickers with a hint of gratitude, but then it dims. "You can't fight her directly," he says on a cough. "Not now. She's too strong. She's gathered Old Gods to her side, gave them freedom from their slumber. She's twisting the Underworld's energies, feeding on them. You'd need something else. Allies." He laughs weakly, a sound like bone scraping stone. "If there are any left."

"Enough," I say gently. "Rest." I motion to Torben to help me remove his chains. With some effort, the shaman's bindings come loose, and Ilmarinen cries out as his arms fall free, fresh blood welling from where the iron cut his flesh. One of the generals pulls out a strip of cloth, and I use it to wrap his wrists. I may be Death, but I'm not heartless. This man suffered for Louhi's gain.

Now, he's our best source of information.

Ilmarinen watches me warily. "You...you're different than I imagined," he says, voice parched. "I thought the God of Death would be colder, crueler."

I almost laugh at that. "I can be cruel," I say. "But cruelty without reason bores me. I prefer order, and I would have you alive rather than lost in Oblivion." I nod at Torben, who nods back. We help Ilmarinen stand; he's weak, barely able to hold himself upright, so I instruct one of the generals to support him.

"Do you know of anything in this palace we can use?" Torben asks. "Weapons, relics, something to give us an edge? We have the Finnish army outside waiting to do our bidding."

Ilmarinen shakes his head slowly. "She took most of what mattered with her, but...the armory might still hold scraps. Old blades, talismans. Not enough to defeat Louhi outright, but perhaps something to protect yourselves. There's a library upstairs too—maybe some knowledge there? My powers are too weak, but I recognize a fellow shaman when I see one."

I press a hand to my temple. More delays, more detours, but what choice do I have? I need every advantage.

"Ilmarinen," I say, surprised by the gentleness in my voice. "Come with us. Show us the armory. Help us if you can. I'll see you safe, I promise." A hollow promise in a realm of shadows, but I mean it as much as I'm able. He nods, resigned, leaning heavily on the general's shoulder.

"What are you doing?" Torben whispers as he leans in to me. "He is too weak to travel. He can just tell us where the armory is."

I give him a steady look. "I know he's weak and discarded, but I don't trust him yet. I can't leave him alone unchained.

Louhi's influence runs so much deeper than one would believe. I should know."

He thinks about that for a moment and then nods.

"Let's go," he says. "I'll help my fellow shaman."

He moves to Ilmarinen and, together with the general, supports him.

"The armory is in the basement," Ilmarinen says, voice a deep rasp. "Follow the stairs all the way down, then to the left."

I lead the group out of the chamber, back through the iron door, and into the half-lit corridor, General Pekka behind me. We hurry down the stairs as quickly as we can without leaving them behind. Amidst the echo of our boots, the palace groans softly, as if resenting our presence.

Hanna's face drifts before my mind's eye—her fierce determination, the way she challenged me. Damn it, I want her by my side again. I need her, and that alone shocks me to my core. I've never needed anyone. Is that love? Perhaps. If it is, let it be a weapon. Let it drive me forward, push me beyond my limits. If I have to stare down Old Gods, break apart Louhi's schemes, and tear down reality itself to reach her, I will.

We reach the end of the stairs and head to the left. As we move, Ilmarinen's breathing hitches. He points down a side passage, where a door carved with sigils stands slightly ajar. "There," he says hoarsely. "Past that hall, down a staircase. The armory is below."

I nod, pressing on. Whatever scraps of power and weaponry we can salvage, we will. Then, we'll leave this forsaken place. Outside, my borrowed soldiers build barricades, ready to hold back whatever nightmares might wander in while we're here. I wonder how long they will last once I release their minds. Long enough, I hope, to matter. Long enough to save Tuonela.

Which, in turn, will save their own world.

But just as I'm about to enter the armory, I hear a stampede of footsteps, and a general calls out from behind us.

"Uh, sir? There are people approaching the castle."

Fuck.

CHAPTER ELEVEN

LOVIA

SORROW CHOKES THE AIR.

Not just sorrow, but anger and grief and frustration at the utmost cruelty and helplessness of it all.

Mielikki and Nyyrikki, Goddess and God of the Forest, are gone.

Brutally murdered in cold blood.

And every single step we've taken is fraught with enough emotion and tension to make the trees break. They bend toward us as we hurry beneath them, bowing to their Gods, grieving the loss just like us. Everything here is connected, and the forest knows how fragile life is now in the Land of the Dead.

Nothing is safe.

Louhi's minions will come for everyone.

And I can't help but wrestle with my own connection to her.

She's my mother.

I'm her daughter.

How could I come from such a wretched being?

How did she not, I don't know, eat me the moment I was

born, like a viper in a den?

Did she ever love my father?

Did she ever love me or Tuonen?

What was our purpose?

What is *my* purpose?

The Magician reaches out and grabs my hand, giving it a squeeze. It instantly grounds me, pulling me out of my thoughts and lessening the weight in my chest.

I glance over at him, finding the stars and planets in his infinite face are still, exuding a certain calmness.

"The past is a prison, Loviatar," he says quietly. "The future is an illusion. Be here now, even if it hurts. It hurts less than the hurricanes you're creating in your mind. They can blow you off course."

I give him a fleeting smile. "I can't help it. I just don't understand how…"

I glance ahead of us. Rasmus is walking slowly, but his movements are freer now since the Magician changed the mycelia so they're only binding his hands at his back. I can tell he's listening, but I don't mind. Out of everyone here, he understands what I'm going through—or at least he should.

Ahead of him, Tapio and Tellervo lead the way out of the forest, broken, defeated, lost to their grief. Once we're out of here, I will step up and take the lead. They shouldn't have to shoulder this burden when they're barely holding it together. I will lead all of us across the frozen void to the Star Swamp and Castle Syntri. I will keep them safe.

I have to.

I don't notice how hard I'm gripping the Magician's hand until he gives mine a squeeze back.

"Sorry," I mumble, trying to take my hand away.

He holds on tighter. "Nothing to be sorry about. I'm in awe of your strength, you know. Not just in a bone-crushing way, but your inner strength. You're so much stronger than you know."

I swallow hard as I step over a twisted root. "I don't feel strong, but I will be, for them." I nod up ahead at the rest of them.

"You already are," he says. He looks ahead to Rasmus. "And I'm starting to see how he might play a part in all of this. You don't have to go through what you're feeling alone. He understands you. He is weighed down by the same thing. You are both products of a disrupter."

"A disrupter?" I snort. "That's what you're calling Louhi? She's a monster."

A shooting star flits across his face. "From a different angle, monsters are just agitators of peace. To view something as a monster, as evil, is looking at it from a place of emotion. A very mortal, human emotion. A deity looks at things from a distance. It sees this chaos as the natural order of things."

I can't help but glare at him. "You know what she's like. You saw what she did. You know what she will do. How can you view any of that from such distance?"

"Because I do. Because that is what I am," he says matter-of-factly. "And you are looking at things from the heart because you *have* a heart, Lovia. A very big one. It's time to embrace that, time to realize you're a Goddess with love to give, one who grapples with morality. You're utterly human in ways you can't even imagine, and that is a blessing. It's time to stop thinking of it as a curse."

I shake my head. "It feels like a curse. Gods are supposed to be above that all."

"And yet, all you need to do is look around and see that the Gods here are fallible. It's their tie to humanity that makes this realm work the way it should. You cannot care for the souls of the dead without relating to them at the same time. Even Louhi has more humanity than you think. She may not carry the capacity for love or kindness, but that doesn't mean it didn't exist at one time. Her soul became corrupted. If you looked at the demon she came from, you'd see it was always inevitable." He pauses. "Her human-like predisposition to ego and vanity and power will be her downfall. You'll see—and you'll only see it because of your own humanity."

I'm so engrossed with what the Magician is saying, I nearly bump into Rasmus, who has stopped ahead of us. We've all stopped.

"This is the end of our realm," Tapio says in a deep, broken voice. He and Tellervo stand at the edge of the forest, staring forward at the landscape unfurling in front of us. The towering trees abruptly give way to thin birch and aspen, to low shrubs of thorns and berries. Frost blankets the hard ground, lacing the grass like icing sugar until it turns white with snow in the distance. The air is colder here, our breath rising in the air. Without the protection of the forest, I already feel painfully exposed.

Tapio turns around and eyes us, his lashes wet. "I hate to leave this place. I think perhaps it would be easier to die here, to become one with my wife and son."

"No, Father," Tellervo pleads, grabbing his burlap cloak in such a way that reminds me of a little girl terrified to lose the one person she has left. "Don't speak like that. We must move on. Please."

After we discovered their bodies, we buried them, performed a ceremony. We took our time even though we knew time was of the essence. The forest responded in kind by swallowing their forms, making them one with the root system and all living things, enabling them to live on forever in some ways.

Still, deep down, we all know the truth, that their souls

are forever lost to the void of Oblivion. It's something I try not to think about—how extra fragile we are now, how we're all one wrong step closer to that eternal agony.

Tapio sighs, a tear falling freely from his eye. I curse the Creator for giving us Gods such human-like emotions. I don't care if it's supposed to be the very thing we can use against Louhi. I'd give anything to be like the Magician, to have such distance from the things we're going through and the things we must do.

I don't want to feel anything, especially not this.

"All right," he says to his daughter, giving her shoulder an affection squeeze. "We continue. It's not as if the forest isn't compromised anyway."

He raises a hand to the trees and looks at them with such gravity, it makes my chest ache. "We will return to you soon, after we avenge Mielikki and Nyyrikki's deaths. Take care of the creatures, big and small, of the living beings from sprout to cedar."

We all take a moment of silence, respecting the forest and their Gods. The birds and squirrel that lived in Tapio's beard reluctantly leave, heading to the trees, chittering sadly as they go.

I let go of the Magician's hand and walk over to the Forest Gods.

"Let me guide you the rest of the way," I say gently, though I make sure they notice my sword at my side. "You have done so much for us already."

He nods, conceding with ease.

I motion for the Magician to join me, but he shakes his head. "I'll stay back here, keep an eye on any trouble from behind." I know he means to keep Rasmus in line as well.

As much as I feel stronger and less alone with the Magician by my side, I know it's time for me to lead. I can't wallow in the fear of it all. If there's no one else left in my family, then I have to step into my role as Goddess and do the things my father and brother can't. I'm sure as hell not leaving that task to my mother.

I start walking with purpose, keeping my pace quick. The further away from the forest we get, the more exposed I feel. Every now and then, I glance behind me at the trees, and I swear I see glowing eyes watching us through the leaves, though I can't tell if they're from the creatures and fairies themselves, wishing our safe return, or something malevolent.

Eventually, the grass disappears and becomes hard ground, and then snow crunches under our boots. The shrubs grow more stunted as we move on, the red of the snowberries standing out against the white, but this is a good thing. Yes, we're more exposed, but when you can't see around the bushes, it only makes you paranoid that something is lurking behind them, waiting to pounce.

After a while, snow starts to fall from the sky, and I can't help but think of my father. If he's here, do his moods still control the weather? What does it mean? Snow is a fairly neutral emotion; I suppose that's better than a thunderstorm.

We trudge on. The further north we go, the thicker the snow gets, gathering on my eyelashes. Every now and then, I look back at the others—Tapio's beard is thick with snow, Tellervo's antlers icicles. Rasmus is shivering, his mortality on full display. Only the Magician seems unbothered, gliding along with ease.

Eventually, we come to a stand of thin trees, the only semblance of a forest in these frozen parts. I decide to skirt around them instead of cutting through, not trusting what could be lurking amidst the spindly trunks, when, suddenly, I hear a wail.

Not just a wail—a blood-curdling scream of anguish.

CHAPTER TWELVE

LOVIA

I FREEZE, RAISING MY HAND TO TELL THE OTHERS TO STOP AND quiet.

The wail came from inside the thin woods.

I glance nervously behind me, wondering what we should do.

I'm about to ask Tapio if he can communicate with the flora outside the Hiisi Forest when he says, "Wait."

"What is it?" I whisper harshly as he slowly walks toward me, his snow-crusted brows drawn together. "What could have made such a sound?"

It was so raw, I still hear it echoing in my mind.

"I'm not sure," he says with a shake of his head. "It's just something I recognize, that I feel. I don't think it's any foe of ours."

I look back at the woods. The spaces between the trees seems to have grown darker. Then, the wail sounds again, loud, powerful, and pitiful.

"I recognize the sorrow," Tapio says. "Someone is mourning. We know our enemies could never feel such emotion."

"Who are you!?" Tellervo suddenly yells into the trees,

causing ice pheasants to fly from the canopy, their wings beating like drums as they head north.

All of us freeze.

"Shhh," Tapio chides her, his eyes blazing with fear.

"But you just said—" she protests.

"I didn't say I was certain," he argues.

"What's done is done," the Magician says from the back. "Call again."

I clear my throat. "Who is in there?" I call out, cupping my hands over my mouth. "My name is Loviatar, Goddess of the Dead. I am passing through, searching for my father. You sound like you're in distress."

My words seem to be swallowed by the snow as silence falls around us.

"Maybe we scared her," Tellervo whispers.

"Maybe *you* scared her," Rasmus chides her. "If it is a her, that is."

I keep a steady eye on the woods, my ears straining for any sound.

"Should we go in or...?" I ask. I know I'm supposed to lead, but a good leader doesn't do anything without consulting their group. Anyway, I'm not sure what we should do, though I don't want them to know that.

"There," Tapio says in a hush. "Look."

I squint my eyes at the trees and realize he must have better eyesight than I do, because it takes a few seconds for me to spot something moving between the white trunks—something blue, tall, and glistening.

Wearing a coral crown broken in places.

"Vellamo!" I cry out. I nearly drop the sword in surprise and start sprinting toward the Goddess of the Sea.

She pauses at the edge of the thicket, and her gaze contains so much sadness, it stops me in my tracks.

"What happened?" I whisper.

She puts her hand to her chest, licking her lips, trying to find the words. I have a feeling she might just collapse into the snow with grief.

Then, she looks over my shoulder at the rest of them, her gaze growing hard when she spots Rasmus, and some sort of dignity returns to her posture. She stands up straight and swallows hard. I take in the sight of her, pearls missing from her grown, her blue seaweed gown torn in places, perpetually wet. She has been through battle.

The short sword in one hand and the pearl-crusted knife sticking between her cleavage is more than proof of that.

"Ahto is dead," she says bluntly.

Yesterday, I would have said it was impossible to kill a God, but after seeing what happened to Tapio's family, I know that's no longer true.

"I'm so sorry," I tell her. Ahto was my uncle, and though I didn't know him well, given his predisposition to the sea, I know my father had deep affection for him. This will certainly hurt.

Vellamo nods and eyes Tapio and Tellervo. "You have lost loved ones too."

"Mielikki and Nyyrikki," Tapio says, his voice breaking. "They were killed by the Old Gods."

"The same for Ahto and so many of my kind," Vellamo says with a deep sigh. "I am very sorry for your loss. Did you witness it?"

Tellervo shakes her head. "We came across them. Perhaps it was a blessing we didn't see it happen. If we had, I can promise you, we would have killed them."

"They aren't easy to kill," Vellamo says tiredly. "I had my sea serpents to aid me, and even then, we couldn't save him. I've never felt so powerless before…"

She trails off and looks away, her eyes glistening. It's hard to see such a stoic, powerful woman feel like this, another fellow God I need to be strong for, and yet I feel like strength is being leached from me by the minute.

Then, she looks at me and holds my gaze for a moment, as if reminding me to be strong. I square my shoulders in response.

"Have you seen Hanna?" she asks.

I blink at her in surprise. "No. We don't know where she is—or my father, for that matter."

"Ah," she says, slowly walking toward us. "Then I at least have some good news for you. Your father is stuck in the Upper World."

"Still?" I exclaim. "That's not good news."

"Perhaps not, but he should be finding a way back with Torben any time now."

I glance over at Rasmus, who visibly stiffens at the mention of his father.

"And Hanna was here," Vellamo goes on. "My mermaids pulled her from a portal at the bottom of the sea. She made it through when the others didn't."

"So where is she?" Rasmus asks, looking around nervously.

"Päivätär took Hanna to the sun realm to claim her powers," she says simply.

"She did *what* now?" I ask.

"The sun?" Rasmus says in disbelief. "What powers? Hanna is mortal."

Vellamo glares at him, her gaze sharp enough to cut glass. "You," she spits, her voice steel. "Your presence here insults me. Why are you even still alive?"

"We have our reasons," I explain, though I still wonder what they are. "What do you mean, *Hanna is on the sun*? What powers?"

"Hanna is Päivätär's daughter."

"Who is Päivätär again?" Rasmus asks, bewildered.

"She's the Goddess of the Sun," Tapio says gruffly. "And it would do you good to keep your questions to yourself. My patience for your existence is running low."

I can't help but shake my head. "I thought...I thought her mother lived in, like, America somewhere. Some mortal. Her father is Torben the Shaman."

"It's a long story," Vellamo says. "One that explains how this Salainen has come into play, how she took Hanna's place at Shadow's End. For now, though, all you need to know is that Hanna has divine heritage. She's even seen her powers begin to take flight here. But she can't become who she needs to be unless she goes to the sun to grow her powers from the source."

"So that means she's coming back," I say, "with powers that might help us fight." The Magician had already said as much—yet another time I wish he could have just come out and said what he knew. Cryptic bastard.

"That is the idea," she says carefully.

"You sound unsure," Tapio says.

"Because there is a risk to all of this, of course," she says. "And frankly, I didn't think Hanna was ready. I'm willing to be proven wrong, of course. I want to be proven wrong."

"What's the risk?" Tellervo asks.

"Losing her humanity," Vellamo says. "To gain the powers of a God, there is a tradeoff. I fear Hanna might not remember exactly who she is after a taste of immortality."

"So she's immortal now?" Rasmus says. He's practically whining, and that's when I realize what his problem is: he's jealous of her. That's all this has ever been; perhaps it's why he willingly kidnapped her to begin with all those months ago, why he was eager to turn against her and do his mother's bidding. Hanna not only has their father's love, but now, her mother is a bona fide Goddess.

"I don't think she's fully immortal," Vellamo says. "But

even so, I don't know how her transformation will affect her humanity."

"As long as it can help us," Tapio says. "As long as she can help us get our revenge."

Vellamo raises her chin, her eyes sparking with determination. "We're going to get our revenge, with Hanna's help or not. This is why I was heading towards north. I want to find the Keskelli and see if they will join our side. Do you happen to have influence on them, Tapio?"

"The Keskelli? I've never even encountered one. They are trolls, are they not? My connection is only to flora and fauna. Anything sentient or close to human is beyond my reach."

"Then you're heading in the right direction," I tell Vellamo, brushing the snow off my shoulders. "The Keskelli are found outside the Star Swamp, and that's where we're headed anyway."

"Why are you going there?" she asks.

"Because Castle Syntri is the last place Louhi would think to find us. Besides, she's taken over my home. It's only fair I take over hers."

"I see your logic," she says. "It's petty. I like it." She places her sword in her other hand. "Lead the way, Daughter of Death."

I nearly tell her she should be the one leading us, but from the steadfast gleam in her eyes, I swallow down my humility and fear and nod.

I start walking again, flanked by Vellamo, the Forest Gods behind us, then Rasmus and the Magician. We march for what seems like forever, past strands of forest, where Tapio communicates with the undead deer who tell us they haven't seen any Old Gods ahead. We go through more thickets of bushes, stopping to snack on the plump, frozen berries to gain enough energy to continue. Rasmus seems to need the sustenance most of all, as the only one of us who is completely mortal. He might have my mother's demon blood, but it doesn't do him much good.

After that, we continue until the bushes fade to straggly sticks, their leaves, berries, and bark stripped by hungry reindeer, which we pass along with grouse and a curious fox or two, who poke their heads out of their burrow in the snow, and then after a while, it's just the frozen void, a landscape of undulating snow and ice.

Until it abruptly ends at the top of a ridge that gently slopes down toward the Star Swamp.

"There she is," I say under my breath. Before us is a frozen wasteland, a bog pockmarked with black holes. Usually, you can see the stars shining in them, similar to the Magician's face, but they've been covered with snow. The only way you know the pools are there is because of the way they indent the landscape.

"Strange," Vellamo says. "I've never seen them frozen over."

She's right. I haven't seen them like this before either.

Rasmus sniffs the air. "There's magic being used. I can smell it. There's a spell keeping the pools frozen."

"But why?" Tellervo asks.

"So we can cross safely," the Magician tells us. "So others can't fall into Oblivion."

I glance at him, feeling hope for the first time. "You mean to tell me someone is trying to protect us?"

"Us, or perhaps just themselves," he says with a shrug. "Either way, this is a good sign. Maybe we'll find our allies at Castle Syntri in the end."

I stare at him for a moment, wishing I could read him better. There's something about his way that makes me think there's something wonderful ahead. I guess I'm just too cynical at this point to believe him.

I keep my hope in check. "Well, let's hurry then before the

magic gives out. Everyone, stay away from the pools, just in case. I don't want to test the theory if we don't have to."

We hurry down the slope and then walk single file, picking our way between the pools, the bog mercifully hard beneath our feet. All of us feel the urgency now, the need to keep going as fast as we can, until, eventually, the icy façade of Castle Syntri rises into view atop a small crest.

At first, I think the place is completely abandoned, but as we get closer, I see movement in the snow. As my eyes adjust, I realize I'm looking at people—hundreds of people, humans, dressed in puffy white-and-black uniforms.

With guns.

"What the fuck?" Rasmus says. "Who the hell are they?"

And that's when I see someone march out of the front doors and stop at the end of the platform, an extremely tall, commanding figure dressed all in black.

My father.

The God of Death.

CHAPTER THIRTEEN

DEATH

I FOLLOW THE GENERAL WHO CALLED ME AND HURRY OUT OF the front doors and under the raised portcullis, heading straight to the end of the barbican where a few troops have gathered.

They're pointing in the distance, in the middle of the Star Swamp, their rifles raised and ready.

There's a small, ragtag group of six people coming toward us single file, and at the very front of them stands my daughter.

Loviatar.

My heart soars, a gasp escaping my lips.

"Should we fire?" General Pekka asks, appearing beside me.

"No," I growl. "Hold your fire! Lower your weapons! That's my daughter!"

I push into their minds briefly for extra measure, and they all lower their guns in unison. At least I know they were more than ready to defend this place. That counts for something.

Lovia waves her sword at me in greeting and then starts

running, her blonde braid whipping behind her. As she gets closer, I see the rest of her ragtag crew.

Vellamo, Tapio, Tellervo, the Magician, and...

Rasmus.

I let out another growl just as Torben comes to stand next to me.

"Oh my Gods," he mutters under his breath. "What is Rasmus doing here?"

I give him a sharp look. "I don't know, but if you let your fatherly instincts get in the way..."

He shakes his head. "I know he's a traitor for his mother," he says. "Even though that's as much my fault as anyone else's."

I grunt. "Sort your family trauma out some other day. Keep that boy in check, or I'll do it for you." I wriggle my fingers at him, implying I'll take off the gloves. "Lovia better have a damn good reason for bringing him along."

Soon, she's climbing up the stairs to the platform and running toward me, troops parting on either side of her to let her through.

"Father!" she cries out. She drops her sword with a clatter and runs straight into my arms. I envelop her, holding tight, as if loosening my grip for a moment might see her slipping out of my arms, never to be seen again.

"Lovia," I manage to say, her name stuck in my throat. I never let myself really think about her much—too afraid, I suppose, of coming across an answer that would devastate me. But now that she's here, in my arms, my only daughter, I realize just how much she means to me. All this time, I think I've been a good enough father, but I've been keeping my children at arm's length, too worried about their duties or their roles to let myself be as involved as I should be.

All of that will change going forward.

Hanna was right. I owe them so much more than what I've given.

"I thought I would never see you again," Lovia says, her words muffled against my coat. "This is the last place I thought I'd find you."

"And I you," I admit. I pull away, holding her by the shoulders. She looks pale, scratched up, a little worse for wear overall, but her eyes blaze with strength. "And Tuonen?" I dare to ask. "Where is he?"

She shakes her head, her mouth set in a firm line. "I don't know. Tapio last saw him at Shadow's End, where Salainen and Louhi have taken your places."

I gulp and give her shoulders a squeeze. "Louhi won't hurt him. She needs him. We'll get him out of there, if he hasn't escaped already. That boy is slippery when he needs to be."

As before, I don't let myself think of the alternative.

"I'm so very glad you're here," I add, giving her a tight smile. "I'm going to need you at my side."

But my joy is short-lived, for the moment I look up and see Vellamo slowly approaching, I know something horrible has happened. I can see it in her eyes, the pain and sorrow swimming in them. They brim with tears; not for a happy reunion, but for grief.

For death.

"Where is Ahto?" I whisper. Usually, my brother isn't too far behind. I glance over at Tapio and Tellervo as they gather around us, but they too share a similar haunted look, their shoulders drooping in defeat.

"Tuoni..." Vellamo says in her low voice. She steps forward, Tellervo taking the sword from her hands, and the Goddess of the Sea suddenly crumbles, dropping to her knees. I catch her before she hits the ground, hauling her up as she cries.

She grasps at my coat, and I embrace her, feeling sick to my stomach as she floods me with tears as strong and plentiful as a river.

And that's when I know my brother is dead.

"No," I say thickly, my chest caving in like a sinkhole. "It can't be. It *can't* be. How?"

She continues to cry, and at one point, I look down to see tiny minnows swimming in the pool of tears she has left on the ground.

"Killed by an Old God," Lovia explains grimly. "The same thing happened to Mielikki and Nyyrikki."

"Probably not the same God," Tapio says, his voice rough. "But they're out there, Tuoni, destroying us one by one. Soon, there will be nothing left of Tuonela."

If I wasn't holding Vellamo, I would crush someone's bones under my hands; the rage that spreads through me is sharp, deep, vicious. Louhi's Old Gods have not only killed my brother, my own beloved flesh and blood, but taken the souls of two innocents meant to protect the forest. Three of my brethren, lost to eternal torture in Oblivion.

I look over at Rasmus, at his flaming red hair, his smug, pallid face that can't hide what he is underneath. Venom overtakes me, and I'm pushing Vellamo into Lovia's arms and striding toward the minor shaman.

"You!" I bark, a ferocious rattle sounding in my chest, like an animal about to escape, about to attack.

About to kill.

"Tuoni, no!" Torben yells, running after me, but it's too late.

I pull my glove off and reach out for Rasmus' throat with my bare hand, prepared to squash his windpipe and send another soul to Oblivion.

Suddenly, without warning, my hand freezes, inches from his skin.

I stare into his eyes, and they peer back at me with nothing but the fear of death. Still, I can't move.

What the fuck is happening?

I look over at Torben, figuring the shaman's magic must be working overtime to try and control me, something I didn't know he was capable of, only to find he's staring at us in shock.

Then, the Magician steps out from behind Rasmus, his black sparkling hand extended from his flowing robe, finger pointed toward me.

"We need him," the Magician says, slowly coming closer. "For more than this moment of revenge. You'd feel powerful for a second, Tuoni, but then his death would mean nothing. It won't bring back Ahto, won't bring back any of them. It won't change the tide."

Fuck. Why does he have to be right?

"You cryptic son of a bitch," I grind out, glaring at his faceless form. "What are you even doing here anyway?"

"I've drawn all my cards," he says, "except for a few up my sleeves. Now, please, refrain from killing Rasmus, as much as you want to. Trust that you need to keep him alive. Focus on saving Tuonela and not on petty revenge."

"How dare you think my revenge is petty!" I let out a roar of frustration when I try to move my hand again. Close—I am so close, but the Magician's magic is impossibly strong. "I should be able to kill whomever I want to avenge my brother!"

"But not him," he says simply.

Now *he's* the one I want to kill.

I bare my teeth at him, hating how I feel like a caged animal.

"This is part of it, Tuoni," the Magician says. "You'll understand it later. You'll even be grateful."

I groan, trying once more to move, but it's futile.

And now, I'm painfully aware of everyone watching me. They've all seen the God of Death bested by the Magician. Why is he here? What is his purpose in all of this?

Finally, I sigh heavily and concede.

I move to drop my hand, and it falls easily to my side.

Rasmus is still staring at me, breathing hard through his nose, wide-eyed and shell-shocked. He knows how close he came to death, at least. For a second, I think about having another go at it, but I decide the Magician probably has a failsafe, some force protecting the ginger fucker.

Never trust a redhead—doesn't the Magician know that?

I grumble and turn away, giving Torben a hard look.

"He's your problem now," I mutter. "Make sure to keep him out of my sight."

Torben doesn't look happy about it either, but he nods.

"So your magic can overpower a God?" Lovia says to the Magician, a tremor of hurt in her voice. "How come you didn't do that earlier?"

The Magician folds his hands in front of him. "Because I only do what I can do when I can do it."

"That makes no sense." General Pekka speaks up.

"Never mind him or any of them," I tell the general before I address the rest of the troops. "You all heard the Magician. No one touches the redhead. No one harms anyone else, for that matter, or you will answer to me, and no one will be there to save you. Now, let's start making this a fortress and figure out our next steps."

Even if I can't have Louhi's son, I'll get my revenge somehow.

CHAPTER FOURTEEN

TUONEN

"DO YOU REMEMBER THE RULES?" THE GIANT'S VOICE COMES booming toward me from down the tunnel.

"Frankly, I don't remember much of anything right now," I admit. It feels like I've been walking through this cave system all day; my bones are weary. I don't dare complain to Vipunen, though. He'd merely laugh, so utterly unaffected by it all.

Must be nice, I think.

Even Rauta has lost his earlier spark and vigor, padding silently beside me, sniffing the air occasionally.

"The most important rule of all, Tuonen," Vipunen chides me. "Come now, you didn't spend your youth training with me to not remember."

Right. The training. All those years with the blind mask and the sword, and for what? For me to be captured so easily, and by my own damned mother? Though I suppose some of it must have come in handy when I defeated that tentacle thing.

"I can't look at you," I affirm. "But I left my blind mask at home. You wouldn't have a spare, would you?"

Vipunen chuckles, making the crystals on the tunnel walls chime. "I will stay hidden. Your sight will be safe from my true form, and you and Rauta will be safe under the mountain until you are ready to fight again."

"Well, am I getting there anytime soon?" I say, wincing at how whiny I sound.

"Patience is a virtue," he says, "even in such urgent times as these. Perhaps especially so."

I ignore that. Virtues are overrated. I'm not that kind of God.

We walk on, my footsteps echoing in the silence, accompanied by the soft scrape of Rauta's claws on stone. The tunnel widens and the light changes—faint glimmers catch on mineral veins in the walls, sending subtle rainbows dancing over the rock. Though Vipunen promised I wouldn't need a blindfold, I'm still wary about how much I might see. He said he would stay hidden, and I trust him not to break that rule. Still, I can't help but feel uneasy, remembering the old lessons, the emphasis on not beholding his true form.

Eventually, we emerge into a broad cavern, and my shoulders relax as the space opens around us. Rauta lifts his head, ears perking up at some distant drip of water. The air is warmer here, the darkness not so absolute. I can see faint patterns in the stone, subtle shifts of color and texture. It's quiet. Peaceful, even. A far cry from the chaos outside.

"Tuonen," Vipunen's voice resonates, not loud now, but steady and calm. I cannot pinpoint its source—he might be above, below, behind any of these shimmering walls. Just as he promised, I see no giant figure looming in the darkness, only diffused light that seems to seep out of cracks and crevices, as if the very stone were alive with his presence. It reminds me of being young and blindfolded, relying on other senses. But now, my eyes are open, even if I cannot fully understand what they see.

Rauta pads closer to my leg, nudging me with a gentle prod. I rest my hand on the dog's metal skull and feel warmth radiating from him—a comfort in this strange domain. We are far under the mountain now—safe, as Vipunen said, but safe for how long, I don't know.

I wet my lips and try to speak, my voice echoing faintly. "Vipunen, I hope you know how glad I am to see you—or not see you, as it were—but I need answers. I need to know what's happening outside. The land is in turmoil. Old Gods awakening, Louhi's forces twisting the realm's fabric. Kaaos is finally here. My father fights a war that only grows more dire. I need…I need to understand what I can do, what role I play in this."

If any.

A soft rumble like distant thunder passes through the cave. "Always searching for understanding," Vipunen says, matter-of-factly. "You know the realm is wounded. Louhi and Rangaista have stirred horrors once laid to rest. The living, the dead, and the Old Gods are entangled in conflict. Your father stands at the center, forging alliances, trying to restore balance. But the scale of this war outstrips mortal or even godly strength. Forces older than memory now stride upon the Earth."

I swallow, heart pounding. So he knows exactly what's going on out there and yet doesn't seem concerned at all. "Then you must know about Sarvi," I say quietly. The unicorn's name is bitter in my mouth. "Louhi captured them, drained their power, and I can't help but feel responsible. If I hadn't been trapped myself, my own horns sawed off for her magic, maybe I could have saved them."

Rauta's ears flick at the sound of my voice. He feels my guilt, I'm sure.

"Sarvi lives," Vipunen replies, voice calm but unyielding, causing a bolt of relief to spike through me. "Though its energy wanes, it remains alive. Louhi uses it much as she once used Ilmarinen—an unwilling conduit of power. Your question is whether to go back and save Sarvi or continue forward, seeking your father, forging ahead in the war. You hesitate between duty and compassion, between the urgency of battles yet to come and the pain of a friend's suffering."

I nod, though he cannot see it—or maybe he can. "Yes," I say. "If I go back, I risk losing ground and being recaptured, and my mother sure as fuck won't let me escape a second time. If I move forward, well, maybe I can help my father win the war...but then I abandon Sarvi to torment."

The thought claws at my chest.

Vipunen's voice resonates through the stone, a steady pulse of truth. "You ask what you should do, but you know I will not command your choices," he says. "I am the Oldest God, older than the troubles that plague your land. My role has always been to observe, to oversee. When you were young and blindfolded, I taught you patience, perception, acceptance of uncertainty. I never interfered in Death's struggles, even though I cared for him when he was small, guiding him as one might guide a seedling into a mighty tree. I do not fight your battles. I do not alter fate's course on a whim."

His words strike a chord of memory. When I trained here, always in darkness, I learned to listen without sight, to move by instinct, to trust I could act without needing to see the path laid out. I always wondered why Vipunen never took sides, never lent a hand when needed. Now, I see—it's not his nature. He's a historian, a witness, a keeper of ancient secrets —one who nurtured my father, yes, but who never took up arms for him.

Too bad for us.

I look down at Rauta, searching for reassurance in the dog's red eyes. He stares back patiently, as if waiting for me to find my own answers. The silence stretches, broken only by a gentle dripping of water somewhere deep in the rock.

"But Sarvi—" I start, voice wavering.

"Sarvi's fate is woven into the larger tapestry," Vipunen interrupts, tone even. "Saving the unicorn now might cost you dearly, diverting you from tasks that shape the realm's future. Pursuing your father instead might mean leaving Sarvi to endure more pain. Such dilemmas define heroism, Tuonen. There is no neat solution."

My hands curl into fists. "So I must choose, then." I know he won't give me a final directive. He never has, never will.

Vipunen's voice softens slightly. "Do you truly wish council from me?"

"Yes!" I exclaim.

"Stay here," he says. "Under the mountain, you are safe from the immediate horrors above. You are weary, uncertain. Patience was always our lesson, was it not? Your father—Death—knows me, and if he seeks knowledge or aid, he will come here. It might even be the only way to reclaim Shadow's End. Eventually, your paths will cross again in this place. Fate has a way of folding back on itself."

I reel at that suggestion. Stay here? While war rages, while Sarvi suffers, while my father struggles? The thought fills me with anger and dread. Yet, Vipunen's logic is sound. Cowardly, perhaps, but sound. Rushing out blindly might achieve nothing but my own downfall. If I can't trust my senses, or if I'm too weak to change the outcome, I might waste the advantage of being here, in this timeless sanctuary, under the watchful eye of the Oldest God.

Rauta nudges my hand again, as if to say *listen. You came here for truth, for safe haven. Vipunen offers both, in his mysterious, detached way.*

Choices are so terribly heavy when they're yours alone to make.

"So you advise me to wait? To trust that, in time, the world will turn, and my father will find me here?"

Vipunen's laughter is gentle, like distant echoes in a deep canyon. "I do not advise, Tuonen. I only state what is. If you remain, you hold a vantage point outside the fray, allowing fate to run its course until the moment you are truly needed. Your father, or those tied to him, will seek knowledge only I hold. When they do, you'll be here, ready to join them. If you leave now, chasing Sarvi or chasing battles, you risk losing this critical junction."

My pulse pounds in my ears. The pain of indecision claws at me. Yet, a strange calm seeps in as well. Vipunen's domain is quiet, eternal. The war outside will continue whether I flail at it or not. I'm no hero who can singlehandedly turn the tide. Perhaps waiting is wise. Perhaps that's the hardest lesson—knowing when not to fight.

I swallow hard, voice cracking. "I'll stay."

Rauta gives a low, affirmative huff. The dog seems content with this decision, as if recognizing that resting and gathering strength might be best. He has already done so much for me; he deserves the rest.

Vipunen's light glows brighter for a moment, only to dim to a comfortable glow. "There are streams deeper in, edible fungi, places to rest. Time flows oddly here; you will not starve or wither. Think of this cave as a womb of stone, cradling you until the moment comes to be reborn into action. That moment will arrive, I assure you. Your father will not forget you, nor will fate's tapestry neglect your thread."

I bow my head, tears slipping free now—not sobbing, just quiet resignation and sorrow for Sarvi, for the realm, for my own helplessness. All the emotions I've tried to keep buried inside come to a head at a most inopportune time.

But there's also a flicker of hope. If Vipunen says my

father will come, I must trust it. My father is strong, resourceful, and surrounded by allies. Plus, he's spiteful as fuck. If there's a way to save Sarvi or to strike at Louhi's heart, he'll find it, and I can rejoin him when the time is right.

"Thank you," I manage, voice low, raw. "I'll wait. I'll learn patience again."

Perhaps I'll have a virtue after all.

Vipunen's presence hums through the stone, a gentle reassurance. "No thanks needed. You walk your own path, Tuonen. I am only the light in the cracks, the old watcher who shaped you long ago. Rest. Regain your strength."

I guide Rauta toward a quieter corner of the cavern, where a small pool of water reflects the faint glow. The dog settles down, laying his iron head on his paws. I kneel beside him, trailing a hand through the still water. The silence is profound but not lonely. I have Rauta, at least, and somewhere above, my father and others fight for the realm.

So, I wait, breathing steadily in the hush of ancient stone and gentle light as time drifts and destiny's pattern weaves unseen.

Unseen by all but the Oldest God.

CHAPTER FIFTEEN

DEATH

The night is dark.

I'm now standing in the cavernous hall where Louhi must have strategized her attack on my world. It's strange how a place can hold echoes of another's presence even after they're gone. Louhi once paced these floors, plotting and smirking and planning my demise. Now, I'm about to use the very space where she schemed against me to plot her downfall. It's fitting in a way, but it doesn't feel victorious. It feels desperate, as if I'm only here out of sheer necessity, which is the cold, hard truth.

The hall is constructed of obsidian and volcanic ash, the walls carved with old runes and sigils I can't bring myself to read right now. Columns rise like inky trunks in a moonlit forest, and strange banners—left behind by Louhi or her minions—hang limp in the still air. The torchlight flickers, shadows dance, and the people I've gathered stand in an uneasy semicircle before me. They look at me expectantly as I pace behind the large, ironwood desk, maps strewn about the surface Torben had found in the cellar.

In the middle of the group, on the other side of the desk,

stands Lovia. She looks strong, fierce, defiant. I'm glad she's here—I need her strength, her fire. Still, it shames me that I have to rely on my own child in this madness. She has proven herself countless times, I know, but I still feel guilty that I've allowed the world to come to this point. I was supposed to protect all of them: my children, my people, my allies. The despair that gnaws at me is relentless. I swallow it down. I cannot show it. Gods must be unshakable, must they not?

And yet, I've already shown too much. My pain over Ahto. My rage at Rasmus. The humble pie the Magician forced me to eat when he wielded magic stronger than a God's.

Missteps, pitfalls, I tell myself. *A glimpse at weakness. You must return to being the all-powerful leader they need.*

Behind Lovia are the other Gods: Tapio, Tellervo, and Vellamo. Tapio, the Forest God, once proud and brimming with quiet strength, is now hollow with grief. The loss of his wife and their son has left him raw; I can feel his pain like an open wound in the air. Vellamo, my sister-in-law, stands next to him, her own loss just as palpable.

Because it's my loss too.

The Magician lurks near a column, galaxies swirling beneath his hood. I know he sees more than the rest of us. He probably knows how this might end. His refusal to share what he knows unsettles me, but I cannot press him. I can't afford to alienate an ally, even an ambiguous one. Still, I hate that helpless feeling, the idea that I must accept riddles when I crave certainty. More than that, I hate that he has magic that makes me appear weak and that he's in charge of when he uses it. I can only hope he does remain our ally; I would hate to see what might happen if he were to suddenly switch sides.

Rasmus and Ilmarinen linger nearby; I've ordered the

generals and a few troops to watch them at all times. The Magician might have faith that Rasmus has a part to play, but I have no doubt that son of a bitch will try to usurp us the first chance he gets. Lovia has explained why they brought him, but he's as trustworthy as a viper in a cradle.

As for Ilmarinen, the shaman is weak, and he speaks poorly of Louhi, but he reminds me too much of Rasmus. Louhi's influence runs deep, and I would be a fool to put all my trust into him just because he suffered at her hands for decades. I know how insidious her ways are, how they can lodge inside you and manifest. We might need Ilmarinen while we're here, but I won't put my full trust in him yet, not when Louhi's magic might still linger.

The generals shift their weight uneasily, representing the hundreds of troops out in the cold flanked around the castle. They know war on mortal terms, but this is a conflict waged on spiritual, magical, and metaphysical fronts. They glance at me with expectation, trying to find in my eyes the certainty they lack. I realize, with a pang, that everyone here looks to me. Tuonela is my realm; I am its God, its King. If I fail, what hope is there?

I draw a slow breath and begin, forcing my voice to remain steady and calm. "We have little time," I say, the words echoing softly in the hall. "Louhi and Rangaista hold Shadow's End. They command the Bone Stragglers, my own armies, and Old Gods who were supposed to be sleeping. We know that, at some point, my son, Tuonen, and my loyal servant, Sarvi, were with them, but their whereabouts are now unknown. We also know Louhi has taken control of my magicked double, my shadow self, and that Salainen, another pawn of Louhi's and Hanna's half-sister, is pretending to be the queen herself."

At the mention of Salainen, Torben sucks in a breath. For a second, I consider glaring at him, since both Salainen and

Rasmus are his fault, but he also brought me Hanna, and for that, I have to be grateful. Besides, I know the man feels shame. I've spent more than enough time with him now to see how deep it runs in his bones.

I clear my throat and go on. "The City of Death has fallen. Inmost has spread to the other layers. There is no order in the afterlife, only Kaaos. This has always been Louhi's final goal, perhaps put in place by her father, the Demon God Rangaista, before she was even born. But now that she has succeeded in getting what she wants, we must figure out both what her next steps are and how we can defeat her and the Old Gods and bring Tuonela back."

"We need a list of our allies," Lovia chimes in. "Who else is there to help us? We could send scouts to find and bring them back here, maybe."

"Very well. So, who else is there?" I ask the room.

"Hanna," Torben says.

"We cannot rely on Hanna's return," Tapio argues.

I give Tapio a sharp look. "We can and we must. Mark my word, she is coming back."

After learning Hanna is on the sun with Päivätär, her mother, I have to admit, I've been more nervous than relieved. Her mother is a different breed of God. She and her sister, Kuutar, have always been distant and indifferent to our struggles, which is why what Vellamo told me was a surprise. I didn't think Päivätär would care enough to give Hanna her powers, but I suppose she must have some stake in our world after all.

Still, I don't know the Sun Goddess like I do the ones of this realm. I worry she might inadvertently hurt Hanna in some way, particularly with Hanna still being mostly mortal. I know she can handle anything thrown her way—she has proven that time and time again—and yet, I can't imagine how she might feel in the realm of the sun, being so far away from everything she's ever known.

Then again, she might be thriving, wielding her powers and testing out her golden wings. She never ceases to surprise me, my little bird.

"There are the trolls," Tellervo suggests. "Vellamo was going to find them."

"The Keskelli," I muse. "Yes, I suppose they could be of help if they are still alive. I haven't seen any in a very long time."

"There are also my mermaids and the sea serpents," Vellamo says.

"They will come in handy, especially around the waters of Shadow's End," I tell her.

"Speaking of Hanna, Päivätär and Kuutar might be of help," Tapio says.

"I wouldn't count on them. And even though Hanna will return, I wouldn't count on her either," I muse. "Oh, Hanna will fight by our side, but I don't want to leave things to chance when it comes to any newfound power."

"What about your sister?" Vellamo asks me.

"Ilmatar?" I say with a sigh. The Goddess of the Air is as flakey as her name. "Perhaps. We'll see."

"Auringotar?" Tapio asks.

"Another one who won't bother with our realm."

"Akka? Ukko?" suggests Lovia.

I let out a caustic snort. "My parents have pretended we don't exist for a very long time. They're off in some other dimension, most likely watching this like some reality TV show."

"Reality TV show?" Tellervo repeats, confused.

"Then Vipunen," Lovia suggests. "The giant is the one who practically raised you."

I nod, running my hand over my beard. "Yes, I have

thought about Vipunen many times. But he's no better than the Magician over here when it comes to knowing how things will go and standing back and letting it happen."

"I'm still here," the Magician says quietly. "If I truly just let things happen, I wouldn't have stopped you from killing Rasmus."

"Then tell me, oh wise one," I say bitterly. "Who are our allies? Can we depend on Vipunen?"

The Magician stares at me for a moment. The room hums with such silence that when Tellervo coughs, it sounds like a gunshot.

"We must try to find Vipunen," he eventually says, "when the time is right."

"And you'll be the one to tell us, huh?" Torben says wryly.

"I will," he says flatly. "But you'll also know yourself."

I shake my head, annoyed again. "Fine. So there are our allies. Are they, plus everyone here and a thousand troops, enough to fight against everything between the Star Swamp and Shadow's End?"

Silence again.

Then, the Magician says, "It's a start."

"Oh, fuck off with that," I tell him. I run my hands down my face and sigh. "All right. So we gather our allies when we can. Then, we must plan our attack. We head for Shadow's End."

A general raises his hand. "My lord, we could go back through the portal and rally more troops from the Upper World. Gather them here at Syntri Castle—"

I shake my head. "No," I say firmly. "The portal would require a shaman to go with you, to ensure it is open for your return, and I can't spare any of them. We have to make do with the troops we have. Besides, drawing too many soldiers here would give away our position. We must stay hidden if we expect to survive this, at least for now."

I don't add that any more mortals brought here would only compound my guilt at having dragged them into this mess against their will.

General Pekka, who has been studying a faded map of Tuonela in his hands, speaks up. "Shadow's End is heavily fortified. Seems the only way in is through Death's Passage. We might be sitting ducks."

"It's not the only way in. We can go by sea as well."

"And there's the underground cave system," Lovia says. "There are access points all along the realm."

"You're correct," I tell her. "But I would approach that with caution. It would be a terrible place to get stuck."

I look around, hoping for more input, but all I see is uncertainty in their eyes and feel the pressure mounting behind my ribs. I wish I had all the answers.

"We must know their weaknesses," Vellamo says. "Their strength is not just in soldiers, or the savagery of the Old Gods, but in twisted magic."

"Ley lines," Torben muses. "This world has them, as does the world above, right?"

"There are ley lines here," I say slowly. "But to be honest, I've never paid them much attention. I know in the Upper World, they are conduits for magic, but here, everything is a conduit. They aren't anything special."

"Except Louhi knew where they were," Rasmus says.

My gaze snaps to his, and I'm tempted to tell him to shut up.

"What do you mean?" Lovia asks.

"*I mean* Louhi knew where the ley lines were," Rasmus says. "There's a map here somewhere of them." He looks around. "Or, I don't know, she probably took it with her, but she said the ley lines were important. It's where the Old Gods would rise from the ground."

I narrow my eyes at him, not wanting to believe a word he's saying.

"He's right," Ilmarinen says, his voice raw and barely audible. "Her magic opened the ley lines. They were a conduit she corrupted."

"Okay, so Rasmus just proved his worth," I say to the Magician. "Now can I kill him?"

General Pekka snorts. At least someone here thinks I'm funny, though I wasn't really joking.

Torben nods thoughtfully. "Perhaps if we restore order to the ley lines, their monstrosities weaken."

"I can forge a device, the sampo, to stabilize the ley lines," Ilmarinen says. "If we combine that with the power of three shamans, we might be able to at least put the Old Gods back in their place."

"And this device you speak of," Lovia says, "how long would that take?"

"A week," Ilmarinen says. "Perhaps."

"We don't have a week," I practically growl. "We'll be found out by then, and Louhi will bring her army to us. We won't have the element of surprise."

"Maybe I can do it," Torben says.

"I was once a skilled blacksmith before I was brought to this wretched land," Ilmarinen tells him. "No offense, but you don't have what it takes to forge the sampo. I would be quicker, but my strength has been drained along with my magic."

"Let's call this plan B, then," I say. "If you can get it done sooner, then great." I look to everyone else. "What else do we got in terms of ideas?"

"When we attack, I can redirect the waterways, flood certain valleys," Vellamo says. "If we channel them into narrow routes, our enemies may be forced into traps."

"Skeletons don't drown," Lovia points out.

"No," Vellamo says patiently, "but where water goes, so do my serpents. They will tear them all apart."

I nod again. "Good," I say, voice quieter now. Every promise of help is a candle in the darkness. "Torben, can you erect wards to protect key positions?"

He sets his jaw and nods. "Temporarily, but I'll try." He glances at Rasmus. "If I have help, even better."

Rasmus nods, looking determined. I still don't trust him, though.

Vellamo straightens, trying to show resolve. "We've lost much. We will not lose more without a fight. I'll see to that."

Tapio murmurs agreement, though he looks as if his heart is ashes. "The forest is under my domain, but only when I'm in it. Still, I do have a connection to the animals of the land. We can use them as scouts, birds especially. And Tellervo's green magic can control plants anywhere in the realm."

"Then that's a start," I tell them by way of dismissal.

The generals begin murmuring amongst themselves, exchanging tactical ideas: ambushes, scouting missions, coded messages. Torben, Ilmarinen, and Rasmus move to a corner, whispering about stabilizing energy currents and forging anchors. Lovia stands near me, her eyes still bright with impatience, but I see the way her hand tightens on her sword hilt.

"I want you to be my general, Lovia," I say to her. I shoot General Pekka a wry glance. "Sorry, mortal, you've been bumped a spot. You'll now answer to Loviatar."

I swear, I see a hint of disappointment in his eyes. Perhaps I'm not controlling him as much as I thought.

No offense, I put the thought in his mind. *You're doing a good job.*

He relaxes slightly, but my daughter's mouth is agape. "General? Are you sure?"

"I have no doubt," I tell her.

She raises her chin at that. "I won't let you down."

"You better not," I say under my breath, to which she laughs.

I laugh too, even though it rings hollow.

I catch a reflection of myself in a polished shield mounted on the wall. I look older somehow, wearier. Grief and guilt have carved out my cheeks, made my eyes darker, like an old silver coin. I must not let them see me falter. I force my posture straight, my shoulders square. I am Death. They look to me as their king, and a king I must be.

I dismiss the meeting with a nod, and the assembly breaks apart. The generals hurry off, eager to begin preparations and to consort with the troops, many of whom are taking shifts getting warmth and shuteye in the rooms of the east wing.

Rasmus stands uncertainly until guards nudge him along. Ilmarinen follows, guarded closely, led to their own rooms for potential traitors. Tapio, Tellervo, and Vellamo linger at a window, heads bowed, speaking softly of routes and weather, grief heavy in their voices. Lovia gives me one last look, one of gratitude, and then strides away after the Magician.

I slip through a side corridor, my footsteps echoing softly. Torches sputter, casting trembling light on pale banners adorned with wings and ram horns, Louhi's crest and emblem. Syntri Castle is foreign to me, a place I never intended to use as a command center, but we are refugees in our own realm now, forced into corners we never imagined. My mind churns with strategies, half-formed plans, desperate hopes. I feel the weight of this looming war pressing down on me like a heavy mantle.

I step onto a narrow balcony high above the Star Swamp. Night drapes the world in quiet darkness, the swamp a blanket of white. A hush has settled over the landscape, the only sound the gently falling snow. Far beyond the swamp lies the Hiisi Forest, still reeling from the horrors that happened there. Beyond that, distant mountains rise as jagged silhouettes against pale skies, barely visible even to my far-reaching eyes. Shadow's End waits beyond those peaks, my former stronghold, now Louhi's lair.

My throat tightens; that was my domain, my seat of power. To think that my enemies roam its halls—her laughter echoing where once my quiet rule held sway—is enraging. But I must not give in to blind fury. I must remain calm, controlled, even when all I want to do is exact my revenge and make it rain blood.

I press my palms against the balcony's stone rail. I remember Ahto's laughter, how he guided the seas of Tuonela, how we would discuss the nature of existence over cups of bitter elixir he procured from clams and seagrass. He never liked the sweetvine wines. Now, he's dead, and I bear that failure like a scar. I was supposed to protect this realm, maintain balance. Instead, Kaaos reigns.

I worry about Hanna. Is she becoming something more, someone capable of aiding us? Or will she remain absent, lost to the realm of light, never to return? I can't depend on her, and it hurts me to the core to admit that. I know I said she would return, but I have been wrong before. I'm not sure what I would do if I was.

A flutter of wings startles me, and I glance to my left, surprised to see a small white bird land on the balcony rail. My breath catches. This bird is no random creature—it's my snowbird, now out of its cage. I thought the damn thing hated me, yet here it is, feathers pure as snow, head cocked, regarding me with bright, curious eyes.

The bird hops closer, as if testing my reaction. Slowly, I extend a hand. It eyes me then takes a small leap and settles on my hand before it flaps up to my shoulder, its tiny claws gentle against my cloak. I stand utterly still, stunned.

In its presence, something in my chest loosens. The snowbird is a sign, is it not? That hope is not lost? That I still have a hold on this land that's supposed to be mine? I feel my eyes sting with emotion I shouldn't show, but here, in the dark, I do.

I close my eyes, focusing on the bird's soft breathing. For a moment, I let myself feel all the sorrow, the guilt, the worry. I let it rise and then settle. I am the God of Death and King of the Underworld. I have endured eons before, and I can endure this too. I must. My people need me. Lovia looks to me with defiance and loyalty. Tapio, Tellervo, and Vellamo grieve but have not yielded. Torben, the Magician, the generals, even Rasmus and Ilmarinen—all pieces on a board I must arrange.

When I open my eyes again, I survey the land spread beneath the starlight.

My land.

I lift my chin. The bird remains on my shoulder in silent support. I will not fail. I will form a plan, strike at their weaknesses, and reclaim my throne. If I have to forge uneasy alliances, so be it. If I must fight without Hanna, I will. My remorse and guilt do not vanish, but they harden into resolve. I may be humbled, grieving, and unsure, but I am still a God. This is my realm. I will not let them extinguish the light of what we have built here.

All of humanity depends on it.

And I refuse to let them down.

I will turn helplessness into strength, guilt into purpose. Let the enemy prepare; let the Old Gods prowl.

We will take Tuonela back.

The snowbird shifts, and I smile grimly into the darkness.

They will learn to fear Death again.

CHAPTER SIXTEEN

LOVIA

After checking in with the Magician, I happened to catch a glimpse of my father on the balcony, the image of that snowbird on his shoulder lingering in my mind. For a moment, I'd caught a rare, unguarded expression on his face. Relief? Hope? Even just a spark of something other than worry. That gives me comfort as I step back into the castle's dank corridors. He's trying to be strong for everyone, but I know how much pain and worry he carries. Hanna's absence, the loss of Ahto, the realm in disorder, and here I am, his daughter, now wearing the mantle of a general.

General Lovia. The idea still feels foreign, no matter how good it sounds. I've always been a fighter. I've always known how to swing a sword, hold my ground, frighten the souls out of those who dared stand against us. But commanding others, guiding strategy, protecting not just myself but an entire force—that's something else. My father trusts me with this. I feel a stirring of pride but also a tightness in my chest. What if I fail him? He's already burdened by so many disappointments and losses. I don't want to add my failure to his pain.

I wander the winding halls of the castle. It's an odd place, carved from obsidian laced with black magic, a palace that tries so hard to be the antithesis to Shadow's End but just feels sad and soulless. Louhi's old banners, her weak claim to the land here, hang limply, ragged and nearly colorless. The corridors have a hush about them, as if even the stones are waiting for something. I remember being here as a child and having that same feeling.

Every so often, I pass a guard who snaps to attention at the sight of me.

That's new.

They used to respect me, of course, as Death's daughter, but now, they treat me like an officer, like someone who might give orders that determine their fate. It's unsettling, even if it's due to my father's mental coercion. I'm used to wielding a sword, not wielding people. As much as I like mortals, I don't want to be responsible for them in this way.

I turn a corner and nearly walk straight into Vellamo. The Sea Goddess glides down the hall with quiet grace, though her oceanic eyes are haunted. We've all suffered losses, but for her to lose Ahto—my uncle—I know how sharp that ache must be. She inclines her head when she sees me, her hair shifting around her shoulders like waves.

"General Lovia," she says softly, though there's a hint of teasing in the lift of her brow. "I keep hearing that title. Feels strange, doesn't it?"

I manage a half-smile. "I suppose I'll get used to it." My voice sounds more confident than I feel.

She gestures to a small alcove near a window. We step aside, letting a patrol of soldiers pass. Outside, the snow shimmers under faint moonlight that pierces the moving clouds. "Actually, I wanted to congratulate you," Vellamo says in that deep voice of hers. "It's a heavy duty to have thrust upon you, but I believe you'll shoulder it well."

I look down at my boots, tapping my heel against the stone to steady myself. "Do you really think so? I'm good at fighting; I've proven that. But leading...I'm not sure. That's not really my thing, if you know what I mean."

Vellamo's gaze is calm and sympathetic. "Leadership isn't just about strategy. It's about caring for those who follow you. You have the passion, the courage. I've seen it. You led Tapio and Tellervo when they needed you most. You led me here. You need to trust yourself." She pauses, a ghost of a smile on her lips. "Your father trusts you. He wouldn't have named you General otherwise."

My heart clenches. "I know he does, but he's lost so much already. If I fail—"

She places a cool hand on my arm. "Your father knows the risks of war. He's not expecting perfection. He expects you to fight for what's right and to do your best. None of us can promise more than that. You carry your own integrity into battle. That matters more than a flawless victory."

I nod slowly, forcing myself to absorb her words. My father, stoic as he is, wouldn't have chosen me if he thought I would crumble. He knows me better than anyone. He must believe in my strength.

Which means *I* have to believe in my strength.

"Thank you, Vellamo," I say, voice quieter now. "I needed to hear that."

She squeezes my arm gently. "We're all uncertain, Lovia. We've never faced enemies like these. We've all been so damn blind, sticking our heads in the snow, toiling in our ignorance. All we can do is stand together and trust in each other's resolve."

I watch her walk away, a sad elegance in her step. She lost her beloved, and yet still, she's trying to comfort me. The depth of her strength astounds me.

Feeling a bit more grounded, I decide to find Rasmus.

He's lurking around this castle somewhere, under guard but not entirely imprisoned. We need him—or at least, the Magician thinks we do. He's still my half-brother, linked by blood. By poisonous blood, yes, and he has been on the enemy's side, brainwashed to bits. He shot me with an arrow, yet my father allowed him to live because the Magician said Rasmus might be of some use to us.

I have to trust in that.

Still, I have this urge to test his loyalties, to see if there's anything redeemable in him. Maybe Rasmus knows something he hasn't shared. Perhaps I can draw him out with conversation, learn his true intentions. If I'm going to be a general, I must also learn the art of subtlety. Of trickery. Of interrogation.

This could be my first test.

I find him in a side corridor near the kitchens, seated on a low bench with two guards standing a few feet away, arms crossed. Rasmus' red hair falls over his eyes as he stares sullenly at the floor. At my approach, the guards straighten, and he lifts his head. Our eyes meet—mine cold, his guarded.

"Rasmus," I say curtly. "Good evening."

He raises an eyebrow; amused or resentful, I can't tell. "General Lovia," he says dryly.

"Don't start," I warn, keeping my tone even. "I want to talk. The guards can step aside." I glance at them, and they hesitate. Despite my new status, they clearly aren't sure if it's wise. But I give them a firm nod, and they move a few steps farther off, still within reach if something goes wrong. Plus, I can take care of myself. Rasmus may have some magic somewhere, but he's just a mortal in the end.

I sit down on the bench beside Rasmus but not too close. I rest my hand on my sword hilt casually, letting him know I'm not stupid. "I want to know something," I say. "About our mother."

His lips twist. "You mean the mother who left me to die?" A bitter laugh escapes him. "You think I know her now? She fucking blindsided me."

I observe his face. There's anger there, hurt. He's just as wounded by her abandonment as anyone would be. "I think you know a part of her none of us do. You spent time with her, didn't you? Long enough to earn her trust, be part of her schemes. She chose you for a reason, and not just because you're her son. She must have confided something in you."

He snorts. "*Son* is a generous term. I was a pawn, a useful extension of her will and nothing more."

I recall how he shot me with an arrow, how he mouthed off. "You certainly acted like you believed in her cause."

He turns his head slightly, eyes narrowed. "I was wrong, okay? Now I see I was just another tool."

I consider his words. He's admitting he was manipulated, but does that make him trustworthy now, or just desperate? "If you resent her, if you truly feel betrayed, then you should help us. She's your enemy as much as ours."

Rasmus looks away, silent for a moment. "You think a few kind words will make me forget who I am?"

"Well, who are you then?"

He doesn't answer.

I sigh. "Listen, I don't expect miracles. I'm just pointing out the obvious. She cast you aside. We saved your life. That should mean something."

He shakes his head. "You saved me for your own purposes. Don't pretend it was charity. If I was of no use, you'd have left me in Yggthra's coils, right?"

"No," I admit. "I went back to save you for reasons I don't really understand, but it wasn't because I thought you were useful. Leaving you to die was the wrong thing to do. Look, we both know what Louhi is capable of. We both know she's tearing Tuonela apart. You might not care about the realm, but you care about your own skin. Aligning with us could keep you alive."

He laughs, a sharp bark with no real humor. "Spoken like a true pragmatist. You know I'm only trying to survive." He runs a hand through his hair. "But trusting you would mean trusting the family I never knew, the family that scorns me. I see how you look at me, Lovia. Like a snake you mustn't turn your back on."

I meet his gaze steadily. "You did try to kill me," I remind him. "You tried to kidnap Hanna. You sided with my mother, who wants nothing more than to destroy everything my father built. Forgive me if I'm a little wary."

A flash of shame, perhaps regret, passes through his eyes. "You're right," he admits quietly. "I was your enemy. I could be again—or maybe not."

I roll my eyes and sigh. I swear, he's being annoying on purpose, if not obtuse.

I lean forward slightly, lowering my voice. "What if we tried something else? What if we worked out a truce—a real one, not just you tied up like a captive? Give us something. Information, a weakness in Louhi's plans, something that proves you're useful beyond your own survival."

He grimaces, shaking his head. "You expect me to just hand over secrets I'm not even sure I know? Louhi didn't exactly leave her plans on a scroll for me to read."

I was afraid of that. He might know nothing concrete, which complicates things. "What about Rangaista or the Old Gods? Did you see anything that might help us understand their nature, their limits?"

"You know their nature, Lovia, way better than I do. We're just talking in circles now." He pauses, eyes distant. "I'm not eager to throw in my lot with you either, but maybe that can change if I see I'm not just a prisoner here, if I see you're at least willing to consider me as more than a hostage."

I study his face. I see hints of sincerity—or maybe it's a clever trick. He has been taught by a master manipulator, after all. But still, I get a sense that he's lost, drifting. He had his entire worldview shattered. That can break a person…or open them to change.

"Rasmus," I say slowly, "we're on the brink of a battle unlike anything our realm has seen. If we fail, everyone loses —Louhi rules a realm of nightmares. If we succeed, maybe we build something better. If you help us, you might find a place in that better world."

"A place, huh? You think I can just reinvent myself? What would I even be?"

I smile thinly. "That's up to you. You could be many things, but I know you're no longer your mother's puppet." I study his face for a moment, seeing Torben in his features. "Perhaps your place is getting to know your real father. I know you and Torben go way back, that he was your mentor in the Upper World, but it's only recently you learned he was your true father. Maybe you being here is less about helping us and more about helping him."

The torches in the corridor flicker, and the guards shift their weight impatiently. They probably wonder why I'm bothering to talk to him—because I must. Because as a general, I must consider all resources, all possibilities. Trusting Rasmus blindly would be stupid, but dismissing him could be a missed opportunity.

I stand, adjusting my sword belt. "I'll leave you to think about it," I say. "I'm not promising we'll trust you overnight, but trust isn't given freely; it's earned. Show us you can be trusted, and maybe we'll meet you halfway."

He watches me go without a word, and I can feel his eyes on my back. Maybe I've planted a seed. Maybe he'll try something cunning. I'll be ready either way.

I stride down the corridor, the stone floor cold beneath

my boots. The weight of my new responsibilities presses on my shoulders, but I feel a strange calmness. I may not be certain of what tomorrow brings, but I'm doing my part. I'm making decisions. I'm learning to trust myself as my father trusted me with this rank. The castle's halls still feel haunted by old fears and old loyalties, but now, I carry a bit more confidence. I won't let fear define me.

The corridor leads me back toward the main hall. Outside, the Star Swamp shimmers softly. My father is likely on some balcony or in a chamber, wrestling with his own doubts, perhaps confiding in the snowbird, but I know he won't give in. Neither will I. We stand on a knife's edge, and I must hold steady.

I let out a slow breath and move on. No matter what doubts I harbor, no matter what chaos lurks outside these walls, I will face it with everything I have. If that means growing into my new title, so be it. I may not be certain I'll succeed, but I'll do my damned best.

For myself, for my father, for all who depend on me.

CHAPTER SEVENTEEN

DEATH

Morning arrives, grey and cold, muffled by a gentle snowfall that hushes the world outside the castle walls. I stand in what now serves as my personal antechamber—a small room off the main hall—holding a cup of coffee close to my chest. The scent drifts upward, rich and warm, and for a moment, I let my eyes close and savor the aroma. This coffee is contraband, really. I had a general smuggle it down from the Upper World, a private indulgence I share with no one. Well, perhaps Lovia, if she asked. Which she thankfully hasn't. The bitterness against my tongue reminds me of a time before all this madness. It's a small pleasure amid so much uncertainty and despair.

Outside, the Star Swamp stretches beneath a blanket of delicate white flakes, the reeds bowed under the weight. All is still, but when you look closely, you can pick out all the troops below, camouflaged in the snow.

I drink slowly, letting the heat settle in my chest. I've already sent my snowbird off at first light. It darted into the pale sky without a sound, heading beyond the swamp to scout the lands. I never imagined relying on that tiny-toothed creature for reconnaissance, but times have changed. Every ally, every resource, must be used.

I finish the cup, savoring the last drop, and head into the hall. We've officially turned it into a makeshift war room now, bringing in tables and chairs from other rooms. Maps are spread across surfaces, plans scribbled on scraps of parchment. My generals wait there, along with Lovia and Torben. Outside these walls, guards patrol in the muffled hush of snowfall. Inside, tension crackles along with the logs in the hearth.

Lovia stands near a map of Tuonela stretched across a long, ironwood table. She taps her fingernails lightly on the wood. Torben leans on a black staff with a raven skull at the end, something he procured from one of the rooms. Perhaps it belonged to Louhi at some point. The other generals have formed a cluster at the far end, quietly debating routes and positions, as if Tuonela is just another part of Finland. As I approach, they all snap to attention. Even Lovia stands a bit straighter, though I catch the hint of a fond smirk on her lips when she sees me.

"Good morning," I say. My voice is calm, a practiced steadiness. "Any updates from last night's discussions?"

A stout general with a scar cutting through his eyebrow steps forward. "We managed to send the messages, Lord Death."

Lord Death. I try not to smile. How I pride myself in making them call me that.

"Runners left before dawn for the Great Inland Sea and to the Frozen Void north of here," he continues. "If we are lucky, the sea serpents and mermaids will respond and the trolls will come to our aid."

Originally, Vellamo wanted to go to the sea to spread the message and Tapio wanted to seek out the Keskelli, but I'm not letting any God leave this stronghold. The Gods are not expendable. Like it or not, the troops are. They're also less likely to be seen. They've been trained for it. The Gods are not used to hiding and will be found out in a second. The troops have written messages infused with Torben's magic, which allows the recipient to hear it in the voice of the God. That way, they're more likely to trust the messengers.

"Very good," I say, nodding. "Torben, have you been able to strengthen our wards around the castle?"

Torben meets my eyes. "I have. I have also discovered a few spells with Ilmarinen's help, ones that might give us extra protection in battle."

Lovia's eyes flick to the map. "We should ensure the wards align with natural choke points—the valleys Vellamo plans to flood, the narrow passes in the mountains, and the edges of the Hiisi Forest. If we can funnel them—"

The generals nod. They're soldiers, so they understand terrain, though this conflict is so far beyond a normal war. They mark down notes, muttering about supply lines and vantage points.

I lean over the map, running a finger along the drawn rivers and ridges. The River of Shadows still flows darkly, a thread through the land, and I worry Louhi's forces might use it. "Speaking of the waterways," I say, glancing at Torben. "Vellamo intends to manipulate the tides, but can we secure the banks? If they come by boat..." I shudder to think of the boat we use to ferry the dead being used by Louhi and her minions.

General Pekka clears his throat. "We can place gunmen and traps along the riverbanks," he suggests. "If Torben can lay subtle wards there too, it might buy us time."

I nod, pleased at the initiative. "Then we'll do that. Every moment they're delayed is a moment we can use."

Lovia steps closer to me, lowering her voice. "What of Rasmus?" she asks quietly. "We know he's not entirely trustworthy, but perhaps it's time to see what he knows, to wring some advantage from him. He was helpful to me the other night."

I straighten, considering. She's right; Rasmus has been a thorn in our side, full of secrets and half-truths. If he knows something—anything—that can help us gain an edge against Louhi, we must have it. "Agreed," I say. "Handle the strategy here for a moment. I'll question him myself."

Time to put my mind-melding powers to the test.

Lovia gives a curt nod. I know she hates being away from action—she's been itching to get out there and fight already—but this is action of a sort. She'll keep the generals focused, and Torben will keep the plans balanced.

I exit the hall through a side door and descend a short corridor to a small chamber, where Rasmus has been kept under watch. Ilmarinen is not here—he's in the armory, forging the sampo—but Rasmus sits on a stool, guarded by two soldiers who straighten when I enter.

"Leave us," I tell them quietly. They hesitate only a second before obeying. The door closes, and Rasmus raises his chin defiantly.

"Lord Death," he says, voice dripping with sarcasm. "What can I do for you today?"

I ignore the mockery. I take my time, crossing my arms and regarding him. He's still bruised, clothes rumpled. He knows he's alive by my mercy—or rather, the Magician's mercy. I loathe how that makes him feel more important than he is.

"You know Louhi better than anyone here," I say evenly. "Or, at least you know this current version of her. You know how she thinks, how she strategizes. You were kept in this very castle by her side. Tell me what plans she might have. I want to know what leverage she counts on."

He narrows his eyes. "What makes you think I'll tell you? Your daughter already tried to interrogate me."

I tilt my head, letting silence and my steady gaze unnerve him. Rasmus may be stubborn, but he's not fearless.

"Because Lovia has told me your fears," I eventually say. "I know you will favor only yourself, but you also know your own mother doesn't care if you live or die. Unfortunately for me, the Magician *does* care. So, while you're here, no harm will come to you."

He continues to glare. "Until my purpose is served."

I take a wider stance. "If your purpose is to help us win, then I personally won't lay a hand on you. And I mean that literally."

He tilts his head, mulling that over. "You're not the only one here who wants me dead."

"No one would dare. They want Louhi dead more," I assure him, though it bothers me that I even have to. "Now, tell me what I need to know to defeat her. I know you know something."

"Or what? You'll try the same Jean Grey shit you've done with the Finnish troops?"

"I don't know who Jean Grey is, but yes."

He sighs, licking his lips as he looks around the room. "You know, this was my room before. I was under lock and key just as I am now. You really think she let me in on her plans? She kept me prisoner."

"You still did her dirty work."

"I didn't have a choice. It was work for her or die. I'm sorry, but all I want is to save my own ass."

I step forward until I'm looming over him. "You know something. Help us help you. Give me something we can use. Anything. What about Rangaista?"

"I never saw Rangaista. Louhi's plan was to raise him in the crypt, some section that runs over a ley line..."

My brows raise. "The Sect of the Undead?"

"That's it. She said she needed some more ingredients before she could call him forth. She said it would also release the saints from their prison."

I picture the macabre statues lined up along the crypt and shudder. To think, that's where Hanna and I got married. "Do you know what she meant by ingredients?"

He swallows audibly, running his tongue over his teeth. "Something about horns..."

Like a sword to the gut, I immediately know what she had in mind.

Either Tuonen's horns or Sarvi's.

Or both.

"Tuonen," I whisper, quiet horror in my voice. "He was last seen by Tapio at Shadow's End."

Rasmus doesn't say anything. He doesn't have to. He knows.

"This won't just be an attack," I say. "It might have to be a rescue mission."

Unless Tuonen escaped, but I can't count on that, or on Sarvi, for that matter. They would be here already otherwise.

"I'd say she wouldn't hurt her own son," Rasmus says carefully, "but I have a couple of cracked ribs that say otherwise."

I clench my jaw so hard, I think I crack a tooth.

"What else do you know?" I manage to ask, my hands curling into fists. Her goal will be to use Tuonen's horns to conjure Rangaista, so she already hurt him. Now, I can only hope she has enough motherly instinct to keep him alive.

Or turn him against you, a voice says. I can't bear to think of that right now. Either way, we're getting him back.

I do my best to rein in my emotions as I bring my focus back on the attack.

"If she has Tuonen, she wants me to come and get him," I

muse. "She knows I won't let go of my son so easily. She expects us, doesn't she?"

Rasmus nods. "Yes. She knows you'll go to her, but she'll be ready. I really don't think you'll get to Shadow's End without going through more than a few battles. The Old Gods are everywhere, as are the Bone Stragglers. Those fuckers have been waiting to exact their revenge on you for a long time, and that's what she's been counting on. You'll have to get through all of them before you can get remotely close. They'll be ready, and once you're spotted, she'll be ready too."

I need to be strategic. "Boats on the River of Shadows—could she use them as a feint while sending another force through the forest?"

Rasmus nods begrudgingly. "You must expect attacks from multiple fronts."

"Vellamo will have control of the river. She can take care of them. We will prepare to fight in the Hiisi Forest. It's the best place for the Old Gods to hide and where Tapio can wield the trees to his advantage." I realize I'm thinking out loud now and don't really need Rasmus at this point. I clear my throat. "Very well. Be thankful you've been useful."

I leave him there, guarded, and return to the hall. The generals and Lovia look up as I enter. "Rasmus confirms Louhi may have used Tuonen's horns in a spell to conjure Rangaista," I say grimly.

Lovia lets out a soft gasp, her lips curling into a sneer.

"I'm sorry," Torben says.

"No matter," I say with a wave of my hand. "I should have expected as much. It means she knows we'll try and pull off a rescue mission regardless. She is expecting us to attack, which means the battles will start long before Shadow's End. I feel the moment we hit the Hiisi Forest is the moment the real battle begins. But we can take control of both the forest and the river through Tapio, Tellervo, and Vellamo. If we can get there before they know we're coming, we'll have the upper hand."

Torben taps the map with his staff, frowning. "Then we must strengthen the wards along the forest edge and the riverbanks both. That means splitting our meager resources."

Lovia's eyes flash. "We'll have to be smarter than Louhi. If the forest is the main thrust, we put a stronger defense there."

General Pekka suggests deploying scouts with signal horns in the forest canopy, but that's too risky. She might hear them before we do. Torben proposes placing enchanted stones along the river's edge to create illusions of safe passage, luring their boats into dead ends. It isn't a bad idea, especially if Vellamo is using the river to flood certain areas.

The planning continues until my head aches with details.

At midday, I excuse myself. Lovia follows me into a corridor, and I beckon her to accompany me outside. "We need fresh air," I tell her quietly. She doesn't argue. We pass through a side gate and down a slippery path to the swamp's edge.

It's colder here, the snow drifting in fine flakes. The Star Swamp, usually half-frozen or at least chilly, now shows signs of thawing despite the snow. Water pools under the crust of ice, reflecting a dull, pale sky. The contrast is unsettling—snow above, thawing swamp below. The realm's natural order is twisted. We must keep Torben's spells strong if we want any hope of stable terrain. If the swamp shifts unpredictably, our plans will crumble, and we'll lose most of our army.

Lovia stands beside me, her breath visible in the cold air. We walk slowly, careful not to slip. "It's strange," she says, voice subdued, "to see the swamp like this, as if it can't decide on a season. As if it's fighting us."

I nod. "Torben may need to reinforce his spells. I'll let him know. The power of Oblivion is strong, even more so in a land where Louhi's influence has held steady for so long. Evil corrupts the natural order of things."

She glances at me sideways. "When this is over, do you think things will ever go back to normal?"

I wish I could offer reassurance, but I've learned to be cautious with promises. "Not the old normal," I say quietly, "but perhaps a new balance. Tuonela will heal, in time, if we can restore what was lost. We might be able to make it even better."

Lovia's gaze drifts over the pale reeds. "I've been thinking about Tuonen," she says gently. "And Sarvi. I wonder if...if my mother would actually kill them..."

The fear gnaws at me, but I can't show it. "Tuonen is clever—he would know to keep his head down until it's safe. And Sarvi is resourceful."

But I don't doubt Louhi would dispose of Sarvi before anyone else. She hates that unicorn. Then again, she hates all things with an allegiance to me. Sadly, that might also include our son.

Lovia nods, blowing on her hands for warmth. "Still, I'm worried."

I stop walking and turn to face her, placing a hand on her shoulder. "I know," I say softly. "I'm worried too." Admitting it feels risky, but I'm her father. She deserves honesty. "I take comfort in knowing they're not reckless. They'll find a way to survive until we set this right."

She meets my eyes, and I see her fear and resolve mirrored there. "You really think we can win this, Father?"

I inhale sharply, feeling the weight of all those who depend on me. "We must believe it," I say. "I'm proud of you, Lovia, for everything you've done. You've fought bravely and faced horrors no one should have to. We may be battered, but we're not broken. You've proven how strong you are, and I'm honored that you're my general."

Her lips curve into a small, grateful smile. It's a rare tenderness, despite the duty and war that has hardened us.

She nods, shoulders a bit straighter. "Well, I've had a great teacher. I won't let fear dictate my actions. You can depend on me, I promise."

A part of me swells with pride. Through everything, my children have shown courage, each forging their own path. I fear for them, but I also trust them. Perhaps that trust will guide us through this horror to come.

We continue walking, careful steps on the slick ground. The silence is peaceful, broken only by distant drips of water as ice melts from branches and the occasional troops adjusting their rifles from their hidden vantage points. The Star Swamp reflects silver and grey in the fading afternoon light, and I think of the forces already gathering somewhere beyond the forest's edge. Did the snowbird find them yet?

Night falls slowly, the sky darkening from silver to charcoal. We return to Castle Syntri, entering through a side gate, where a guard nods respectfully. Inside, torches are lit, the hall warmer than outside. The generals and Torben have dispersed for now, each to their tasks. I sense that everyone is resting before the inevitable storm.

I settle by a window that overlooks the swamp, Lovia at my side. We say little, just watching the darkening landscape. My mind wanders to Tuonen and Sarvi again, hoping they remain safe, hoping this war won't claim them too.

Then, my thoughts drift to Hanna. The longer she's away from me, the more desperate I am to hold on to her. I wish there was some way I could communicate with her, just to remind her I'm here and waiting for her return, but the realm of the sun is like another dimension entirely. I have to find comfort in the idea that she might be watching me, right now, from all the way up there. I'm tempted to give her a wave, but I think Lovia might think I'm nuts.

A faint flutter of wings in the distance catches my eye, and I straighten and peer outside. There, approaching through the dim twilight, is my snowbird. It flies low, ghost-white against the dark. I hurry outside to the balcony where it first reappeared to me, Lovia trailing behind. We stand in the cold, watching as the snowbird glides on silent wings and lands on the railing.

Its eyes gleam with urgency. I raise my hand, and it steps onto my wrist, breathing fast, feathers ruffled. "What did you see?" I whisper, as if expecting it to answer. It cannot speak words, but I know how to read its mannerisms.

It lifts its head, pointing its beak toward the forests to the north. The message is clear: the Hiisi Forest. Something stirs there. Then, it flutters, turning to point toward the river's direction. Two fronts. Two armies. I feel a chill, and not just from the winter air.

"They're coming," Lovia says quietly, her voice tense. She understands the bird's signals as well as I do.

I nod grimly and look back to the bird. "Are they holding fort, or are they on the move, heading for us?"

The bird goes raises both wings straight up, a motion that says halt.

For now, they aren't moving. At least there's that.

"We have little time," I say softly, stroking the bird's head. It relaxes slightly at my touch, as if glad to have delivered its message. "We must prepare. If they're already out there, expecting us, then this changes everything."

Lovia's eyes burn with fierce determination. "We must alert the others. Call an emergency council."

"A general's job," I remind her before she nods and runs off into the castle.

I face the dark silhouette of the distant land, heart

pounding with dread and resolve. Hopefully, we'll hear back from Vellamo's allies, as well as the Keskelli, soon.

I inhale the cold night air, my lungs filling with resolve. "We'll make them regret coming," I say out loud.

The snowbird chirps in response.

I glance at it. "I need you to go on another mission," I tell it. "Find my sister, Ilmatar. Let her know Ahto is dead and we need her help. Perhaps that will spur her into vengeance. You can communicate with her, yes?"

The bird nods. My sister has always been able to communicate with the beings of the air. It is her birthright.

"Good. Then tell her we require her assistance here immediately. After that, I need you to fly to Shadow's End. Fly above the clouds so you blend in and see if you can find Tuonen or Sarvi. Tell them the plans. If not, find the giant Vipunen and put forth a request for aid."

The bird tilts its head. Perhaps all of this is a pretty tall order, but I'm counting on someone somewhere to understand this flying, furry dinosaur.

Then, it flies off into the darkness.

"Good luck, you tiny terror," I say.

As I walk back into the hall, this time in darkness lit by torches, I feel the faint thrum of panic beneath my breastbone, but I also feel purpose. The final struggle looms, and though I'm scared—though I grieve and fear for those I love—I know I will not yield.

CHAPTER EIGHTEEN

LOVIA

I STAND IN A CORNER OF THE MAIN HALL, ARMS CROSSED, staring at a map pinned to the wall with a dagger. The hall is lit only by torches, their flames sputtering as the wind sneaks in through cracks in the stone. Snow drifts against the tiny, high windows of the castle, and the walls seem to hum with tension. The others—my father, Torben, Vellamo, Tapio, Tellervo, the Magician, and a handful of generals—are gathered around a long table. They talk in hushed, urgent tones, planning what's to come. Soldiers move quietly down the corridors, checking armor straps, sharpening swords, and muttering prayers.

I tap my foot, exhaling hot breath into the cold air. Outside, it's snowing more heavily, the weather shifting, pulled by my father's emotions. The snow muffles all sound, dampening every noise except the crackle of torches and the scrape of metal.

The tension in my chest builds. I know what I want to say, what I think we should do—I'm just afraid to put it into words, afraid to be wrong.

I take in a deep breath and stride forward, inserting myself into the huddle. The generals make space for me, cautious respect in their eyes. I nod at Tapio and Tellervo; they look weary, grief etched into the lines of their faces, but determined all the same. Vellamo stands beside them, her eyes distant and sad. Torben clutches his staff, frowning at the map. Rasmus is down in the armory, helping Ilmarinen forge the sampo, the device that will apparently help uncorrupt the ley lines. He's been given a bit more freedom now, though he's still guarded by the Magician. At least I trust *him*.

My father stands at the head of the table, arms folded, face set. He looks calm, but I know him well enough to see the strain in his posture, the flicker of uncertainty in his eyes. He glances at me as I approach, his gaze expectant.

I clear my throat. "We know they're coming," I say, voice steady. I'm trying not to let my frustration seep out. "We know the Hiisi Forest is infested with Old Gods, probably Bone Stragglers. We know they're marching, that boats are coming down the river. Why are we still sitting here, practically waiting to be attacked? We should advance toward the forest and strike first."

My father's jaw tightens, as if he expected me to just blindly agree with his strategy. The generals look at each other, brows raised.

I press on, my voice rising. "Tapio and Tellervo's powers are greatest in the forest. They can wield trees, roots, and vines against the skeleton armies. Vellamo can control the river and the beasts within—turn their approach against them. If we push into the Hiisi Forest before they set their ambush, we can catch them off guard, make them regret coming at us."

No one says anything, so I keep talking. "We need to hurry. Don't you feel the urgency? The snowbird told us they've halted, but for how long? We need to move, and we need to move now."

"We are still waiting to hear from our allies," Torben says.

"Well, how long are we supposed to wait? Forever? What if they never come? What if they're..."

I don't want to say gone, but from the hollow look in Vellamo's eyes, I know she's thinking it. She might be the last of our kind from the sea.

For a moment, I think my father might agree. His eyes flick to the Magician, who stands off to the side, galaxies swirling beneath his hood, silent and unreadable.

Then, my father's voice comes, quiet but firm. "No."

The single word makes my heart sink. He doesn't snap or shout, but his tone leaves no room for argument.

"Why not?" I demand, hands on my hips, feeling less like a general and more like a petulant child who isn't getting her way.

"Because of what Torben just said. We are waiting for allies; without them, we don't have the numbers," he says, meeting my gaze. "We're too few, too fragmented. Fighting in the forest leaves us vulnerable to being surrounded. Tapio told us how his wards no longer work there, which means the forest itself has been compromised. We know Louhi's forces are brutal and numerous, if not cunning. If we leave the safety of Castle Syntri, we gamble on controlling terrain that might already be corrupted beyond recognition."

My frustration sparks. "But the Forest Gods—"

He shakes his head. "Tapio and Tellervo are weakened by what's happened. They can still use their powers, but not like before, and Vellamo's hold on the river is tenuous without Ahto. We risk too much by going out there. Here, we have walls, high ground, and time. Torben can unfreeze the Star Swamp at the right moment, turn the terrain into a deathtrap beneath their feet. We control this place, Lovia. If we leave, we control nothing."

I clench my fists, wanting to argue. I want to remind him that being passive is what got us into trouble before—all those decades of my mother slowly forging her plan, piece by piece, while we sat back and let it happen.

But I see the logic in his eyes, the grim resolve. He's right —we're outnumbered, something Louhi would be counting on. My pride and fury struggle against his reason, but in the end, I inhale, hold my breath, and slowly exhale.

"Fine," I say, forcing calm into my voice. "We'll do it your way."

A relieved murmur passes among the generals. Torben gives me a sympathetic nod, as if thankful I didn't press the fight. Tapio and Tellervo look disappointed but resigned while Vellamo closes her eyes, perhaps remembering a time when we held more certainty, more power.

We finalize the plan. We'll stay in Castle Syntri, use the swamp as our trap. Torben will hold his magic in reserve until the army is fully committed and then break the ice beneath them. Vellamo and Tapio will assist by luring them closer then striking with their own magic. If the sampo is ready before then, the shamans might be able to open the ley lines to lure and swallow the Old Gods.

If Rangaista happens to be amongst them, all the better.

Night falls down on us like a final curtain. Earlier, I felt impatient that we were doing nothing, sitting still, waiting for allies who might never show. But then, there was still daylight, even one covered in snow, and that brightness was enough for me to ignore my fear and focus on the things that needed to be done.

But now that darkness has fallen, everything has changed. The fear creeps in with the cold, and I'm not the only one who feels it.

I stand off to the side in the main hall, trying to steady my breathing as the others scatter to make final preparations. The torchlight quivers over worn stone, throwing shadows that dance like uneasy ghosts. The firelight glints off battered armor and sharpened steel, off anxious eyes and trembling hands. Outside, the snowfall thickens as the storm intensifies with my father's brooding mood, and a knot of worry tugs at my stomach.

"Lovia," my father calls softly, and I turn to face him. He's at the table, still pouring over the map with Torben and the generals. He knows Tuonela like the back of his hand, but I feel he's busying himself to keep his mind off the same things I am. At least it won't hurt for the mortals to know the land by heart.

He nods at me, a wordless instruction to head to my assigned position. The tension thrums between us—he knows I disagree with waiting, but I must obey his orders. After all, I'm the head general for a reason, and it's not just because I'm strong. It's because he's my father, and I'll support him no matter what. I give a curt nod and step away, allowing them space to finalize the plan.

I move slowly through the corridors, passing soldiers hunched in quiet prayer or steeling their nerves by whispering amongst themselves. The air smells of metal and lamp oil, and my breath fogs in the chilly drafts. I slip into a storage alcove where I can be alone for a moment. For a few heartbeats, I let the tension roll through me, trying to release it as I exhale into the dim light.

I think of Hanna, my friend, my mother-in-law—a fact I still have a hard time wrestling with—somewhere beyond these wars, transformed by the sun's power. Will she return? And if she does, what form will she take? I picture her smiling face as I remember it—bold, warm, reassuring. A little cocky, too. If she arrives too late, or not at all, we must face the enemy alone. I push that fear down. There's no room for helplessness now. If my father can manage to stay strong without her, so can I. It's a slippery slope to put all your hope into one person.

I straighten and head outside. The courtyard is filled with hushed activity: soldiers carrying bundles of arrows brought from the armory, a makeshift hospital corner where Tellervo arranges bandages and herbal salves, already anticipating casualties. I catch her eye, and she gives me a determined nod. She has been quiet ever since the loss of her mother and brother—using her healing powers is probably a good distraction for her.

It's not just her who looks determined. I see it grimly painted on every face. No one jokes or jests; the night smothers all levity. Snow swirls over broken flagstones and grotesque statues made in my mother's image, all bat wings and curled ram's horns. I watch the flakes dance in the torch-light then turn toward the ramparts.

On the walls, archers test their bowstrings and squint into the distance. The forest and swamp lie hidden by whirling flurries.

The trap is set.

All we need now is for the enemy to come. The waiting is a slow torment, each second stretching like hours, and the longer it takes, the more fear seeps into my marrow.

A hush spreads through the halls, a hush that gnaws at my

nerves until they're left exposed. Soldiers march quietly along the corridors, the metal of their swords and spears dulled with soot and ash to prevent unwanted gleams. Some of them check and recheck their rifles and ammunition. I see a young soldier, barely more than a teenager and so painfully mortal, fumbling with the straps of his breastplate. He sets his jaw, trying to hide trembling fingers.

We all wait.

We are all afraid.

A familiar hum of energy fills the air, and I glance sideways to see the Magician emerging from the gloom of the castle and out into the weather. He glides toward me with that silent grace of his, snow gathering on his hood. If he knows what will happen tonight, will he say anything? When it was us in the forest, I felt closer to him than ever before, but ever since we've arrived at the palace, I've felt distance between us. I know it's because we're both busy, but I still need him, especially in ways I don't quite understand.

"Lovia," he says, voice low enough that it doesn't carry. He stands close, and my shoulders immediately drop with relief, grateful for his presence. Everyone else is too wrapped up in fear to offer comfort. He's still calm and distant, yet somehow reassuring.

"You know what's coming," I say softly, studying the swirl of impossible stars, "don't you? Will you tell me if we survive this night? Can you tell me if *I* survive this night?"

A faint shift of colors plays across the darkness within his cowl—indigo to silver, constellations rearranging themselves. He tilts his head. "You know I can't," he replies gently. "Some futures must remain uncertain, even to those who can see them. To speak them aloud would risk changing their course."

Of course, he would say that. I clench my jaw. I want to beg him for reassurance, for a hint that all won't be lost, but I know better than to press. He's made of secrets and cosmic riddles and things far beyond my limited understanding. It's who he is.

The tension in my chest doesn't ease, though. The wind picks up, tugging at my cloak, sending a flurry of snowflakes dancing around us. My fingertips are numb against my sword's hilt. "I hate this waiting," I admit softly, voice shaking a little. "I hate standing still, letting fear crawl under my skin like bugs."

The Magician raises a hand as if to comfort me, but he hesitates, uncertain. Then, as if making a quiet decision, he steps closer. The scent of old books and rain and smoldering fire clings to him, or maybe that's just my imagination. He lifts his other hand, fingertips brushing gently against the curve of my jaw. It's a small, unexpected kindness in a night filled with dread.

"You carry too much weight, Loviatar," he murmurs. "Courage and doubt are both heavy on your heart." His voice, so calm and quiet, seems to still the snow for a moment. "I wish more than anything I could show you the path ahead, relieve you of this burden, but I cannot. To do so would change what needs to be."

I growl internally at his vague prose. I want to cry, to demand he stop talking in riddles, to just tell me something real and certain. But looking at him, I see understanding in that shifting darkness, as if he truly cares.

Before I can respond, he leans in and presses his lips to mine—a sudden, gentle kiss, warm and unexpected in the icy night. For a heartbeat, I yield to it, closing my eyes, forgetting the storm, the enemy, the weight of everything. The world narrows to the soft press of his lips, a spark of beauty in a chaos of gods and monsters.

He pulls back slowly, galaxies still swirling in that hood. I'm breathless, heart pounding. I knew he was solid thanks to his hands, but I'd never touched his face before, let alone his lips. As I stare at him, I find no features at all, but I felt his lips like I would any other.

He's manipulating matter to become real.

He's becoming what I want him to be.

What I need him to be, even if just for a moment.

"Thank you," I whisper, voice cracking slightly. I don't know what I'm thanking him for—the kiss, the moment of comfort, or for just being present in a landscape of uncertainty. Maybe all of it.

"The pleasure is all mine," he says softly, reaching for my hand. We stand a moment longer in silent accord, snow drifting around us, holding on to each other. In the distance, I hear a muffled clang as a soldier drops a shield, a hushed curse as another fumbles with arrows, the sound of a rifle being loaded. Reality seeps back in. The Magician's galaxies swirl slower, as if reluctant to leave this shared instant of warmth.

"I must go," he says at last, regret in his tone. "There are illusions to prepare, positions to take. We are all needed tonight, every single one of us."

I nod, biting back the urge to beg him to stay, to tell me more, to give some final reassurance. I won't trap him in my fears, though. He has his role. We all do.

He fades into the gloom, disappearing soundlessly down stone steps. I lean against the parapet, the icy stone pressing through my cloak. The taste of his kiss lingers, a strange sweetness amid bitterness. For a moment, I feel braver—not because I know what's coming, because I don't, but because I know I'm not alone in my anxiety, in this silent vigil before the storm.

I take a steadying breath and return to my patrol, footsteps crunching softly on newly fallen snow. I pass the archers and gunmen again, meeting their eyes with a firmer gaze. I must show them strength, must be ready to lead. My father has put me in this position because he believes in me. If the Magician can offer comfort without certainty, I can at least offer courage, even without guarantees.

The storm intensifies, flakes coming faster, heavier, as if the sky itself conspires to hide our fate. The wind picks up a mournful note, whistling through arrow slits, tugging at Louhi's old banners that hang limp and frosted. I might need to talk to my father about keeping the visibility open, but this might not be all of his doing.

I make one last round, checking that the troops along the western walls are in place. They nod to me as I pass, their eyes weary but resolved. My father must be expending so much energy to keep them in line, and I have to wonder how much they truly understand. I know they're afraid, but they still don't have total autonomy.

Luckily, I know my father will follow through with what he said, that in the end, he will reward all of them with seats and places across the land when they eventually die. Hopefully, that won't happen here, but rather after they return to the Upper World, when they're ninety. They won't even go to the City of Death—if there is to ever be a City of Death again. They will be gods in their own right.

I stand near the battlements once more, sword at my hip, and try to imagine dawn breaking over this field. Will it be a dawn of victory or a pyre for us all?

How much longer do we have?

No answers, only silence, snow, and the distant hush of shifting wind.

But I have something more than I had a moment ago: the memory of that gentle kiss, a reminder that even here, at the edge of doom, there can be tenderness. It sparks a tiny flame of hope in me—hope not for promises or certain outcomes, but for the strength to face what comes and find meaning in our struggle.

I close my eyes, focusing on that feeling, and wait in the deepening night, heart steadying. Let the enemy come. We have our plans, our courage, and the quiet bonds between us —even those forged in silence and star-swirled shadows.

That will have to be enough.

CHAPTER NINETEEN

LOVIA

A HORN SOUNDS SOFTLY FROM A WATCHTOWER, WAKING ME from my slumber.

I sit up fast and straight. I'm in the grand hall, having fallen asleep in the chair next to the fire. Across from me is Vellamo, her watery eyes wide and gleaming in the firelight. She's dressed in armor that once belonged to my mother, black steel covered in spikes. She would look formidable if not for the fear in her eyes.

The horn sounds again, and now, I'm fully awake, hit with a spear of terror.

"Something is happening," Vellamo says to me, quickly rising to her feet.

I pick up my sword, adjust my own armor, and hurry up a winding staircase to a balcony high in the castle's spires. Soldiers with bows and spears line the battlements. I lean over the stone railing, straining my eyes into the darkness. The snowfall lessens here, as if a dome of clearer air surrounds the castle, granting us visibility.

Beyond, in the gloom, shapes move.

Oh gods.

They're already here.

They come from the top of the ridge that slopes down toward the swamp, dark figures that move quickly, running toward us. I estimate we have only a few minutes before they're upon us.

"They're here!" I yell. "On the other side of the swamp! They're here!"

My cry is carried on the wind, amplified by the troops and generals and other Gods, followed by another blast of the horn.

"Where is your father?" Vellamo asks, looking around.

"I don't know," I cry out, holding my sword so tightly, I'm afraid my palm might fuse to it. I thought I was strong and brave and ready to be a general, but I've never been so afraid in my entire life. I can barely breathe.

This is it. *This is it.*

They come closer, enough for me to start picking out their forms amid the dark and blowing snow. The first line is one of skeleton warriors, their bones rattling, swords and axes in bony hands. They wear piecemeal armor, and in the dim light, their hollow eye sockets glow with eerie green fire, a sign of Louhi's control. Behind them, towering silhouettes loom—a mass of Old Gods with too many limbs, twisted heads, and bodies that ripple as if made of shadows and nightmares. I see what might be antlered skulls floating atop writhing masses of bone. Strange, pulsing lights flicker around them as they advance.

Overhead, wingbeats fill the air, putting a chill down my spine. Looking up, I see dark shapes against the cloudy sky—flying unicorns, their bodies stripped to bone, manes of shadow, horns glistening with malice. They circle slowly, searching for prey.

"Oh, fuck," I whisper. I didn't count on those. Gods, I hope Sarvi isn't among them.

Louhi and Rangaista are not visible because of course they aren't—they send their minions first. They must be holding back, waiting for a perfect moment, or simply letting their forces soften us before they strike themselves.

My mouth goes dry. We're truly facing an army of nightmares. Below, soldiers shift nervously, muttering prayers and curses in equal measure. I scan the crowd for Rasmus, only to find him lurking near a supply wagon. He's not fighting yet—he's hesitant, or maybe just terrified. I can't blame him, but if he wants to survive, he'll have to choose a side soon.

My father suddenly appears beside me, silent and grim. I steal a glance at him; his expression is stern, a skull mask pulled over his face, carved from blackened bones. The wind picks up, blowing his cloak. I wonder what he's thinking, what regret or fear hides behind that mask. He chose this ground to stand on. Now, we must prove it was the right choice.

The enemy advances slower now as they close in, cautious. They know we're here; they must sense the trap. Below on the barbican, Torben steps forward, staff in hand, beginning a low chant. When they're close enough to let them think they can breach our walls, he'll unfreeze the swamp. They'll tumble through ice into blackened mire and drown, whisked straight to Oblivion. They won't all fall, but it will be enough to break their formation. It's our first line of defense.

But something's wrong. Torben's chant falters. He frowns, the runes on his staff glowing dimly. He tries again, voice rising as I watch intently.

"What's happening?" I whisper to my father. "Can't he do it?"

"I don't know," my father says grimly. He glances at Vellamo. "Run to Rasmus over there, tell him to help his father."

Vellamo gives him a look as if to say, *really? Rasmus?* but she does as he asks.

Now, I'm giving my father that same look.

"We need that ice to crack," he says defensively. "Whatever it takes."

Well, this is a now-or-never moment for Rasmus to prove himself.

We watch as Rasmus runs over to Torben and joins in on his chant.

But still, the army advances and the ice doesn't crack. I can see Torben's knuckles whiten on the staff. "Come on, Torben," I hiss under my breath. "We need that ice to break."

A hush falls over the battlements. Soldiers glance at each other. Across the parapet, Tapio grips a wooden talisman, hoping to conjure whatever animals he can in the fight, while Tellervo stands at the edge with an arrow knocked and ready to fly.

Still, no result. Torben curses softly, words I don't understand, and Rasmus chants even louder, his hand sharing the staff with his father. Then, a sound reaches our ears—an arrow lancing off the castle walls.

They charge.

I barely have time to shout a warning before the skeleton warriors surge forward at a run. They come in a wave of clattering bones and scraping metal. Arrows whistle from our archers and gunshots fill the sky, striking some skeletons down, if only temporarily. Still, many keep coming. The Old Gods behind them lumber forward, limbs twisting, jaws snapping. The flying skeleton unicorns descend in a macabre swoop, shrieking like banshees as they come for us.

The battle begins.

The first unicorn dives as quick as a lightning bolt, about to pierce their horn through my father's chest when, suddenly, it hits an invisible shield with a loud thud, knocking itself unconscious and landing on the skeletons below. I didn't think it was possible for Torben to protect us with wards while trying to unfreeze the swamp, but when I look to my left, I see Ilmarinen, hands in the air, his brow furrowed as he throws up as many shields around us as he can.

Guess he's on our side after all.

But the wards are small, just enough to protect my father and those of us standing around him, leaving everyone else in the open. The soldiers along the castle walls cry out, losing arrows, lowering spears. Gunshots fill the air, along with the sound of steel on bone, splintering wood, and the eerie clamor of the undead army. I draw my sword, adrenaline flooding me. I know I'm protected where I am, but I also want to get out there and fight.

To our right, I see Tapio raise his arms, and roots slither from beneath the snow, entangling skeletons in knots. Tellervo calls upon the birds, sending a flurry of sparrows into the enemy ranks, their murmuration enough to blind them.

Vellamo tries something with water, summoning a mist from the swamp's edges. It drifts toward the enemy, obscuring their vision. Some skeletons stumble, confused, while others slip on the ice, but it's not enough.

I break through the ward, to which my father yells at me to stay. I ignore him as I leap down a short staircase to the courtyard, joining a group of soldiers. Their eyes widen as I stand with them—the daughter of Death, fighting at their side. I nod, and we push forward, meeting a skeleton as it tries to climb the wall. My blade flashes, cutting through bone, dismembering them. The skeleton collapses into a heap, but another takes its place.

Above us, I see my father raise his hands. The snow intensifies again, pushing a thick curtain of white toward the enemy lines. Wind howls and some skeletons fall, but there are so many enemies. Too many.

Torben, frantic now, tries again to unfreeze the swamp. I see him muttering spells, the runes on his staff flaring bright and then dimming. It's as if something, or *someone*, resists him. Perhaps it's the staff itself. After all, he found it in this castle. It might be working against him; the ice remains solid, giving the enemy stable ground to charge on.

An Eldritch-like horror slams into the castle's outer gate, splintering wood. Soldiers rush to reinforce with shields and spears as I climb the stairs again, needing a vantage point. I see Rasmus stepping away from Torben. For a moment, I think he's going to run, but then he looks at me, swallows hard, and picks up a long pole with a hooked blade at the end. With shaking hands, he pushes it through a gap in the wall, hooking a skeleton's spine and yanking it off the ledge. The skeleton falls with a clatter. It's a small gesture, but it shows he has chosen our side.

For now.

The Magician finally appears, gliding to the end of the platform. I watch him raise a hand, and a swirl of starlight flickers beneath his hood. Suddenly, a section of the enemy line falters, as if they've stepped into quicksand. Skeletons sink, their bony arms flailing as his black universe pulls them down. One of the Old Gods lurches sideways, distracted, and our archers take advantage, firing a volley that shatters several undead skulls.

Still, they keep coming.

The Finnish troops—these mortal warriors—fight bravely. I see them in the courtyard, shoulder to shoulder, faces grim. They thrust spears into rib cages, smash shields into skulls, blast bodies apart with close-range gunfire, but they're also casualties to the undead. Some fall, their screams cut short, and my heart clenches. These soldiers are dying to protect this place, to protect us, and they're going straight to Hell. I have to do something, have to fight harder than this.

I leap into the fray, slicing through bone, dodging a blade as it whistles past my ear.

High above, a flying skeleton unicorn dives at me, its horn aimed like a spear. I roll aside at the last moment, the creature's horn scraping stone, leaving a trail of sparks. I lunge upward, slashing at its bony flank. It screeches and flaps away, missing one of its rear leg-bones.

We can't last forever like this. We need Torben's spell. The plan was to unfreeze the swamp and send half their army plunging into the Oblivion below. Without that, we're overwhelmed. I see General Pekka shouting orders, rallying troops, sweat and blood staining his face. He's fighting two skeletons at once, hacking them apart, but an Old God, a towering beast of molten rock and fire, lowers a fist of stone on top of him, crushing his head.

General Pekka is reduced to a pancake of blood.

My stomach twists. We are losing people. We are losing ground.

"Torben!" I shout over the din. "We need that swamp broken now!"

He grits his teeth, eyes blazing. "Something resists me," he calls back. "I need more help."

"Drop the staff!" I yell, but it's swallowed up by the noise.

I look around frantically. Who can help him? *Ilmarinen*. If anyone can assist with complex magic, it's him. The only problem is, I don't think he'll be able to keep the ward going at the same time.

Still, I run toward him, cutting through a pair of skeletons on the way, ignoring the slice that tears through my armor's shoulder strap.

"Ilmarinen!" I shout. "Torben needs you. He can't break the ice alone. I think his staff is compromised."

Ilmarinen glances at me. "I can't hold the wards at the same time."

"I'll be fine!" my father booms. "But no one else will if you don't thaw the swamp."

The shaman nods and grabs a small pouch from his belt, the energy of the wards fizzling. My father brandishes his sword, ready for the next unicorn to try anything.

Ilmarinen and I push through a knot of soldiers toward Torben and Rasmus.

"I can amplify our power," Ilmarinen says, voice calm despite the chaos. "If the staff is indeed magicked against us, this will help."

He rummages in his pouch and pulls out a handful of runic nails. "Hold them," he instructs me. I do so, cupping them in my palm, feeling them vibrate with faint power.

He takes one, presses it against Torben's staff, and whispers something I can't hear over the battle roar. The runes on the staff flare brighter, and Torben tries again, voice carrying a strange harmonic note as the ground beneath us shivers.

Below, the skeleton army surges again, pushing closer. More soldiers fall, screams torn away by the wind. I see my father spearing a unicorn in the chest with his sword as Tapio conjures grasping roots that ensnare legs. Tellervo's birds swoop and soar, dodging and wasting the arrows that were meant for us. The Magician's galaxies swirl brighter, warping space so an Old God with five legs stumbles into a wall, as if misled by illusions.

Still, there are too many.

Then, I feel it. A deep crack resonates through the stone under my feet. Torben's and Rasmus' chanting rises in pitch, the runes glowing like wildfire. Ilmarinen drives a nail into the parapet stone, and there's a sound like thunder as, beneath the enemy army, the ice splits apart.

What had been a solid, frozen surface over the swamp

now fractures into jagged shards. Sections of the enemy ranks suddenly lose their footing as skeleton warriors slip, tumble, and crash through the breaking ice, plunging into the dark Oblivion beneath with their weapons. I watch entire columns of enemy soldiers collapse into the swamp's depths, dragged down by armor and tangled limbs. Old Gods screech as they flail, trying to climb back up, but it is no use.

Infinity has its hold on them.

The flying skeleton unicorns, startled by the sudden shift, swoop lower, only to meet a barrage of our arrows, bullets, and spears that knock them from the sky, each one landing on the skeletons, taking more of them out. Cheers rise from our troops. Hope is on the wind. The enemy numbers thin as a third of their force falls into watery Oblivion, and for a moment, hope flares in my chest. Maybe we can hold Castle Syntri after all.

But they keep coming. Louhi's forces seem endless as more undead spill from over the ridge. The few horrors that avoid the pools surge forward, smashing at our walls, forcing us back. Archers run out of arrows, gunmen out of bullets, soldiers tire, and many of our troops lie lifeless in the snow.

"We're being overwhelmed!" a general cries.

I grit my teeth, slashing at a skeletal warrior who dared climb the wall. It falls apart under my sword, but for every one I cut down, two more appear. The courtyard is littered with broken bones and shattered shields.

My father stands on the highest battlement, summoning storms and hail, but even a God can tire. I see him falter, shoulders slumped, as if carrying a great weight. Tapio and Tellervo cling to each other, their powers waning as the night drags on. Vellamo tries to stir the water again, but the enemy no longer trusts the frozen swamp and stays on firmer ground. The Magician creates illusions, but illusions alone cannot stem a tide so vast.

It's too much. Even with Torben's and Ilmarinen's success, we cannot hold forever. The enemy is pressing in, and I see soldiers retreating through the inner courtyard. Screams fill the night. My sword arm aches, my breath coming in ragged gasps. I search for my father's face again, only to see pain and dread there, his mask pushed up on his face. He knows we're losing ground.

This can't be it.

Rasmus appears at my side suddenly, hooking another skeleton off the wall with that pole-blade. He's shaking, eyes wide, but he's helping. "We need a fucking miracle," he gasps, voice cracking.

The castle is about to fall. The soldiers form a last ring of defense around the inner gate as my father lowers his hands, looking defeated. My stomach turns cold. We've done everything we could, but the enemy is too strong.

We have too many mortals and not enough Gods.

Then, a bright light appears in the sky above the castle, cutting through the swirling snow. It's blinding, pure, and warm. At first, I think it's a trick, another illusion put forth by the Magician to blind our enemies. But then, I feel heat radiating from it, a gentle warmth that pushes back the cold and the darkness. Soldiers stop fighting to stare upward, mouths agape as skeletons recoil, their glowing eyes dimming.

"Hanna," I whisper, heart pounding. It must be her. It has to be her. The Sun Goddess' blood flows in her veins. If she has returned, maybe we have a chance.

The light intensifies, casting long shadows of bones and broken weapons across the courtyard. Under its radiance, I see Father lift his head, disbelief and hope mingling across his face. Tapio and Tellervo gasp, and Vellamo's eyes shine with something like relief as Torben lowers his staff, awestruck. The Magician tilts his hooded head, as if he knew this would happen but still marvels at the sight.

The enemy army halts, uncertain. The light grows brighter, and I can almost see a figure within it, with angel-like wings of radiance, and flames streaming from her hair. The snowstorm falters, flakes glowing gold before they melt into soft droplets. The darkness that clung to the castle recedes.

We needed a miracle, and we got one.

Hanna is here.

CHAPTER TWENTY

DEATH

THE SKY IGNITES WITH A BRILLIANCE AND BEAUTY THAT DEFIES this world. Moments before, the fields around Castle Syntri lay dim beneath storm-wracked clouds and swirling snow, the world reduced to howling winds, desperate screams, and the relentless clatter of the undead. Now, the darkness recedes, and a radiance too pure for twilight spills over the battlements, painting every broken stone with shimmering gold.

I stand atop a fractured parapet, the wind tugging at my cloak, ice crusting in my beard. Pain throbs in my shoulder from an earlier clash, and sweat freezes on my brow. I dare not look away from that sky, not now. I know that light. I know the shape emerging from it as intimately as I know my own breath.

It's Hanna.

My wife.

The Queen of Tuonela.

But she doesn't descend. Instead, she hovers high above, wreathed in halos of shifting color—pinks, oranges, ambers —with glowing wings of light protruding from her back. Her silhouette is tall and regal, arms outstretched. I see her hair aflame with strange brilliance—chestnut and amber and blonde—and though I cannot make out her face, I imagine her eyes shining with sunlight. The cold wind softens slightly in the radius of her glow, melting the flakes into droplets. Yet, she stays distant, as if observing from a height.

A gasp echoes along the battlements, and I hear Lovia choke out her name. Soldiers pause mid-strike, undead falter mid-lunge, and even the Old Gods waver, their monstrous forms twitching uncertainly in the sudden glare. The darkness Louhi's hordes brought with them quivers before Hanna's arrival.

My heart pounds. Relief, joy, and a thousand unanswered questions surge through me. Weeks of fear and loss peel away at the edges of my mind as I stare into that luminous figure. Hanna is back. She returned.

Yet, this isn't over. The battle has not ended.

We must still fight.

Thankfully, with her at our side.

Snarls and screeches rip me from my reverie. The enemy hasn't vanished—far from it. Old Gods flail tentacles and chitinous limbs, shrieking to rally the undead ranks. Flakes of grey snow swirl on the far edge of the battlefield where Hanna's light does not yet reach. Skeleton legions, rattling swords and spears, try to press their advance. They push back against the sudden warmth, steeling themselves with the ancient hatred that animates their bones.

I tighten my grip on my sword. We must seize this moment. "Hold the line!" I shout, voice cracking across the courtyard. "Don't falter! The sun is with us!" It's a phrase I never thought I'd use, but now, it feels right. Hanna is the sun, or at least touched by it. We must stand firm.

My allies respond with renewed courage. Torben lifts his staff into the sky, runes flaring brighter than before.

Ilmarinen traces shapes in the air with his fingertips, creating pockets of protection here and there. Lovia leaps onto a ledge, her blade gleaming, rallying the soldiers around her. Tapio and Tellervo draw upon what remains of their power to summon roots, vines, and birds to harry the enemy flanks. Vellamo clenches her jaw and coaxes streams of water from melting snow, forming icy shards to hurl at encroaching horrors.

The Magician stands at a crooked tower's edge, face obscured by his hood. He conjures illusions that glimmer with flecks of sunlight, tricking the enemy into stumbling into ambushes. Rasmus struggles to reload a crossbow with trembling fingers. Though he was a traitor, he now fights beside us, the fear of death etched into his face. The redhead might be good for something yet.

The Old Gods are various in form and substance, but all are colossal nightmares—some fusions of bone and chitin, barnacle-encrusted limbs and too many eyes, while others resemble giant deer with the body of a man with antlers that soar ten feet in the air. One wades through a collapsed section of wall, snapping at defenders with a beaked maw dripping black ooze. Another hovers on membranous wings above the courtyard, screeching and dropping twisted carcasses that explode into swarms of ravenous insects. I choke on the stench as I swing my sword, severing a skeletal warrior's spine. The creature crumples at my feet before I hack apart the rest of him, disabling him for good.

Hanna remains above, silent and godly. She raises one hand, and sunbeams stab downward, piercing the gloom. Where the beams land, undead hiss and crumble into ash. A tentacled horror tries to shield its eyes, keening as parts of its flesh scorch and peel, but even this divine intervention doesn't simply wipe the enemy away. The Old Gods are clever enough. One curls behind a toppled tower and vomits out a thick, inky cloud that dims the sunlight in a patch of the battlefield, allowing skeletons to rally within that shadow. Another creature with lobster-like claws and a carapace of petrified wood smashes into our left flank, scattering wounded soldiers. Screams rise, and I flinch, desperate to help them.

I rush down broken steps, joining a knot of defenders wrestling with the snarling mass of horned skulls and scythe-like arms. The thing flails wildly, cutting down a soldier before I slam my sword into its side, feeling bone give way beneath the blade. The creature howls, and a shaft of light from Hanna lances it in the back, causing it to shrivel. I glance up, wanting to meet her gaze, to thank her, but she's too far, her face lost in the glare.

On the eastern parapet, Lovia fights two horrors at once. One resembles a monstrous serpent wreathed in leech-like growths that snap at her ankles while the other stands like a hunched giant made of bone shards. She ducks under a spiked limb, counters with a clean slash, and then calls for archers. Arrows whiz by, followed by bullets, many helped by Torben's magic. The serpent squeals as arrowheads puncture its hide, green ichor spraying across the stones.

Tapio staggers, panting. His attempt to grow entangling roots falters as an Old God's scream shatters the delicate magic. Tellervo hurls a spear of spectral ivy that crackles with emerald energy, impaling a skeletal champion who'd been rallying troops. Vellamo summons a spinning vortex of meltwater that topples another cluster of undead. Ilmarinen's wards deflect a volley of cursed arrows spat by an Old God that resembles a giant tick, its abdomen festooned with skulls. The tick-thing scuttles along a wall, toward Hanna's light. When a sunbeam sears off two of its legs, it screeches and leaps down among us. Soldiers scatter, and I lunge forward, sword raised, shouting for a shield wall from Ilmarinen.

But it's Rasmus who surprises me, darting forward and hooking the tick-thing with his pole. The Magician sends a mirage of fire dancing along its flank, making it think it's aflame. Distracted, the horror flails at empty air, giving me time to drive my blade into a gap in its chitin, foul blood spilling out. The monster collapses under our combined assault, twitching until another shaft of sunlight from above reduces it to char.

Despite these victories, the battle rages on. The enemy is legion, and not all can be felled by a single beam of light. Some Old Gods burrow beneath the rubble, emerging behind our lines. One enormous, centipede-like horror clambers onto a rooftop and vomits a torrent of maggots that strip flesh from a soldier's arm before rifles drive it back. I grimace at the brutality of it all. Even with Hanna's help, this is no effortless bout. Every inch is paid for in blood and sweat.

The courtyard turns into a swirling chaos of shrieks, roars, and clangs. Skeleton warriors fight with unnatural tenacity, their shattered limbs still crawling after us. I watch in horror as a headless torso drags itself toward a wounded guard until Lovia crushes it beneath her boot. Thick smoke from burning monsters clouds the air, stinging my eyes. Still, Hanna floats far above, raining down shafts of solar fury whenever an Old God gathers enough strength to threaten us anew.

I just don't understand why she doesn't come closer. I long to see her face clearly, to hear her voice, to feel her presence beside me as we once fought side by side, like we were fated to. I mean, it is her, isn't it? Or has the sun changed her? Is she preserving her strength by staying aloft? My questions find no answers in this frenzy.

A roar shakes the battlements. One of the mightiest Old Gods—a towering behemoth of bone, antlers, and horns—lumbers toward the main gate. Its hollow eyes glow green, and it raises massive claws to tear down what remains of our defenses. Soldiers cry out in dismay. If that horror breaches the gate fully, we're done for.

"Focus on that one!" I bellow.

Hanna responds with a column of light so bright, I must shield my eyes. The beam hisses as it strikes the behemoth's crown of skulls, cracking them open. The creature howls, staggering, and I race forward, sword raised high. Lovia joins me, blade gleaming. We attack its flank, carving into a joint.

With one final heave, I drive my sword deep into the creature's chest cavity. The smell of rot and old bones engulfs me. Lovia slashes its tendon, causing it to collapse in a heap of debris and dust. Before it can recover, Hanna's light intensifies, reducing the behemoth to a pile of ash drifting on the breeze.

A ragged cheer goes up. Is this it? Are we winning?

Have we won?

The undead army, leaderless and battered, begins to falter. Without the Old Gods to push them forward, skeletons mill in confusion. Some attempt to retreat, clattering away towards the south, while others simply collapse into inert heaps. Flying horrors, once so bold, spiral away, wings tattered by sunbeams.

I peer over the broken wall. The enemy is in disarray.

But we have survived.

The courtyard, once hellish, now lies strewn with broken bones and steaming ichor. Soldiers stumble and cough, some crying tears of relief. Tapio and Tellervo sink to their knees, exhausted. Vellamo presses a hand to her chest, breathing hard. Ilmarinen wipes sweat and soot from his brow while Torben slumps against a parapet, staff rattling on the stones.

The Magician folds his arms, galaxies swirling faintly, as if pondering the odds of what just transpired. Rasmus, chest heaving, looks at me in stunned disbelief.

I turn my gaze upward, heart pounding. Hanna still floats there, lined by fading brilliance. The fierce glow begins to dim slightly, letting me see more of her form. She descends, not swiftly like a joyous return, but slowly, deliberately, as though considering whether to grace us with her presence. I wait, hands trembling, longing to touch her.

Lovia and I move closer together, father and daughter standing atop a shattered tower. The light that guided our salvation now seems distant and uncertain. Hanna's feet touch down on a high parapet bathed in half-light, and the sunbeams retract, leaving faint halos around her shoulders. Her hair, once dark, now shifts with hues of gold and red, like embers at dawn. Her eyes—oh Gods, her eyes—are not the warm brown I recall, but pale, molten copper.

I swallow, stepping forward. "Hanna," I say quietly, voice breaking. "You came for us."

She tilts her head, studying me with an odd detachment, as if I am something curious rather than familiar. Lovia's breath catches. Even the cries of the wounded and the grieving seem to fade, as if waiting for her response.

Hanna's gaze sweeps over the courtyard, taking in the wounded, the dead, the lingering beams of sunlight. Her expression is blank, eyes distant. She offers no smile, no word of comfort.

Nothing.

I force a step forward, pain in my muscles a reminder of all we've done to reach this moment. "Hanna," I repeat, softer this time. "Please. Join me."

For a long moment, she does not respond. Then, her lips part, and I expect a flood of relief or apology, an explanation for her strange magic and long absence. Instead, she speaks a single word in a language I do not recognize—harsh and clipped, like sparks struck from flint. The sound scrapes over my heart like a blade.

My chest tightens with dread.

"Hanna?" Lovia says. "Are you all right? It's us."

Hanna regards us both as though we're strangers and she's where she doesn't belong. Her posture is regal, spine straight, but there's no sign of love in her face, no flicker of recognition. The final rays of her conjured sunlight fade from the stones, leaving only the dim, natural twilight and distant fires burning in heaps of slain horrors.

A chill runs through me. Could the sun's power have changed her beyond recognition? Did her trials in the celestial realms strip her memory?

Her compassion?

But no, that can't be. She saved us. That's compassion.

She knows we're worth saving.

Doesn't she?

The silence stretches, and my allies shift uneasily below. The Magician tilts his head, as if unsurprised by this terrible twist. Torben's knuckles whiten around his staff as he stares at his daughter.

"Hanna? It's me, your dad," he says.

Hanna lifts a hand toward him, and I instinctively brace myself, unsure if it's a gesture of greeting or a threat. She utters another low phrase in that unknown tongue, and her eyes flick to my sword, then to Lovia's blade, then across the corpses of the slain Old Gods. Her gaze returns to me, staring as if I am some puzzle to be solved.

My heart plunges. After everything—our desperate stand, the miracle of her return, the light that saved us—the woman I knew does not look back at me. She does not run into my arms. She does not weep with joy or whisper my name. Instead, she stands apart, distant as the sun itself, and I realize we may have won the battle but lost something far more precious.

A sharp wind stirs the ashes below. Around us, soldiers and Gods alike wait, breath held, for her next move. I try once more: "Hanna, please. It's me. It's Tuoni. Your husband. Your king."

No flicker of recognition. Her eyes narrow slightly, as though irritated by my words. She takes a step back, foot scraping stone, and spreads her arms. A subtle glow sparks at her fingertips.

My heart turns to ice. She doesn't know us. She doesn't remember.

Or worse—she chooses not to.

Before I can utter another plea, Hanna's gaze hardens, and I see a gleam of alien light behind her eyes. Everyone tenses, weapons raised with uncertainty. I stand there, sword slack in my hand, my voice locked in my throat.

"You must be Death," she says.

CHAPTER TWENTY-ONE

HANNA

The God of Death stares back at me with what can only be described as hurt on his face. How have I hurt him? I just saved him and his land. Why isn't he happy?

I look at those surrounding him. There's a pretty girl with long, blonde hair, her face cut and bruised. I feel something inside me call to her, a hint of recognition. She must be Loviatar, Death's daughter. I wonder what she means to me, for she stares at me in a similar way to her father. She too looks like I have betrayed her somehow.

I do not understand.

I look to the others. A young man with red hair gazes at me with a mix of awe and contempt—such an interesting combination of feelings, something to be wary of. There is also a tall, stately woman in black armor, her torn gown flowing like the sea. She comes across as a Goddess herself, and I figure she must be Vellamo. I have a brief memory of the two of us together before Mother Sun whisked me to my home. She didn't want me to leave; she was worried, but what for?

Then, there is the man who said he is my father. It is

looking at him, at his watery blue eyes lined with life, that I feel something in my chest, a pang where a heart should be. This man, I trust. I once felt love, innocent love, without conditions, and I felt it for him. He is the only one who doesn't look hurt at my appearance; if anything, he looks relieved. I smile at him, hoping it comes across as sincere.

In the distance stand two others I recognize as Gods: an aging man with skin like bark and a long, bushy beard leaning against a wooden staff, alongside a girl with tangled red hair, tiny antlers springing from her head. They watch me warily, on guard.

"I mean you no harm," I say to them, to everyone. "I have come to help."

The God of Death holds out his hand for me, and I eye it. There's something about this I have to be careful of, but I'm not sure what. It's just his hand, gloved in leather.

I take it, and he squeezes it. I stare up at his formidable form, at the skull mask shoved up over his forehead, curling horns sprouting from the top, as if he has been fused with an animal. His hair is long and black, flowing over his shoulders, his beard ending in a small braid. His eyes are alive with many emotions, a dark silver that gleams against his brown skin, accentuated by lines of black kohl. The furry collar of his cloak is just low enough for me to spot shimmering veins of silver running over his neck, disappearing beneath.

He is handsome in the intimidating way only Gods are. Somewhere in my crystalline core, I feel a tremor of something for him. Is it emotion? It's a curious feeling—perhaps not emotion, but a physical response. My blood seems to warm in my veins, becoming molten gold, my breath shaky. This God has an effect on me still.

"Hanna," the God of Death says to me, his voice like roughened silk. "Do you know where you are?"

He squeezes my hand, as if that will help.

"I am at Castle Syntri," I tell him, hoping he will be satisfied with my answer. "This was Louhi's stronghold before she took over Shadow's End."

His gaze narrows slightly. "And you know who I am to you."

"You are my partner," I tell him. "The king to my queen."

"I told you this could happen," Vellamo whispers to Lovia.

I bring my eyes to her. "Told them what could happen?"

A flash of shame comes across the Sea Goddess' face before she raises her chin proudly. "You are not the same Hanna I saw leave with Päivätär. You have changed. The power of the sun has lessened your tie to humanity."

I stare at her, wondering if I'm supposed to feel a certain way about that.

"I still have mortal links," I counter. "My mother explained I might forget those I walked beside before, but I do remember you all. Slowly, you are being revealed; from a distance, but I do. I am unsure what it is you want from me, because you all stand around as if you were wanting someone different. For that, I'm sorry. I can't be the Hanna I was, but that Hanna wouldn't have been able to save you in the way I did. It is unfortunate there is such a trade."

"We are grateful, dear daughter," Torben, my father, says to me warmly. "I'm just glad you're okay."

"I am better than okay," I tell him. "I am the prophecy, the one to unite the land."

"The one to touch Death," Tuoni says in a grave voice.

"Yes," I say, giving him a small smile. "I remember now. I am the only one you can touch with your bare hands. I have now become the thing most needed to save Tuonela."

There are a few murmurs in the crowd. There are many mortals here, soldiers, and they look relieved, far more than the Gods do. They know the odds have now turned in their favor.

Still, Vellamo's words hang in the air like a shimmering veil of accusation. My tie to humanity has lessened? I think of what that means. Humanity: that messy, heated swirl of emotions, memories, vulnerabilities. I remember how, before Mother Sun took me, I was someone with feelings that burned like coals, sparking wild fires, often out of control. Now, I feel…refined, focused, powerful—and distant.

Did I lose something vital in gaining so much strength?

I study their faces again. My supposed family and allies are a wounded, wary circle around me. Tuoni—my partner—still holds my hand, as if afraid I'll slip away. Lovia, his daughter, watches me with bruised suspicion. Vellamo's eyes glitter like the surface of a stormy sea. The red-haired young man—Rasmus, I think—regards me with wary awe, as if I might burst into flames at any moment. And at the edge of the courtyard, the Forest God and the antlered girl stand tense, as though expecting violence. There's a brittle calm here, tension humming through the icy, broken spires of Castle Syntri.

I clear my throat. "I am still here to help. I remember enough to know Louhi must be stopped, that this realm hangs by a thread, and that we cannot afford to fail."

"All right," Lovia says, coming over and taking my other hand in hers. She gives Tuoni a pointed look, and he reluctantly lets go of me. "We should get you settled. We have a lot of work to do around here and people to help, and you need… Well, you need clothes."

I glance down. The gown I'm wearing is nothing more than gossamer, my body on full display. "What's wrong with this?" I ask.

"You're kind of naked," she whispers.

I raise my brows, as if to say *so what*? What kind of Gods have such an issue with nudity?

"Perhaps it would be good for you to get settled," Tuoni says. "You are planning to stay, aren't you?"

I meet his eyes. "That is my purpose."

He makes a grumbling sound and then nods at Lovia.

She gently takes my hand and leads me down the dim castle hallways. It is only now I realize how loud it was outside with the cries of the wounded, the stench of the dead. I saved them, but I arrived too late.

"Well, I know that wasn't the welcome you were expecting," Lovia begins as we walk down the hall, past a couple weeping soldiers.

"I wasn't expecting anything," I interject.

"I see," she says. We step around broken columns, walking past chunks of stone punched out from the roof above, snow falling inside. "Regardless, we're all glad you're here. I was worried you might never show. So was my father. He really, really missed you, even if he doesn't show it."

"Show it," I echo, pontificating the words. "He shows more than you think. You humans think you must wear your feelings like a cloak, but it is there for everyone to see."

"Humans?" she cries out with a snort. "I am not a human. I'm a God."

I look her over—the fire and pain in her eyes, the set of her jaw. "You are more human than God. That is your weakness."

"I don't have a weakness," she says sharply, letting out a grunt of annoyance. "Come on, let's go to my mother's chambers. She left an array of dresses behind."

She leads me up a spiral staircase of shimmering onyx to another level. I look around with interest. This place is the opposite of the sun—dark and soulless. And yet, my memory tells me it's new to me even still, that I've never been here before.

Lovia takes me into a cavernous room with a couple of torn chairs, their guts pouring out of them, and a bathtub in the corner. She leads me over to a wide bed with a black bedspread. One of the windows is broken, snow blowing inside. I sit on the edge of the bed while she starts rummaging through a wardrobe in the corner.

Suddenly, I am hit with a memory. I may have not been here before, but I have done this with Loviatar. My mind skips back, like looking over photographs or a reel of film, still more objects from a previous life.

And then, it stops on a specific scene.

I remember when I was first brought to Shadow's End.

I had traded my life for my father's.

I had promised to become Death's bride.

I had been brought to his stronghold, placed in my own room, prisoner but not a prisoner, and Lovia had been kind enough to dress me so I looked good for her father, for the dinner.

I knew I immediately liked her, even as other memories roll in—how I kicked her off the boat in the River of Shadows and stole her sword while battling some swans. The swans were akin to a Goddess like myself, and I feel a flash of shame that I killed one of them as a mortal.

"Here," Lovia says, turning around with a black gown in her hands. Tiny beetles scurry off the fabric and onto the stone floor, running for a hole in the wall. "Uh, ignore the bugs."

I take the dress from her, staring down at it.

"I know you're pretty tall for a human..." she begins, and I give her a sharp look. "Ex-human?" she stammers. "Either way, it's still your body and you're tall. But my mother was taller, bigger all around. You know, muscle. Not that you aren't muscular; you really do look like you work out.

Anyway, what I'm trying to say is it might be too big and too long, but we can always make it work with some sashes and a pair of scissors."

I stare at her, all the memories flooding back. I feel like I'm watching a movie in which I care about the characters, but because it's not happening to me, I'm indifferent.

"You don't like the dress?" Lovia asks, her brows knitting together.

"I think the Hanna I was would appreciate it," I admit, running my fingers over the fabric. "I am remembering how we were. The two of us. When you took care of me at Shadow's End."

Her eyes widen with excitement. "So you do remember!"

"I do. Not everything—just pieces."

"Well, that's great. That means you haven't lost your humanity."

I look down at my hands. On the sun, they had strange runes on them, but here, they look normal. "I remember, but I do not feel."

She tilts her head, bright eyes studying me. "Do you want to feel?"

"Perhaps," I tell her. Then, I sigh; everything feels heavier now, so much more than it did when I first arrived and set about fulfilling my purpose. "But won't that make me lose my gifts? That is why I'm here. I'm not here to be a wife or a stepmother or a friend. I'm here to help you win. Feelings seem like a complication we can't afford. I am probably better off without them."

She makes an unsatisfied noise with her mouth. "Well, for now, at least you remember. That's a start. Why don't we get you dressed, and then perhaps we can use your logic and distance to help me and my father formulate our attack. There is more than one way you can help us win our battles."

I nod and stand up. The gossamer veil I was wearing

instantly disintegrates as Lovia makes me step into the inky gown. It is a little loose and too long, but Lovia makes quick work of it by wrapping sashes around my waist to pull the dress in before taking scissors and cutting off the bottom so it comes to my ankles in jagged edges.

"I might as well have a bath," she says. "I'll need a clean dress to wear after, for this little respite before we have to fight again. Do you want me to draw you one?"

"I don't need it," I say. I'm still purified by the sun.

"Suit yourself," she says, going back to the wardrobe. More insects scurry out of the way.

"You and your mother were not close," I say in both a memory and observation.

She tenses for a moment. "No. We certainly weren't."

"You did live here briefly."

"I did, back when my parents first split."

"And now, your mother is the one responsible for bringing all of the realm to its demise. That must be very complicated for you."

She exhales heavily, her fingers grasping one of the dresses, a blackish blue. "It is, but it's also helpful to not think of her as my mother. It's better for me to think of her as Louhi."

"You worry about how much of her is in you. You worry what she thinks of you. You worry that, in the end, you won't matter to her at all, that maybe you never did."

She turns around and gives me a tired look.

"You worry too much," I finish. "What good has worrying ever done?"

The corner of her lip curls up. "Oh, if only the old you could hear you now."

"She worried a lot?" Hanna already feels like someone else, a human I was once close to instead of myself.

"Like it was an addiction," she says with a laugh.

"She mustn't have been very happy."

Lovia stops laughing, her gaze turning soft. "Actually, I think she was."

CHAPTER TWENTY-TWO

DEATH

All around me, horror slowly reveals itself. The wounded cry out, smoke billowing from the festering remains of Old Gods, soldiers weeping openly for their fallen comrades as snow falls on the dead. My friends and allies are trying to figure out what to do next, looking to me for guidance, but my attention has already been stolen.

All I can do is think about Hanna.

Lovia took her into the castle to get her changed, no doubt into one of Louhi's dresses. I'm not sure how that makes me feel—my wife wearing my ex-wife's clothing—but it's better than Hanna being naked all the time while hundreds of troops leer at her.

Not that I can blame them. To see her appear so suddenly, her body on display, brought too many primal urges to the forefront. I acutely remember the feel of her beneath my bare hands, the carnal way she submitted to me, the raw pleasure in her eyes as she came time and time again. Sometimes, she looked at me like I was her lover, sometimes her God, often times both, and it was in those intimate moments that I came to know how much she meant to me.

And seeing her before me in a way I only knew, I realized I never had the chance to tell her any of that, not before it was too late.

Because now, she's a stranger to me, and I'm a stranger to her.

And my brittle heart is slowly breaking, one hardened piece at a time.

"Lord Death," one of the soldiers says.

I look over at him. He's holding his hat between his hands, his face marred by blood and dirt, his eyes heavy. "General Pekka is dead. Who should take over his command?"

I saw the general's gruesome death from my vantage point. I've been trying not to think about it. He was young and he trusted me. Everyone here did.

"What's your name?" I ask.

"Captain Suvari."

I pat him on the shoulder. "You're General Suvari now." I gesture toward the gathering of Gods. "Time to convene with the others about our next steps. I'll make sure Lovia joins you shortly."

But as I step into the castle, I don't seek out Hanna or Lovia right away. I need a moment to think.

I head to the room I've been using as my chambers and bar the door behind me. Then, I sit on the corner of the bed, ripping my mask off in a sudden rage and tossing it so hard, it shatters against the wall. That was stupid. I had Tellervo make it for me and it was the only one I had here.

But wearing that mask never did me any good, not in this new realm.

I exhale heavily and put my head in my hands as I try to think.

This was only the first battle, and yet we have lost so much.

The only reason we won is because Hanna saved us in the end.

What happens next time?

Hanna could destroy the Old Gods, but could she destroy Rangaista? Could she destroy Louhi and all her black magic? Salainen? Even with that win, can we count on her?

Do I want to count on her?

All I know is that I want is to bring her back to the way she was, the way we knew each other. To see that version of her in her eyes, instead of the alien gleam of a Goddess. It's terribly selfish, I know.

But I am a selfish God.

I let out a ragged sigh, my heart water-logged. Sitting alone in my room isn't going to help anything. I can't hide from my wife. It's my job to make her remember she's my queen.

I get up and leave the room, about to head up the stairs, when I run into Lovia.

"Where is Hanna?" I ask.

"In Louhi's room," she says. "I drew a bath for myself but decided she should have it. I have soldiers to take care of."

I nod, giving her shoulder a squeeze. "You don't mind, then, if I take a moment to talk to her?"

"Take all the time you need, Father. I'll handle everyone else," she says before she hesitates. "She remembers some things, but it's like she's remembering a book she read. It doesn't mean anything to her." She gives me a quick smile. "I know this is out of your skillset, but you should try and win her over."

Then, she runs off down the hall.

I grumble to myself. I know how to win people over. I know I won Hanna over at one point.

Sex, I think. *It was the sex.*

Well, perhaps that's not off the table.

I climb the winding stairs to Louhi's room. Aside from pilfering it for clothes and other necessary items, no one has been using it. It feels too close to evil, like we're cursed for even stepping inside.

I knock on the door, and Hanna's firm response tells me to enter.

I open it and poke my head inside. She's standing by a broken window, snow flying in and coating her black dress like stars, her hair, darker now but not quite her natural color, blowing back from the wind.

I stop and stare at her, feeling dumbfounded by her grace, her power, her overwhelming beauty. There's a faint aura around her, a glow that shifts from pink to gold to copper like a sunset, and it only adds to her divinity.

"May I come in?" I ask. My voice comes out gruff, annoyed I have to ask, and I make a note to soften it.

But Hanna only nods, not affected at all.

I step inside the room, closing the door behind me. With my back to her, I close my eyes for a moment, breathing deeply through my nose. I need to compose myself; I feel too unmoored, like I don't know how to act around her.

When I turn back around, she's staring at me curiously.

"Lovia drew me a bath, but I don't feel like being still," she says. "Would you like to take it?"

"Perhaps some other time," I say, though I definitely need one after that battle.

"Very well," she says as she motions to her gown. "Do you like the dress?"

It's such a normal question, I can't help but laugh.

"The dress?" I repeat, looking her up and down. It doesn't even look like Louhi's when it's on her. "You look good in everything, fairy girl."

She frowns and slowly walks toward me, her hands clasped at her middle. "Fairy girl?"

"One of my nicknames for you, only you turned out to be more than a fairy, didn't you? A true Goddess of the Sun. I should have seen it coming."

"Oh? How so?"

I walk across the room toward her, stopping a foot away, unsure if I should touch her or not.

"Because you've always been such a clever, stunning creature. Doesn't hurt that you look like a fairy with those big eyes and your ears that stick out a little."

At that, she touches her ears with her fingers, not insulted, but curious.

"But I think my other nickname is more fitting," I tell her, reaching out and putting my hands over hers. I pull them away from her ears, which, in my opinion, are perfect.

"And what is that?"

"Little bird," I tell her, gazing down at her.

"Little bird," she repeats, rubbing her lips together as she looks away in thought. "Yes. I remember now. You did call me that. It is rather fitting. My mother is considered the protector of birds."

"And she protected you when you needed it most," I tell her. "She brought you to the sun when you were ready to be transformed."

She frowns. "But you're not happy about this transformation. None of you are."

"Let me explain." I gesture to the bed and sit on the edge of it, the mattress sinking under my weight. "Sit," I command. "Please," I add hastily.

She sits beside me, close enough that I put my hand on her thigh.

"Is this all right?" I ask, noting my hand.

She gives me a sidelong look, her mouth twisted into a very Hanna-like smirk. "I get the impression you're not used to asking."

I chuckle. "It's rare someone says no to me. I always get what I want, or at least I used to...until my whole world fell apart."

"I'm sure you asked for my return," she goes on. "And yet, you don't seem pleased."

My heart sinks in my chest, and I squeeze her thigh. "I am pleased, Hanna. I'm relieved, more than relieved, that you're all right, that you're alive and strong, and I'm grateful you showed up and saved us." I swallow uneasily, my heart pounding in my head. "I just...I missed you," I say, my voice tentative, as if I'm afraid to say the words. "I still miss you, and you're right in front of me. To see the woman I...the woman I care so deeply about, my heart and soul...for you to look at me and not really see me for who I am..."

My eyes drop to my hand and stay focused there. Even though she's not exactly Hanna and won't judge me or take my words to heart, I still have a hard time admitting this to her.

"I see you for who you are," she says in a low voice. "I remember, Tuoni. Not all at once, but the memories are there. They just belong to someone else."

"And that someone else is who I want by my side," I admit quietly.

"I'm not good enough?"

I glance up, meeting her eyes. There's a spark of hurt there, and as much as I don't want to hurt her, that spark has to be a good thing. It means she feels.

"You are more than good enough. You are still Hanna," I tell her, my other hand cupping the side of her face and angling it toward me. "And I have faith I will get through to you eventually. As I said before, I always get what I want."

She swallows hard and leans into my hand. "My mother said that each time I use my gifts, I lose a bit of myself." She takes a beat, eyes flicking over my face in thought. "She also said the more I feel, the more connected I feel to this realm, the more I could lose my powers. It seems like an unfair situation to you."

"And not to you?" I ask, my hand falling away.

"I don't want to feel," she says with a firm set to her chin. "It is too complicated and messy. I want to do my job. I want to help save the realm, fulfill the prophecy. It's why my mother had me. She knew I had more of a chance than anyone else. She said my mortal side would prevent me from becoming too powerful. It's the only thing holding me together when I use the sun."

"You're saying the power would corrupt you?"

Absolute power corrupts absolutely. That's what the mortals always say.

"Corrupt is too human of a word. I don't think I would be overtaken by evil, for evil is just a concept to me. Rather, this world and other worlds and the people in them wouldn't matter to me at all. I could destroy the universe if it pleased me."

I don't like the sound of that. I clear my throat. "Well, then you can clearly see why your humanity is important, Hanna."

"But so is winning," she says. "I am uncertain if we can have both."

"Then I hope you don't mind, but I'm going to try and see if we can have both. You, in love with me. I never realized how much I needed your heart until it was gone…" I trail off, shifting uncomfortably. One would think it would be easier to admit such things to someone who doesn't feel or judge, but it isn't. I just want my little bird to hear it, to take it in, to have it mean something to her.

I want to affect her.

"Can I ask you a question, Tuoni?"

"Anything."

"Were we happy together? In our union? In our marriage?"

The question catches me off guard. I wasn't expecting that.

"Happy? Yes, I think we were quite happy…"

Funny; it's something I never really thought about. I guess I was always just taking it one day at a time. I guess there was always something getting in our way.

"Good," she says. "You seem like someone I want to make happy."

At that, my heart lurches against my ribs. "You did make me happy. You do."

"Was it always that way?"

"Well, no," I say with a huff, scratching at my beard. "Not at first. I'd say our coupling wasn't under the best circumstances. For you, anyway. But you got under my skin, Hanna. You got in and you stayed there, through everything thrown our way. Even at the end there, when we were trapped in the Upper World with all the silly mortals, I felt closer to you than ever before. All I needed was to step out of my realm and feel what it was like to be human, and it made me admire and respect you even more. You showed me who you really were, and I…I…"

I loved you.

No, I love you.

Present tense. Here and now.

Words I'd never said to Hanna, words I'd never even said to myself.

I was never supposed to fall in love.

But I know I love her, even with my heart that seems too hardened at times. I can't pretend anymore, can't pretend it's something else when I know the truth. It took feeling completely lost without her by my side to know she captured my heart long ago. It just took time for the rest of me to realize it was missing.

And now, more than ever, I wish I had said those words to her. She had told me she loved me, and I felt it, deep and raw and real, and now, I want her to hear those words from me.

But the woman across from me wouldn't care for those words. They wouldn't mean anything.

I swallow the thickness in my throat. "If there is a way for me to bring the Hanna I desire to the surface, would you let me do it?"

She ponders that for a moment. "Only if you recognize the risks. That, in exchange, I might not be able to use my full powers, perhaps no powers at all. Then how would you battle Louhi and win? How will you get your son back?"

"We will figure something out. You saved us once, and that might be enough for us to save ourselves next time. Besides, maybe your father can grant you some of his magic, enough to keep some of your powers accessible. It might not be such a black-and-white situation."

"I see," she says. "What do you propose, then? How could you bring me back?"

I give her a sly grin. "In the most debased, primal way humans do to connect. One of the most human acts we have."

She gives me a blank look. "You are talking about sexual coupling."

"However you want to say it," I tell her. I raise an expectant brow, having no idea if this course of action appeals to her. "Does that…entice you?"

Shit, I sound like a fucking imbecile.

She smiles faintly, and I swear I see something glittering in her eyes, though that's probably just her powers. "Perhaps. I might need some time to consider."

"Take all the time you need," I tell her, getting to my feet.

"Something tells me you're not a very patient God either," she says, staring up at me.

"I'm not," I say gruffly. "But I've learned to be one for you."

CHAPTER TWENTY-THREE

LOVIA

THE AFTERMATH OF BATTLE IS ALWAYS QUIETER THAN YOU expect. The sounds don't vanish; they just change. Instead of clashing steel and roaring commands, we have the moans of pain, soft weeping, hushed prayers, and the shuffle of boots on blood-stained stone floors. Instead of bellowing horns, we have the wheezing breaths of wounded soldiers and the distant crackle of fires still burning in the wreckage—fires sparked by Hanna's radiant blasts. Yes, we've won, here within the broken walls of Castle Syntri, but it doesn't feel like victory. It feels like survival.

And it's a fragile fucking thing.

I pass through the ruined courtyard where the fighting was fiercest, stepping over fallen beams and twisted scraps of armor. Parts of the castle halls are now open to the sky, smashed by Old Gods, letting in a greenish haze of filtered daylight from the swamp beyond. We made our stand here when Hanna returned—changed, distant, haloed by strange light—and with her help, along with the rest of us, we pushed back Louhi's invading forces. The cost was steep. The bodies of our allies lie in hastily cleared alcoves while the wounded occupy what remains of the castle's interior chambers.

My sword hangs at my side, scabbard rattling slightly as I navigate collapsed corridors and toppled stone arches. What was once a hidden stronghold is now a half-ruined sanctuary. I should be grateful Hanna is back; her solar magic helped turn the tide, shattering enemy lines and scorching their ranks, but I haven't really spoken to her since she returned and I helped her get changed. She has become a distant figure, a sunlit presence hovering in the old gallery windows, her emotions unreadable. I'm glad she's alive, but I wonder what she's feeling, if anything. She's more Goddess than mortal now, and while I know my father has been spending most of his time with her, I don't know if he has been able to reach her. I sure wasn't able to.

I head toward the first aid area—one of the old banquet halls near the eastern wall. The roof there collapsed when one of the Old Gods was shot down, and we've strung tarps and canvas between cracked columns. Vines from the swamp have already begun creeping inside, called forth by Tellervo's green magic to aid her. Lanterns hang from broken rafters, and fresh moss and ferns have been laid as bedding. Not only is there not enough bedding to go around in the castle, but Tellervo says the organic matter will be better for healing.

As I approach, I hear muffled sobs and Tellervo's hushed, soothing voice echoing off the stone. The daughter of Tapio is kneeling among the wounded, her antler-like horns now entwined with withered blossoms instead of fresh ones—she has been working tirelessly for hours, exhaustion circling her eyes.

I duck under a sagging tarp and step inside. The smell hits me first: sweat, dirt, blood, and the sharp tang of poultices. Rows of makeshift cots line the edges of the chamber, where soldiers lie moaning or unconscious.

Tellervo hovers her hands over a soldier's abdomen. Vines of chartreuse light spiral from her fingertips, coaxing torn flesh to knit and blood to flow evenly again. The soldier's grimace softens, and soon after, his breathing steadies. The lanternlight flickers over helmets piled in a corner, shields propped against fractured walls, uniforms stained with mud and crimson.

I linger near the entrance, not wanting to disturb her work. All around me are men, though I spy a couple of wounded women. Some bear Louhi's crest, breastplates taken from the armory below. Ironic, considering she's the one who gave the blows.

I have to admit, it pains me to see them like this—so many wounded, so many who won't ever return home whole. Even though we won this battle, it looks more like a disaster narrowly survived.

A young soldier whimpers to my left. She looks only a few years younger than me, her arm twisted at a hideous angle. I kneel beside her, voice low. "Can I help?" She tries to speak, but only tears fall. I take her good hand, holding it firmly. "Hold on," I say. "Tellervo will see you when she can."

The Goddess hears me and nods from across the room. She finishes closing one wound then moves on to the next patient. But Tellervo can't be everywhere at once. There are medics from the Finnish army, but they can only do so much as well. I watch Tellervo's shoulders droop under the weight of impossibility. She uses her forest magic—faint sparks drifting around her knuckles—but some wounds are too massive, too grotesquely complex. Simple lacerations or shallow burns yield to her healing touch, but shattered bones, ruptured organs, or infected injuries demand more time than we can spare. She cannot exhaust herself entirely; she might pass out if she tries to save everyone. She told me that bodies might become immune to her skills.

A strangled cry from the far side of the hall makes everyone tense. Several soldiers huddle around a cot near a collapsed archway. Tellervo stiffens and moves quickly, and I follow, heart pounding. The soldier on that cot gasps for air, blood bubbling at his lips. A deep chest wound, poorly bandaged, has reopened, a medic trying in vain to help as crimson soaks his tunic and drips onto chipped floor tiles.

The medic moves aside as Tellervo kneels, pressing glowing hands to the wound. "Stay still," she whispers. He tries, but his eyes roll wildly. He coughs, and blood spatters Tellervo's forearms. I can see she's fighting a losing battle. His injuries run deep, and time is measured in heartbeats.

She calls on her magic again, chanting softly in an ancient tongue that echoes off the cracked walls. For a heartbeat, I think I see hope flicker in the soldier's eyes. Then, his body convulses, blood pooling in his mouth. Tellervo tries once more, pushing energy through her trembling fingers, but it's like pouring water into a sieve. The lanternlight seems to dim as we all realize it's too late.

His breathing rattles then stops. The silence that follows is crushing. Tellervo bows her head, withdrawing her light. "I'm sorry," she murmurs, her voice bouncing softly off the cold stone walls.

A soldier at my side breaks into sobs. Another curses and stomps away. My eyes burn; I've seen the dead all of my life, but I've always handled them from the other side. I don't see their deaths; I merely deposit them into their afterlife. This last while, though, it's everywhere I turn.

Tellervo closes the dead man's eyes, her hand shaking. She has saved countless lives today, but I can tell this one weighs on her. I rest a hand on her arm. "You did all you could," I say, my voice hushed.

She nods, knuckles white, sorrow shining in her eyes. "Others need help," she whispers, rising and turning back toward the rows of wounded. She can't afford the luxury of mourning now; none of us can.

I step back, struggling to breathe normally. The damp smell of mildew and old stone presses in. Despite winning, despite Hanna's return, despite forcing Louhi's troops to retreat from Castle Syntri, we're still mired in suffering. The war is far from over.

I move toward the exit, where a doorway with a missing doorframe leads outside. I see my father standing beneath a broken arch, his cloak smeared with ash and dried blood he hasn't bothered to wash off. He beckons silently. I cast one last glance at Tellervo and the wounded and then follow him out into the fractured courtyard.

Outside, the late afternoon sun slants through cracks in the castle's defenses, finding passage between the dark clouds. Parts of Syntri's towers now lie in heaps of ice and stone. My father leans against a toppled column. He looks exhausted, silver eyes shadowed, but there's a firmness in his posture that wasn't there before.

"I have news," he says, voice low and measured.

I swallow, heart still heavy from the scene inside. "Good news, I hope."

His lips twist into a small, tight smile. "Yes, surprisingly. One of our troops got through to the Keskelli. They've answered our call for aid and are on their way. They should arrive within a few days."

Relief washes over me. The trolls could tip the balance of this war, or at least give us equal footing. "That's...a mercy," I say, my shoulders relaxing slightly. "We're stretched thin now."

He nods. "I don't know how many there are, but in the old days, there were hundreds of them. We could use every last one to take back Shadow's End."

At that name, my chest tightens. Shadow's End, my

former home, now Louhi's lair. It stands waiting, a dark beacon of her power. "We're still going there, aren't we?" I ask softly. "To get Tuonen?"

He meets my eyes, expression grim. "We must. As long as Louhi holds Shadow's End, she has the upper hand. We cannot let her rebuild and strike again. Time isn't on our side."

I think of the wounded inside, their moans drifting through the broken corridors, and my mouth twists bitterly. "We have so many injured," I say. "If we move too soon, we leave them behind, vulnerable. But if we wait, Louhi might be at us faster than we can blink with even more reinforcements than before. She might come herself."

I shudder at the thought of what she can do now with all that power.

My father sets a hand on my shoulder. "The Keskelli's arrival changes things. With their reinforcements, we can leave a small garrison here to protect the wounded, maybe even send the most critical cases away from the front. Perhaps Torben could open the portal and they can go through to the Upper World to be treated. It's not perfect, but it's safer than dragging them into another battle."

"Is anywhere safe now?"

He sighs, gaze drifting over the broken battlements. "No," he says bluntly. "But we've made progress. Hanna's return, even if she keeps her distance, unsettled Louhi's plans. We caught them off guard here."

"How is she doing?" I ask gently.

My father sighs, his gaze sliding to mine, looking weary. "She's too much like her mother now, too much of a Goddess, but I feel I'm getting through to her. She's still half-mortal, half-human, and that's the side I need to appeal to." His voice lowers. "In every way possible."

I decide I don't want him to elaborate on that. At all.

He clears his throat and goes on, "If the Keskelli are indeed coming, we won't have to hold this position for long, but we must stay vigilant. Louhi might try to strike before our allies arrive."

I nod, stomach knotting. "I'll convene with the others, see what we can come up with. We need to see the enemy coming if they try a surprise attack."

He nods, satisfied. "You're a general now, Lovia. I trust your judgment."

The weight of that trust settles on me like an anvil. "I'll do my best," I say softly.

He offers a faint smile and then moves off to speak with other officers. I stand there a moment, letting the breeze carry the scent of smoke and swamp over me. Reinforcements are on the way; that's one spark of hope, but we can't linger too long. Eventually, we must push onward to Shadow's End and confront Louhi face-to-face. The thought sends a shiver of anxiety through me. We're caught between caring for the wounded and the urgency of pressing our advantage.

I step back inside to find the young soldier I spoke to earlier. The hall is quieter now, save for low groans and Tellervo's murmured spells. The girl looks up as I approach. "Your name?" I ask again, kneeling beside her.

"Ismena," she says, voice still trembling.

I offer a reassuring smile. "Listen, the Keskelli are coming. Allies. Reinforcements. You're not alone."

Her eyes widen, relief flickering through the pain. "That's…good?" she whispers. Obviously, she has no idea who or what the Keskelli are.

I squeeze her hand gently, wishing I had my father's powers of coercion. "Tellervo will tend to your arm soon, and then maybe we can find a way to get you to safer ground, perhaps back to your world. Just hold on."

Tellervo, now examining another soldier's burns, glances my way and nods. She'll do what she can. I stand, turning my gaze to the wounded mortals who fought for Tuonela—for my father's cause, and now, as I hold command, for mine. I must justify their suffering by leading wisely. When the Keskelli arrive, maybe we can transport the worst cases out, secure a fallback position, and move forward without leaving them to Louhi's mercy.

I walk among the injured, offering quiet words of comfort or praise. I'm no healer, but I can at least show them we value their sacrifice. It's the absolute least I could do. They watch me, eyes filled with trust and doubt, hope and fear. I'm new to this role, but I can't afford to falter. I must find a path that balances mercy and strategy, compassion and steel.

Outside, the evening light slants over the broken stones. Soldiers clean weapons near a collapsed tower, some whispering prayers in Finnish to the fading sky. They sound lost and hopeless.

I run a hand over my hair, smoothing it back, forcing resolve into my spine. I know who I am and who I need to become. I've stepped into a role I never imagined for myself, but I'll meet this challenge head-on.

For my father, for my brother, for the realm.

CHAPTER TWENTY-FOUR

DEATH

"Tuoni," Torben says as he steps out of the hall, his staff in one hand, his spellbook in another. "Is this blizzard your doing?"

He nods at one of the few windows in this damned castle that wasn't broken during the battle. Snow slams against the thin panes, whirling like a hurricane outside.

I raise my chin. "Sometimes, the weather does what it wants." Then, I hurry off down the corridor before he has a chance to analyze me any closer.

Truth is, it is my doing. For the last two days, ever since Hanna in her Goddess form arrived, I've been doing my best to quell my nerves, but now, I feel it's a losing game.

I'm *anxious.*

About going upstairs to my wife and fucking her memory back into her.

Naturally, I can't tell the old man that, given Hanna is his daughter and all. I also wouldn't want him to think I'm not the confident, controlling God he thinks I am and knows me to be.

But this storm is a betrayal of my true feelings.

This morning, Hanna took her breakfast in my bedchamber—we have been sleeping in separate quarters. She noted the shattered skull mask in the corner, something I haven't bothered to clean up. What's the point in a ruined place like this? But she was curious about my anger. She suggested that perhaps I needed a better place for my emotions to go.

Of course, I only had one thing in mind, and I told her that. There is no use mincing words around Hanna, no matter what version of herself she is. I always got my emotions together, arranged in an order I understood them, through sex and sex alone.

"All right," she had said over the cup of coffee she had barely touched. "Tonight then, come to my bedchambers, and perhaps you can make me the wife you need again. If not that, at least it might spare you another broken mask."

And so, here I am, climbing the stairs to her room, sweat gathered at the back of my neck, feeling as if I'm about to face another battle, this one hewn by sweat and skin, lust and pleasure. One where I want us both to win.

I knock at her door, and she tells me to come in.

I open the door to see Hanna standing by that window again, the blizzard flowing in and covering the room in a thin layer of frost and snow, as well as coating her dress and hair.

"Aren't you cold?" I ask as I close the door behind me. "You know we can board up the window."

She shakes her head, her ethereal face lit by the flickering torchlight. "I am perpetually warm. The snow feels nice this evening. Is it too cold for you?"

"Nothing is too cold for me," I tell her. "I am Death."

She gives me a small smile and gestures to her dress, one of Louhi's I haven't seen her wear yet. It's dark green and adorned with tiny black skulls from some small rodent with horns. Goat rats, perhaps. It's a little too macabre for the Hanna I know, but right now, it suits her.

"You look lovely," I tell her. Especially when she still has a bit of her radiance to temper the darkness, though I must say, it seems to be dimmer than before. That gives me hope. Her humanity is thrumming just beneath her glowing skin.

She raises her brow as if to say, *shall we?*

I have to wonder what she knows of sex. Surely, she remembers us together if she remembers everything else. Will her body know before her heart does?

I approach her like a young colt, skittish and shy, two things I have never been in my life. I am nervous, actually fucking nervous, about coming on to my wife.

She stares at me from across the room expectantly, her eyes dancing between the molten copper of the new Hanna and the old Hanna, deep brown and warm.

She knows I'm her husband, her king, her lover. She knows our history.

And yet, she still looks at me like I'm a stranger.

I plan to fuck that right out of her.

"Come here," I command, unfastening the collar of my cloak and letting it fall to the floor. Time to take control.

She stiffens slightly, cold air rushing in through the broken window, but I don't think her posture changed because of that.

Could she be nervous too? Afraid? She said she doesn't have those feelings.

This is a good sign, is it not?

"Come here," I say again, this time with authority. "Kneel before your God."

She hesitates for a moment, uncertainty in her eyes. But then, she closes the distance between us, her steps measured and cautious, like a wild animal sizing up a predator.

She stops before me, and I stare at the graceful lines of

her swan-like neck and see her pulse pounding there, a sight that immediately makes me hard.

Then, she kneels before me, as I instructed, her dark dress spreading out against the scattered snow like a stain, her gaze never leaving my face, and I grow harder still, my cock straining against the flat of my pants. Her copper eyes seem to glow in the flickering torchlight that casts grotesque shadows on the stone walls around us.

I stand before her, feeling powerful and yet also exposed and vulnerable. My heart beats strong with resolution as I reach down and cup her chin, tilting her face upward to meet mine. Our eyes lock, the connection electric between us in a visceral way, as if faint beams of light are connecting her to me.

"You are not just any Goddess," I say softly, my voice a deep rumble that vibrates through my chest. "You are *my* Goddess. There is a difference."

She swallows visibly, a hint of a shiver running over her shoulders at the possessive tone in my voice. It's been so long since we were husband and wife—just Tuoni and Hanna—but I have to try to bring that back somehow, to remind her of who I am beneath the godly exterior she now sees me in, to remind her of who she is under her own divine façade.

Strangely enough, I can see longing in her eyes, a need for normalcy that might haunt her every thought. But there is also a fierce determination there, a spark of rebellion that makes me both proud and fearful of her. Sometimes, she's too rebellious for her own good.

"Hanna," I say softly, running my fingers gently down her cheek and feeling the warmth of her skin beneath my touch. "My little bird. It's all right. You don't have to be afraid of anything. I have you."

She looks down, unable to meet my gaze, but then she surprises me by leaning forward and reaching for the fly of my pants. I stiffen, watching with bated breath as she wraps her hand around my cock, pulling it out into the chilled air and taking me into her mouth.

Oh, *fuck.*

The sensation is overwhelming, like being hit by a tidal wave. Her lips are soft and warm, her tongue dancing around me in a way that sends shivers down my spine. I reach out and run my fingers through her hair, feeling the silken strands between my fingers as she works her magic on me, making me feel like I'm a God coming undone.

I didn't expect this. She must know how natural this feels, that she was made to worship me, just as I was made to worship her.

The world around us fades away as we lose ourselves in each other. She hums softly against me, her breath hot and wet as she focuses her attention on the task at hand, sucking me off in the expert way she used to do. I close my eyes and let go of all my worries, feeling only the raw desire coursing through my veins. This is what it means to be human—to feel something so intensely that it consumes everything else. Perhaps my humanity is what's coming to the surface here, more than hers.

And I will revel in it.

As I continue to lose myself in her, I can barely feel the snow that gathers on my shoulders, nor the cold coming in through the broken window, the blizzard dying down. All that matters is the heat of her mouth enveloping me, the way she sucks and strokes me until I feel like I'm about to burst.

I grip her hair tighter in my hands, making a fist as she moves faster and faster, her eyes wide and wild as she takes me deeper into her mouth, keeping her fiery gaze locked on mine. The sight of her like this—so desperate, so needy—only gives me hope and fuels my own desire.

"That's it," I groan, my hips bucking involuntarily as she hits just the right spot. "Oh Gods, Hanna..."

She moans, a low sound vibrating against my cock that sends shivers directly through my shaft and over the rest of my body. It's not long before I can feel it building up inside me, that rush of heat and energy that threatens to consume me whole. We may be surrounded by ice and snow, but together, we are an inferno.

"I'm going to... *Fuck...*" I gasp, clutching at her hair as wave after wave of pleasure crashes over me until the tension is razor thin.

And then, it happens. I let out a loud roar as I come, one that shakes the entire room, spilling myself into her waiting mouth. She gulps it all down eagerly, never missing a beat as she continues to suck and stroke me until the very last drop.

When I finally come down from my high, I nearly collapse, unsteady on my feet.

She stares up at me, pulling my spent cock from her mouth, smiling in such a coy way that, for a moment, I think she's back to being my very naughty wife.

But she still has that distant, alien gleam in her eyes.

And so I know I'm not done with her yet.

I'm going to fuck her back to who she was.

I pull myself together, reclaiming my kingly composure. I know she needs me, and I need her too. We both need to remember who we are to each other.

I walk over to the bed and sit, my half-hard cock visible as I pull down my pants, discarding the rest of my clothes. Her eyes widen at the sight. I must admit, admiration from a Goddess feels like nothing else.

"Take off that dress," I tell her, my voice strong and authoritative.

She stands before me, her eyes fastened to mine as she slowly undoes the clasp of her dress. The fabric falls away from her body, revealing a sight more beautiful than any painting I've ever seen. Her skin is flawless, like a golden statue smoothed by the eons, and she glitters under the snow that pours into the room.

I watch as she stands naked before me, her body a masterpiece of muscle and curves. She is so much more than just a woman—she is a Goddess, an otherworldly being who has somehow found her way into my life again, and I am determined to make sure she never leaves again. Not because she can't, but because she won't want to, because she'll realize how much she loves me.

Gods, please, let her remember she loves me.

I beckon her toward me and then lie back on the bed, cock jutting straight up at the ready, twitching with each breath. She hesitates then climbs onto the bed, straddling my thighs and positioning herself above me.

"Your gloves," she says. I barely hear her, instead concentrating on the sight of my cock jerking in front of her cunt. "Can you take them off?"

I swallow hard. Part of me is wary, fearful that with her in her Goddess state, I might not be allowed to touch her.

"I am the prophecy," she reminds me, reaching for my hands. Before I can protest, she's yanking off one glove, her fingers wrapped around my bare skin.

Nothing happens except that I melt at her touch.

She gives me a quick smile, relieved, maybe proud, and removes the other glove.

I reach out and caress her hips, feeling the warmth of her skin against my fingers. I've missed this so much. She shivers under my touch, but it's not from the cold; it's from desire—raw, unbridled desire.

I'm getting through to her, I know I am.

Her eyes lock with mine as she lifts her hips, firmly gripping the base of my cock before she lowers herself onto me.

The sensation is intense, almost overwhelming, as she takes me inch by inch. She leans forward, adjusting her position, and her breasts brush against my chest, nipples hard as ice, her hips moving in a slow, rhythmic dance that builds between us.

I can't help but moan, deep and long, unable to put what I'm feeling into words of any kind.

I reach up and wrap my arms around her, pulling her close. She is so fucking *warm*, inside and out. The feel of her body against mine is as if we are two halves of a whole, fused in the most potent of ways.

As we move together, my hips jerking up to meet hers, I can feel the raw heat building inside me once again, a fire that threatens to consume us both. Her eyes stay focused on mine, her expression one of utter concentration and lust. She's as determined as I am.

Her movements become more urgent now, her hips bucking against me, and I realize she's not just trying to make me come. She wants to come too. The bed rocks, and the room is filled with both the blizzard intensifying again, snow blowing over us, and the sounds of our passion, the soft moans of pleasure, the slapping sound of skin against skin, the ragged breath that signals how close I am to the edge.

"Oh fuck, Hanna," I murmur, my voice hoarse with desire. "You are…you are everything to me."

She gasps at my words, her eyes flashing with desire and something else—a spark of recognition, perhaps? A sign she remembers who I am to her?

Either way, it only fuels my passion further, driving me onwards as I thrust into her, feeling the heady heat of her body enveloping me.

"I need you," I whisper gruffly. "I need you like I need air to breathe."

She moans in response, arching her back and pressing herself against me. She leans down, her hands gripping my shoulders, her nails digging into my skin. The sensation is so intense, it's almost overwhelming—like a storm of unsaid words and pent-up lust battering both of us.

"Give it to me," she whispers, a fierce determination glinting in her eyes. "I want to feel it all."

"As you wish," I grunt.

And with that, I let go—I give myself to her completely, my hands a vice on her hips as I rock her back and forth on my cock, fingers digging deep, each movement more aggressive than the last as I seek to connect with her on a deeper level and pull her out of her divinity. The world around us fades, leaving only the two of us, lost in each other's embrace, wrought with determination.

Her cries fill the room, her body tensing and relaxing in rhythm with our movements. It's not long before I can feel the tension building inside her too—a rush of energy that threatens to consume us.

But before it can, the urge to be in control takes over.

Some things never change.

I grab her by the waist and pull her off me, dragging her down onto the bed, deftly flipping her over onto her stomach and straddling her from behind. I gather her wrists behind her back and push her head into the pillow, my aching cock pressed against her ass.

"Do you remember this?" I ask gruffly. "Do you remember, my little bird, when I would come into your room at night and fuck you? You were waiting for me, and I never even took off my mask. I had my way with you time and time again, and you would let me because you wanted it, you wanted me, even though you hated me at the same time. You wanted it because you knew I was your destiny. You knew I was your king." I tug at her hair and pull her up so my lips are at her ear. "Do you want to know what that felt like? Here and now?"

"Yes," she cries out softly, a whimper more than anything, and I grin at the sound, shoving her head back down as I push her thighs apart with my knee and ready my cock at her entrance.

"I didn't quite catch that," I tease.

"Yes," she moans, her voice muffled in the pillow. "I want to know. Show me. Make me remember."

I can feel the heat of her body against me, her wetness coating the tip of my cock as I position myself at her cunt. Her hips buck involuntarily, her body begging for me to take her, to fill her up in the way only I can.

"Then tell me to fuck you. *Mean it*," I growl.

"Fuck me like you did before," she moans, her voice a mix of longing and desperation, no longer sounding distant and cold, but like she's *here*. "Make me remember who I am."

I nod, my heart pounding in my chest. This was the Hanna I knew—bold, passionate, desperate for me. My cock throbs at the thought of claiming her this way, just like old times.

I squeeze the base of my shaft, feeling the slickness of her desire as I push forward. She gasps, her body arching beneath me as I slowly sink into her.

Fuck, she's tighter than ever.

"Yes," she moans, writhing beneath me. "That's it. Fuck me like you mean it."

I raise my brows at her language. She's so close now, I can smell it.

I begin to move within her, my thrusts slow and deliberate at first, her ass jiggling with each push, but building in intensity as we both grow more feverish with desire. Her moans fill the room, mingling with the sounds of our bodies slapping together.

"Tuoni," she cries out, gripping the sheets tightly as I thrust harder into her. "More, please."

Fuck.

She's a wicked little Goddess, isn't she?

And so, I give her more. My rhythm becomes more frantic, each thrust more powerful than the last as I drive myself into her with renewed fervor. Her cries grow louder, more urgent, and I know she's close to release, close to her old self.

I lean down, my lips brushing against her ear as I whisper gruffly, "You want it, you want me, and that's all that matters now. Let go of everything else and just feel this."

Her body responds to my words, her muscles tensing and relaxing in perfect sync with my movements. Her moans become more fervent, her knuckles white as she grips the sheets, and I think I might just fuck her straight through the bed.

"Oh, Gods," she cries out again into the pillow, her voice a mix of ecstasy and desperation. "Oh, yes, Tuoni. Please, don't stop."

But I have no intention of stopping. My thrusts become wilder, more feral as I drive myself deeper into her. Her body bucks beneath me, matching my rhythm perfectly as we begin to move as one. Sweat spills off my body, splashing onto her, melting the snowflakes that have gathered on her back.

"Ah!" she cries out again, her muscles tightening around me as she nears her release. "Please."

And that's all it takes—the utterly raw and deeply human sound of her voice, the feel of her body around me, all the passion and desire we had been denying ourselves for so long coming to a head in this one, fiery moment.

"Fuck!" I roar, my orgasm surging through me like a raging fire as I thrust into her deep and hard. My body trembles above hers, every muscle strained as I come, every fiber of my being focused on this one perfect moment between us.

She comes too, her cries piercing the air, her limbs convulsing and shuddering beneath me. Her walls squeeze my cock harder and harder, making me lose my breath, my *mind.*

And yet, through the spinning throes of my release, all I need to know is if I brought her back.

CHAPTER TWENTY-FIVE

HANNA

"Are you my Hanna yet?" Tuoni growls in my ear, his cock throbbing inside me as my body continues to pulse around him, my release creating a torrent of feelings inside me.

I don't know who I am.

I can barely breathe, barely think.

The memories sink into me like the falling snow blowing around us, covering the bed in a sheet of frost.

When I first met him long ago, I called him Death. He had said, "You can call me Death, and I will call you mine."

I am his now, I feel that. There's something sparking inside me, like two pieces of flint scraping against each other, just waiting for the fire to spring.

I'm so close to being Hanna again.

And fear is my first emotion.

Because it scares me to become a mortal, a human.

What if that means I give up my destiny?

What if this messes with the prophecy?

What if we lose because I chose to feel love?

Isn't it better to just enjoy that I feel desire and lust?

Isn't that enough?

It's not enough, a voice inside me says. Perhaps it's Hanna's voice. *You need more. Your soul needs more.*

My soul. Is that what's missing?

"I'm not giving up on you," Tuoni says, voice rough as sandpaper. "I'm going to keep making you come until you don't have a choice."

His soft, strong hands grip my waist, making me feel dainty and petite, even though I know that, in my Godly form, I am more powerful than he is. He flips me over on my back.

He stares down at me for a beat, his dark, damp hair hanging off his face, his brow furrowed with determination and laced with sweat, the dark kohl liner around his eyes smudged with our frenzied coupling. His skin is brown with a beautiful bronze sheen, laced with silver lines I know represent the souls who pass into the land, his frame huge and muscular beyond reproach. The body of a true God.

His gaze burns so intensely, I nearly look away, but I force myself to stay connected to him, because this is the only way forward.

He stares at me like he might die without me, and I'm starting to believe it.

But is it because I am meant to save him and his realm?

Or because it's my love, my heart and soul, that he needs to truly rule?

He places his lips on mine, and I gasp against them. Gentle and tender at first, they meld into wild fury, my heart racing as our bodies entwine. The taste of him is intoxicating, reaching something deep within me, the smell of his skin, of something rich and warm, overwhelming me with desire. I can feel my walls still contracting from my orgasm, and yet I'm yearning for more, craving him.

My husband's hands caress my body, slowly and deliberately, sending shivers down my spine. His touch is electric, his fingers tracing patterns that send my mind reeling with lust and longing. He knows what he's doing, and I can't help but submit to his control, wanting to revel in every inch he explores.

As we continue to kiss, he slowly pulls back, his eyes gazing into mine, a storm brewing within them. The more I stare into the tarnished silver of his irises, the more it seems like there's a blizzard inside them too. "Do you remember yet?" he whispers hoarsely. "Do you feel what you once did?"

I shake my head slightly, unable to form words, but I do feel. My mind is a whirlwind of mortal emotions: fear, lust, desire, swirling together all at once. I don't know if I'm ready to embrace my humanity fully, but the way Tuoni looks at me, the way he touches me...I want to give into it. It already fulfills me in ways I couldn't have imagined.

I want to be here with him forever.

He leans in again, his lips brushing against mine gently. His full, soft mouth travels down my neck, leaving a trail of kisses and nibbles in its wake. "I won't let you go," he promises as he returns to my lips once more. "Not without a fight."

As his lips meet mine again, I feel a surge of warmth spread through my body. His dark promise fills me with a sense of security and belonging that puzzles me. On the sun, with Mother, I finally felt like I belonged somewhere. But here, with my husband, my king, I wonder if it's he I truly belonged to all this time.

He lowers his head to lick at my breasts, sucking my nipples into his mouth, giving them little pinches of beautiful pain. His hands trace the curves of my stomach, my waist, down the slope of my hips. Every touch is a reminder of what we once shared—a bond that transcends time and space.

"I'm not giving up on you, fairy girl," he repeats, his breath warm on my skin as he laps at my breasts with long, teasing strokes of his flat tongue. "I'm going to keep bringing you back to this place until you're my true wife again. My queen."

His words send a shiver down my spine, and I can feel the first tendrils of my old self beginning to form. Our past, our love, everything we've experienced together—it's all coming back to me now. The more we explore each other's bodies, the more memories resurface.

And it's more than just the memories.

It's the feelings in them.

Slowly, so slowly, I'm becoming less of a bystander to my past and more of the main character.

"Keep going," I whisper to him. "I'm close to something..."

Tuoni's fingers continue to trace patterns on my skin, his touch sending waves of pleasure coursing through me, brow furrowed in concentration. He knows exactly what he's doing. He knows how to ignite this fire within me; he has done it so many times before.

He keeps his silver eyes on me, eager to witness my transformation as he moves down my body, my thighs parting for him. He licks his lips, and I shiver, knowing and needing and wanting what comes next.

His lips slowly descend towards my most intimate part, and I can't help but hold my breath. The anticipation is almost too much to bear, his eyes never leaving mine.

As he takes his first, tender lick along the length of me, I'm slammed with the sensation, my body shivering as I let out a soft moan that resonates through the room. His touch is so gentle, yet it sets off a firestorm of need within me. He repeats the motion multiple times, each pass of his tongue causing another small gasp to escape my lips.

With each controlled movement, I feel myself becoming

more and more aroused, my legs widening for him, my desire dripping out of me. Tuoni seems to sense this, for he starts to explore further, gently teasing the entrance to my core with his tongue before delving deeper. His hands hold my legs apart, his grip bruising as his tongue thrusts inside me, thick and hard, claiming every inch with precision and care. This is not just an act of physical pleasure for him but an exploration of our connection—a deepening of our bond through this intimate exchange.

The sensations are overwhelming as he continues his worship of my body. Wave after wave of pleasure crashes over me like the tide against the shore, each one building on the last until I feel like I might explode from sheer ecstasy. My fingers dig into his thick hair, pulling him closer, as if attempting to draw him even deeper within me.

Gods, I want, I want...

Then, he brings his fingers to my entrance, inserting one inside, two, three, until I'm gasping, making fists in his hair, bucking up my hips for more.

I'm...greedy.

Is this what being Hanna is like? Forever wanting more of this?

His fingers move in and out of me in a rhythm that matches the pulsing of my heart. His tongue continues its dance, lapping at my clit with an intensity that leaves me breathless. Each touch, each lick, is like an electric shock coursing through my veins.

His fingers curl slightly, brushing against the most sensitive part of me, causing me to arch my back and let out a soft cry. My husband responds by increasing his pace, his fingers digging deeper into me with each thrust. I can feel myself getting closer and closer to the edge, the need building to a point where it feels almost unbearable.

Then, he suckles my swollen clit into his mouth, and I

can't take it anymore, my body tensing, preparing for what's to come.

Without warning, Tuoni starts humming softly, a low and resonant sound that seems to vibrate right through me. It's as if he's using his entire body to please me—not just his hands and mouth, but his very soul too. My body starts to tremble, my breath hitching as I feel the orgasm building within me. He senses this and adjusts his movements accordingly, increasing the intensity of his touch and lick until I can no longer hold back.

I am coming.

I am *becoming*.

The orgasm hits me like a freight train, overwhelming me with pleasure so intense, it feels as though I'm going to burst. My entire body shudders, my muscles tensing and relaxing in waves of ecstasy. I cry out Tuoni's name, lost in the intensity of the sensation, feeling like I'm soaring through the dimensions beyond on a wave of pure bliss.

It keeps coming and coming and coming.

Gods.

Where am I?

As I come down from my high, Tuoni's hands never falter. He continues to touch me gently, even as my body quivers and shakes in the aftermath of my orgasm. His touch is tender and caring, a reminder he is here for me in every sense of the word.

Finally, as my breath begins to steady and my heart rate returns to normal, Tuoni raises his head to look into my eyes once more. The fire that burns within him seems even more intense now, searing and searching.

So much hope.

"Little bird?" he says softly, my desire shining on his lips. "Have you flown back to me?"

I close my eyes and breathe in deeply, feeling the heat of

my divinity start to fade away into the darkness until it's just a kindling, a single flame. It promises to burn there forever, but for now, it's no longer wanted.

I want to be Hanna Heikkinen.

I want to be the Goddess of Death.

I want to be the wife of this God between my legs.

I want to be human and all that entails.

I want to love and *be* loved.

Tears suddenly flood my eyes, spilling over and down my cheeks as a sob of joy rattles through me.

"Yes," I cry out, feeling it, everything, all at once. "Yes."

I am home.

CHAPTER TWENTY-SIX

DEATH

A HUSH DRAPES OVER CASTLE SYNTRI'S CORRIDORS, A QUIET unlike the tense silence that ruled before the battle. This hush is heavy with exhaustion and grief, but also with a fragile sense of relief. It has been three days since we drove the Old Gods and Louhi's undead legion back, long enough for the numbness of shock to wear off. Now, the pain settles in: the loss of General Pekka and so many troops who trusted me, the wounds that may never fully heal, the knowledge that victory was only a reprieve, not the end of our struggle.

I stand at a narrow window in one of the castle's smaller towers, looking out over the courtyard. Snow still clings to the ramparts, though the storms have calmed ever since Hanna reclaimed her mortality, and in turn, her personality. I have a fucking wife again, which is the only thing that soothes me in this uneasy aftermath.

The Star Swamp beyond lies quiet, its surface crusted with new ice. We fractured the enemy's forces here, but they will return, stronger, and if I know Louhi, with newfound vengeance and brutality. I can feel it. It will not be long before she unleashes another horror upon us, making sure to really make it hurt this time. There's nothing worse than a demon woman scorned—I should know.

The morning light filters through thin clouds, casting a cool glow over my gloved hands. Three days past, those same hands gripped a blade that sliced through Old Gods' flesh, directed gunmen, tried to hold our fragile alliance together. Today, they tremble slightly; not from fear, but from the weight of what lies ahead. Even though my role as God has been to welcome and steer the souls of the dead, I find myself burdened with their fragile hopes. It's not just the dead of the whole world, this one and the one above, but these troops I have manipulated into being here. I wonder if that makes me no better than Louhi.

But desperate times…

I glance up at the sky and wonder if the snowbird will ever return. So far, I haven't seen any sign of my sister Ilmatar. I wonder if the bird got as far as Shadow's End or if it met its demise along the way. Another soldier lost.

Footsteps sound out from behind me, and I turn to see Hanna entering the room. She halts in the doorway, her eyes scanning my face. For a moment, I see the fear in them, and it cuts me to the core. She might be her old self, but the cost of invoking her sun-gifted powers still haunts her. She has told me how, in that blazing moment of unleashing solar wrath, she nearly lost herself for good. How she'd looked at us with no recognition, how the world had become alien. Now, restored to herself, she's terrified that using her powers again might erase her memories once more. She says the powers are still there, burning inside her like coals, ready to flare.

I beckon her closer. "Hanna," I say softly. Her name

carries a thousand emotions. Just a few days ago, I feared I'd lost her forever. Now, she's here, her expression anxious but determined. So damned beautiful.

"My queen. My little bird," I add. "Be with me."

She steps forward, her hand tightening around the doorframe before letting go. She has regained her dark hair, her eyes their familiar chocolate brown.

"Where have you been?" I ask.

"I've been trying to think," she whispers, voice low. "I know what we have to do next, but I'm…" She hesitates, words catching in her throat. "Well, I'm fucking scared, Tuoni."

I reach for her hand, and she lets me hold it. I feel the tension thrumming in her fingertips. "I know," I answer gently, curling her fingers between mine. "Your powers saved us, but they took something from you as well. No one expects you to wield them lightly again."

Or at all.

She swallows, nodding, her eyes glistening like dark pools. "It's like a living nightmare. I can't stop seeing it play out like some bad movie. I remember looking down at you all and feeling nothing. It was as though the sun's power scorched away my ties to this place, to you, to even my own father. That can't happen again. If I forget myself, if I forget you…" Her voice trembles. "Well, I think I'd rather die than face that emptiness."

My little bird has always had a flair for the dramatic, but I don't like how grave she sounds.

"You won't lose us again," I promise, though I feel it's a promise that might not be kept. "We will find another way. We have new allies to consider, remember?"

I gesture down to the courtyard, where soldiers re-pack supplies. Further down in the armory, Torben and Ilmarinen refine the sampo—their device to purify the ley lines and take down the rest of the Old Gods. If that works, maybe we can fight without relying so heavily on Hanna's solar wrath.

She nods, biting her lip. "Yes, the sampo thingy. Whatever the hell that is. And the trolls, right?"

"That's right."

Her eyes dance with disbelief. "Like, for real? Actual trolls? Like straight from the Hobbit, or...?" She pauses. "Wait, you've probably never seen that one."

"I have seen all three Hobbit movies, thank you very much," I tell her. "That was a whole day I'll never get back. And yes, like those ones. Maybe a little less ugly, and certainly not dumb. They'll be good to have on our side."

She laughs, a sound I've missed so terribly much. "Well, that does make me feel better about not being able to go full Goddess for you when you need it. So where are these not-ugly trolls?"

I smile wryly. "They arrived earlier. I have word they're in the war room currently. We'll go meet them together."

The Keskelli are twenty-foot-tall trolls who once roamed lands beyond the Star Swamp. They got our message late, or so they claim, having sheltered in ice caves within the Frozen Void. Now, they come to offer their help. I'm curious what shape that help will take.

Hanna and I leave the tower, walking side by side through the halls, torches sputtering in drafty corners. Soldiers salute quietly as we pass. Some smile at Hanna with relief and respect—she is the one who turned the tide of the battle, after all. Others still show fear in their eyes, awed by her brief transformation. She acknowledges them with a nod, face carefully composed.

Such a queen, especially with her wearing one of Louhi's leftover dresses, this one black with silver trim that matches my eyes. They look a million times better on Hanna. Everything does.

I sigh internally.

I'm certainly smitten, aren't I? Certainly doomed, at any rate.

We enter the war room where the others are waiting. Lovia leans against a pillar, arms folded, trying to look calm, but I sense her impatience. Tapio and Tellervo sit close together, the Forest God's beard threaded with leaves that have lost their color and grown brittle from stress. Tellervo's antlers are adorned with a few stubborn flowers, wilted but still clinging to life. Vellamo stands a bit apart, her gaze distant, as though listening to unseen ocean waves. Torben is at one corner, staff propped beside him. Ilmarinen sorts through a crate of small metal components—arrowheads, runes, possible artifacts for the sampo. Rasmus, that redheaded weasel, hovers near Ilmarinen, eager to help, trying to prove himself. The Magician drifts near the back wall, galaxies swirling in his hood, inscrutable as always.

And in the center of it all, standing because there are no chairs sturdy enough to seat them, are the Keskelli.

All five of them.

Only five of them.

They are broad-shouldered, with rough, bluish skin, tusked underbites, and thick fur-trimmed garments. Their eyes gleam with curiosity and a certain gentleness you wouldn't expect from twenty-foot-tall trolls. We exchange nods as we approach.

One Keskelli raises a hand in greeting, and his voice rumbles like distant thunder. "Greetings, Tuoni," he says, pronouncing my name with unexpected familiarity. "I am Kaleva, elder of our small clan." He taps his chest with a weathered hand. "These are my kin: Uljas, Mieli, Sihvo, and Tenko." He points to each in turn.

Uljas looks stern and silent. Mieli has softer features and kind eyes, Sihvo is scarred and wary, and Tenko sports a bone necklace that rattles softly. Each bows slightly, as space allows.

Hanna's eyes widen slightly, impressed by their presence.

"Kaleva," I say with a nod. "We're glad you've come. We feared our message hadn't reached you."

He rumbles a low laugh that shakes dust from the rafters. "We received your plea late. We were hidden deep in ice caves within the Frozen Void when the Old Gods rose. It took time to journey here, but we come as friends. Your fight is ours—this land's fate affects us all."

A murmur of approval passes through the room. We can use their strength. If these trolls can help us navigate the forests or hold against another assault, it might make the key difference. Still, there were hundreds of Keskelli at one point, and sheer numbers was what I needed.

"I don't mean any disrespect," I say carefully, "but I thought there were a lot more of you."

"That was true, many moons ago," Mieli says. "Back when we lived here, around the Star Swamp. Before Louhi slaughtered many of us. Those who remained took off to the frozen north to hide. But ever since the Old Gods rose, more of us have been lost still."

Silence fills the room. I had no idea Louhi was doing this, but it explains a lot. I have to wonder what other creatures she destroyed in her battle for dominance here. Some God I am; I should have been protecting them.

I clear my throat, stepping toward the table. "We've survived one assault," I begin, my voice echoing in the quiet hall, "but Castle Syntri can't withstand another. The walls are cracked, our supplies low. The enemy knows our position, and they will return. We must move, and soon."

"Where?" Kaleva asks.

"The Hiisi Forest awaits," Tapio speaks up, "though it has been corrupted. We know it once bettered our enemies, but now… We must tread carefully. If we move under cover of darkness, maybe we can avoid direct confrontation. The Old Gods might be regrouping."

Tellervo's voice is soft but resolute. "The forest could offer some advantage still. My father and I can coax some of the trees, roots, and vines to our cause. They can regenerate under the worst-case scenarios. They always come back."

Vellamo crosses her arms, shifting her weight. "Meanwhile, the river and the sea routes are waiting. With Ahto gone, my grip on the waters is diminished, but I can still guide small groups and my mermaids, maybe see if I can conjure the Devouress, Ved-Ava, and Näkki. If we split our forces—some through the forest, some by sea—we might surround any lurking threats or find safer passage."

Hanna stands quietly beside me, listening. I sense her tension. I know she wants to help, to use her power. I squeeze her hand gently—no one demands she burn her memory away again. We have other tools now.

Lovia pushes off the pillar and steps forward. "We have the sampo being refined by Ilmarinen and Rasmus. If it can uncorrupt the ley lines, we might weaken the Old Gods' hold. That was our original plan, wasn't it? To lure them toward the Hiisi Forest and then break their power at its source?"

Torben clears his throat. "The sampo is close to completion. If we deploy it properly, we can restore balance to at least some portion of the land. That might strip Louhi's minions of their unnatural strength. But to do that, we must be near the ley lines' convergence in the forest. We cannot do it from here."

"Then we must move tonight," I say decisively, letting my voice ring out. "We can't linger a moment longer. The castle's walls are too damaged, and we have too many wounded. We have already waited too long. Another assault, and we'll be trapped inside a ruin. We leave under cover of darkness, scattering our approach so we aren't a single target."

Hanna's hand tightens in mine. I sense her nerves—night travel is risky, but staying is worse. The others consider my words. Tapio nods slowly as Tellervo lets out a breath of relief. Vellamo narrows her eyes thoughtfully then gives a curt nod.

Kaleva of the Keskelli rumbles, "We will follow your lead. We know hidden ways near the forest's edge—paths less trodden. If some of us travel with Vellamo by sea, we can guard her flank. We Keskelli are strong swimmers, even in icy waters."

That's good news. I raise my eyebrows in surprise. "You would split your numbers?" I ask, concerned. "There are only five of you."

Kaleva and his kin share a look. Uljas grunts, "We are five, but each of us can stand against a hundred Bone Stragglers. Dividing our strength still leaves us formidable."

Mieli's voice is gentler. "We want to be of use. The Old Gods threaten all life. We cannot hide forever in ice caves if we wish to preserve the future."

I nod, touched by their resolve. "Very well. Two of you go with Vellamo by the sea route, three remain with us on land. I'll let you decide who."

Kaleva considers then points to Mieli and Tenko. "You both go with Vellamo." Mieli smiles softly, Tenko's bones rattling as he nods. "The rest of us will go through the forest."

Hanna exhales, easing her posture. She raises her chin and addresses the room. "Then it's settled," she says firmly, and everyone looks surprised to hear her speak. "My father, Ilmarinen, and Rasmus will carry the sampo with the main group. The Magician can help hide our movement with illusions. Tapio, Tellervo, Lovia, Tuoni, and I will move through the forest, guiding the main force. Vellamo and her flank of Keskelli travel by sea, meeting us later near the forest's far side before it reaches the Gorge of Despair."

My heart blooms at her determination, at her taking control, getting involved and giving orders, like the true Queen of Tuonela.

My cock grows hot, and I have to swallow down my lust for her. This isn't the time nor the place, but later, whenever we get another chance, I'll remind her again that she's my queen in every way.

The Magician inclines his hood. He says nothing, but I know he approves of this plan. He probably already saw it coming, that riddling bastard. Lovia stands straighter, ready for action. Torben and Ilmarinen exchange a look, determination etched on their faces. Rasmus swallows hard but nods —he has accepted his fate, cast his lot with us.

I consider the timing. Nightfall isn't far. "We have a few hours to pack and prepare," I say. "Gather only what you can carry. We travel light, swift, leaving nothing for the enemy to reclaim. The wounded who can fight, we take with us. The severely injured… We will find a way to keep them safe, even if it means reopening the portal."

A heavy silence follows. The reality is grim—some may not survive the journey. Still, no one challenges me. We know what mercy and loyalty mean in times like these.

Vellamo steps forward, voice soft. "I will select a small band of troops to accompany me and the two trolls by sea. We will find a boat that can navigate the coastline. The Old Gods lurk in the waters, but I've faced them before, and they aren't as numerous as the ones on land. If we're lucky, we'll slip past them."

Tapio and Tellervo exchange glances before Tellervo speaks, "We will do our best to coax safe passage through the forest. Even corrupted trees remember ancient pacts. They may not open paths easily, but we can at least avoid the worst snares."

Hanna looks down at her hands, flexing her fingers. I know what she's thinking—that a single flare of her solar power could carve a safe route, but the cost is too high. She meets my eyes, and I shake my head slightly. Not this time. She nods, looking relieved and guilty all at once.

Lovia breaks the silence. "I'll organize the archers and gunmen for the forest group. We'll need eyes that can see in the dark, or at least follow faint moonlight. The Magician can help with that?" She glances at the hooded figure.

The Magician's galaxies swirl. "I can weave gentle illusions to mask our scent and footsteps, perhaps sharpen eyes a fraction, but no grand spectacles—we must remain subtle, lest we attract unwanted attention. That goes for the shamans as well. Magic must be used with caution."

The meeting lulls as we each absorb our roles. Outside, a gust of wind rattles the shutters. The mood in the room is grim but purposeful. We have a direction now, a plan to follow. Remaining here would mean inevitable defeat. We must move, strike where we have an advantage, and pray the forest grants us mercy.

I gaze around at each ally. Until recently, many of these faces were strangers or distant acquaintances. Now, we're bound by blood, battle, and sorrow.

And the biggest factor of all: revenge.

"Go now," I say firmly, ending the silence. "Prepare as best you can. Eat, rest if you can, tend to the wounded. We have only this chance. Make no mistake: the enemy will come again, harder. We must not be here when they do."

As the gathering disperses, everyone filing out to begin preparations, Hanna lingers by my side. The Magician remains a moment, galaxies twinkling softly. I consider asking him again if he foresees success, but his silence is answer enough. He tips his hood and vanishes into the castle.

Now, it's just Hanna and me, and I close the door softly, letting the muffled sounds of activity fade. She steps closer, searching my face.

"Tuoni," she whispers. "I *want* to help, to burn the hell out of our enemies and ensure we never lose anyone else. But I can't risk forgetting you, or anyone else, ever again. I don't know if that makes me a fucking coward or what."

I pull her into a gentle embrace. She rests her head on my shoulder. "We don't need a blazing sun," I say softly. "Just your presence, your guidance, your heart. We will find another way. I want you beside me, alive, remembering who you are, rather than wielding power that costs us your soul. Besides, I've seen you fight. You're, as they say in your world, a badass."

She nods against my chest, relaxing into me. "I don't feel very badass anymore." She sighs. "All those MMA lessons I took made me feel powerful once upon a time, but now that I know what having true divine power is like? I've gone from Conner McGregor to, like, I don't know… Someone who weaseled their way in, like Logan Paul."

I don't bother telling her I don't know who those men are, but I hold her until her breathing steadies. Outside, the castle resonates with quiet urgency—footsteps rushing through halls, the clank of armor being readied, frantic whispers of what to do. The walls still bear scars from the battle, scorches where Old Gods screamed, fractures where horrors tried to climb. The memory of that violence weighs heavily, but we must move past it. The future lies beyond these wretched stones.

Eventually, we step apart and follow the others. We spend the afternoon in grim preparation—gathering what food remains, stocking weapons, organizing squads. I check on the wounded; some can walk with support while others must be carried on makeshift stretchers. The Keskelli offer to carry them, but the truth is, none of the wounded can go with us. They'll slow us down and probably die in the process.

"We need to leave them behind," I tell Lovia. Her face falls, but she nods, because she knows it must be done. "Go get Torben and have him open a portal to the other side. It's their best shot. If we leave them here, they will die without anyone to look after them. At least once they pass into the Upper World, they'll regain agency. I can't say what they'll remember, but they won't be able to return here. They'll be safe. They'll find the trucks they abandoned in the forest. They'll be able to get to the nearest hospital. We'll send a few of their medics along with them, just in case, and keep a few for ourselves."

At that, my daughter scurries off to find Torben. I feel bad about sending them back and having them fend for themselves in the middle of nowhere, but it's the best thing for them, the only chance they get. I make a silent vow to uphold my promise, to offer them seats at the table when they pass. If I can give them all the most peaceful deaths in their golden years, then that's even better. May they all die on the beach, old and grey, Mai Tais in their hands.

With Torben creating a portal, the troops guided by Lovia and some of the generals, Tapio and Tellervo confer with Rasmus about how best to coordinate signs—bird calls, flashes of foxfire—to guide us in the dark. Vellamo selects a handful of sailors from among our troops and plots a course to a dock in the Great Inland Sea that has a few boats we can push through the waterways.

I find Ilmarinen hunched over a small metal contraption in a side room. The sampo's main component—two intricately etched metal spheres that grind against each other—

sits in Ilmarinen's lap as he polishes runes on its surface. It looks strange and fragile for something so crucial. If it works, we can restore the land's balance along the ley lines. If it fails…well, we'll find another way.

Night approaches faster than I'd like, the sky dimming to a pale grey. The snow outside glows faintly in the twilight. Gunmen line the walls one last time, scanning the horizon, making sure the enemy hasn't returned prematurely. The wind howls softly, as if mourning our departure from these half-broken walls that sheltered us for a time.

In the great hall, I give quiet orders: torches doused, everyone ready to move at my signal. Soldiers stand in clusters, whispering farewells to the castle. They had gathered by the portal earlier, saying goodbye to their wounded brethren as they disappeared into the Upper World.

We take what we can: food, medicine, weapons. The Keskelli kneel, allowing supply packs to be strapped to their backs. Mieli and Tenko prepare to follow Vellamo across the Star Swamp to the west, Torben freezing the swamp over once more for good measure. I break my façade and pull Vellamo into an embrace, making her promise to meet us on the other side of the forest. My sister-in-law gives me a warm smile and says she will do her best.

Then, she and her chosen band slip away to the sea route, two giant trolls padding silently beside them, as if creatures of myth stepping into a forgotten saga. We watch them vanish into a drift of snow and night air. I already lost Ahto; I hope to the Creator I don't lose her too.

Hanna draws a deep breath, her hand in mine. "We can do this," she says, voice steadier now. "Right?"

I nod, pressing a kiss to her knuckles. Lovia stands to my other side, gaze sharp, determined.

At last, I give the nod. The last of the torches are extinguished, and we move out in a careful hush, heading across the frozen Star Swamp.

I glance back at the castle over my shoulder

Good riddance, I can't help but think.

It provided what it could, but I hope I never again return to this damned place.

CHAPTER TWENTY-SEVEN

HANNA

We travel by moonlight, Tuoni's moods stable enough for the clouds to part, the way lit by Kuutar, the Moon Goddess. I can feel the moon's rays burn on my skin as if the sun itself, briefly illuminating the heavenly runes and sigils my powers once embossed on me. They are dormant, but they're there, just under the skin, and I'll be damned if I haven't been wrestling with this dilemma every step of the way.

It has been hours since we left Castle Syntri, passing over the Star Swamp, past frozen plains where the wind bites, past sparse woods of aspen, where sleeping reindeer lay beneath the trees. We're now within sight of the Hiisi Forest, a dark shadow in the distance beyond these low shrubs laden with berries. I can see it all clearly—I guess being a Goddess also means having night vision, which is a pretty cool perk.

I glance over at Tuoni as we walk beside each other. His focus is straight ahead at the looming forest, brow furrowed in stark determination. The two of us walk at the front, a few generals, Tapio, and my father flanking our sides. To our left, a couple hundred yards away, is another set of troops, led by

General Suvari, Tellervo, and Ilmarinen, along with two trolls. To our right, across the same distance, is Lovia, leading Rasmus, the Magician, and the remaining troll with the rest of the troops. Somewhere far beyond them and unseen to us is Vellamo, two trolls, another garrison of soldiers, and hopefully a few sea creatures, all traveling on the waters. We don't actually know if Vellamo is there, but we have to believe she is, preparing to meet us on the other side of the forest where the river dips in.

I look over my shoulder at the troops as they march behind me, silent and stern, some with rifles at the ready, but more with bows and arrows, since bullets are in short supply. Many carry swords and shields, making it look like a couple of timelines in history have gotten mixed together.

It's unethical, what Tuoni is doing. I've told him that much. To manipulate the minds of innocent soldiers and force them into battle is a little, well...let's just say that has never panned out well in the annals of history.

But perhaps ethics don't count for much when it comes to saving the afterlife. This is one part where I think Tuoni wishes I'd squash my morals and think a bit more like the unfeeling Goddess I am. Perhaps he's right. When I was off doing my Doctor Manhattan thing and viewing the world and the humans in it as something trivial and insignificant, morals definitely didn't come into play.

I don't want to go back to that, though. I fear it. In that state of grace where I had no emotional ties to this land or these people, there was something profoundly empty inside, even if I didn't know it at the time. Yes, being with my real mother, getting to know her as well as I could and stepping into my true birthright gave me a true sense of belonging, one I felt I was missing my whole life, but the power overshadowed the truth: I already belonged. With my husband, with my father, as the queen of this land.

This Hanna, this me, who I really am right now? This is my destiny.

This is the prophecy.

I'm the one to touch Death and unite the land.

As if he can feel what I'm thinking, my husband glances over and gives me a quick, reassuring smile before it fades back into a firm line.

We keep marching forward through the darkness, the only sound the breathing of hundreds of troops and footsteps crunching over snow.

When the forest looms above us, dark and mysterious and deadly, we all come to a stop with a raise of Tuoni's hand.

He looks to my father. "Do you have wards at the ready?" he asks in a hush.

My father nods, gripping his black staff, magicked nails hammered in the sides.

Then, Death looks at Tapio. "Are you able to communicate with the forest yet?"

Tapio squints at the tree line. "I have. I don't sense any dangers. The trees tell me it is safe, and I am inclined to believe them."

"Good," he says. "Then we must press on. We'll travel a good ways in until you find us a good place to camp, perhaps one that already has your old wards in place, ones Torben can strengthen. If it can connect near a ley line, all the better. We won't be able to cross the entire forest in one go." He looks to everyone else. "We must be on high alert at all times. Watch for snaking vines and roots underfoot, for unnatural stillness, a sense of being watched by something malevolent. If something feels off, let us know."

"In other words," I say to the troops in my best airport PA voice, "if you see something, say something."

"Yes," Tuoni says, frowning. "That's literally what I just said."

I shake my head. Yet another thing he doesn't understand—though, frankly, I am impressed he made it through the *Hobbit* movies. Maybe one day, if we get out of this alive and save the realm, I'll make him sit down and watch all the *Lord of the Rings* movies back to back. I doubt he has seen the extended editions.

"Let's go," I command.

Signals are made to the garrisons to the left and right of us, and we start to enter the forest.

We slip into the Hiisi Forest, spaced out in several single-file lines, the towering silhouettes of ancient cedars and ironwood lit by moonlight. Snow crunches underfoot, the cold having seeped into the woods, and we move slowly, cautiously, as if expecting the trees themselves to lunge at us. No one speaks; our breaths are clouds in the chilled air. Even Tuoni, usually so confident, holds his silence, scanning the darkness with wary eyes.

I stay close to his side, aware of the soldiers branching out behind us, while Tapio leads the way at the front. He's quiet, his attention fixed on the subtle language of leaves and roots. Every so often, his head tilts, as if listening to a whisper we can't hear. Tuoni's tension eases minutely whenever Tapio gives the slightest nod. That means the forest approves of our passage, or at least tolerates it. We're guests here, not enemies. Not tonight.

After an hour of winding down narrow deer paths and ducking beneath low branches, I feel my pulse calm. No ambush springs from the gloom. No Old Gods surge from beneath the snow. There's only the murmuring hush of a winter forest. The tension thins, though no one relaxes completely. We all know danger can strike at any moment.

At one point, I lag behind Tuoni by a few steps, my boots treading carefully on a patch of ice. They're a couple of sizes too big, taken off the feet of a dead soldier, which I try not to dwell on. The moonlight slants between trunks, illuminating patches of moss and lichen. My fingers start to itch as I feel the power inside me, that dormant solar gift kindling deep down. Could I try it again? Just a little spark, a test? If I can control it here, in the quiet, maybe I'll trust myself more when the time comes to fight. Maybe I can be useful in the end.

I close my eyes briefly, imagining a delicate thread of light flowing from my core to my fingertips.

Just a spark, I tell myself, breathing slowly.

My hand warms, and I open my eyes. A faint glow hovers above my palm, no brighter than a candle's ember. It flickers nervously, like a timid animal ready to flee. Fear nips at my heart—what if it flares out of control? But it doesn't. It stays small, obedient. When a soldier glances my way, I quickly close my fist, smothering the glow. Good. I can manage something tiny without losing my head and turning into Doctor Manhattan again. It's a start.

We press deeper into the forest. The trees thicken, their tangled tops blocking out the moon. My father walks at the flank, his black staff tapping gently against roots, as if in conversation. He's placing wards, I realize, small, protective spells that settle around us like invisible blankets. I sense them more than see them—strands of energy that hum in harmony with the hush of the woods. I wish I could speak to him about it, compliment his craftsmanship, tell him how proud I am of him, but I feel the need to stay quiet. Still, he glances my way, and I give him a smile that hopefully says a lot.

At last, Tapio halts before a clearing lit by a strange moss that glows faintly green. Snow drapes over a cluster of old stones in a half-circle, like a forgotten altar. The Forest God touches a trunk, listens, and then turns to us. "This place was once a grove of power," he murmurs. "My wards from long ago linger. Torben can reinforce them. We'll be safe here."

Tuoni exhales and gives a curt nod. Immediately, the soldiers set to work, murmuring quietly as they clear a space for tents and bedrolls, extending beyond the clearing and into the rest of the forest, making room for everyone. I can feel the collective relief—no traps, no monsters, no sudden screams, just a night's rest in the heart of a forest. I never really did trust this place, considering what I've been through before (hello, giant spider that almost ate me) but tonight, I feel a sense of calm—though perhaps it's the calm before the storm.

As we settle, my father kneels to anchor the wards by sprinkling ash and salt on the ground around me and Tuoni while Tapio hums softly, coaxing the trees to watch over us. The other garrison has joined us now, and the Magician stands at the edge of the clearing, galaxies swirling beneath his hood, a silent sentinel. Lovia checks on the troops, shoulders squared against lingering doubt, while Rasmus offers to help gather firewood.

I can't help but watch Rasmus as he goes. He catches my eye for a moment, and in his gaze, I see both shame and fear. Good. Let that asshole fear me; it's the least I deserve. Seeing him alongside my father—*our* father—as well as Death and Lovia, was a hard thing to understand. Frankly, I still don't get it. He was a traitor in so many ways, and I don't care what they all say. He is *never* to be trusted.

Part of me wants to follow Rasmus into the woods to make sure he's not going to alert Louhi's gang or something, but then I see the Magician trailing behind him, and I know he's on the case. I suppose he's the only one who truly knows what Rasmus is going to do.

I take a seat on a fallen log beside Tuoni. He doesn't say

much, just reaches for my hand. I squeeze it back, and we watch the moss-glow shimmer in the darkness.

"This is the first time we've been camping," I whisper to him. "You don't strike me as someone who likes roughing it."

"I only like roughing it in bed," he says with a smirk before he kisses my cheek. Then, he takes a look around; satisfied no one is looking, he places my palm on his crotch, his cock hard against his fly.

I roll my eyes. I shouldn't be surprised.

"Care to take a walk with me?" he whispers.

I should say no. I'm tired, we're surrounded by soldiers, and our enemy could strike at any minute. But I also know this is one way to keep my humanity humming.

Besides, all the adrenaline is making me hard up for it.

I nod slyly and get to my feet. He pulls me into the forest, though we have to walk quite aways before we're away from prying eyes.

The trees swallow us in their embrace, the shadows thickening as we venture further from the camp. Tuoni's hand is warm in mine, his touch grounding me amidst the uncertainties lurking beyond the trees. A sense of freedom washes over me as we walk, a brief respite from the weight of our mission and the dilemma clawing at my insides.

We find a small clearing illuminated by a cluster of fireflies dancing in the night air. The ethereal glow flickers around us, casting a soft light on Tuoni's face, highlighting the lines of worry etched there. I reach up to trace his jawline, feeling the stubble beneath my fingertips.

"This is terribly romantic," I tell him. "Did you plan this?"

"Just divine luck," he says before he grabs my face and kisses me deeply.

I melt into his embrace, the tension of the war melting away as our lips move in synchronicity. Tuoni's touch ignites a fire within me, a primal need that eclipses any danger that might lurk just beyond the trees.

The urgency of our kiss propels us backward until my back meets the rough bark of a towering pine. His hands roam over my body, and even with his gloves on, his touch sets my skin ablaze with desire, the scent of pine and soil filling my senses.

With a swift movement, Tuoni lifts me effortlessly, my legs wrapping around his waist as he presses me against the sturdy trunk. The rough texture of the bark scratches against my skin, a delicious contrast to the silkiness of his touch.

Want and need course through me like wildfire, primal and insatiable. Our breath mingles in the cool night air, fogging between us as my husband explores every inch of my exposed skin, igniting trails of heat in his wake. His lips trail down my neck, leaving a searing path of kisses that send shivers down my spine.

Then, he pushes the layers of my dress out of the way, and the thick head of his cock teases me, rubbing against me in slow circles that send waves of raw lust coursing through my veins.

I reach up, running my fingers through his hair, feeling the silken strands against my skin. His breath quickens at my touch, and when our eyes lock, I can see the raw need in them, a need only I can sate.

With a low growl, he thrusts into me, filling me completely. I gasp at the stretch, so thick and deep and right that it takes my breath away. He pulls back slightly then thrusts again, each movement sending shockwaves of pleasure through me like an electric current.

I wrap my legs around him tighter, feeling his muscles ripple with exertion. His eyes latch onto mine once more, his gaze deep and intense, silver glowing in the moonlight. He thrusts harder now, desperate for release, desperate to take me with him.

My body responds to his urgency, matching his fervent desire with equal intensity. We move together as one, each movement perfectly synchronized. The sound of our ragged breaths mingle with the rustling of leaves and the gentle whine of wind passing through the forest.

The heat between us builds until it bursts like a supernova, washing over me in waves of pure, blinding pleasure, followed by a rush of emotion that swells, threatening to spill over. I can't find the words to express what I feel in this moment, so I press my lips to his, pouring all my love and longing into the kiss. The world falls away around us, leaving only the echo of our heartbeats and the whisper of the branches overhead.

As we break apart and he pulls out, lowering me back to the ground, a rustling in the underbrush startles us. Tuoni tenses, his hand instinctively reaching for his sword, but instead of an enemy lurking in the darkness, a small fox of fur and bone emerges, its golden eyes curious as it regards us.

I can't help but let out a soft laugh at the unexpected visitor. Tuoni relaxes beside me as it runs off into the night.

"We might have scarred that poor fox for life," I tell him. "Think of the things he'll tell Tapio."

"Animals understand it better than anyone," he says to me, doing up his pants and helping me smooth down my dress before he takes my hand and leads me back to camp.

CHAPTER TWENTY-EIGHT

DEATH

Morning in the Hiisi Forest comes quietly and bitterly cold. Our makeshift camp rests in a glen where the ancient trees, at Tapio's urging, have bowed their great limbs to shield us from the skies. I hunch over by a low-burning fire, the smoke locked in place by a ward Ilmarinen placed over the campfires, carefully nursing a tin cup of coffee between my gloves, a small luxury that makes camping in the wild worthwhile.

Hanna sits across from me, perched on the broad root of a gnarled tree. My wife. My queen. The Goddess of Death and the Sun, ruler of Tuonela at my side. It still jolts me to think of her fully like this, after everything we've been through.

But I see the hesitation on her face, the way her fingers hover over the cup I offered her. She put on a brave face, but now that the morning is here, she's afraid—afraid that if she calls too strongly on her powers of the sun, the gift that makes her so formidable, it might strip away her true self again. Her mind, her love, her identity—fragile things balanced on the edge of that divine fire.

She sips the coffee anyway, her dark lashes lowered, chestnut brown hair braided loosely over one shoulder, ends tied together with vines courtesy of Tellervo. The greenish light of the Hiisi Forest canopy makes her look pale, but I know how much strength she carries inside.

I wish I could take that fear from her. I'd carry it myself if I could, but even Gods have limits.

Lovia has gone for a walk with the Magician. I trust Lovia, and I trust the Magician, in his own cryptic way. Still, their relationship concerns me a little. I noticed it before, back at Castle Syntri, and thought nothing of it, but since we've come to the forest, they've been inseparable. Perhaps the two of them search for answers, for a path through the Kaaos threatening Tuonela. Or maybe it's something more than that. If that's the case, I should talk to her, because the last thing I need is for my daughter to lose her head over... well, I don't really know what the fuck the Magician is. It doesn't matter—she needs to keep her focus on what's at hand, like the general she is.

The rest of our small army stirs quietly in the dawn. Soldiers rake coals back to life, sharpen blades dulled by too many battles, check their guns, and whisper hopes of winning any next battles. Still, I think they're happier here than they were at Castle Syntri—if you can call their stern, glum faces happy. Then again, they are Finnish and hard to read.

Outside the forest's protective canopy, it's snowing lightly, and a few stray flakes drift down through the woven branches.

In the dim light, Ilmarinen crouches near a mossy rise, preparing to use the sampo. This morning, he found a ley line right there—one of the vital currents of power Louhi and the Old Gods have twisted out of shape. If the sampo works, the Old Gods will lose some of their strength, if not all of it. We desperately need that edge, especially with Hanna's power out of the picture.

Hanna shifts, and I catch her eye. I see the flicker of determination and fear in her gaze as she glances at Ilmarinen's preparations.

"Is that thing really going to make a difference?" she asks softly.

I shrug. "It better," I say as I rise, stretching sore muscles. The night's rest on the forest floor wasn't kind to my bones—I'm feeling less like a God by the day—but we survived another night. That alone is a blessing.

I walk over to Ilmarinen, damp moss squelching underfoot. he kneels with his ear to the ground, muttering to himself. Soldiers form a loose perimeter, watching silently, curiously. Torben appears, yawning deeply, Rasmus by his side, his hair a mess from sleeping, both ready to help if needed.

"So?" I ask Ilmarinen.

He looks up, thinning hair pulled back, cheeks smudged with dirt. "So," he echoes, "I can feel it pulsing beneath us. This spot is as good as any."

I glance back at Hanna. She stands behind me, silent, her presence an anchor. My hope rekindles, small but steady.

Ilmarinen positions the strange device with reverence. It gleams faintly, a complex work of metal and crystal and grinding parts etched with ancient runes. I feel its hum, as if hearing a distant choir singing beneath the soil.

He spins one of the spheres and begins a soft chant. Soldiers tense, hands on hilts. The forest hushes. For a moment, I imagine this working smoothly: ley lines stabilizing, the Old Gods losing their stranglehold. Then, we can push forward to Shadow's End and challenge Louhi on more even terms. Hanna's hand drifts near mine, as if seeking comfort. I brush my knuckles against hers.

A sudden creak of wood snaps me back to reality. The ground vibrates, and Ilmarinen jerks upright, hands stopping the sphere.

Suddenly, vines and roots at the edge of the clearing heave as if alive, dirt flying through the air. The ground near us splits, moss and ferns sucked under. Soldiers shout in alarm.

"Yggthra!" Rasmus yells as a blackened trunk rises from the ground, an Old God of twisted roots and tangled vines. It must sense us trying to mend the ley lines. Thick, wooden tentacles surge upward, lashing out. Ilmarinen leaps out of the way with his sampo as soldiers quickly spring into action, hacking at roots as thick as a man's arm. Hanna lifts her hand, golden sparks dancing at her fingertips, then hesitates. I see the conflict in her eyes. She could obliterate these roots with solar fire—but at what cost to her memory?

"Do what you must," I say, pressing my sword into my palm. I charge forward, slashing at a thrashing root. Sap and black ichor splatter the moss. Hanna draws a careful breath and then unleashes a narrower beam of radiance—less than what she's capable of, but enough to scorch a cluster of roots. She's holding back, rationing her power.

Yggthra's limbs keep coming, writhing in fury. Soldiers form a line, shields raised. The Magician and Lovia return from the forest depths, the Magician weaving mycelia up from the ground to slow the roots, Lovia's sword flashing in the dim light. From the way she charges at the creature, it's apparent she has fought the Old God before.

Tapio and Tellervo join in, summoning vines and other roots against the beast. I strike down two more twisted coils, my blade humming with each swing.

"Allow me!" Kaleva the troll says, running through the forest toward it, the ground shaking with his heavy footfalls. The soldiers jump out of the way just in time as Kaleva throws himself on the Old God, punching it hard enough to break wood, bark flying.

Well, well, well. Thank the Gods for the Keskelli.

However, it doesn't kill the Old God, only disables it enough for it to flop and writhe on the ground, its roots still reaching for people but slower now.

Then, I hear the dry rattle of bones. Skeleton soldiers appear from the shadows between trees, encircling us. We're flanked. The undead hordes press in, their hollow eyes glowing green, shields and swords raised. The timing is perfect—too perfect. We're caught between Yggthra's thrashing roots and the skeleton army.

Hanna stands at my side, jaw tight. She could incinerate them all if she let the sun loose inside her, but she doesn't. Instead, she summons controlled bursts of light, firing them at the undead, killing some of them.

Meanwhile, Kaleva continues to tear Yggthra apart with a roar as the soldiers hack off the roots, the mycelia dragging them into the ground. The skeletons keep coming, jabbing spears, swinging cleavers, their mouths clacking. Soldiers cry out, and I bark orders, trying to keep them organized. Lovia fights valiantly, cutting the undead into pieces while Torben and Rasmus try to protect pockets of soldiers with shimmering wards.

Suddenly, the sky darkens. Clouds race overhead, and within moments, we are plunged into blackness, like a candle being snuffed.

"What's happening?" Tellervo yells, green vines growing from her fingertips.

Someone else cries out, confused by the sudden night.

But I know this trickery can only belong to one Old God. Zelma, the Night-Binder, has arrived. Zelma thrives in darkness, weaving webs of shadow that drain life and hope. I feel a crushing lethargy settling on my limbs, soldiers nearby yawning and drooping, as if under a spell. A total eclipse swallows what little light filtered through the canopy, and Hanna's faint glow and the embers from the fires are all that remain.

Hanna's eyes meet mine, wide with fear. She knows this darkness will demand more light from her if we hope to survive. She clenches her fists, golden veins flickering under her skin. Another memory risk. Another test of her resolve.

Then, a horrible, otherworldly cry joins the fray—a swirling, spectral storm at the edge of our camp. I have heard of this one too, an Old God called Thaerix, the Screaming Vortex. It howls with the voices of lost souls, driving some soldiers to clutch their heads in agony. The wind tears at tents and flings debris. The darkness is absolute, the screams mind numbing. Skeletons advance, Zelma's shadows weigh us down, and the spectral winds of Thaerix scatter our formation. We are pinned beneath a perfect storm of horrors.

I slash blindly, feeling my sword bite into something solid —bone or bark, I can't be sure. Soldiers shout and fall silent. The Magician tries to form a barrier of starlight, but Zelma's darkness and Thaerix's shrieks shatter his concentration. Lovia curses, swinging her sword wildly. Tapio's and Tellervo's powers wane in the suffocating gloom.

Hanna stands near me, trembling with indecision.

"Hanna," I say, voice cracking. "If you can, we need more light."

She hesitates, tears in her eyes, torn between saving us and saving herself. I want to tell her we'll find another way, but I know time is slipping through our fingers. Skeleton blades clatter against shields, and I hear Ilmarinen shout from the darkness. I can't see him, only sense he's in trouble. The sampo must be protected. If we lose it, we lose our only chance to end all the Old Gods at once.

Zelma's laughter is a low hum, and I feel sleep tugging at my mind. The spectral storm's scream threatens my sanity. My sword arm grows heavy. Around us, soldiers slump, eyes rolling back into unconsciousness while Bone Stragglers finish them off with their spears and cleavers.

I glance back at Hanna and she gives me a stiff nod then closes her eyes, tears glittering on her lashes. Her aura brightens. At first, it's just a faint glow—enough to see her face. Then, it becomes brighter, brighter still, forcing back Zelma's darkness. Threads of shadow recoil, and skeletons stagger.

I hear Hanna gasp. Her face contorts with pain and fear. She's tapping into the sun now, summoning power that could unravel all she has worked for. I reach for her, grabbing her hand, and it's like grabbing a hot poker, searing through my skin.

"I'm here," I whisper. My voice is lost in the chaos, but maybe she hears it. Maybe this is enough for her to stay.

A flash of brilliance tears through the camp, revealing the grim tableau: soldiers wounded, some dead, skeletons cringing at the sudden glare, Zelma shielding itself with spidery arms of darkness, and Thaerix's funnel thinning, as if under a strong wind of its own. We have a chance. If Hanna can hold this for just a moment longer, Ilmarinen might plant the sampo. We might turn the tide.

I move toward Ilmarinen to clear a path for him. The Magician and Lovia fight at my flank, their swords and illusions carving through the confusion. Tapio and Torben rally a few soldiers, skeletons shattering under blades and guns and fists. Zelma hisses, trying to weave new shadows alongside the Screaming Vortex.

Hanna's radiance flares again, a heartbeat of pure, blinding light. In that moment, I catch a glimpse of her face —anguished, determined, and terrified. She's losing herself. I can feel it—memories slipping, tears falling, her sense of self fading away.

"Hanna," I tell her. "Stay with me little bird. You can do both."

Then, the light dims. Darkness encroaches again, not as absolute as before but still strong. The eclipse hasn't passed. Hanna's strength wavers. She stands rigid, and I can tell she's trying to keep her identity intact, to remember why she fights.

In the distance, I think I hear a horn, a faint echo. Could it be the Vellamo and the other Keskelli? Is Ilmatar finally making her appearance? Or a trick of Thaerix's screams? The sound repeats, clearer this time, cutting through the cacophony. The skeletons pause, heads tilted.

Hope flickers in my chest.

But we are still trapped. Hanna's light flickers uncertainly. She's fighting not only the enemy but her own mind. Soldiers around me breathe raggedly, struggling to hold positions. Ilmarinen clutches the sampo, trying to edge closer to the ley line's heart.

I slash at a skeleton, feeling my muscles burn. The horn sounds again, louder. Is help truly on the way? If so, can we hold out until they reach us? We balance on a knife's edge, caught between salvation and annihilation.

"Hanna," I whisper again, not sure if she can hear me. "Remember who you are." If she can remember me, if she can remember Tuonela and all we've built, maybe she can hold back the madness of forgetting. Maybe she can shine again without losing herself.

I steel myself. Whatever happens, I won't abandon her. Nor will I abandon these soldiers, this land, or the future we've all fought for. If this is the end, we'll face it together. Still, I hold out hope that the horn heralds allies rushing to our aid. That Ilmarinen will find a moment to plant the sampo. That Hanna can balance on this razor's edge a little longer.

We stand at the brink, shadows and screams pressing in. My sword feels heavy, my breath ragged, but still, I raise it, prepared to strike at whatever comes next. We will not surrender. We cannot. The underworld's fate depends on this.

I will not be defeated.

A skeleton lunges at me, and I swing. The world hangs, unfinished, uncertain, on the edge of a blade.

CHAPTER TWENTY-NINE

HANNA

When I was younger, I liked to think that if I was ever in any kind of emergency, I would turn into one of those people where others would say, "Wow, she was so calm and poised. She really kept her head." Of course, I didn't really have many emergencies back then, but it was tested when I thought I left my phone behind in an Uber. Turns out, I do not keep my cool when tested. I completely lose my shit.

Which was why, when I was able to harness the sun and swoop down onto the battlefield outside Castle Syntri and literally smite everyone like the fucking God I am, I actually felt like I was finally one of those people. I mean, I sent those bitches up in flames, and I did so without my pulse even quickening.

Cool as a cucumber.

Of course, that only happened because I didn't really know who these people were or understand what they meant to me. Being a Goddess of the Sun means you're a little *too* cool instead of hot. The irony.

Regardless, I wish I could have kept some of that fortitude, because even though I'm able to call upon my powers a tiny bit, like a glorified night light, I'm internally losing my shit.

The battlefield has become a place of darkness and howling winds, of screaming souls and clashing swords, and I am lost to the chaos, floating between fear and purpose. This eclipse brought on by an Old God presses at my senses, trying to smother the memory of sunlight. My father, Lovia, Tellervo—everyone is struggling blindly in the blackness. I feel my powers flicker inside me, waiting to be unleashed, yet doubt coils around it, yanking it back like a choke chain. I know what I should do, what I could do, but I would lose these people and who they are to me.

I watch as Tuoni drives his sword through a couple of skeletons and then slices at the darkness that is the moving eclipse. Fighting erupts from all around me, and I have no idea who is winning. I pick up a sword from the ground, wanting to rely more on it than my powers, and step back away from the front line, trying to figure out what to do next.

I stand shoulder to shoulder with Tapio, barely able to make him out in this suffocating darkness. I sense the Forest God more than see him—he smells of pine and damp leaves, a living fragment of these woods. He's trying desperately to rally his domain, forcing green sparks from his fingertips, coaxing half-dead branches and wounded trees to fight back. But the eclipse overhead mocks him, the Old God twisting night and shadow into something that smothers all growth.

A skeleton lunges at him. Tapio cries out and parries with his wooden staff, snapping one undead limb, then another. He's good, much better than I gave him credit for, but then a root lashes out from the darkness. Yggthra? It coils around his leg, biting into flesh. He gasps, horror coloring the sound, his eyes gleaming as he stares at me for help.

I feel the sun-gift flare inside me. If I unleash it, I might burn through this darkness—briefly. But what if I lose control and scorch my allies too? That would be even worse than losing any sense of my humanity.

The thought paralyzes me.

"Help!" Tapio's voice scrapes the air. Panicked, I step forward and raise a trembling hand. I could fire a clean beam of sunlight, cutting the snare off him.

Do something! Anything! I yell at myself.

I hesitate, heart pounding, before I raise my sword and run at him. I start hacking away at the root, trying to slice it in half. I call for help, for someone to pull Tapio away while I try to get the monster to let him go.

Tapio cries out again, weaker, being dragged downward. Zelma's eclipsing night thickens, shadowy shapes closing in. My muscles shake as I continue to hack away at the root, panicking, unsure of what else to do. A soldier runs over and grabs Tapio, holding on to him, but that soldier is dragged away too, heels carving ruts in the dirt.

"Father!" Tellervo yells, running toward him. Her palms are out, coaxing the forest to help, but only a few vines shoot up and wrap around his arms, not enough to make a difference. The rest of the forest is too weak and corrupted by the battle.

I force a spark of light onto my palm—I could free him.

The fear has me in a vice, but I know what I must do.

I raise my hand.

Too late.

In that instant, an Old God I've never seen before erupts from the dark—a looming silhouette of chitin and tendrils. It moves too fast. One dreadful slash, and Tapio's scream cuts through me. A wet crack, a splatter—then silence. The Old God vanishes as swiftly as it appeared, leaving nothing but dripping gore and empty space where Tapio once stood.

I surge forward, grasping at nothing. Tears sting my eyes;

I had the power to save him, but fear held me back. Now, he's gone. *He's gone,* torn apart in seconds.

"No," I whisper, hands shaking. "No!"

But my useless words are swallowed by Tellervo's awful scream as she collapses to her knees beside what remains of her father.

"Hold the line!" someone shouts nearby. Everything becomes a blur while my heart lurches in horror. My own father's voice rises in strange syllables, and I glimpse faint glowworm lines of ward magic taking shape. Rasmus joins him, their chants blending. Together, they push back Zelma's crushing shadows and Thaerix's shrieking winds—not banishing them entirely, but carving out a bubble of safety. Soldiers stumble into this pale sanctuary, gasping with relief.

But the relief doesn't reach me.

I stand at the edge, shaking, guilt clawing at my throat. Tapio is dead because I froze. The wards flicker around my father and Rasmus, my father barking orders, Lovia's blade flashing, the Magician twisting galaxies beneath his hood. They all rally as best they can.

Ilmarinen appears, bloody and breathless, clutching the sampo. "I must try now! The ley line's here!" he yells. My father, battered and grim, nods. Ilmarinen sets the sampo down, runes glinting, and I stand there, hollow, replaying Tapio's death again and again. I can't stop seeing it.

My father and Rasmus deepen their chant, straining to hold this fragile bubble of calm as the skeleton army hammers at the wards. Soldiers brace for another strike. The Magician mutters about fate. Lovia paces, staring down the enemy, blade at the ready.

A soft chime from the sampo cuts through the chaos. The ground trembles, energy racing up my legs as the sampo's crystal core swirls with color, tapping into the ley line. The Old Gods sense it—Zelma's shadows tremble, Thaerix's vortex howls in panic, skeletons rattle forward. The wards waver.

"Hanna!" a voice cries out. I can't tell who, but I know I'm needed. My fear still grips me, but I force out a faint glow of warmth, just a drop of sun. It fuses with the ward, holding back spears and clawing hands. It's not much, but it's better than nothing.

Ilmarinen works frantically. The ground cracks, ley energy sparking like fireflies. The Old Gods recoil; Zelma's eclipse loosens, Thaerix's winds falter, skeletons stumble.

For the first time, hope surges.

Then, the sampo's glow flickers. Ilmarinen curses, adjusting the spheres. A crack appears in the crystal, and he tries to steady it, but it's too late. The sampo vibrates, fractures webbing across its surface. "I can't hold it!" he shouts, leaping back.

A flash of multicolored light blinds us, hurls us to the ground. I gasp for air. When my vision clears, I see skeletons collapsing into bone piles, Zelma's darkness thinning, Thaerix's vortex narrowing to nothing. The Old Gods, momentarily sealed away by the broken sampo's surge, are sucked into the cracks, vanishing underground. Silence falls, broken only by ragged breathing.

We did it.

The sampo worked.

We survived.

But at what cost?

Tapio is gone. Too many soldiers have died. Despite working enough to disable the Old Gods, the sampo is shattered, leaving the ley line half-fixed, our victory incomplete. Ilmarinen kneels amidst crystal shards, trying to gather them with shaking fingers. Soldiers groan and wipe sweat from their brows, some of them waking up from the sleep Zelma put them in. My father and Rasmus, drained, lean on each other as the Magician stands apart, silent.

Did he see this all?

Did he know?

I push myself up, numb, limbs shaking. Tellervo's anguished cries burn into my soul. She sees me, eyes blazing with accusation. "Hanna!" she sobs. "You could have saved him!"

My throat locks. I have no excuse. I'm not a Goddess—I'm a coward. My terror killed him as surely as that Old God's claws. She turns away, cradling her father's staff, hatred radiating from her every sob. The forest itself seems to cry along with her, branches shaking violently, leaves and needles falling to the ground like tears.

I drop to the cold ground and fold inward, hugging my knees, tears sliding silently down my face. I'm the Goddess of both the Sun and Death—and I failed. I had one chance to save Tapio, and I froze, choking on fear. Now, he's gone, and I've lost more than an ally. I've lost trust, confidence, and perhaps the right to call myself their savior.

Tuoni comes to my side, hauling me up to my feet and putting his arms around me. He holds me tight, telling me it wasn't my fault, that I did the best I could, but I don't believe a word he says. I'm not sure he believes it either.

As the camp tends to wounds and grieves, I remain hollow and ashamed. The Old Gods retreated for now, but there will be others in our future. The path to Shadow's End remains perilous, the ley lines broken, my courage and conviction beyond shattered.

I don't know how to face them—or myself.

In the silence that follows, I weep into my husband's arms, holding my guilt close, like pressing on a wound that won't stop bleeding.

CHAPTER THIRTY

LOVIA

WE HUDDLE BENEATH FLICKERING WARDS THAT HUM QUIETLY in the darkness. The skeleton army stands beyond, unmoving, a grim army of hollow gazes and rusted blades. I can't see them through the shimmering barrier, but I know they're there, waiting all day for a chance to break through. I can almost taste the tension in the air—the knowledge that this fragile bubble of magic is all that keeps us from annihilation. We're survivors in a shrinking circle of safety, clinging to hope that might not last the night.

I sit on a fallen trunk near the camp's center, muscles aching, mind heavy. My father stands a short distance away with the Magician and Hanna, who wears her grief and guilt like shackles, controlling her every move.

Torben hovers at the edge, exhaustion carving lines in his face. His red-rimmed eyes turn occasionally toward Tapio's makeshift grave, where Tellervo stands by herself, staring at the spot where her father's body vanished into the moss and roots. The funeral just ended. The forest itself performed it—a silent, green magic that reclaimed Tapio without flames or fanfare, his form sinking gently, nature weaving him into the soil. This is the third God I've watched be buried here, and it doesn't get easier. If anything, the pain is amplified.

I want to say something to Tellervo, to offer comfort, but I can't. There's nothing to say. I couldn't say anything to bring back her mother and brother, and I certainly can't say anything to bring back her father.

Besides, right now, she's drowning in anger. Every time I think of approaching her, my throat closes. She blames Hanna for Tapio's death, and I can't argue with her. Hanna could have acted sooner. She could have saved him, if not for her fear, her uncertainty. I understand her hesitation, know the impasse she faces within, but understanding doesn't banish anger, at least not for Tellervo. The shoulders of the last Forest God trembles now and then, and each subtle shake of grief drives a wedge deeper into my heart. I feel powerless, trapped in hesitation. I'm supposed to be the general; where was I when all of this was happening? I should have been at Hanna's side, ready to step in. I should have been protecting the other Gods. Instead, I was battling skeletons, easy prey. I had no idea that one of our own was so close to death.

But I should have.

The wards glimmer faintly as Torben and Rasmus adjust their spells. They strain to maintain this thin shield, sweat shining on their foreheads. Soldiers cluster in uneasy knots, cradling mismatched weapons. Ilmarinen tinkers with the shards of the broken sampo, his eyes narrowed in obsessive focus. I catch the strange intensity in his movements, the way he mutters under his breath. Something about him now unsettles me, reminds me of something, but I hold my tongue. One crisis at a time.

My father finishes speaking with Hanna and the Magician then turns toward me, meeting my gaze. He doesn't need words to convey his message: we must endure, we must press forward. We must not break. I nod stiffly, summoning a ghost of resolve. I'm trying to hold us together, just like he is.

Then, my father puts his arm around Hanna and leads her away to converse in private. I truly hope he can lessen the guilt in Hanna's heart. I can't imagine what she must be going through.

The Magician comes over to me now, and for a moment, I feel a hot spark of anger at him. He must have seen this. He must have seen Tapio's death. Why the fuck didn't he warn us? Why didn't he say something? Why does he continuously step in for Rasmus but no one else? Tapio deserved to live more than Rasmus.

"You're angry with me," the Magician says in a cool, hushed tone. "I accept that."

I swallow down my rage and take a deep breath, not wanting to have a fight with him here in the forest. "You could have told us. You could have warned him."

He gives his head a shake, and even the stars seem to dim. "I did not know."

"Bullshit. You know everything."

"I don't know everything," he says. "I see different paths. I thought…" He looks around and then lowers his voice. "I expected Hanna to use her powers. That was the path I saw before. She didn't, which means threads have been altered and a new tapestry is being woven as we speak."

I glare at him. "You and your fucking metaphors."

He reaches out and grabs my hand. "Sometimes, I wish I wasn't what I am, but I can't change that. Not yet."

"Not yet? What does that mean?"

"It means there is always a plan," he says, squeezing my

fingers. "And that you are, right now, exactly where you need to be."

Then, he lets go of my hand and walks away.

"Well, thanks," I snarl after him. "I hate it here."

I sigh and look back to the scene unfolding. Tellervo doesn't turn from her vigil. No one dares interrupt her grieving. Eventually, Torben and Rasmus settle, having reinforced the wards as best they can, even though the presence of the army beyond the shimmering borders makes my stomach twist. My father returns with Hanna and motions for all of us to gather quietly.

The plan is simple, if not desperate. Ilmarinen needs time to work on the sampo's remnants. We must hold the wards and wait for a chance to break out. We can fight the skeletons head-on but not any Old Gods that may join them. Without the sampo, we're weaker. Without Tapio, we're missing a vital ally.

But what choice do we fucking have?

I listen, arms crossed, as Hanna nods silently, agreeing to help as she can. She says nothing about her fear or her earlier inaction. She doesn't need to. We all know what happened.

We disperse to our tasks. Soldiers rest, some murmuring prayers. Torben and Rasmus watch over Ilmarinen as he hunches over the sampo shards, cursing softly. Hanna edges near me, hesitant, searching my face for understanding. I offer a thin, weary nod. We're all hurting; maybe that's enough to say right now.

Night deepens. The wards crackle softly, the skeletons remain still. The forest creaks and sighs, as if breathing in the scent of our sorrow. We must keep going, find a way forward despite broken tools and broken hearts. One day, maybe Hanna will reclaim the confidence she lost. Maybe Tellervo will forgive her. Maybe I'll find words to comfort them both.

That's what a good general would do, isn't it? Mend her soldiers?

For now, I stand guard, gripping my blade and scanning the darkness. We're trapped but not defeated.

Let the night pass.

Let dawn bring another chance.

We will endure as best we can.

And hope it's enough.

CHAPTER THIRTY-ONE

DEATH

It happens in the dead of night, when the camp should be at its quietest. I have been sleeping lightly—no one can sleep deeply here, not with the skeleton army outside and the wards shimmering like fragile glass around us. My eyes snap open when I sense a change in the air, a subtle trembling in the wards. I sit up quickly, heart pounding, and look around. Hanna sleeps deeply beside me, her brows twisted together even as she dreams. Lantern light flickers over tense faces. Soldiers stir, muttering questions, hands on weapons.

I see Torben and Rasmus at opposite edges of the camp, each hunched in concentration. Their wards have protected us since yesterday, but now, the barrier crackles with instability. Sparks dance in the dark. I rise to my feet, stepping over sleeping rolls and scattered gear, making my way toward Torben.

He looks up, sweat beading on his brow. "They're failing," he says, voice tight with strain. "I don't understand. Something's sapping our strength."

Rasmus echoes the sentiment from across the circle, voice

shaking. "It's not just us—something *inside* the wards is interfering."

My heart sinks. I look around for Ilmarinen, expecting to see him working on the sampo—he has been focused on the device with an unsettling intensity—but I see no sign of him. The makeshift table where he had been tinkering is empty. Tools lie scattered, and the pack of parts and shards that once held the sampo is gone.

My blood runs cold at the sight.

"Ilmarinen!" I call, voice low but urgent. Soldiers pick up the alarm and begin searching the woods, but he's nowhere to be found. Hanna sits up, looking around in confusion as Lovia calls for the missing shaman and starts searching. I don't think poor Tellervo slept at all; she's standing apart from the group, arms crossed, face still etched with grief—she barely glances up, her antlers drooping.

The wards sputter again, sending a shiver of green and blue sparks. A soldier yelps as a spark grazes his arm. The skeleton army outside stirs, as if sensing weakness, and the rattle of bone and rusty metal scrapes at my nerves.

"We must hold them," I tell Torben. "Is there no way to reinforce the wards? Another spell?"

He shakes his head, grim. "They're collapsing from within, destabilized with black magic. Without Ilmarinen or the sampo, we have no stable anchor."

"And he's just gone..."

Torben nods, his mouth twisted with betrayal. "He's just gone."

I clench my fists. It's possible Ilmarinen has been taken, but we would have known. Others would have been taken too. There's no way Louhi's minions would have taken or killed him but let the rest of us live.

Which means he sabotaged us. A fucking traitor. But

why? Did he serve Louhi all along, or did the sampo's dark magic corrupt him? What was he really crafting?

I have no time for these questions now.

Survival comes first.

"Everyone!" I shout, my voice carrying over the crackle of wards. "Prepare for attack! The wards are failing, and we don't know how much longer we have!"

The sound of weapons being drawn fills the air. The Magician steps into the dim light with Lovia beside him, sword at the ready. Hanna stands near me, pale and tense. I see Tellervo's jaw tighten—she says nothing, but she lifts her hands, and I can sense her calling on the forest again, coaxing them to protect their last remaining God.

With a final crackle, the wards fail. The shimmering boundary pops like a bubble, leaving us exposed. Torchlight and lantern glow reveal a half-circle of skeletal warriors, their hollow eyes glowing. They surge forward with clacking jaws and clattering armor, and behind them, I sense more shapes lurking, perhaps Old Gods waiting for the right moment. For a second, the thought weighs on me like a hammer, and I'm so fucking weary of it all, tired of this continuous fight.

But my resolve only bends for a moment. I think of Tuonen and Sarvi and driving a sword through Louhi's eyeballs, and that's enough.

"Form ranks!" I bellow, stepping forward. My sword gleams dully in the uncertain light. Soldiers close in, shields raised as the skeleton horde rushes us. Steel clashes with bone as we meet them head-on. Sparks fly, shouts and curses filling the air. I parry a skeleton's spear, shatter its ribs with a swift strike, and move on to the next one.

Hanna deflects a sword stroke aimed at Lovia's back, her eyes fierce despite her lingering guilt. Lovia stands strong, cutting down two skeletons with fluid grace. The Magician weaves strands of starlight to snare a knot of skeletons, holding them still while Rasmus and Torben hurl bolts of spiritual energy to shatter them, their magic now freed since they no longer have the wards to contend with.

But more skeletons pour in from the sides. The forest confines us, roots and trunks limiting our movement. We fight desperately, pushing forward to escape the choke point. One of the Keskelli hurls her spear at a tall Bone Straggler, splintering its skull.

Meanwhile, Tellervo stands behind us, arms raised, calling a name I've never heard her utter: "Olso!"

The ground trembles in response. A deep growl resonates through the forest floor as branches creak and leaves quiver. A colossal shape emerges from the darkness—a giant bear the size of a troll, thick with fur and moss-laden, eyes glowing with old magic. Olso, summoned by Tellervo's plea. The bear bellows, a thunderous roar that shakes skeletons apart. With massive paws, it swipes a line of the undead into splinters.

Our soldiers cheer. With Olso breaking their ranks, we gain ground. Step by step, we push through the forest. The skeletons press in from all sides, but the bear's sheer strength carves a path while Torben creates a ward around it that deflects swords and spears. I fight near Hanna, watching the hesitant but determined strikes from her sword. She still struggles with her power, I can tell, but she's here, helping in any way she can.

We crash through a thicket of brambles, driven forward, the skeletons moving back. The forest thins, the undergrowth clearing with it. Ahead, I see open space, the edge of the Hiisi Forest. Beyond lies the Liekkiö Plains, the vast desert where demon children burn with eternal flame. They roam at night, biting and clawing travelers, but we have no choice. Sticking to the forest means less space to maneuver—

plus, I have no qualms about kicking those fiery kids' heads clean off.

We burst into open ground under a sky just starting to lighten with a false dawn. We continue to drive the skeleton army backward, rattling and clacking, while Olso lumbers behind us, growling and swiping at anyone who dares to approach. Tellervo is pale, her lips pressed tight in concentration—controlling or guiding the giant bear must cost her dearly.

The Liekkiö Plains spread out in front of us, flat, dusty, eerily silent, and thankfully devoid of any demonic brats. Perhaps they fear the approaching undead—or maybe they're waiting for a better moment.

A shout goes up from a soldier on the flank: "Look! Over there!"

I turn, squinting. In the distance, I see figures approaching—a column of allies, led by Vellamo and her trolls and the small contingent of troops running toward us across the dusty plains. I had told her to wait by the river, but I've never been so grateful she's stubborn.

We wave them in, signaling for them to approach carefully. Vellamo greets us with a curt nod, relief in her eyes. I notice the horn in one of the Keskelli's giant hands. It must have been them we heard the other day, but they were too far away. It doesn't matter; we are stronger now, bolstered by fresh blades and sturdy trolls.

But our respite is short-lived. I feel a rumble beneath my feet, a sick twisting sensation in the ground. Old Gods are stirring again, no doubt drawn by Kaaos. Without the sampo's stabilizing influence, we have little to hold them back.

The ground cracks and heaves as greenish fluid seeps up. Yggthra's roots appear again, snaking across the plains as Zelma's darkness stirs at the edges of my vision and

Thaerix's winds whisper on the horizon, stirring up red dust.

Oh, for fuck's sake. Them again? These Old Gods refuse to let us escape. Ilmarinen must have let them loose, or maybe their destruction had always been temporary.

Vellamo steps forward, pearl-crusted spear in hand, her face contorted in anger. "They will not take this land!" she vows. She kneels, pressing a palm to the dusty ground, and I feel a shift in the air—moisture gathering, pressure building. She's summoning water, asking the River of Shadows to flood these plains. It's a daring move, considering the river isn't close, but one that might give us an advantage. The undead and Old Gods might be hampered by water, and that river flows right from the Great Inland Sea, which means its power is limitless.

Cracks appear in the dry soil, and then water gushes forth in glistening streams. The river floods upwards, rising from aquifers beneath the desert floor. Within moments, puddles form, then pools, before a shallow flood spreads across the plains, soaking our boots. The skeletons look around in confusion.

The Old Gods rise from sinkholes of mud and muck, their bodies half-formed of root, shadow, and storm. Now, they must contend with water swirling around their anchors. Vellamo raises her arms, and a serpentine shape emerges from the newly formed flood—a massive serpent with too many teeth, the Devouress, twisting sinuously through the knee-deep water. Alongside it swims other water creatures—Näkki, a female water spirit with sharp claws and webbed fingers, a creature called the Ved-Ava. They dart in and out, dragging skeletons under the surface.

We fight half-submerged now, sloshing through rising water. Soldiers adapt quickly, lashing out with polearms and spears as the trolls wade in, their great legs stable in the flood, smashing skeletons with mighty blows. Olso the bear stands chest-deep in water, snarling and swinging massive paws to fling enemies aside.

Still, the Old Gods try to lash out. Yggthra's roots attempt to grip the mud but slip and slide. Zelma's shadow tries to blot out what faint light we have, but the water's reflection and the shimmer of warding spells defy total darkness. Thaerix's vortex hovers above the plains with a howl, but the moisture in the air dampens its force.

My attention swivels to Torben, the shaman trapped between two skeleton soldiers, struggling to maintain balance in the swirling currents. The ugly Old God who killed Tapio suddenly pops up out of the water, lurking behind the shaman, claws extended. My heart clenches. If Torben falls, we lose a crucial ally, and I lose my father-in-law, someone I never thought I'd care for, considering our fraught beginnings. But now, I cry out and surge forward, sword raised, pushing through water and debris.

It's too late. I'm too far away, and the Old God lunges for him.

"No!" Hanna's voice pierces the chaos. She stands on a slight rise of packed dirt, water streaming around her legs. Her eyes flare with panic and resolve. I see her raise her hand, trembling.

She doesn't hesitate this time.

A burst of light erupts from Hanna, bright as a solar flare, piercing through Zelma's gloom. She cries out like a warrior, like a Goddess. The light intensifies, banishing shadows, reflecting off the floodwaters until the entire scene is bathed in radiance. The Old God about to strike Torben shrieks, recoiling as its chitlin-like form smolders and cracks.

Hanna's body changes, her outline blurring into a figure of molten gold and flame. She is incandescent, painfully bright, terribly beautiful, a living star in the midst of battle. I shield my eyes, tears leaking from the corners. Around me, soldiers gasp, some crying out in awe or fear.

Under Hanna's blazing aura, skeletons crumble into ash. Yggthra's roots recoil, scorched and blackened, and Zelma's webs of darkness burn away like cobwebs in a furnace. Thaerix's vortex screams once more before it unravels, the winds scattering to nothing.

The Devouress and the Näkki pause, momentarily disoriented by the sudden brilliance. Even Olso the bear bows his great head, whining softly. Our soldiers shield their faces, squinting through their fingers.

Hanna sweeps her gaze across the battlefield, and wherever she looks, enemies ignite and disintegrate. The water steams, rising in pale clouds, and in moments, the battle is over. The Old Gods burst into flames, the skeleton army gone, nothing but drifting flakes of ash on the water's surface.

I stand transfixed, pride and love battling with fear. This power is immense, greater than any I've wielded. Hanna has saved us all—but at what cost?

All I know is that she chose to do this. She chose to save her father.

She knew what the cost was and decided it was worth it.

As the last enemy falls, Hanna's glow dims. Her radiant form trembles, and I try to reach her, sloshing through the lukewarm floodwaters. When I come close, the glow fades further, revealing her face contorted in pain and confusion.

She looks at me, eyes wide and unfocused. "Did it work?" she whispers, voice thin.

I catch her as she collapses, pulling her into my arms. She's lighter than I remember, as if hollowed out. The water laps at our knees, bodies of our allies pushing closer, trying to see if she's all right.

"Hanna, stay with me," I plead, my heart pounding. She

blinks, tears in her eyes, but not of sorrow—of emptiness. I see no recognition there, only hollow bewilderment.

"What happened?" she asks, voice eerily calm.

A knife twists in my chest. I've lost her again to the cost of her transformation. I cradle her close, my throat tight with unshed tears.

Around us, the floodwaters recede slowly as Vellamo eases her magic. Soldiers gather, wounded and weary, as Tellervo walks away, reeling, perhaps from seeing Hanna save Torben but not Tapio. Lovia and the Magician approach, concerned, while Torben stands in silent awe of his daughter, a hint of guilt on his face as he rubs the bruises on his arms, alive only through Hanna's intervention.

Hanna stares at me with blank eyes. I run a hand through her damp hair, the colors lighter again, forcing a smile I do not feel. "It's all right," I say softly, though it isn't. "You're safe now."

She tries to speak, but words fail her. She looks past me, at the soldiers, at the scorched remains of battle with a look of detachment. She's a stranger wearing my wife's face, holding unimaginable power in fragile hands.

I hold her tighter, though she's no longer trembling. "We'll help you remember," I whisper, voice thick with emotion. "You'll come back to me again, little bird. We'll find a way. I promise."

She doesn't respond; she just closes her eyes and hesitates before she rests her head against my chest. I feel her breath, shallow and uncertain but alive. Alive is something. Alive and safe for now.

Everyone looks to me, waiting for the next command. I feel their expectations, their fears, on my shoulders like a weight.

"What now, Lord Death?" General Suvari asks, looking wet and tired, swaying on his feet.

I square my shoulders and try to steady my voice.

"We move on," I say, quiet but firm. "We'll get Tuonen and Sarvi. We'll restore what's lost. We'll protect each other." My eyes sweep over them, seeking solidarity in their weary faces. They nod, some murmuring in agreement.

Hanna's condition pains me, but I must be strong for her, for all of them. We must reach safer ground, regroup, maybe find shelter beyond these plains. The demon children have not appeared, and I can only hope our luck holds a bit longer. Once we find stable ground, we'll plan our next steps.

The air smells of damp soil and lingering ozone from Hanna's fiery magic. The sun tries to rise beyond the horizon, its pale rays reflected on shallow pools. We wade through the receding flood, carrying our wounded and collecting our fallen. The forest lies behind us, battered and violated by the Old Gods. The plains stretch before us, empty except for scorched ground and distant shapes.

Beyond that lies the Gorge of Despair.

Then, the City of Death.

But there is one place between them where we might find safe passage.

For now, we march forward, a weary band in a world gone mad, guided by the faint hope that we can still save Tuonela from the darkness seeking to consume it. I hold Hanna's hand as we go, as if by keeping her close, I can anchor her to who she once was. She walks quietly, trusting me despite not knowing why.

That trust will have to be enough for now.

CHAPTER THIRTY-TWO

LOVIA

"We'll camp here for the night," my father announces, his voice fraught with the weight of our journey. We've been walking all day after the battle in the Hiisi Forest, crossing the Liekkiö Plains without much fanfare. I waited for those terrible, flaming ankle-biters to appear and swarm us, but they didn't. I have to wonder if the Magician destroyed them all for good when we encountered them last.

Now, the last light of the sky bleeds behind thin clouds that threaten rain and snow that never comes. We're just past the Gorge of Despair, the canyon in our wake, taking shelter on a plateau rimmed with windblown trees and brush, giving us cover while also providing an uninterrupted view of the land around us. Unless Louhi has more unicorns up her sleeve to attack us from the air, we'll be safe here.

I pick up my tent and head into the brush, away from the rest of the camp but still close enough. I feel like keeping to myself tonight and being alone with my thoughts. From the hushed silence, I can tell everyone else feels the same way.

"Need any help?" the Magician asks me, hanging around a straggly pine.

I roll the tent out and up before I get down on my knees to stake it. "I can manage."

"I know you can manage," he says, "but help is being offered if you want it."

I can't help but laugh, even if it rings a bit hollow. "You certainly have a way about you, don't you?"

"Is it a way that you like?" he asks.

I hammer down the last stake into the hard ground before I get up and dust my hands off. I stare into the void of his face, wondering what his deal is. "Did you really come here to help me?"

He nods, gliding across the forest floor toward me. "I did." He stops a foot away and extends his velvety black hand, reaching out to cup my face. I briefly close my eyes at his touch, melting against his palm, cool but strong. I've needed this contact more than I care to admit.

"I want to understand you, Loviatar. I want to know what your heart feels like, what your *soul* feels like. I want to know what it's like to be more human than I am."

I swallow uneasily, not sure what he's talking about. "Okay..."

"This is important," he says, his voice slipping from its usual melodic cadence and taking on a sense of urgency. "It's important to me and to you." He pauses, his thumb running over my lips. It smells like rain. "Haven't you wondered what it's like to become one with the universe?"

My heart skips a beat, heat tightening my skin. "Yes," I whisper, even though I've never wondered that. However, *now* I am.

"Good," he says. He nods at the tent, his hand falling away, leaving my skin feeling bereft. "Now, go inside that tent and wait for me. I'll appear at nightfall. Try not to fall asleep."

"No promises," I tell him, though my voice trembles with

nerves. I watch as he turns and walks back between the trees, disappearing from view.

What in the realm was that all about?

Wait for him? In the tent?

Become one with the universe?

My brain is starting to go wild. He can't possibly mean what I think he means, can he?

So, I stand there for a few minutes, staring at the trees. Night falls slowly, the light beyond the canopy still grey. Around the edges of the plateau, a few troops patrol in a single file, but they don't pay me much attention. Further inward, soft chatter and the crackle of flames drift from the camp.

Eventually, I start to feel the tiredness seep into my bones. It has been a long day, having woken in the middle of the night when the wards failed, battled, and then walked all the way here. I've seen too much death, including a God whom I liked very much, whose lost spirit I still mourn.

I crawl into the tent before night falls, and even though I'm supposed to stay awake, I promptly fall asleep, my body too exhausted to hold on.

My sleep is deep and sound until...

"Loviatar," a voice whispers. It belongs to the Magician, but I'm hearing it as if he's speaking from inside me. "Open your eyes."

I open my eyes to darkness, but it's not the dark of the tent. It's black and it stretches on forever. I raise my hand, expecting to reach the sides of the canvas, but there's nothing there.

"Hello?" I say, slowly sitting up. The darkness hums, and light slowly emerges in pinpricks, looking very far away. Too far away to be inside the tent.

Panic claws up my throat. Where the fuck am I?

"Don't be alarmed," the Magician's voice said, sounding

from all around me in echoes. "Everything is as it should be. Just relax."

"Relax for what?" I say, feeling around me, only to find nothing but inky darkness and sparkling stars. "Where am I? What's happening?"

"You're with me," he says. "Just lie back and open yourself. Let me take care of everything."

"Wait." I feel around me with my hands, and that's when I realize I'm not wearing any clothes. "I'm naked. Why am I naked?"

What the fuck is happening?

Silence stretches on before he says, "I can put your clothes back on if you'd like."

"You took them off? You undressed me?"

"It's nothing I haven't seen before, Lovia. I have seen everything and all. But no, I didn't physically remove them. I just made them no longer exist. You are in a place where articles like those don't matter. All that matters is you. You don't even need a body, but it's better to experience it with one."

"Experience what?" I cry out.

"Our union," he says. "That is what you've wanted from me, isn't it?"

I swallow hard, my heart drumming a beat against my ribs. "I—I don't know."

"If it isn't, then you can tell me. I can end this."

"No," I say quietly. "I just... Are you talking sex?"

"I'm talking a union of unearthly delight for you."

Well, that sounds like it could be sex.

"You have an awfully high opinion of yourself," I mutter.

"As I should," he goes on.

"All right." I clear my throat, my curiosity getting the best of me. "If that's what I get out of it, what do you?"

"I told you before—it's important for me. Being inside

you, wholly and completely, will let me feel what it's like to be you. You will give me my much-needed humanity."

"You sound like Hanna," I comment.

"We aren't too dissimilar," he says. "But I am searching for something that will help me in the end. You have morals, Lovia. You are a great judge of character."

"So are you. You've been the real judge, the one dealing the cards to the newly dead all this time."

"It's not the same. There is no love in that. You hold love, Lovia. I want to know what that feels like."

But I don't know if I love you, I think to myself. *Can you love the universe?*

"It's not about loving me," he says, reading my thoughts. "It's about love. You *are* love. I must know what it tastes like. I want to hold your humanity in each and every star."

"And it helps me how?"

"As I said…"

"Right. The union of unearthly delight."

Silence falls between us again while I think it over.

Honestly, at this point, I'm so exhausted, my heart so heavy from grief, my mind so fraught with worry over what's to come, that spending some time with the Magician in this way might be the distraction I need.

"All right," I whisper. "How do I do this?"

"Like this," he says, and, suddenly, his voice is right in front of me.

I feel his hands on my face as his petrichor scent fills my nose, blossoming inside me before he presses his lips to mine.

Like the kiss before, it envelopes me like a cloud, my breath trembling as his tongue sweeps against mine. Desire rockets to my core, butterflies unleashed in my belly, and I reach for him, surprised when it makes contact with his form.

I open my eyes, and I can't see him at all. It's all just an endless black void speckled with stars and the occasional galaxy that flies past, but I can feel him. My fingers dig into his strong shoulders, run down the muscled length of his arms, down across his rigid abs.

What is happening? I think. *Is this what he really feels like or what I want him to feel like?*

"I'm arranging myself for you, to be what you want, to be what fits you best," he says, his voice now a whispered echo in the dark. "Does it please you?"

I can't help but laugh, staring into the infinite universe as my hands go lower until they feel what can only be his cock. I gasp at the feel of it, hard, long, and cool, reveling in the detail.

"Does that feel good?" I whisper, suddenly overpowered by the need for him to feel good. My ego craves the idea of being the one to make the universe see stars in a truly different way.

"It feels good to me because it feels good to you. Now, lie back."

I feel his hands around me, pushing me back to the ground.

Except, there is no ground.

There is nothing behind me.

I am floating in space.

And his lips are on me, everywhere. Not just my mouth, but my neck and my breasts and my stomach and between my thighs. He's everywhere all at once, like I'm being kissed and licked by multiple men.

I flail into the nothingness, my head going back, letting the Magician devour me, tongues and lips and hands exploring every inch of my body, over and over again.

Then, my legs part, and he enters me, filling me with something indescribable, something both warm and cold, soft and hard, something that fills every crevice. It snakes in between bones and seeps into my veins, and I'm being fucked by the universe in every way possible.

I cry out, but it's in my mouth as well, thrusting deep, meeting somewhere in my ribs, wrapping around my heart and squeezing. I am shattering into a million pieces yet held together by stardust. Every last inch of me is explored and kissed and teased until I am writhing, endlessly and forever, until time doesn't exist.

And it doesn't stop. It keeps going, and I keep falling and rising and I am flying and I am here and there and everywhere at once. I am myself and I am beyond myself. I am a soul in the world; I am the world.

"I feel you," the Magician's voice surrounds me as I feel him singular again, lips at my neck, his cock pounding inside me, coaxing orgasm after orgasm from me. "I feel who you are, Lovia, and you are lovely."

"I don't want this to end," I cry out. It could go on for infinity. I am infinity.

"It has to at some point," he says. "Let me feel you again, one last time."

And so it begins once more, the onslaught of mouths and lips and hands and cocks, filling me until I burst into starlight, until I'm just a former Goddess spinning into another galaxy.

I whirl and turn, and I am one and I am everywhere.

And then, I feel hard ground behind my shoulders.

And I am no longer everywhere, but *somewhere.*

In my tent.

Staring up into the dark. No stars.

"Magician," I whisper into the dark. I slowly sit up, my head brushing against the canvas. I run my hands over my legs and feel my tunic and trousers.

I am me again.

Alone.

And yet, deep inside me, fragments of the universe still burn.

THE NEXT MORNING, I sleep in and don't wake until Vellamo shakes my tent.

"Get up, Lovia," her deep voice says. "We're ready to move on to the Iron Mountains. It's starting to snow."

I let her know I'm coming and then quickly get ready, my body sore, my mind groggy from the wildness of last night. By the time I'm all packed up and hauling my tent over to the main camp, where someone loads it into a supply wagon, everyone is staring at me like I'm holding them back.

"Sorry," I apologize sheepishly.

My father gives me a stern nod. "I suppose even generals need their rest sometimes," he says gruffly, but his eyes are kind.

We start walking, and I look over to see the Magician. I go to him, falling in step beside him.

"So..." I start, not wanting to say too much since we're surrounded by people.

"I take it you slept well," he says in that smooth, blank voice of his.

A shivery feeling takes hold of my chest. "Very well. I had very unusual dreams. I was floating in space, one with the universe."

He glances at me, and a shooting start curves up in a smirk. "That's funny. I could have sworn I had that same dream, except in mine, I gained something invaluable. Of course, I don't dream, but I'm glad you had a good one."

And at that, he moves a little quicker, as if he's trying to leave me behind. I'm about to rush after him when I sense Torben at my side.

"Peculiar fellow, isn't he?" Torben comments. I study his weathered face to see if he's being facetious, but he seems sincere.

"Very," I say.

The plan for the day is to walk into the Iron Mountains and then down to my father's secret cave, into what he calls his Mountain Lair. From there, we should be able to travel all the way to Shadow's End hidden in the cave system. Of course, there are risks involved, one being that we could end up trapped and ambushed, but I doubt even my mother knows about the existence of these caves. For now, my father believes it's the best option for us, and as his general, I agree.

Of course, the mountains themselves are no small feat, especially with the weather systems that usher in snow and freezing rain.

We've been walking for a while now, the wind getting colder by the second, funneled through the looming slopes of the mountains. Our troops trudge forward in a narrow column, the sound of boots scraping over loose stones echoing between sheer cliffs. I'm at the back of the line, walking a good distance behind the main group. I volunteered for this position—someone must watch our rear, make sure nothing follows us. It's a quiet vigil, but I find some comfort in isolation. It gives me a chance to think about what happened in my tent last night.

That had been real, hadn't it?

As we snake around a switchback, I can see the rest of the line ahead, my father's silhouette barely visible as he leads the others, cloak flapping in the wind. Hanna, still distant in more ways than one and glowing faintly, walks near him. The Magician hovers at their side, choosing to be up ahead instead of back here with me. I figure maybe he needs some time apart to think. I just hope he doesn't regret anything.

Rasmus is usually closer to the front with them, but today, he lingers at the rear with me. I sense his hesitation—maybe he thinks I still don't trust him, or maybe he wants to prove something. We've barely spoken since we left the forest. I feel like he has consistently been trying to redeem himself, quietly aiding in small tasks. He's still a shaman, still powerful in his own right, and maybe he wants me to see that.

Maybe he just wants forgiveness.

I glance over my shoulder at him. He's a few paces to my left and behind, boots crunching on loose gravel. He should be in front of me, but I can still keep an eye on him this way. The sky is a sickly grey above us, clouds scraping the peaks. Snow drifts lazily—not enough to blanket the ground, but enough to blur the edges of the world. The soldiers between us and the main party are distant shapes bobbing along the jagged path. I feel oddly alone, despite knowing they're not too far off.

Rasmus notices my attention. He tries a tentative smile, one that flickers and fails. I give a short nod, acknowledging his presence. Words feel heavy in my throat. I'm still not sure how to treat him. Like a brother? A friend? An ally? Is he any of those things? Time and battles have dulled the sharp anger I once held, and yet, trust doesn't come easily to me. But we share a purpose now, don't we? Survival and revenge. Perhaps that's enough.

We move slowly, careful not to slip. The path isn't wide, and below us is a steep drop that gives me a rush of vertigo. The sound of distant water echoes somewhere, a hidden stream or a melting snowfield. The hair on my neck prickles, and I feel a looming sense of dread, though I don't know what of. Everything seems fine, but I know enough to never let my guard down.

I pause, listening. There's something odd about the silence. The wind whistles and stones clatter under Rasmus' boots as he catches up, but beyond that...no birds, no distant calls. I grip my sword hilt tighter, scanning the crags and ledges. Nothing moves. The columns of soldiers have disappeared around a bend, leaving me and Rasmus almost entirely alone.

"Lovia," Rasmus says quietly from behind me, voice carrying despite the wind. "Should we hurry to catch up?" His tone is respectful, cautious, like he knows I might snap at him.

Before I can tell him yes, the ground trembles beneath my feet and my stomach drops.

An earthquake?

Or something worse?

We lurch backward as the ground splits open behind us, hurling shards of rock in a violent spray. I cry out, feet sliding on loose stones, and beside me, Rasmus lets out a string of expletives. A jagged fissure yawns wide, and a blast of bitter, frozen air hits my face.

From the craggy gap, something emerges—an Old God of stone and ice, as though the mountain's marrow has formed into a living nightmare. It rises, hulking and immense, its body a mass of cracked granite shot through with icy veins. Shards of frost hang in jagged protrusions from its limbs, and where a face should be, there is a cavernous hollow rimmed with jagged blood-red crystals.

My heart leaps into my throat, terror sparking through my veins. I have my sword in hand before I know I've drawn it, fingers numb against the hilt. I back away, trying to find space, but the path is narrow, the drop behind me unforgiving. Rasmus stands near me, eyes wide and panicked.

Can we run fast enough?

The creature lunges before we can move, an arm of ice-crusted stone swinging toward me. I duck at the last moment, feel the rush of frigid air. My blade lashes out, sparks dancing where steel meets granite. The impact jars my arm, nearly twisting the sword from my grip. It lets out a grinding shriek like glaciers groaning under their own weight. As I block its second strike, the force rattles my bones.

"Get back!" I shout at Rasmus, but he doesn't flee. Instead, he spreads his hands and chants, wind howling around him as sigils flicker in the air. I sense elemental power stirring as he attempts to bind it, slow its movements, give me a chance to finish it.

The Old God roars, a hollow echo rolling through the cliffs. Its icy limb lashes out again, razor-like shards scraping across my forearm. My armor deflects some of the blow, but pain flares hot under my skin. I grit my teeth against a scream.

Rasmus steps between us, his chanting intensifying. I can feel the air grow dense, a hush of magic that sets my hair on end. The monster hisses—an eerie sound of stone grinding on stone—and swings low. Rasmus leaps aside but not far enough. A hammer-like fist of ice and rock clips his leg, spinning him off-balance.

"Rasmus!" I snap, slashing wildly at the creature's flank, desperate to draw it away from him. My sword skitters, carving shallow grooves into ice and stone but not nearly enough to cripple it. I'm fighting gravity, fear, and pain all at once.

Rasmus recovers, gasping. He thrusts a hand forward, and faint lines of runes blaze momentarily, his sword raised in his other hand. The Old God recoils as if whipped by invisible chains. For an instant, I catch my breath. Warm blood dampens my sleeve. We must end this now, or we won't survive. The others are too far ahead, their footsteps lost in the wind. No one will come to our aid.

The Old God rumbles, swinging a massive limb in a sweeping arc. I duck then lunge, trying to strike deeper. My sword sinks a few inches into stone and ice, meeting stubborn resistance. The creature shudders but does not fall. It whips its arm, knocking me backward. My boots skid on loose gravel, and I nearly plummet over the edge before I catch a sharp outcrop of rock.

Rasmus yells something I can't decipher and hurls a bolt of energy. The Old God shrieks, a crackling sound like ice splitting, as part of its stony hide fractures. I see a chance, try to move forward, but the monster bucks violently as rocks rain down from the cliffs above. One strikes my helmet, knocking it off, clattering over the mountainside. Stars dance in my vision, dizziness swamping me.

Too slow. The Old God lunges, a limb of serrated ice and granite aimed for my exposed head. I'm off-balance, sword raised too late. Panic grips me as I see my death in that frozen limb.

Rasmus cries out, a desperate, wordless sound, and throws himself in front of me, sword at the ready.

But the Old God's blow impales him cleanly through his head. My stomach lurches at the sickening crunch, the spray of blood on the stone.

"No!" I scream, voice tearing free of my throat. Rage and grief fuse into vicious strength. I hack at the creature's arm, and this time, my blade bites deeper, fueled by fury. Something cracks. The Old God howls a splintering cry, and I strike again, shattering ice and fracturing stone. The limb falls away, twitching uselessly, and while it's distracted, I shove the sword right into the glittery maw until red ichor sprays me, every crystal shattering at once.

The Old God staggers, wounded at last, and stumbles backward to the edge of the cliff until it gives way. Within seconds, it's gone, falling thousands of feet down, leaving only a bitter wind and scattered shards of ice and rock. Its impact below shakes the ground, the explosion echoing off the mountainsides like a bomb.

I drop to my knees beside Rasmus, who lies crumpled by a river of his own blood. His eyes flutter weakly. I raise my trembling hand above the gaping wound—half of his scalp shaved off, blood and skull and brain exposed.

Oh gods, oh gods.

I don't know what to do, panic throttling my chest, vomit stuck in my throat. He tries to speak, blood on his lips. I lean closer, tears flooding my vision.

"Why?" I choke out. He saved me despite everything.

His voice is ragged, almost inaudible. "You deserved better," he manages, each word a struggle. "You're still…my sister…still…my family." He coughs, blood staining the stone. "I'm sorry…" he whispers, eyes distant now, gaze slipping beyond me.

"No," I plead, terror clawing at me. "Don't go, don't go."

I shake him lightly, but the life fades from him, the spark leaving his eyes. He grows still, limp in my arms.

Rasmus is gone.

Sobs wrench from my throat. The wind keens around us, as if in mourning too. I've lost another ally—no, a brother—here in these cold, indifferent mountains. The others, far ahead, do not know; I am alone with Rasmus' body, the echoes of our battle, and my grief.

For a long moment, I cradle his head, tears hot on my cheeks, letting his warm blood stain me as I turn cold in the wind. It shouldn't have ended this way. So many regrets hang in the silence.

But I must stand, must keep moving. I cannot remain

here. The path is dangerous, and I must warn the others of the Old God below in case the fall didn't kill it. I must carry this burden forward, tell them how Rasmus gave his life for mine.

With trembling hands, I close his eyes and whisper a quiet farewell. The wind scatters my words. I rise slowly, arm throbbing, soul hollow. The cliffs tower around me, impassive witnesses. I take one last look at Rasmus then turn and continue along the trail, following the distant shape of my father's party. My steps are heavy, each one a painful reminder of what I've lost.

I walk on, alone and broken, tears freezing on my cheeks, determined to survive and make his sacrifice meaningful.

There's no turning back now.

CHAPTER THIRTY-THREE

DEATH

The redheaded bastard is gone.

One moment, we were trudging forward over the serpentine ridges that make up the Iron Mountains, heads down against the wind and snow, and the next, Lovia was running up, pushing through the line of troops with tears streaming down her face, her shoulder bleeding, to tell me Rasmus had died.

At first, I didn't know what to feel. Rasmus has always been a wily nuisance, a thorn in my side. He stole Hanna away from me and tried to corrupt her in the name of Louhi. He was a shifty shaman apprentice who couldn't be trusted as far as I could throw him (though I could throw him very fucking far).

But when Lovia told me what happened, that Rasmus had risked his life to save hers, I realized that perhaps I was wrong about him. Perhaps he'd deserved more of my trust. It was apparent that, in the end, it wasn't his own survival that was the most important thing to him—it was my daughter's. It was all of us. He wasn't as selfish as he pretended to be, and he proved himself worthy too late.

Torben, of course, took the news the hardest, the poor man. Rasmus had always been like a son to him because he *was* his son. He was his flesh and blood, as well as his student in the magical arts, and while their relationship was complicated ever since Louhi entered the fray and fucked things up, as the she-devil does, I could tell he loved him greatly. I got to know the old shaman against my will when we were stuck in the Upper World, and while he certainly makes more mistakes than the average mortal, he carries them inside him.

But for now, we all carry on. We have to.

We continued down the mountain, Lovia and Torben leaning on each other in their sorrow, the path narrow and fraught with dangers. Loose scree and falling rocks sent a couple of soldiers to their deaths, and around every corner, we imagined the Old God that killed Rasmus would rise again.

Eventually, we made our way down to the alpine forest following the base of the mountains, finally reaching our destination at the edge of the shadowy trees.

"The Mountain Lair," I announce to the party, poised beneath a sheer rock face. I meet their gazes, expecting at least one of them to laugh, since Hanna thought the name of my secret caves was hilarious.

But everyone just looks at me expectantly, even Hanna, who, in her Goddess state of mind, doesn't find anything humorous. It's what hurts me most of all about her loss of self: the Hanna I know and love is the funniest person I've ever met, even though she doesn't know that herself. Her quick banter, her pithy remarks, playful comments, and sarcastic snorts—those are some of the things I love most about her. Without her sense of humor, she's beautiful but blank, missing something vital, something I never knew was so important until it was gone.

Perhaps you should have told your wife that when you had the chance, I chide myself. *Maybe you should tell her that anyway.*

Gods, what happens if she never returns to me? The thought strikes horror into my battered heart. I swore I would never leave her side, even if she remains stately and cool (in her brief moments of clarity, she kept comparing her other self to some Doctor Manhattan, yet another—potentially nerdy—pop culture reference I don't understand), and I plan to uphold that promise. Still, it would certainly lead to an emptier, colder, more boring life without the real Hanna by my side.

I push the thoughts away—the garrison still stares at me, waiting for something—and look back to the steep rock face. Normally, I have a key to unlock the magic veil and make my lair visible, but who the hell knows where that is at this point?

I have to dig in deep, see if I can remember any of the magic the Book of Runes has taught me over the years. For a moment, I feel a spear of panic at the idea of Louhi corrupting it, but at this point, I doubt that would change anything.

"Lord Death?" General Suvari asks, clearing his throat. "Are you all right? You're staring at nothing."

"Just a minute," I grumble, raising my hand to tell them to be patient. Since when did the general learn to talk back like that?

I close my eyes and concentrate, trying to remember some line or stanza.

Then, Hanna puts her hand on my shoulder.

"I remember this place," she says in her calm, quiet voice. "Allow me."

As I open my eyes to look at her, suddenly, the world erupts in bright white, the source being her open palm. I squint, but the light fades quickly, revealing the true nature of the mountainside when it's gone.

The steep cliff looks the same at first, but when my eyes adjust, I can see the narrow stairs made of glossy obsidian carving up the face, leading all the way to the metal door. Yet another thing I need a key for.

"I will take care of that too," she assures me.

I give her a tight smile of thanks, feeling a little small after that show of power. I can't even find a fucking key, and she's out here doing her own magic tricks.

We march to the base of the mountain, shadow stones rearranging themselves to show us a clear path, then start up the glassy black stairs. I remind everyone to be careful and, once inside, to not touch the skull snails.

"They're poisonous," I add.

At the top, Hanna puts her glowing hand on the door and unlocks it with ease. I glance at her before I enter, searching her face for a smirk or a sign of arrogance, anything that would tell me there's still a spark of *her* underneath. Oh, how I yearn for her to tell me how *badass* she's being, besting a God.

But there is nothing, just Hanna's beautiful but blank gaze of molten copper.

Still, I give her a nod of thanks and step inside the cave while the rest of the party continues up the steep stairs.

Once inside, the troops murmur their surprise. The cave system is elaborate and long with high ceilings—not at all what they were expecting, I'm sure. I lead everyone through the lair, pointing out the different rooms and caverns where they can hunker down. Some of them are made up for entertaining and sleeping, a home away from home with animal skin rugs and furniture made of bones, but most of the spaces are empty. Still, it's better than sleeping unprotected in the forest. At least here, everyone will be safe and can finally get a good night's rest.

"Where shall I go?" Hanna asks me.

I grab her hand and squeeze it tight. "You're with me, my little bird. Come. I have a surprise."

Her brows raise quizzically, and I lead her down a tunnel to the left, the torchlights magicked to flame to life with a wave of my hand. We pass by my chambers, sparsely decorated with only a handful of furnishings, and I point it out to her before leading her further down the passage.

"Where are we going?" she asks idly.

"You'll see."

She points at the skull snails climbing up the sides of the walls, each one the size of a fist, a different tiny animal skull housed on their back. "Do you have an infestation problem?"

"They cleanse any bad energy," I tell her. "Helpful at a time like this."

The tunnel leads to a narrow set of stairs, and damp, warm, sulfur-scented air rises to meet us as we descend.

"Here we are," I say to her, gesturing around the small cavern that spreads out from the bottom of the stairs. The air is thick with warm humidity as a steaming creek runs through it, glowing a bright greenish blue as it gathers in a small, bubbling pool. "My private hot springs."

I lead her to the edge and then start taking off my clothes as I nod at her to do the same. "We are both filthy," I tell her. "And normally, I like that, but even I know when enough is enough. Take off your dress."

"I am to go in there?" she asks, eyeing the pool.

"*We* are to go in there. To cleanse. The heat will help our muscles too. You must be sore."

She gives me a haughty smile. "I am always clean and warm, Tuoni, and my muscles don't need any help."

I let out an exasperated sigh. "Fine. Then we're doing it

for me, and I want my wife naked beside me so I can fuck her."

She frowns. "You could have just said that to begin with."

I laugh, taking off my tunic and slipping out of my trousers, the cloth stained with blood and ichor, until I'm completely nude. Naturally, my cock is at full attention.

"I suppose that's very Hanna of you," I tell her. "Never mincing words. Now, take off that dress, or I might have to take it off for you. Better yet, I *will* take it off for you."

I stride over to her, cock bobbing as I walk, which draws her attention. At least I see heat in her eyes, and not the type that comes from the sun. She might not be fully human, but this Goddess still has her primal urges, which is the most human thing of all.

I stop in front of her and reach for her dress. I'm impatient and my fingers are too large for such intricate laces, so I end up ripping the corset laced up over the dress right down the middle, the sound echoing through the cave. The dark red gown, torn, dirty, and a few sizes too big, falls from her shoulders with ease, pooling at her feet like a blood stain.

I growl at the sight of her naked body, the urge to take her here and now nearly too powerful to contain, rumbling eagerly in my chest. Still, I contain myself, waiting for her to take off her boots before I grab her hand and pull her to the hot springs. I enter the water first, steam rising from the glowing aqua, then beckon her to follow.

I wade to the opposite end, where a bench has been carved out, and sit, my arms stretched out over the rim of the pool. I watch as she steps hesitantly yet gracefully into the steaming water. I already feel a million times better. All the horrors I've seen, all the souls that have been lost under my watch in this endless battle for my kingdom, they all seem to fade from my heart and mind as the hot water seeps deep into my muscles, soothing me.

Hanna stops in the middle of the pool, lowering herself so the water is up to her neck. Her hair flows around her like a golden cape, her skin shimmering in shades of gold under the surface.

She's so beautiful, it nearly kills me, but what drives the knife in deeper is that the most beautiful part of her, the essence of all that she is, is gone, frosted over with divinity.

And yet, she swims over to me, fire in her eyes that rivals the heat of the hot springs. She puts her hands around my neck and clasps them there, staring at me as if to say, *well? Are you going to fuck me or not?*

I can't help but grin at her, reaching out to run my thumb over her lips. She takes it into her mouth, sucking slightly, sending a jolt straight to my cock as her eyes hold contact with mine.

"Do you want to remember?" I ask her, voice rough and raw with need. "Do you want to remember who you are?"

She swallows, and I pull my thumb out of her mouth as she says, "Yes."

"Are you sure?" I ask, licking her spit off the side of my thumb, savoring her taste. "Because I feel like this doesn't work if it's not something you want."

"I am certain," she says, raising her chin.

That's all I need.

I grab her face and kiss her deeply, claiming her as mine with each violent sweep of my tongue, forcing her mouth wider, to take as much of me as she can. Our lips meld, wet and building with pent-up frustration, tongues sliding against each other, spurred on by urgency and need.

My hands drop into the water, roaming over her skin, tracing the curves of her body with reverence and care, fingers sinking into her flesh with hunger. Her skin is hot beneath my touch, radiating heat not only from the water but from her core.

"Tuoni," she murmurs as she pulls her lips from mine, her voice barely above a whisper. "Is it so terrible that I don't go back to being Hanna? Can't I just please my body through you?"

Her words make me pause, unraveling something inside me. I try to keep my voice steady as I reply, "We don't have to talk about it right now. We can just be."

Once upon a time, I would have loved to have her as something akin to a mistress, a woman to whom I would pledge no allegiance except through my cock, someone to fuck, someone who wanted me for pleasure and nothing else.

In the beginning, I believed that's what Hanna was to me.

But I am not that God anymore.

I want every single fucking part of this woman.

"Then I need you," she whispers as she kisses down my neck, lust surging through me. "I need you to become her. To become what you want."

I swallow thickly, my heart swelling against my ribcage with love for her, and I kiss her deeply again, my hands exploring every inch of her I can reach. I can feel the rhythm of her heart beating in sync with mine.

But I want you to want it too, I think.

As we float in the hot springs, our bodies entwined like two magnets, my desire for her grows stronger with each passing moment. I want to be inside her again, to feel the true warmth of her body surrounding me once more.

"I will do what I can," I whisper against her skin, kissing her collarbones, savoring the taste of her. "I will give you my all, fairy girl."

She moans softly, her body trembling in response to my touch. Her hands grip my shoulders, pulling me closer to her.

Taking her hips in my hands, I position myself at her cunt, her legs spreading wider, knees settled on the bench. Her body welcomes me, her muscles clenching as I push inside her tight opening and begin to move within her. She's wet as sin, a slippery slickness that makes my eyes roll back in my head. The rhythm of our bodies is in sync with the sound of the rushing water around us, like we are one with the cave and the elements.

"More," she moans, her voice ragged with desire. "Deeper."

Her words are a passionate prayer, fueling my desire for her as I move. Each thrust is filled with a fierce urgency, as if we are trying to escape the world around us while also finding ourselves.

As we continue, our moans mingle with the sound of the water, creating a symphony of lust and need that echoes throughout the cavern. Hanna's body tenses beneath me, and I know she's close.

"That's it," I whisper into her ear, taking the lobe between my teeth. "Let go. Let me take you there. Fly with me, little bird."

She responds to my words, her muscles gripping me tightly as she surrenders to the pleasure that courses through her veins. Her cries fill the air, each one more fervent than the last as her body trembles wildly, her back arching, her neck exposed.

"Tuoni!" she shouts, her voice music to my ears, the echo crumbling a stalactite in the distance. Her words ignite a fire within me, and I thrust harder, deeper, my cock pulsing with the need to claim her completely. My heart races in time with our movements as I bury myself inside her once more.

"I won't stop," I promise her, my voice hoarse with desire. "I'll never stop as long as you want me."

She moans, in the middle of her release, hips bucking to meet each thrust, her body arching beneath me in perfect harmony with my movements as the water sloshes around us. Her eyes are closed, lost in the passion of the moment, but I can see emotion on her brow, the hunger, the need, the pure, unadulterated, raw pleasure that overtakes us.

As we continue to move together, faster, deeper, the water whirling around us in a violent frenzy, I feel myself nearing my own release. The sensation is intense, overwhelming. I'm dizzy with it.

Dizzy with my feelings for her as they overtake me like a storm.

"I love you," I whisper hoarsely into her ear, feeling terribly vulnerable as I share the words for the first time. "I've loved you since the moment I saw you, and I'm sorry I never told you sooner. I didn't know. I was a fool blinded by his own power and ambition and ego, and I didn't know."

Her eyes flick open, and she looks at me with an intensity that takes my breath away. I sense Hanna just underneath, sense her taking stock of my admission and what it means, but she's still buried beneath a sheen of indifference.

I grab her face in my hands and stare at her, willing her to appear. "I just want you to love me again, Hanna," I plead, heart on the line. "It's all I want in the end. You and your heart and your soul, all things you once gave me so freely, all things I hope still burn for me somewhere."

She gives me a wan smile, desire slowly fading from her eyes.

"And I hope I can give you that someday," she says.

Some day, but not today.

CHAPTER THIRTY-FOUR

TUONEN

It's impossible to measure time in this godsforsaken cave. I know days have passed because I feel it in my bones—a numb ache in my ankles from pacing, a dull throb in my head from the stale air. Vipunen's cavern is vast, dripping with echoes, but it has no markers of day or night. The only light comes from bioluminescent lichen that glows faintly along the walls. I've counted their patterns until madness lurks at the edges of my mind.

Did I say lurks?

I meant to say the madness has already overtaken me, for I am going fucking *stir-crazy*.

Rauta, the best of all dogs, lies curled at my feet, whining occasionally. He's restless too. He misses the Library of the Veils and the steady supply of dog bones at Shadow's End. I run a hand over his wiry fur, grateful he's here to ground me, my only friend. Without him, I might have lost track of reality altogether, drifting into the murk of memory and fear. I'm worried about Sarvi, about my father, about Lovia, about Hanna, about the war raging aboveground. Waiting here feels like a betrayal. I want to move, to do something instead of sitting on my haunches and twiddling my damn thumbs.

Vipunen, the giant, remains as cracks of light in the stone, his hidden form blurring with the darkness. When he does speak, it's always in cryptic riddles and vague admonitions. He insists we must stay. He claims the Creator has a plan. He insists that deviating leads to unpredictable ends. I've tried reasoning with him, begging for more information, but his light only dims in response, as if I'm a child with no grasp of destiny.

But I'm not a child, and I don't want to believe in destiny anymore.

I rise to my feet, Rauta stirring at my movement. My spine cracks as I stretch; I've had enough of this waiting. My father is out there, facing who knows what horrors, and I'm stuck in this cave with riddles and silence. Every hour here feels like a blade twisting in my gut. I can't stand it. Either I go forward and join my father in his war, or I go backward and try to save Sarvi. Either way, I have to *go*.

Rauta stands too, ears perked, as if sensing my resolve. He has waited patiently, only dozing fitfully. At least we've had some meager food—dried, bitter strips of fungi and water dripping from stalactites, gathered in briny pools—but it's not enough to blunt my hunger for change. I pace toward the lights in the stone, fists clenched.

"Vipunen," I say, voice echoing. "I'm leaving."

Silence fills the cavern. The water drips and echoes.

"You must stay," he intones, voice like distant thunder. "The Creator has set their pieces on the board. Your role here is essential."

I bare my teeth, frustration boiling over. "Essential? I'm doing nothing but rotting in the dark. My family needs me. The war outside might be spinning out of control, and I can't just sit here waiting for your cryptic approval."

Rauta growls softly, as if agreeing. I place a hand on the dog's back to calm him—not that it helps me much.

The light dances. "Deviations from the plan bring uncertainty. The more you stray, the less certain the outcome. The tapestry frays with every thread pulled."

I laugh, a harsh sound. "You think I care about your tapestry? I care about my father, my sister, about Sarvi. If staying put was so crucial, then why isn't the world safer yet? Why do I feel like everything is unraveling while I waste time here?"

"Impatience leads to ruin," he says.

"I'm already ruined!" I snap, voice cracking. "My horns have been butchered! My mind is being torn apart waiting here! I need to act." I shake my head, resolve flooding through me. "I'm going, and you can't stop me."

I know I sound like a child, but I don't care.

Vipunen sighs, a gust of wind that blows back my hair. "If you go north through these caves, you follow paths not meant for you yet. You risk meeting fates unplanned." He sounds almost sorrowful.

"Then I go south."

"A worse path yet."

I turn away, refusing to engage further with his nonsense. I pick up my sword and beckon Rauta. The dog follows, tail low but determined. Together, we work our way toward the northern tunnels. Vipunen says nothing more. Maybe he knows I won't listen. Good. I'm done with his fucking riddles.

The passage narrows as I head deeper. The ground becomes uneven, stones jutting out at sharp angles. Water drips, a steady plink that marks my progress. Rauta sniffs at the walls, ears twitching, sometimes pausing to look back, as if expecting Vipunen to thunder down the passage after us in a ball of lightning. Yet, no one comes. The giant remains behind with his mysteries.

I press on. My mind reels, though moving is better than sitting. My feet are sore, my stomach hollow. I keep going, using anger and worry as fuel. I imagine my father's face—that stoic determination. He wouldn't wait idly by while I was in danger. He'd move mountains to find me. The thought strengthens my resolve, knowing I'm acting as he would.

Eventually, I hear something. Voices. At first, I think it's a trick of echoing water, but as I move forward, it grows clearer. Voices, human voices, and the faint flicker of torchlight beyond a curve. My heart quickens. Could it be allies?

Or enemies?

Rauta stiffens, ears forward. He looks up at me, tail wagging uncertainly. I slow my steps, pressing against the damp cavern wall, creeping closer. The tunnel widens, opening into a huge space, and I step through a rocky arch before stopping dead in my tracks.

A gaping hole in the cavern's ceiling lets in a shaft of greyish light. Snow must be falling somewhere high above, though I see only swirling mist. The cavern is enormous, large enough to hold an army, and on the opposite end, where torches and lanterns cluster on one side, that's just what I see.

A mass of silhouettes—then a few familiar shapes.

My eyes sting as I realize who they are: my father's tall, looming figure, Lovia's warrior form, Hanna...who seems to be glowing? I keep looking, my mouth agape as I take in the Magician's hooded shape, Vellamo's proud stance, Hanna's father, Torben, leaning on a staff, Tellervo with her antlers, plus five trolls and hundreds of soldiers—mortals!—gathered in tired clusters.

They made it here, into the mountain's heart.

They made it to me.

Relief floods me so intensely, my knees almost give way. I found them. Against all odds, I found them.

"Father!" I call, voice echoing sharply. Heads turn, weapons rising briefly in alarm. I rush forward, Rauta at my heels, barking happily. I see Lovia's astonished face, see Hanna's eyes widen, see my father's stern features melt into shock and joy.

"Tuonen!" his voice cracks as he strides across the cavern. The others part for him as I run to meet him, tears blurring my vision. When we collide, my sword clatters to the ground, and he pulls me into a fierce embrace. I cling to him, feeling like I'm a child again, sobbing into his cloak. It has been so fucking long with so much uncertainty. His hand palms the back of my head, respectful of my horns, his strength holding me together.

"Son," he says to me warmly, pulling away, his own eyes wet.

Lovia steps close, tears glistening on her cheeks as she pulls me into another boisterous hug.

"We found you," she cries into me. "Oh, gods, I had hoped you were all right." She pulls away, and that's when I notice how beat up and broken she looks, one shoulder bandaged and soaked with blood. "We were coming to get you."

Vellamo, Tellervo, and others hover nearby, unsure but hopeful. We embrace, a huddle of worn Gods reunited.

We have only a moment's grace. The cavern feels too still, as if holding its breath, and there's urgency in the air. I pull back to look at them, scanning faces. Everyone is thinner, more worn. They carry visible wounds and invisible scars. My father's eyes flick past me. "How did you escape?"

"It wasn't easy," I admit. I look down at Rauta, who wags his tail proudly. "I had help."

My father gives his dog a proud smile before his grin fades. "And Sarvi?" he asks, fragile hope in his tone.

I shake my head. "My mother… She took both our horns for her magic, to unleash the saints and conjure Rangaista."

"Shhhhh," Tellervo hushes me, a finger to her mouth, looking around warily. "Don't utter that name here."

"Why not?" Hanna asks. Her tone sounds strange, and I notice her hair is lighter, her eyes burning like liquid metal. What the hell happened to her?

"Because we're too close to Shadow's End," Tellervo says, whispering frantically. "Can't you feel it? We should leave this place."

I frown at her. "Where is Tapio and the rest of your family? I know you left Shadow's End in the middle of the night before Louhi could get to you. I hoped you all…"

I trail off. Her eyes brim with tears, and when I look to everyone else, they look equally haunted.

"What happened to them?" I ask quietly.

"Slaughtered by the Old Gods," my father says, his teeth grinding together.

"Fuck," I gasp, feeling sick with sorrow. "Was it—?"

"Not the one we shouldn't speak of," he says quickly before nodding at Tellervo. "You're right, we shouldn't say his name. Not here, under the ground in which the Old Gods used to slumber." He eyes me up and down. "Where did you come from, anyway?"

I jerk my head back. "Vipunen. He kept me confined to his cave for who knows how long. I wanted to go back to rescue Sarvi, or come and find you, but he told me I should stay. So I did until I couldn't take it anymore."

His eyes brighten. "So Sarvi is alive."

"As far as I know. They've been captured by *her*, used for her own gain, but we'll get them back."

My father puts his hand on my shoulder. "That we will."

He looks over the rest of the troops, who stare at him as if awaiting their next command. Who are these humans, and where did they come from? I have so many questions.

"All right," my father says to the crowd. "We move forward and—"

Before he can finish, Rauta growls.

We freeze before a sudden commotion makes us all jerk upward. The hole in the cavern's roof darkens, shadows twisting through it. A foul stench fills the air, followed by a mounting pressure that makes my ears pop. There's something familiar about the smell and, with horror, I realize why I recognize it.

"It's him," I whisper in horror. "It's *him*."

"Enemy incoming!" my father yells, thrusting his sword into the air. "Hold the line!"

Soldiers scramble, raising swords and spears. The Magician, whom I've never seen away from the City of Death, steps forward, hands raised, face a void. Hanna clenches her fists until they burst into flames—most unexpected—while Lovia sets into a fighting stance and readies her blade.

Something massive and malevolent appears at the lip of the hole above, peering down into our sanctuary with glowing crimson eyes. It's the hulking outline and monstrous silhouette of none other than Rangaista.

So, we meet at last.

A hiss, low and dreadful, reverberates through the cavern, filling it with the terrible smell that makes everyone cough, fragments of rock raining down over our heads. Rangaista's burning eyes fix on us, and time slows. I see Hanna move closer to my father, Lovia stepping protectively near Torben and Tellervo. Vellamo's hand tenses on her spear. The Magician's stance shifts, readying some sort of magic. Soldiers form ranks despite the shock. Fear crackles in the air.

The demon's presence sends waves of unease washing

through me. I realize I left Vipunen's cave because I couldn't stand waiting. Now, we're trapped here under the gaze of this monstrous being. The irony isn't lost on me. Vipunen warned me about deviations leading to unpredictable outcomes. If I hadn't left...would this confrontation be happening differently? It's too late to question it now. We've been dealt these cards, and now we have to play them.

Rauta snarls, hackles raised. I rest a calming hand on the dog's back, though I can't calm myself. My father's grip on his sword is white-knuckled, his jaw set. Lovia stands tall, shoulders squared, no hesitation in her stance. I quickly pick up my sword and hold it firmly in my grip, adrenaline spiking through me.

Rangaista shifts, dislodging stones that clatter down around us. Its massive form partially blocks the opening, and I see flashes of a stormy sky beyond. The demon's voice, if it can speak, hasn't manifested yet. Instead, it watches, a predator toying with prey. I recall stories of this demon—how it's the epitome of evil, how no spell can fully contain its wrath.

It's unbeatable. Unstoppable.

And my grandfather.

Lovia glances at me, a thousand words unspoken. I nod slightly, understanding. The blood of that beast runs in us. We must stand together, no matter what comes next. I left Vipunen's cave to act, to stop waiting. Now, action finds me in the form of a nightmare looming overhead.

Perhaps the final battle.

The one that might end us all.

Rangaista shifts, tendrils of darkness rippling around its form as a guttural rumble escapes it. Soldiers tighten their grips on weapons, and I feel Rauta tremble beside me. The air grows colder, as if the demon's presence sucks warmth from the world.

Hanna steps forward, raising a hand that glows faintly. Whatever she has become, whatever has happened to her, there is no doubt she's powerful, the only one here who doesn't seem to show any fear. My father aligns beside her, Lovia on the other side. I take my place next to my sister, shoulder to shoulder with my family, forging a line of defiance. We might be outmatched, but we are not alone.

Rangaista lets out a sound like distant thunder. The cavern's silence breaks as soldiers swear under their breath. The Magician's stars flicker, Torben's staff hums faintly, and I think of Vipunen's warnings.

Deviations and unpredictable ends. Maybe we are off-script now. Maybe destiny itself trembles, the same destiny I cast to the side.

Either way, the demon descends.

Coming for us all.

CHAPTER THIRTY-FIVE

DEATH

THE CAVERN TREMBLES AS RANGAISTA COMES DOWN, ITS massive frame blotting out the grey light from the opening above. Stone crumbles beneath its weight, the sound like grinding bones. The demon's glowing eyes, fierce and unrelenting, scan the cavern, as if savoring its prey before striking. Shadows writhe around its colossal form, tendrils of cold creeping across the ground, swallowing what little light remains.

Every instinct in me screams to act, to protect, to fight. My sword is already in hand, the worn steel humming with latent energy. Around me, soldiers stiffen, shields raised, weapons trembling in their grips. They've fought against Louhi's undead hordes and the Old Gods, but this is different. This is something ancient and primal, something that carries with it the weight of despair itself.

This is Rangaista, the devil in the flesh.

Or, as Hanna once called him, the final boss, though frankly, I don't think he's the boss of anyone.

Hanna steps closer, her light flickering faintly in the gloom. She glances at me, her golden eyes clouded with hesitation. I know she feels it—the fear that if she uses her power, she might lose herself forever, that whatever humanity is waiting to emerge might be buried for good. She doesn't say it, but I see it in the way her fingers twitch, in the way her breath catches.

I want to tell her it's okay, that I'll still love her no matter what she becomes, but the words won't come. I don't have the luxury of reassurance. Not now. Not when this monstrosity threatens to destroy everything.

"Hold your lines!" I shout, my voice cutting through the growing chaos. "Do not falter!"

The soldiers respond with a collective roar, a feeble attempt to rally against their terror. I glance at Lovia, who stands firm beside me, her blade drawn, her face grim. She meets my eyes, and in that moment, I see both a fearless warrior and my daughter, someone who has endured so much and yet refuses to break.

Rangaista roars, the sound reverberating through the cavern like an avalanche. Its slick claws rake across the walls, sending more debris raining down, landing on the cave floor like bombs. Soldiers scatter, some tripping over themselves, others instinctively charging forward.

"Keep your formation!" Lovia yells, her voice sharp and commanding, a true general.

The first wave of spears and arrows flies through the air, striking Rangaista's hulking body. Most bounce harmlessly off its shadowy black hide of fur and hard, puckered casing, but a few manage to embed in the softer gaps between joints. It doesn't flinch. Instead, it lashes out with a massive arm, its claws cleaving through soldiers as though they were paper. Blood splatters across the cavern floor.

"No!" Vellamo cries, rushing forward, her black armor gleaming as she strikes at the demon's leg with her spear. Her blow lands, chipping away a fragment of its hard leathery casing, but Rangaista reacts instantly. Its tail, a spiked, serpentine appendage, whips around and slams into her side.

The force sends her flying across the cavern, her scream cutting through the chaos. She crashes into the far wall, crumpling to the ground. Her arm—her entire left arm—lies severed a few feet away, blood pooling around it.

"Vellamo!" Lovia shouts, starting toward her.

"Stay back!" I bark, stopping her. "She's still alive. Focus on the fight!"

Lovia hesitates, fury flashing in her eyes, but she obeys. I glance at Vellamo lying there. She's a Goddess; she has the strength to pull through. I have to believe that.

Hanna steps forward, her hands glowing faintly. She looks at me again, and this time, there's a question in her gaze, a plea for guidance.

"Do it," I say, my voice steady despite the storm of emotions inside me. "Whatever it takes, Hanna. We need you."

She nods, her face hardening. She raises her hands, and a burst of light erupts from her palms, cutting through the darkness. The cavern floods with a golden glow, and for a moment, Rangaista recoils, its jagged form steaming as if burned. The soldiers cheer, emboldened by the sight of their queen's power.

But Hanna's light is not the sun at full strength. It's controlled, restrained. She's holding back, and I know why. The fear in her eyes speaks to the humanity still within her.

Rangaista takes the moment to lunge at her, its claws slashing through the air. I move without thinking, intercepting its attack with my sword. The impact reverberates through my arms, but I hold firm, driving the blade into its tough, leathery hide.

"Now!" I shout to the soldiers.

They charge again, swords and arrows aimed at the creature's exposed joints and vulnerable spots. Lovia leads the charge, her strikes precise and relentless, followed by her brother, both fighting with the skill and grace Vipunen instilled in them in their youth.

If I wasn't so focused, I would be damn proud.

The Magician hurls bursts of black void, each impact creating rivers of a starry night sky that wrap around the demon's body, squeezing it. Torben frantically chants, weaving protective wards that shimmer faintly around us.

The battle is chaos. Soldiers die horribly, crushed underfoot or impaled by Rangaista's claws. The demon's tail lashes out, sweeping through our ranks, leaving carnage in its wake. The air is thick with the stench of blood and burning hair.

Vellamo, despite her injury, rises to her feet. Her face is pale, but her right hand grips her pearl spear with unyielding determination. She plunges it into a weak spot in Rangaista's side, drawing a roar of pain from the beast.

"Hold it down!" I command, lunging forward. My sword finds purchase in a gap near its shoulder, and I twist, trying to sever whatever unholy sinew holds it together.

Hanna's light intensifies. She steps closer, her golden aura shimmering, her hands trembling. I can see her resolve wavering, the fear battling with her instinct to protect.

"Don't stop!" I call to her. "You're stronger than this thing. End it!"

She takes a deep breath and then raises her hands again. This time, the light explodes outward in a blinding surge as it tears a violent scream from her throat. It engulfs Rangaista, searing into its flesh. The demon howls, its form cracking and splintering into two pieces like a too-hot log on a fire.

"Hanna!" Lovia shouts in awe, shielding her eyes from the brilliance. "You did it!"

The light grows unbearable, filling every corner of the cavern. Soldiers fall back, retreating from the heat and radiance. I force myself to stay close, my blade still buried in the demon's upper side, making sure it's dead.

With a final, deafening roar, Rangaista collapses into the ground, cleaved in two, creating a fissure of fire that runs across the cavern, steam and acrid smoke rising from the crack. Silence falls save for the ragged breathing of the survivors, everyone watching to see if the demon has truly been destroyed.

Then, the fissure opens, slowly at first, flames licking out, giving us enough time to run before it opens wide enough to swallow the back half of beast, leaving the head behind, a long, black, furry tongue rolling out.

Now, it's over.

It's done.

Hanna collapses to her knees, her light fading. I rush to her side, pulling her into my arms. She's trembling, her skin hot to the touch.

"You did it," I say, my voice soft. "You saved us."

She looks up at me, her eyes filled with exhaustion. "I'm not sure I did."

I blink at her, confused. We made it, didn't we? Around us, the soldiers begin to gather, checking the wounded, retrieving the dead. Lovia kneels beside Vellamo, who clutches the stump of her arm, blood pouring through her fingers, her face pale but resolute, Tellervo already trying her green magic to help it heal.

Then, I hear it: a distant voice, faint and echoing.

"Father!"

I whirl around, my heart plummeting.

Tuonen?

Where is he? He was with us when the battle began.

"Tuonen?" I call out, my voice echoing through the cavern.

"Over there!" General Suvari shouts, pointing toward the

far side of the chamber.

I run as fast as I can, panic pressing against my chest. The soldiers part for me, their faces pale. I see the fissure in the ground, the edges scorched and crumbling.

And there is Tuonen, inside the crevice, his head barely above the fire, his arms hanging on to the edge for dear life but slipping, slowly slipping.

"Tuonen!" I scream, running and diving onto the ground, sliding across the cave floor, arms outstretched for him.

My fingers just brush the tips of his.

I almost reach him.

I almost have him.

I almost...

Then he screams as he slips, disappearing into the fires below until his screams abruptly snuff out.

"No," I whisper, staring at the dark void. My son. My boy.

"No!" I roar, scrambling so I'm staring over the edge into flames that fan and then fade into nothingness.

Lovia reaches my side, her face pale and stricken. "He was fighting alongside me," she says, her voice trembling. "He was here. I turned away..."

She breaks off, her composure shattering.

I stare into the abyss. The cavern feels impossibly silent. The victory, the relief—it all turns to ash in my mouth.

"Tuonen!" I shout, my voice raw. It echoes back to me, hollow and mocking.

Lovia places a trembling hand on my shoulder. "He...he might still be alive," she says softly. "There might be a way to..."

Her words falter, but I seize on them, clinging to the faintest hope.

"He's not gone," I say, rising to my feet. "I'll find him. I'll go after him."

"Tuoni..." Hanna begins, but I cut her off.

"I *will* find him," I say, my voice resolute. "This isn't over."

The others exchange uneasy glances, but no one argues. The weight of the moment presses down on us all. We may have defeated Rangaista, but the cost was higher than I was ever willing to give.

My son.

My son!

As the cavern grows darker, I stare into the void, my resolve hardening. But the void stares back at me, silent and impenetrable. My heart pounds against my ribs, each beat a hammer of denial. Tuonen cannot be gone. My son cannot be lost. He is too strong, too clever. He has survived too much for it to end like this.

The silence mocks me. Even the echoes of my calls have faded, swallowed by the abyss. Hanna's hand tightens on my shoulder, her touch warm and grounding, but I feel no comfort. Around us, the soldiers shift uneasily. They are afraid—not just for what we've lost, but for what comes next. Where am I leading them? How can I protect them if I can't even protect my own son?

How does a God of Death grieve for his own blood?

Lovia stands frozen beside me, her eyes locked on the fissure, her chin trembling. "We'll find him," she says, her voice hollow but insistent. "There has to be a way."

Before I can respond, the ground beneath us trembles. A deep, guttural noise rises from the fissure, a sound like stone grinding against bone. Soldiers step back, weapons raised, their nerves frayed to the breaking point. The cavern feels alive again, pulsing with a dark, ominous energy.

Then, with a violent burst, something erupts from the crack. Rocks and debris fly into the air, and everyone ducks for cover as a wave of acrid heat washes over us and the cavern fills with a choking, sulfurous stench. I shield Lovia instinctively, my body reacting before my mind can process the moment.

When the dust settles, I see it: not a monster or another attack, but a lifeless form.

Tuonen.

His body lies sprawled on the ground, thrown from the depths like an offering—or a mockery. His skin is marred with deep gashes and searing burns, one of his horns is broken in half, jagged and raw, and his once bright eyes are dull, staring at nothing.

"Tuonen!" Lovia screams, rushing to his side. She collapses beside him, her shaking hands hovering over his chest, as if afraid to touch him, afraid to confirm what she already knows. Her breath comes in gasps, sharp and ragged. "No, no, no..."

I stand frozen, the world narrowing to this single, impossible sight. My son, my blood, lies before me, lifeless. The cavern feels colder, emptier, as if the air itself mourns. Slowly, I kneel beside Lovia, my hands quivering as I reach for him.

"Tuonen," I whisper, my voice breaking. "My boy..."

My fingers brush his face, cool and unresponsive. There is no trace of the mischievous spark that once lit his eyes, no sign of the defiance that had driven him to challenge me. He is gone, and the weight of that truth crushes me until I fear my heart is lost to Oblivion too.

Lovia presses her hands to his chest, as if she can will his heart to beat again. "He can't be gone," she chokes out. "No. No, no. He can't be. He's Tuonen. He's strong. He always comes back. He—" Her words dissolve into sobs, raw and desperate.

Hanna steps forward, her face pale and grief-stricken. She kneels on Tuonen's other side, her hands glowing faintly with golden light. "I can try," she says, her voice tight with determination. "I can try to bring him back. Perhaps I have that power."

I don't stop her. I watch, my breath caught in my throat as she lays her hands on his broken body.

But nothing happens, even as she closes her eyes and hums, her hands glowing with the sun's rays.

The light can't reach him.

There is nothing.

Nothing but death.

My son has been taken me, forever gone.

"Stop," I say sharply, my voice cutting through the tension like a blade. Hanna freezes, her light flickering. "It's too late. His soul is gone," I say, forcing the words past the lump in my throat. "I would feel it if he was still here. He's beyond even your power. He's beyond this world."

Her light fades, and she sits back, her hands falling to her lap, staring at him with empty eyes.

The soldiers around us are silent, their faces pale and somber. Rauta, my trusty hound, howls in agony before he lies down next to Tuonen and whines pitifully. Even Vellamo, despite her own pain, watches with an expression of profound sorrow. The Magician stands at a distance, his hood pulled low, galaxies swirling in his unseen gaze. For once, he offers no cryptic words, no riddles. There is only silence.

Lovia leans over Tuonen's body, her forehead resting against his. "You can't leave me," she whispers. "You can't... You promised." Her tears fall onto his burnt and blood-stained clothes, her grief raw and unrestrained. "You promised you would always take care of me."

I reach out, my hand resting on her shoulder. "Lovia," I say softly, though my voice shakes. "He wouldn't want you to break. He fought for us, for all of us. We have to honor that."

She turns to me, her face streaked with tears and rage.

"Honor him? How? By letting him die while we keep going? By pretending this is just another loss?"

"No," I say firmly, though the words tear at me. "By finishing what we started. By making sure his sacrifice wasn't in vain."

Her anger falters, replaced by a crushing despair. She nods slowly, her head bowed. "I can't do this without him," she whispers.

"You can," I say, trying to give her strength I don't feel. "You're stronger than you think. And he believed in you. That's why he fought so hard for us."

The cavern feels impossibly quiet, the weight of Tuonen's death pressing down heavily into our chests. I look at Hanna, her gaze blank. Still, she steps closer, her hand brushing mine. It's a small comfort, but it steadies me.

"We need to give him a proper burial," Vellamo says gently. "He deserves that."

"We do. In his home," I tell her. "We're taking him to Shadow's End."

Though the thought of laying him to rest feels unbearable, I lift Tuonen's body in my arms, his weight both familiar and alien. He feels lighter than he should, as if, even in death, he refuses to burden me. Lovia walks beside me, her steps heavy, her shoulders slumped.

The soldiers follow in silence, their heads bowed. We move toward the far end of the cavern, continuing toward the end.

CHAPTER THIRTY-SIX

LOVIA

GRIEF FEELS A LOT LIKE WHAT I IMAGINE DEATH TO FEEL LIKE.

At times, terrible and violent; at others, slow and insidious. But in the end, it's a severing of something vital inside you. A door that closes, never to be reopened.

The cavern air is thick and damp, clinging to my skin like a funeral shroud. Our procession moves in solemn silence, the only sounds the crunch of boots on gravel and the distant drip of water echoing through the tunnels. My father walks ahead of me, his shoulders heavy beneath his cloak as he cradles Tuonen's lifeless body in his arms. Each step he takes is deliberate, the weight of grief and responsibility bearing down on him.

I walk a few paces behind, the Magician and Hanna flanking me, Torben, Tellervo, and Vellamo at my back. Every step feels like it echoes in my chest, reverberating against the hollow space where my brother used to be. Tuonen's absence is a wound I can't stop pressing, and every time I glance at my father, the sight of him holding Tuonen's body drives the blade deeper. I thought losing Rasmus was the worst thing that ever happened to me, but I was wrong.

I was so fucking wrong.

No one speaks—the air is too heavy with loss for words. Vellamo staggers alongside the rest of us, her severed arm hastily bandaged with some of Tellervo's green poultice after Rangaista's attack. She doesn't complain, doesn't falter, but I see the strain in her jaw and the way she clutches her side for balance. Tellervo walks close to her, offering silent support, her small frame trembling with every step.

I glance at the Magician. His face is a black void, the stars faint, as if all the life has been drained from him. And yet, he's the only one who doesn't appear crushed by the weight of what happened. It should comfort me, but it doesn't. He said that things change, and perhaps this is the new path, one he didn't see coming. It would explain why he didn't do anything about Tapio, about Rasmus.

But if he knew about Tuonen and didn't tell me... I can't bear to think of it. I know the Magician has been inside me in ways I can't even explain, making me writhe in heavenly ecstasy and bend time, but if he knew about Tuonen, I would probably kill him, or at least attempt to. How does one kill the universe?

Hanna occasionally quickens her pace to keep step beside my father, brushing his arm. She's trying to offer comfort, though I can't tell if he accepts it. He hasn't spoken since we left the cavern where Tuonen fell, his silence more suffocating than the air down here.

The caves seem endless, a labyrinth of shadows and echoes. My torch flickers weakly, casting feeble light on the jagged walls. I've always hated the caves, the oppressive darkness, the feeling of being buried alive. Now, it feels even worse. Every corner, every shadow, feels like it's watching us, waiting for a moment of weakness to strike again.

We eventually reach another cave, nearly as big as the one before. There's something strangely familiar about it and I'm about to voice this when Hanna stops and says, "I know this place. I've been here before."

My father halts at the entrance, his grip on Tuonen tightening. He looks up at the empty rock face, his jaw clenched, his eyes shadowed. "Vipunen," he calls, his voice steady but low. "We've come back. Show yourself. If you had anything to do with this…" his threat trails off.

Vipunen! That's why this place is familiar. I've been in here many times before, fighting with the giant, except I was always wearing a blind mask, so I never really saw what the cave looked like—nor Vipunen, for that matter. Apparently, if we lay eyes on him, we die.

"Maybe we don't want him to show himself," I say to my father. "Remember?"

But it doesn't matter. The only response is the faint rustle of air through the tunnels, then silence.

"Do you think he's gone?" Tellervo asks softly, her voice trembling.

My father doesn't answer. Walks forward and sets Tuonen down gently on a flat slab of stone, his movements careful, reverent. Hanna stands beside him, her face pale and drawn, but the aura around her still glows, reminding us she's no longer the Hanna she once was.

I have to admit, I'm actually envious of her. I would give anything to not feel what I'm feeling right now, would give anything to just have this horrible, crushing weight lifted from me even for a mere second.

"I'll scout ahead," I say, unable to bear the stillness any longer. My legs itch to move, my mind desperate for distraction.

"No one should be alone," the Magician says, his voice calm but firm.

I glare at him. "If you know something, say something," I snap at him, hand on my sword. "I'm not going far."

He doesn't argue, but I feel his gaze follow me as I move toward the far end of the cavern. I hear my father ask, "Where is she going?" but I keep walking.

The air grows colder as I step deeper into the shadows. My torch flickers, casting distorted shapes on the walls. My heart pounds, and I tell myself it's just the weight of everything that happened, not fear. Not weakness.

Then, I hear it.

A whisper.

It's faint, almost like a breeze slipping through cracks in the stone, but it carries a strange cadence, as if forming words I can't quite understand. I freeze, my grip tightening on my sword.

"Vipunen?" I call, my voice barely above a whisper.

No answer.

The whisper comes again, softer this time, curling around my ears like smoke. It seems to beckon me, pulling me toward a narrow crevice in the rock. My pulse quickens, and despite every instinct screaming at me to turn back, I step closer.

Surely, if something bad was to happen, the Magician would have said something, right?

"Vipunen?" I say again, louder this time. "Give me a warning if that's you, I don't want turn to stone, or whatever it is you do."

The whisper doesn't respond, but it grows clearer, sharper, as if leading me somewhere. I squeeze through the crevice, the stone scraping against my armor and my injured shoulder, making me wince. On the other side, the tunnel widens into a small chamber. It's dimly lit by a faint blue glow emanating from veins in the rock.

The whisper stops.

I turn in a slow circle, my sword and lantern raised, searching for the source of the sound. The chamber is empty, but the air feels wrong, heavy with a presence I can't see. My breath fogs in the chill, and I feel the hair on the back of my neck stand on end.

"Vipunen, if this is one of your riddles, I'm not in the mood," I say, my voice echoing off the walls.

A low chuckle answers me.

My blood runs cold.

"Not Vipunen," a familiar voice says, smooth and icy.

I whirl around, but I already know who it is.

She steps out of the shadows, her pale green, ageless face looking extra sickly in the blue light. Her giant ram horns curl back from her knobby forehead like black sentinels, her eyes gleaming with triumph as her leathery wings tuck in behind her tall form. She looks almost ethereal, like a nightmare made flesh.

"Louhi," I breathe, my voice tight with hatred.

"My daughter," she says, her tone dripping with mockery. "You've grown strong, just like I hoped you would."

I grip my sword tighter, every muscle in my body tensing. "Stay back."

She tilts her head, her expression unreadable. "Is that any way to greet your mother? After all, I've come such a long way to see you."

"You're no mother of mine," I snap, stepping back toward the crevice. "And I'm not going anywhere with you."

Louhi moves faster than I expect, her hand shooting out to grab my wrist. Her strength is inhuman, her grip like iron. I try to pull away, but she holds me fast.

"You've been running from your destiny long enough," she says, her voice a venomous whisper. "It's time you embraced what you were born to be."

"I'd rather die," I hiss, twisting in her grasp.

"So dramatic, just like your father," Louhi smirks, her eyes flashing with cruel amusement. "My dear, you have no idea what's in store for you. But don't worry—I'll make sure you understand. In time."

Before I can react, shadows rise from the ground, coiling around my legs and arms. They move like living things, cold and unyielding, pinning me in place. I struggle, panic surging through me, but the shadows only tighten their grip.

"Let me go!" I shout, my voice echoing through the chamber, my sword and lantern crashing to the ground.

Louhi leans in, her face only inches from mine. "Don't fight it, Loviatar. This is your destiny."

The shadows drag me backward, their cold tendrils pulling me deeper into the chamber. Louhi follows, her laughter echoing around me like a chilling melody.

"Help!" I scream, my voice raw. "Someone help me!"

But the shadows swallow my cries, and the last thing I see before the darkness claims me is my mother's triumphant smile.

CHAPTER THIRTY-SEVEN

HANNA

VIPUNEN'S CAVE IS VAST AND SHADOWED, ITS WALLS HUMMING with faint energy, but the glow that once emanated from the stone giant is gone. The absence feels wrong, as if something sacred has been extinguished. I stand near the center of the space, trying to absorb the silence, but it grates against me. I thought when I used my powers to destroy Rangaista, I would lose all ties to my humanity, for good this time, but now that I'm surrounded by grief and loss, it's starting to creep back, prickling at the edges of my consciousness.

I welcome it, but the threat of feeling my own grief makes me hesitate.

It scares me.

But fear is a human emotion, is it not?

I glance at Tuoni. He's seated on a stone ledge, holding Tuonen's lifeless body as if he could still protect him. His broad shoulders are hunched, his head bowed. I feel a flicker of sadness, but it's distant, like hearing a song through water. I should feel more for this moment. Tuonen was kind to me when I felt like an outsider to the family. He was funny, playful, always wanting more from life, even in this land of the dead.

But now, he's gone, and I am...I am the sun, aren't I? I'm supposed to be above the complicated lives of these humans and lesser Gods, these very beings scattered throughout the cavern like ants.

Vellamo leans against a jagged pillar, her severed arm crudely wrapped in cloth. Tellervo sits beside her, whispering quiet reassurances. Rauta lies near Tuoni, his massive head resting on his paws, his red eyes fixed sadly on the boy he was too late to save. My father and General Suvari huddle nearby, speaking in low tones, their words a murmur in the oppressive stillness.

Slowly, very slowly, we become less and less.

How many of us will remain in the end?

I move to the edge of the cavern and peer into the darkness of the surrounding tunnels. My steps echo faintly, and I force myself to listen for something—anything. It's instinct, I think, or maybe just a way to distract myself from the emptiness gnawing at my chest.

Then, I realize something's wrong.

"Where is Lovia?" I ask, my voice cutting through the quiet.

Heads turn. Tuoni lifts his gaze, and I see the panic in his eyes before he composes himself.

"She headed in that direction," the Magician says, pointing at the corner of the cavern.

I run to the nearest side tunnel. "Lovia?" I call, my voice sharp. The air feels colder here, heavier. Something isn't right.

Up ahead, I spot a narrow crevice, just wide enough for someone to slip through. My heart—or whatever remains of it—tightens as a whisper curls through the air, faint and disjointed. I don't catch the words, but I feel their weight and familiarity.

"Lovia!" I yell again.

I squeeze through the crevice, scraping my arms against the rough stone, but I feel no pain. I never do anymore. On the other side, the chamber opens, dimly lit by veins of faint blue in the walls. My gaze lands on the ground first—a patch of disturbed dirt and moss, as if there was a struggle. Then, I see it: a broken lantern and a sword.

Lovia never goes anywhere without her blade.

I rush forward and kneel, my fingers brushing the hilt. The whisper comes again, clearer this time.

Pick up the sword and try again.

My breath catches. The words are unmistakable. It's what Vipunen used to say to me when I failed in training. I turn, searching the chamber for any sign of the giant, but it's empty.

"Hanna!" Tuoni's voice cuts through my thoughts. He appears in the crevice, his frame filling the narrow opening, his eyes scanning the room.

"She's gone," I say, holding up the sword as proof.

Tuoni strides forward, his movements sharp with urgency. He kneels beside me, his gloved hand brushing the dirt as his nostrils flare and his face darkens.

"The air stinks of Louhi," he growls.

Of course. Who else would be behind this? My stomach twists, a flicker of rage breaking through my detached calm.

Tuoni rises abruptly, moving toward the crevice. "I'll follow her," he says, his voice low and dangerous.

"No," I say, standing and blocking his path. "It's a trap. Louhi wants you to follow. She knows you'll come for her."

He glares at me, his silver eyes gleaming like storm clouds. "She has my daughter, the last of my children."

"And she'll have you too if you go," I snap, my voice rising.

"We don't have time for this. Lovia wouldn't want us to walk into her mother's trap. She would want us to stay on course."

Tuoni's hands clench into fists, and for a moment, I think he'll argue. But then, he exhales sharply, his shoulders sagging. He nods, albeit reluctantly.

Pick up the sword and try again, I hear the whisper once more.

I look down at Lovia's blade still in my hand. It feels heavy but also right, as if it belongs with me now. I tighten my grip and slide it into the belt of my torn dress. "We'll find her," I say, my voice steady. "But not like this."

We return to the main cavern where the others are waiting. They look up as we enter, their faces drawn and weary. Tuoni says nothing, but his expression is enough. They know Lovia is gone.

"We move," Tuoni says after a long silence. His voice is hard, unyielding. "Vipunen isn't here. Louhi has taken Lovia. The Crystal Caves are our only path now."

No one argues.

We gather what little we have and head into the tunnel leading to the Crystal Caves. The air grows colder as we descend, the walls glinting faintly with crystalline veins. The passage narrows, forcing us into a single file, Tuoni leading the way. He carries Tuonen's body wrapped in a cloak, his steps measured but relentless, the weight of his grief making his movements heavier with each passing step.

I follow close behind, my father just ahead of me, his staff clicking softly against the stone floor. The others trail in silence, the echo of their footsteps the only sound. Even Rauta moves quietly, his ears pinned back.

When the tunnel opens again, the sight takes my breath away. I've been here before, but even so, it doesn't fail to impress. The Crystal Caves are otherworldly, their walls shimmering with countless facets of light. It reminds me of the sun, except here, the crystals are cold and pastel. Waterways cut through the stone, their surfaces glittering like liquid diamonds. The air is crisp, filled with chimes and the faint sound of trickling water, as if the world itself is whispering a melody.

Tuoni halts on the crystalline shore, his gaze sweeping over the scene. A small boat rests on the moss and sand, its hull battered but intact, as if waiting for us. With a sinking feeling I realize this is the boat Tuonen probably took to escape from Shadow's End, and from the weight on Tuoni's brow, I know he realizes the same.

Without a word, he strides toward it, placing Tuonen's body gently inside. For a moment, he lingers, his hand resting on the cloak covering his son. Then, he straightens, his expression hardening.

"Get in," he says to us, his voice low but commanding. The boat is small, only able to fit a few bodies. He looks to the troops behind us, still filing out into the cave. "The rest of you, stay behind and wait for further instructions from my scouts. You should be safe here," he adds, though I can tell he doesn't believe it. "Otherwise, if you're a good swimmer, you'll be taking a dip. Perhaps, Vellamo, you can provide some assistance?"

"Of course," Vellamo says as she approaches the edge of the water, closing her eyes and chanting something that causes the water to ripple away from her. She does this for a minute while the Keskelli, standing nearby, exchange nods before wading into the water, their massive forms breaking the surface like living boulders. They kneel, allowing some of the braver troops to climb onto their shoulders.

Vellamo then raises her remaining hand, and the water stirs. A massive shape rises from the depths—a whale made of bones, its skeletal frame gleaming in the crystalline light.

The soldiers gasp as it emerges, silent and imposing, its empty eye sockets glowing faintly.

"Some of you can ride with my kind," Vellamo says, her voice quiet but commanding as she gestures to the whale.

The troops move quickly, climbing onto the whale's back as Vellamo steps into the water, her form blending seamlessly with the currents. She glances at Tuoni, her expression unreadable, then begins to swim alongside the whale, her movements graceful despite the bandaged stump of her missing arm, until she dives beneath the water and disappears.

The boat rocks gently as I climb in beside Tuoni. My father takes the seat opposite me, his staff resting across his knees, the glow of the shimmering walls reflecting faintly on his lined face. Tellervo, her expression solemn in the dim light, sits behind us, General Suvari taking up the oars, in charge of the rowing. Rauta jumps in last, heading to the prow, where he proudly stands on patrol, his red eyes scanning the water.

The boat pushes off, gliding silently along the waterway. The trolls swim beside us, their broad shoulders breaking the surface, four or five armed troops riding each Keskelli. The bone whale follows, its hollow eyes glowing faintly beneath the water, even more soldiers clinging to its back.

For a time, there is nothing but the sound of the water and the faint echoes of our passage. The crystalline walls shimmer with an ethereal glow, casting fragmented light across our faces. It should be beautiful, but the air is heavy with grief. I can feel it pressing down on all of us, unspoken but undeniable.

It feels like it's coming for me, waiting just below my skin.

The boat glides silently across the water, with only the faint sound of oars cutting through the glassy surface. I stare ahead, focused on the shimmering walls, the reflections dancing below, trying not to let the weight of everything press too heavily on me. Then, I hear a soft splash.

At first, I think it's the oars hitting the water, but then, something darts beneath the hull—a flash of kaleidoscopic light. My breath catches. Another splash, closer this time, and a fish breaks the surface.

No, it's not a fish. It's a mermaid, no larger than a doll, with iridescent scales and delicate features. She swims beside the boat, her luminous form glowing faintly in the dim cavern light.

"Bell," I whisper, my voice trembling with recognition.

"Hanna?" Bell chirps, her voice high and curious. She tilts her head, studying me. "I told you I'd see you again! Vellamo put out the call, and here I am. Did you miss me?"

Tuoni glances down at her briefly, his silver eyes distant, as if he has already dismissed her presence. Bell stares at him, unimpressed, and sticks out her tongue when he looks away. Her bright eyes narrow, scrutinizing me. "What's wrong with you?" she asks. "Why are you glowing? You seem…off." She pauses, looking past me to the others. "Everyone is off. What happened?"

I can't answer. Her words pierce through something in me, striking a memory buried beneath layers of divinity. I stare at her, and for a moment, I feel the weight of who I used to be. There's a flicker of emotion—affection, maybe? She was my friend, wasn't she? But it's distant, as though I'm viewing it through fogged glass.

Before I can respond, the water ahead churns violently.

"There!" Tuoni cries out, pointing at the water as ripples spread out in wavering circles, and a low, menacing growl reverberates through the cavern. I straighten up and freeze as a massive shadow rises from the depths.

Rauta starts barking like mad as the water explodes in a spray of foam and brine. A monster from the depths emerges, its grotesque form a monstrosity of jagged fins, twisting tentacles, and barnacle-encrusted flesh. His molten eyes glow with a terrible, ancient rage, and his roar shakes the very walls of the cavern, sending cascades of water down the crystalline stalactites.

"Iku-Turso!" my father yells. "The Old God of the sea! Everyone, hold on!"

The boat rocks violently, nearly capsizing. Soldiers cry out as the bone whale rears back, its skeletal form dwarfed by the leviathan. Bell shrieks, diving beneath the water as a massive tentacle lashes out, slamming against the boat and sending a spray of water over us.

Tuoni jumps onto the prow in front of Rauta, his sword drawn, his silver eyes blazing. "Hold steady!" he commands, his voice cutting through the chaos.

I spring into action, reaching back to grab the tiller, my hands trembling as Iku-Turso's massive form towers over us. His tentacles writhe, slamming into the water with thunderous force. Bell resurfaces briefly, her tiny form darting frantically, but a massive tentacle sweeps down, snatching her from the water.

"Bell!" I scream, my voice raw and desperate. I lunge forward instinctively, but there's nothing I can do. The Old God's gaping maw opens, jagged teeth glinting, and in one brutal motion, he devours her whole.

The sounds of her scream and snapping bones fill the air.

Something inside me shatters. The grief is immediate and all-consuming, breaking through the cold detachment I've clung to. My chest tightens, and I feel my humanity surge back to the surface, raw and overwhelming. Tears blur my vision, and for the first time in what feels like an eternity, I feel pain—real, crushing pain.

Bell.

Tuonen.

Tapio.

Even Rasmus.

All gone.

And if we don't fight this beast, I'll lose the rest of them too.

Tuoni doesn't hesitate. He leaps from the boat, his sword flashing as he lands on Iku-Turso's massive back. The creature roars, twisting and thrashing, trying to dislodge him. Tuoni clings tightly, his blade carving deep into the beast's barnacle-encrusted hide. Each strike sends a spray of brackish water and ichor into the air.

The boat lurches as another tentacle slams into the water beside us, sending waves crashing over the sides. I tighten my grip on the tiller, trying to keep us steady, but the chaos is relentless. Soldiers fire arrows and throw spears from the backs of the trolls, their weapons barely scratching the Old God's impenetrable hide.

Vellamo rises from the water, her remaining hand glowing with an eerie blue light. She summons a massive wave, directing it at Iku-Turso. The water crashes into him with the force of a tsunami, momentarily staggering him as it rocks our boat. But the Old God roars in defiance, his tentacles lashing out wildly.

One tentacle sweeps toward the bone whale, striking it with devastating force. The whale fractures, its skeletal frame crumbling into the water. Soldiers scream as they're thrown into the depths, their cries quickly swallowed by the chaos.

Tuoni climbs higher on Iku-Turso's back, his sword flashing again and again. He reaches the beast's head, driving the blade deep into its molten eye. Iku-Turso howls in agony, his thrashing growing more violent. The boat pitches dangerously, and I cling to the sides, my knuckles white.

"General Suvari!" Tuoni shouts, his voice carrying over the cacophony. "Take the helm! Hanna, do your worst!"

The general scrambles to my side, taking the tiller as Tuoni leaps back into the fray. But instead of summoning my sun power, I grab Lovia's sword. It's what Vipunen would have wanted me to do.

I run to the front of the boat as it rocks back and forth then take aim and a deep breath before I fling the sword toward the beast, as easy as throwing a knife. It spins through the air, and the blade strikes true, embedding itself in another eyeball. Iku-Turso roars, his massive form writhing in pain.

Vellamo raises her hand again, summoning another wave. This one is smaller but more precise, slamming into Iku-Turso's face and forcing him backward. Tuoni seizes the opportunity, driving his blade into the beast's skull with all his strength.

The cavern trembles as Iku-Turso lets out a final, guttural scream. His massive body collapses into the water, sending a tidal wave that nearly capsizes the boat. Soldiers cling to the wreckage of the bone whale, and the trolls swim desperately, gathering the wounded.

Tuoni pulls both swords from the monster and then leaps back into the boat, soaked and heaving breaths. His silver eyes meet mine, fierce and unyielding, as he hands me Lovia's sword. "We need to keep moving," he says, his voice low and urgent.

I nod, taking the sword in my hands, my body trembling with exhaustion and grief. The boat steadies, and we push forward, leaving the shattered remnants of the battle behind. The crystalline walls seem dimmer now, their light muted, as if mourning the loss of Bell and the others.

The grief remains, heavy and suffocating. Bell is gone. Tuonen is gone. Rasmus is gone. Lovia is missing.

I am no longer the unfeeling Goddess.
I am Hanna Heikkinen, and I feel everything.
It's fucking *awful*.

CHAPTER THIRTY-EIGHT

LOVIA

When I open my eyes, the first thing I notice is the stifling stillness. The air is thick and musty, heavy with the scent of aged parchment and something darker—like ash and decay. Shadows dance across the stone walls and towering bookcases, cast by flickering, sputtering torches mounted high above. My arms ache, my wrists bound by cold, unforgiving chains that bite into my skin. I tug instinctively, but the iron holds fast as I look around.

I'm in the Library of the Veils.

I'm home.

The realization sends a chill down my spine. This used to be one of my favorite places in Shadow's End. I would come here often when I wanted to get away from the hustle and bustle of the castle. Rauta used to sit by the Book of Runes at the entrance, guarding it, but he would often follow me around as I wandered through the stacks, running my fingers over the endless array of books, each one harboring countless souls in the pages. Even though I wasn't supposed to, sometimes, I would take the books down and find a comfy spot in the corner to flip through the pages, marveling at all the lives these mortals lived.

But now, this place has taken on an insidious gloom that permeates the literature. It's full of evil and black magic and suffering.

I glance beside me and spot my companion in misery.

Sarvi, the skeletal unicorn and my father's loyal aide, lies crumpled on its side beside me, a once-proud frame bound by iron chains. Its skull is tipped at an angle, hollow eye sockets seeming to regard me with dry humor even in this dire state.

About time you woke up, Sarvi's voice enters my mind, dry and sardonic. *I was starting to think I'd have to endure Louhi's endless monologue alone.*

"Sarvi!" I whisper. "You're here."

I wouldn't sound too excited. That also means you're here and you have to listen to her too.

"Great," I mutter under my breath, wincing as I shift my position. "A two-for-one special. My mother *and* her theatrics."

Sarvi chuckles weakly. *Careful, child. She's in a mood, and it's not the fun, dramatic kind that runs in your family. More the grind-my-horn-into-a-potion variety.*

I'm about to respond, ask how the hell one could be so glib after they've clearly been tortured, their sawed-off horn proof of that, when the sound of footsteps echoes through the library. They're slow and deliberate, heels clicking on the hard floor. My heart sinks.

Louhi emerges from the shadows, her elegant yet imposing figure shrouded in a black gown that seems to writhe like living smoke, wrapping up and over her horns like a cloak. Her pale green-grey face is expressionless, but her sharp eyes gleam with cold malice. In her hands, she holds a mortar and pestle. My stomach turns as I realize it must contain the remains of Sarvi's horn.

"Ah," Louhi purrs, her voice as smooth and cutting as a blade. "You're awake, Loviatar. Good. It would have been a shame for you to miss the final stages of my preparations."

"You mean desecrating Sarvi?" I sneer.

Her lips curl into a faint smile. "Sarvi's horn contains remnants of divine magic, tied to both your father and the underworld. It's a rare ingredient, and as much as I find its commentary tiresome, the creature has proven useful."

Flattery will get you nowhere, Louhi, Sarvi's voice cuts into my mind.

Louhi's smile tightens, but she ignores them. Instead, she walks to a stone pedestal in the center of the room. Upon it rests the Book of Runes, its pages rippling faintly as if alive. Shadows writhe around the edges, curling like smoke. Like everything else in this place, it appears to be corrupted.

"Do you know where you are, my daughter?" she asks, her tone almost casual.

"Obviously," I reply. "Do you?"

"Mmmm," she hums, setting the mortar down with deliberate care. "Each soul, each memory, each whisper from the dead, is contained within the pages of these books. Do you feel them watching you? Listening? Wondering if you'll join them?"

I let out a growl of frustration. I'm running out of time, and I'm already tired of her talking. "I'm not here for story time."

Her eyes narrow, the faintest twitch of irritation breaking her composed exterior. "You don't even know why you're here. It's because you're a pawn, Lovia, a mere piece on a chess board you don't even comprehend."

"Tuonen is *dead*," I spit out venomously, wanting it to hurt her like it hurts me. "Did you know that when you kidnapped me?"

She freezes, her eyes widening briefly. For a moment, just a second, I see a flash of sorrow, of maybe remorse, her wings lifting. Perhaps she didn't know.

Then, she lifts her chin, and her bat wings fold back against her. "He brought that on himself. If he had stayed in the dungeon where I had kept him, he would have stayed safe."

"Well, he didn't. Because he didn't know if he'd end up like Sarvi here. He left to help save the realm, to help my father, to save all the souls who'll end up here one day. He died a hero, even if it was at the hands of your own father."

She swallows thickly. Could it be she didn't know it was Rangaista that killed him?

"Thankfully, his sacrifice wasn't in vain. Rangaista is now dead," I say. "And it was Hanna who killed him," I add, the words tumbling out before I can stop them. "You're down one major piece, Mother. Maybe *you're* the one who doesn't comprehend the board."

Her face hardens, and for a moment, there's a flicker of something in her eyes. Rage, perhaps. Maybe fear. "Rangaista's death is...inconvenient," she admits carefully. "But it's far from the endgame. You think your precious stepmother's victory matters? It changes nothing."

I open my mouth to retort, but before I can speak, the large metal doors to the library creak open. The air grows colder, the light dimmer, as another figure steps into view.

Salainen.

She's Hanna's reflection, her dark twin. Where Hanna radiates warmth, especially now, Salainen exudes an unsettling chill. Her dark hair is twisted into harsh, sharp waves, and her black eyes gleam with cruelty. She moves with predatory grace, her presence commanding and terrifying.

"Mother," Salainen says to Louhi, her voice low and venomous. "I trust all is ready?"

I nearly snort at that. *Mother.* Salainen's real mother is the black magic Torben called upon to create her in a baffling attempt to hide his affair with Päivätär. But Louhi raised Salainen in secret, molding her into a weapon of hate, so I suppose she's my sister in a way, though not one I'll recognize.

Louhi nods, gesturing toward the pedestal. "The potion is nearly complete. When the time comes, I will lead the strike. Tuoni and Hanna will come for their precious daughter, and when they do, well, you know what to do."

I tense, my heart pounding. Louhi turns her gaze back to me, her lips curling into a sinister smile. "You see, Lovia, your father is predictable. They'll walk straight into my trap, believing they can save you, but they've underestimated Salainen. She's stronger than Hanna ever was."

I highly doubt that, I think, but I keep that to myself. I don't know how much my mother knows about Hanna's new status as the Goddess of the Sun, but if it can remain a surprise, then we might have an advantage.

Salainen steps closer, her eyes locking onto mine as she takes out a selenite knife, the same one that belonged to Hanna. "You've served your purpose, Lovia," she says, her tone cold. "You're bait, nothing more." She gives me a sour smile. "Now do you understand what it's like for your parent to turn their back on you? To cast you aside when you no longer provide any use?"

She's trying to hurt me in the way she was hurt by Torben, to make me feel something over the fact that my mother clearly doesn't care if I live or die. But the truth is, I don't feel any different.

No, actually, I do. My mother might not care if I live or

die, but I just want my mother to *die*. And if by my own hand, the better.

I lift my chin, refusing to let them see the fear they crave. "My father loves me more than you'll ever comprehend."

And Hanna's stronger than you think.

Salainen's laugh is sharp and mocking. "Perhaps. But that love won't last forever, not when I send them to Oblivion."

Louhi picks up the mortar again, grinding Sarvi's powdered horn into fine dust. "Salainen will ensure that neither Hanna nor Tuoni leave Shadow's End alive," she says. "And once they're gone, the final components of Kaaos will fall into place, locked in for eternity."

My chains clink as I shift, glaring at her. "You'll never win, Louhi," I say through gritted teeth. "You think you're in control, but you're just clinging to power that doesn't belong to you—power you conjured and corrupted, power you'll never be worthy of. It only makes you look cheap."

Her eyes flash with fury, and she steps closer, her shadow looming over me. "You'll see how wrong you are, daughter," she spits, her voice low and dangerous. "When the time comes, you'll wish you had never been born."

I don't respond, meeting her gaze with defiance. Sarvi's voice cuts through the tension. *I'm starting to think a mother's love is overrated.*

As Louhi and Salainen turn away, speaking in hushed tones, I take a deep breath, steeling myself.

I may be chained and outnumbered, but I'm not defeated.

CHAPTER THIRTY-NINE

DEATH

THE BOAT SCRAPES AGAINST THE STONE DOCK, AND I STEADY myself as the small craft rocks gently to a stop. The cavern beneath Shadow's End is vast, its high ceilings lost in darkness. What light exists comes from scattered veins of phosphorescent stone that streak the cavern walls like ancient scars and the tunnel at the opposite end leading out to the wild sea, dimmed by a lowered portcullis.

I stand, stepping onto the dock with Tuonen's body cradled in my arms. The weight is nothing compared to the heaviness in my chest. Behind me, the others disembark in silence. Hanna, ever radiant and severe, moves with purpose, her golden aura a stark contrast to the gloom. But despite the glow that speaks to her divinity, her eyes are wet with tears, as if she's sad and grieving, which gives me pause. Could her humanity be seeping back after all? I don't have time to even entertain the question.

Vellamo climbs out of the water and walks beside her, her spear in her one hand, her only hand, her steps tense and deliberate despite her missing limb.

Rauta pads silently at my side, his ears pricked, nose

twitching. The dog senses it too; Shadow's End is not as I left it. Already, the air feels heavy, oppressive. This place, once my stronghold, the beating heart of Tuonela, has been twisted into something unnatural.

I glance at the others. Torben clutches his staff, looking at the weeping stone walls with disdain. Tellervo lingers close to Torben, seeking him like a father now, her small antlers catching the faint glow of the cavern walls. The Magician follows silently, with General Suvari near the rear, his broad shoulders squared as he takes stock of the troops and trolls that climb out of the water.

With a sinking sense of dread, I realize there's barely anyone left. Many of the troops died in the water with Iku-Turso's attack. The lucky ones stayed behind in the caves. I'll have to send for them later, when it's safe.

After our victory.

Ahead, the entrance to Shadow's End yawns like the mouth of a beast I had once tamed but may now turn against me.

We move cautiously, our steps echoing against the stone. The air grows colder the further we go, the oppressive stillness pressing down like a suffocating hand. The walls, once adorned with intricate carvings of my reign, are now covered in dark, pulsing veins of shadow, as though the castle itself is decaying, rotting from the inside out.

The first chamber we enter has us pass by the crypt, the macabre theater for the Sect of the Undead. Statues of saints stand outside the chapel, their faces frozen in expressions that look like serene repose at first glance, but the light from our lanterns reveals their true state: their eyes have been hollowed out, bleeding trails of crimson wax down their faces. Dozens of candles are melted onto their bodies, pooling at their feet, and the wax glimmers like fresh blood.

I've always hated these fucking things.

"What the hell?" mutters General Suvari as he and the rest of the troops stare at the statues in disbelief.

"Stay alert," I say, my voice low but firm. "This is no sanctuary."

We move deeper into the chamber, the shadows stretching and shifting unnaturally. I glance back at the statues, unease prickling at the back of my neck. Something isn't right. I swear, their empty eyes are watching me.

Tuonen said Louhi was attempting to free the saints, but they don't look like—

A scream cuts through the silence.

Not a human scream, nor even that of a beast. It's a twisted, otherworldly wail, like the tearing of metal mixed with the agony of lost souls. The sound makes the air vibrate, and every hair on my body stands on end.

The statues move.

One by one, they jerk to life, their wax-dripping limbs cracking and splintering as they lurch forward. Their eyeless faces turn toward us, mouths opening wide on screams that echo off the walls. From the hollowed sockets of their eyes, black snakes pour out, writhing and hissing as they hit the stone floor.

"Defensive positions!" General Suvari bellows, his sword flashing as he steps forward to meet the onslaught.

Chaos erupts. The statues swarm us, their waxen forms surprisingly fast and strong. One lunges at me, its stone fingers reaching for my throat. I pivot, still holding Tuonen as I drive my sword upward into its chest. The blade sinks deep, and with a shuddering scream, the statue crumbles to the ground in a heap of wax and stone.

Another comes at me, swinging a jagged arm that glints with embedded shards of marble. I block the blow with my gauntlet, the impact rattling my bones, and drive my sword through its face. The statue's scream falters then dies as its body disintegrates into a pile of ash and melted wax.

Hanna steps forward, her light blazing as she sends arcs of golden energy at the writhing snakes. They hiss and sizzle, curling in on themselves as the light burns them away. Vellamo fights beside her, her spear a blur as she hacks through the serpentine forms and strikes down another statue.

Despite our efforts, the statues keep coming. They claw and bite, their movements erratic and horrifying, and they don't seem to fucking stay dead. Soldiers fall, their screams mingling with the unearthly wails of the statues, but we can't afford to lose any more of them. The snakes slither underfoot, striking at exposed flesh, their venom causing agonizing seizures.

"Focus on the statues!" I shout, slashing through another attacker. "Destroy them, and the snakes will follow!"

The battle is brutal but brief. One by one, the statues are reduced to rubble, their screeches fading into silence. The last snake hisses as Vellamo spears it cleanly in two.

Then, the chamber falls still.

We stand amidst the wreckage, breathing hard, our weapons dripping with wax. The faint light of our lanterns flickers, casting uneasy shadows across the walls. The crypt is silent once more, but the damage is done. Several soldiers lie dead, their faces twisted in pain, their bodies coiled from snake bites.

Fuck. We couldn't get more than a few feet into my damn home before losing more comrades. You'd think their deaths would be easier at this point, after all that I've lost, but it isn't.

We press on, leaving the desecrated crypt behind. The air grows colder as we ascend the winding stairs. I can feel the castle's lifeblood, the very essence of Tuonela, drained and twisted. Every step is a reminder of what Louhi has stolen from me.

At the top of the stairs, we enter the grand hall, its vaulted ceiling stretching high above. The air here is colder still, biting at my skin even through my armor. Louhi's corruption is everywhere—the walls are lined with skeletal remains, and shadowy tendrils pulse through the stone-like veins.

The sound of clattering bones draws our attention. Skeletons step out from the shadows, their hollow eyes glowing faintly. At their forefront are my former servants, the Deadmaidens—tall, veiled figures with gloved hands. Once, they were the silent guardians of my castle, loyal to me and my family alone. Now, their veils are torn, showing monstrous faces underneath, their movements jerky and unnatural, and their gloves are gone, showcasing various claws. They lurch forward with a hungry growl and the sound of snapping jaws.

"How could you?" I murmur, my chest tightening. "You were mine."

Hanna steps to my side, her expression unreadable. "They're hers now."

There's no time for hesitation. The skeletons and Deadmaidens charge, their movements unnervingly synchronized. The clash is immediate and ferocious, blades sparking against bone as our group meets the attack head-on.

Vellamo's single-handed spear flashes as she carves through the skeletons with precision. Tellervo uses a sword to parry them off as Torben steps in and uses his staff as a baseball bat, knocking a few heads down the hallway.

I focus on the Deadmaidens. Their speed and unpredictability make them formidable, but they're no match for me. Without letting go of my son, I drive my sword through one's ribcage. The Deadmaiden lets out a piercing shriek before crumpling to the ground.

Another leaps at me, its movements impossibly fast. I pivot, catching its claws with my gauntlet, and slam my sword into its neck. The blow decapitates it cleanly, and its body collapses into a heap of bones and tattered fabric.

The battle ends as quickly as it began. The last Deadmaiden falls under General Suvari's blade, its veil shredded, its face caved in. The hall falls silent once more, but the echoes of the fight linger in the air.

I survey the scene. The floor is littered with broken bones and tattered cloth, the remnants of my former servants and the skeletal army. The soldiers regroup, their faces pale but determined. We didn't lose anyone this time.

"This is only the beginning," I say, my rage festering. "She has turned my home into a graveyard."

We push through the rest of Shadow's End, the walls closing in around us as the castle twists and tightens like a predator's maw. The cold air seems alive, carrying whispers of despair that curl around my ears. Hanna leads the way, her golden glow illuminating the dark stairwell as we climb, the others following close behind. My thoughts are singular—find Sarvi, find Lovia, and end this nightmare.

Then, I see her.

The nightmare herself.

Louhi.

Her shadowy form darts up a staircase toward the private wing. Her dark dress billows like smoke, her wings raised behind her as she moves with inhuman speed. My grip on my sword hilt instinctively tightens with rage.

"There!" I snap, halting the group. "She's heading to Sarvi's room."

Hanna turns, her golden eyes narrowing. "Let's go! We'll—"

"No," I interrupt, shaking my head. "This is my fight."

Her jaw tightens, a flicker of hesitation crossing her face. "No, please."

"I have to," I say firmly, already stepping toward the staircase. "Once, she was mine to wed, and now, she's mine to kill. You find Sarvi and Lovia. Save them. I'll deal with my ex-wife."

She doesn't argue further. Instead, she nods, a spark of trust in her gaze. "Don't die."

I don't respond. Words are wasted here, but I give her a look that tells her not to die either.

I pass Tuonen to General Suvari, then bolt up the stairs, my heart hammering like a war drum.

Sarvi's chambers are at the highest point of the castle, a place of seclusion and solace. But now, as I storm in, they are steeped in darkness and malice. Chains hang from the walls, remnants of Louhi's cruelty, and the air reeks of something old and rotting.

Louhi stands in the center of the room, her back to me as she gazes out the window, giving me a clear view of her terrible wings. She turns slowly when she senses my presence, a cruel smile curling her lips. Her dark gown flows like ink, her green-grey skin pale in the dim light. The rams horns that curl back from her head shine with oil—or maybe it's blood.

"You're persistent, I'll give you that," she says, her voice low and venomous. "But persistence doesn't change fate, Tuoni. You can't change what's already been done. But gods, you have such a hard time taking no for an answer."

Every single word has me ready to explode.

"It ends here, Louhi," I grind out, stepping forward, my blade gleaming in the faint light. "No more schemes. No more death. None except your own."

Her laughter is sharp, cutting through the air like glass.

"You always were a fool. Do you think you can stop me? Your realm is crumbling, your son is dead, and soon, very soon, you will join him."

"Don't you dare fucking speak of Tuonen like that," I growl, anger tearing through my throat. "He was your son too. Your son, and you killed him. You. Killed. Him."

Without warning, she moves. Shadows burst forth from her hands, coiling like snakes as they lash toward me. I dive to the side, rolling to avoid their strike. My sword comes up instinctively, slicing through one tendril as it snaps too close. The severed shadow dissipates with a hiss, but more take its place. This magic is new to her, powerful, and it makes me sick to know it was probably conjured with Tuonen's horns.

And so, I will show her no mercy.

I charge, swinging my sword in a wide arc. She blocks with a conjured weapon of her own, a jagged black blade that seems to absorb the light. Sparks fly as our swords clash, the force of the impact reverberating through my arms. She grins wickedly, pushing me back.

"You're weak," she taunts, lunging at me with inhuman speed. "You're not a God! You're nothing but a man."

I parry, narrowly avoiding her strike. Her blade grazes my shoulder, slicing through fabric and grazing flesh. Pain flares, but I grit my teeth and retaliate, forcing her back with a series of rapid strikes.

"If I'm a mere man, then it will be *really* embarrassing for you when I win."

She moves like a serpent, her movements fluid and unpredictable. I have to focus on every step, every angle. She has black magic on her side that's more powerful than I could have imagined.

We crash through the doors, metal and wood splintering, and onto the stone platform outside, the place Sarvi would use as a landing pad. The wind howls, biting at my skin as the open air engulfs us. The platform stretches high above the castle grounds, with sheer drops on all sides. Louhi's grin widens as her shadowy wings unfurl behind her, dark and menacing.

"This is where you fall, Tuoni," she sneers.

Her wings beat once, lifting her off the ground. She hovers just out of reach, her eyes gleaming with malice. She swoops down, her blade slashing at me. I dodge and counter, my sword cutting through the air, but she is faster. She circles me like a predator, striking and retreating before I can land a blow.

The wind roars as she dives again. This time, I brace myself, my blade meeting hers mid-swing. The impact sends a jolt through my arms, but I hold my ground. I shove her back, forcing her to land a few feet away.

"Still standing," I say, my voice steady.

She hisses, her wings flaring. "Not for long."

Shadows surge around her, forming jagged spears that shoot toward me. I roll to the side, narrowly avoiding them. One grazes my leg, cutting through the armor and drawing blood. I stagger but keep moving, lunging toward her on a fierce strike. My blade catches her side, slicing through fabric and skin. She screams, more in anger than pain, and retaliates with a flurry of blows.

We trade strikes, the platform trembling beneath us. She has the advantage with her wings, using the air to maneuver around me, but I hold my ground, each swing of my sword pushing her back inch by inch.

Then, she moves faster than I can track. Her foot sweeps my legs out from under me, and I hit the stone hard. Before I can rise, she kicks me toward the edge of the platform. I scramble for purchase, my fingers scraping against the rough stone as I teeter on the brink.

She looms over me, her blade poised to strike. "Goodbye, Tuoni," she says, her voice cold and final. "Your reign is officially over."

She thrusts, but I roll at the last second, her blade slamming into the stone where my chest was a heartbeat ago. I rise, spinning to face her, but she is already airborne again. Her wings beat hard, sending gusts of wind that nearly knock me over the edge.

I leap forward, grabbing her ankle as she tries to ascend. She lets out a startled cry as I drag her back down, both of us tumbling onto the platform. We grapple, her claws tearing at my armor as I fight to keep her pinned.

With a powerful shove, she throws me off. I skid across the platform, coming to a stop just before the edge. She rises, her wings flaring again as I scramble to my feet, readying my blade for one final attack.

But she is too fast. She swoops in, her clawed hand catching me by the throat. With a mighty heave, she lifts me off the ground and hurls me over the edge.

The wind rushes past me as I fall, the castle walls a blur of stone and shadow.

My mind races, a single thought burning through the chaos.

This is the end.

But then, just as suddenly as I fell, I stop.

Something catches me with a thump that knocks the wind out of me, and I quickly wrap my arms around a warm, thick neck, hanging on tight to a mane blowing in my face.

Large wings beat steadily as Sarvi's voice cuts through the wind. *Hold on!*

"Sarvi!" I cry out. "You're alive."

Why wouldn't I be? Sarvi says. *But I'll have to make this quick; my strength isn't what it used to be.*

Relief floods through me as the unicorn quickly rises

through the sky, lifting me back toward the platform. Louhi's expression shifts from triumph to fury as she sees us ascend. She dives toward us, her blade gleaming.

Sarvi twists, avoiding her strike, but Louhi quickly flaps her wings, propelling her up so she lands on the unicorn's back right behind me, her claws digging into the hide. Sarvi lets out a cry of pain, wings faltering as we fall through the sky until we're aloft again. I reach back and grab hold of Louhi's arm, pulling with all my strength, but she slams me backward, pinning me against Sarvi's flank.

I reach for my sword, but it's gone—lost in the chaos. Louhi's blade rises, aimed for my heart.

"Should have known the God of Death wouldn't die easily," she snarls, her eyes blazing with victory. "Luckily, I'm not a quitter."

I grin at her. "Neither am I."

With a final, desperate act, I tear off my glove with my teeth and reach for her. My bare hand meets her throat, and she freezes as I start to squeeze her neck. Her wings stiffen, her eyes widening in shock.

My touch is death itself, the end of all things.

And oh, have I longed to use it on her.

Louhi's body braces as I strangle her, her shadows unraveling. She lets out a piercing scream as her form begins to disintegrate, her essence fading into the wind. She tries to claw at me, to fight back, but it's too late. She crumbles into ash, the sinister mire of her soul snuffed out, floating away into nothing.

She's finally gone.

Good fucking riddance.

I collapse against Sarvi's back, my chest heaving. All is silent except for the sound of the wind and Sarvi's beating wings as we fly back to the castle.

"It's over," I whisper.

For now, Sarvi replies, their voice low and pricked with fear. *Hanna freed me and Lovia from the library, made me leave to help you, but I fear she's fighting Salainen now.*

"Hurry," I command. "We don't have a second to waste."

CHAPTER FORTY

HANNA

We sprint through the hallowed halls of Shadow's End, our footsteps echoing against the stone. The air is heavy, laden with the scent of damp rot and old magic, though not at all the way I remember it.

My home. This used to be home, more so than California, Finland, or any place I lived in the Upper World, and now Louhi has taken it from me, from Tuoni, from everyone.

I growl to myself, hoping, praying that he's able to defeat Louhi. It took everything in me to not go after him to help, but I know rescuing Lovia was his priority, and I'm sure she's heavily guarded. Still, I worry. My Goddess side is retreating, letting my emotions out in full force, and right now, the anxiety is drowning me. I would give my left tit for some lorazepam right now.

But Tuoni is counting on me as much as I'm counting on him.

So, I lead the way, Vellamo close at my side. My father grips his staff behind us, his chants a low murmur as he strengthens our path with wards against whatever dark forces might try to snare us. I've told him several times that he should hang back, watch for any attackers, but my old man is as stubborn as I am, and so he's right behind me.

As is Tellervo, General Suvari holding Tuonen's body, the Magician, and the remaining trolls and troops, who form a tight group around us, weapons at the ready. Rauta darts ahead, his nose to the ground, growling softly, as if he senses danger in every shadow.

We push onward, deeper into the heart of the castle, toward the Library of the Veils. I can feel its pull, a strange hum in my bones, like a chord struck in a hollow chamber. The library is a repository of souls and lost knowledge and, for now, our best hope of finding Sarvi and Lovia. I can feel it.

We burst into the library, and I stagger to a halt. The Library of the Veils is vast, its vaulted ceiling soaring above us. Shelves carved from black stone rise like jagged cliffs, crammed with ancient tomes and scrolls. Flickering orbs of blue light hover in the air, casting eerie shadows. Despite the grandeur, the space feels suffocating, the weight of Louhi's magic pressing down on us.

And then, I see them.

Sarvi and Lovia.

They're chained to the far wall, their wrists bound by enchanted manacles glowing faintly with dark runes. Lovia hangs limply, her head tilted forward. Sarvi's one white eye flickers open as we approach, their gaze frantic. The sight of the skeleton unicorn is enough to bring tears to my eyes, another wave of emotion that threatens to pummel me into submission.

Hanna! Sarvi's usually blasé voice is raw, trembling with relief and fear.

I don't hesitate. I sprint across the room, the others fanning out to secure the space. Reaching Sarvi first, I grip the chains and summon my power. My hand glows faintly with sunlight, the heat biting against the cold iron. The manacles resist, the runes flaring angrily, but I push harder, my light searing through the darkness. The chains shatter with a metallic wail, and Sarvi stumbles forward. Their sawed-off horn is a sorry sight but, otherwise, the unicorn seems all right.

"Go!" I cry out. "Go! Tuoni followed Louhi into your room. He needs you."

Sarvi doesn't even hesitate; they instead nod and immediately gallop off, hooves striking the stone with a steady rhythm as they race out the door.

I turn to Lovia, crouching in front of her. Her eyes flutter open, clouded with pain but sharpening when she sees me. "Hanna..." she croaks.

"Hold on." I work quickly, breaking her chains with the same heat and light. She slumps forward, and I catch her, pulling her into a brief embrace.

"You're okay," I say, brushing blood-matted hair from her face. "Stay with the others. You'll be safe now."

Before Lovia can answer, the air shifts. A wave of icy magic sweeps through the library, and I whirl around, pulling Lovia to her feet. Black mist surrounds us, curling like living tendrils as the temperature plummets, and my breath fogs in front of me.

"Hanna!" my father calls out, his voice sharp with warning.

The mist thickens, swallowing the faint blue light. Shadows twist and coil, separating me from the others. I can just make out Vellamo's shout, the trolls' roars, but their voices seem to come from a great distance. The darkness presses in until I'm alone.

And then, *she* steps from the shadows.

Salainen.

She's a mirror image of me yet entirely wrong. Her

features are identical, but her skin is ashen, her eyes pools of liquid darkness. She wears a mocking smile, her movements smooth and predatory.

"Hello, *sister*," she purrs, her voice laced with venom. "Did you miss me?"

I draw my sword, its light flaring weakly in the oppressive gloom. "Salainen," I say coldly. "We meet again," I add; it seems like the thing to say.

"How is it that you don't die, dear sister? You're like a cockroach—a cockroach who somehow gets everything she wants. A loving father? You have it. A powerful husband? He'll kneel before you. Powers of the sun? Well...perhaps that one, I'll need you to prove."

Before I can respond, she lunges. Her shadowy blade slices through the air, and I barely block in time, the force of her attack driving me back. Her strength is monstrous, her movements unnervingly fast. Our swords clash, light against shadow, sparks flying with every strike. What the fuck? Has she been taking black magic steroids or what?

Salainen's laughter echoes as she presses her advantage. "What's wrong, Hanna? Is the mighty Goddess of the Sun afraid of a little darkness?"

I'll use the sun if I have to, but I know I can beat her even on mortal terms.

I grit my teeth and retaliate, slashing at her with quick, precise strikes. She dodges effortlessly, her form twisting like smoke. The shadows around us writhe, and then she steps back, raising a hand.

More shadows solidify, forming duplicates of her. Two, then three, then five. Each one wields a blade identical to hers, their eyes glowing with malice.

That bitch. She's using Death's shadow magic to fight me.

"That's cheating," I growl.

They attack as one, a storm of blades and shadow. I parry,

block, dodge—every movement a desperate attempt to stay alive. My sword flashes in the dark, cutting through one duplicate, only for two more to take its place. Their blades are cold, their strikes relentless. One slashes across my arm, another catches my leg. Pain flares, but I push it aside, refusing to fall.

"You can't win," Salainen taunts, her voice coming from everywhere at once. "I've bested you before, and that's when there was only one of me."

"Shut the fuck up!" I snap, spinning to sever another duplicate. It dissolves into mist, but more emerge, their laughter chilling.

I can't suffer for my pride anymore. I call on my power, reaching deep into the kindling inside me and summoning light to burn them away. A golden flare erupts from my hand, but it barely pushes back the shadows. The duplicates absorb the light, their forms solidifying, as if feeding on it.

My power flickers, falters.

I'm losing.

Desperation claws at me. Salainen's blade whistles past my ear, her grin widening as she lands another blow. My knees buckle, blood staining the stone beneath me. I can't keep this up.

Then, I see it—a glint of white on her belt.

My selenite knife.

The blade I carried before she stole it, the one gifted to me. She doesn't see me notice it, too focused on her relentless assault.

I feint right, drawing her attention, then dive forward, grabbing the knife from her waist. My fingers close around the hilt, and I roll to my feet, raising it just as she lunges again.

I stab downward, and the selenite blade cuts through her shadowy form. She lets out a piercing scream. Her duplicates falter, their movements jerky, before they begin to dissolve.

"No!" Salainen shrieks, clutching at the wound. Her dark eyes blaze with fury and fear. "You can't—"

I don't let her finish. I drive the blade further into her chest, the selenite glowing with a brilliant light, not unlike the sun. The duplicates shatter, their forms evaporating like smoke. Salainen stumbles, her eyes wide with disbelief.

"This... isn't... over..." she gasps, her voice a faint whisper as her body begins to disintegrate.

"Oh, I think it fucking is," I say, my voice steady despite the exhaustion in my limbs.

Her form collapses into shadow, and then, she's gone.

The oppressive darkness lifts, the library returning to its eerie stillness.

I drop to my knees, the knife falling from my hand. My chest heaves, my body trembling with the aftershock of battle. I wish I had some snappy catchphrase or one-liner to mutter, but her death will have to be enough.

The shadows at the edges of the library stir, and then the others burst through, their faces tight with worry.

"Hanna!" Vellamo reaches me first, her hand brushing my shoulder. "What happened?"

I look up, my gaze meeting hers. "It's over," I say softly. "The dumb bitch is gone."

Vellamo frowns at my choice of words.

"Sorry, I meant Salainen is gone," I clarify.

"I know that's what you meant," she says with a raise of her chin. "But I'm certain the Goddess of the Sun wouldn't use that language."

"No, that's one hundred percent my daughter," my father says with a sigh. But when I meet his eyes, he breaks into a broad smile and comes over to help me to my feet. He pulls me into a quick hug, squeezing tight. "Welcome back, sweetie." He looks me over. "Are you hurt?" he asks, his voice tight with concern as he looks over where I'm cut and bleeding.

"'Tis but a flesh wound," I say through a wince. "We need to keep moving. Louhi's not far. Tuoni needs us."

The urgency in my voice spurs them into action. The group regathers, their expressions grim but determined.

I cast one last glance at the spot where Salainen fell, her essence reduced to nothing. The selenite knife lies on the ground, its blade dulled and cracked. I pick it up, slipping it into my belt—a piece of my past reclaimed, a reminder of what I've endured.

Of who I've become.

All of us run back out of the library, tensions high, ready to continue fighting.

Only to run right into a battered and bleeding Tuoni, Sarvi behind him.

My husband's victorious gaze meets mine over the sea of heads who rejoice around him.

He grins at me, tired and grieving but relieved.

And I grin at him.

We won.

The realm is ours.

We are the King and Queen of Tuonela again.

CHAPTER FORTY-ONE

HANNA

TUONEN WAS LAID TO REST AMID THE WAVES UNDER A STONE-grey sky.

It's ironic that funerals aren't common in the land of the dead, but a ceremony was given for Tapio and words and tears were shed for Rasmus, and so for Tuonen, the beloved Son of Death, we gave him a beautiful sendoff.

In the end, Tuoni chose to bury him at sea. We set out on boats from Shadow's End, the few Louhi and her cronies didn't inadvertently destroy when they stormed the castle, and went out not far from shore.

Tuonen was wrapped in a shroud and his father's cloak, with burlap sacks full of crystals tied around his ankles and neck. The crystals themselves were giant chunks of lapis lazuli, carnelian, turquoise, and jade, enough to weigh his body down in an eternal watery grave, the crystals themselves acting as conduits for good passage. It doesn't matter that Tuonen is floating in the eternal hell that is Oblivion; we all pretended that his soul was still around and would finally be at peace.

Vellamo called her mermaids forth to help guide the body

to a coral grove at the bottom of the sea—all of them except Bell, that is. I cried for her loss, in addition to Tuonen, in addition to Tapio, and even Rasmus.

Rasmus. Even though part of me still hated him, right up until the end, I mourn the fact that I never gave him a second chance. He proved himself worthy of being called an ally, maybe even a brother. He risked his own life to save Lovia, and he lost it for her. I remember how it was when he first saved me from Noora and Eero at my father's viewing, how he accompanied me into Tuonela to get him back, and I like to think that, at that time, Rasmus wasn't compromised. He truly wanted to save my dad, someone he loved and looked up to, never knowing the truth, and for that, I kind of owe him everything.

But wishing things were different doesn't change anything.

As we sat on the boats, bobbing up and down in the glassy waves, watching Tuoni's beloved son sink into the depths, tears streaming from our eyes, we were all wishing for so many different things.

I wish my Goddess powers could help lessen the blow of grief, but they haven't. Which is funny, considering that's all I originally wanted. I wanted to be human, wanted to feel—well, I fucking got it.

"Still not hungry?" I ask Tuoni, coming around the back of his chair at the head of the table. I drape my arms around him and kiss the back of his head. We're in the dining hall, or what's left of it, at least. After the funeral, Vellamo, Tellervo, and my father had their meal here, but nobody else seemed hungry, especially not my husband.

The troops have been busy, their duties now going from fighting a war to making everyone food. Thankfully, there's still enough in the pantries to feed us for a while. I don't think Louhi ever ate, which would explain why the stockpiles weren't touched.

Tuoni moves his head to kiss my arm. "No. They don't know how to cook." I glance down at his plate of spaghetti and bite back a smile. I think the troops have been cooking the pasta just fine; it's Tuoni who doesn't know what good Italian food tastes like. He thinks spaghetti should be as hard as sticks.

"Perhaps you should think about sending the troops back, then," I tell him. "They've proved their worth. It's not really fair to have them hang around Shadow's End."

He grumbles and leans back against me. "I need them to help clean up this place."

"You have enough of us to clean it up. It's my home, Lovia's home too. We'll get it spic and span. Besides, if you get my father to open a portal to send the troops through, maybe he can go with them and sneak you back more chocolate and coffee."

He twists his head to glance up at me. "You think Torben would go and come back?"

I nod. "I already talked to him. He says there's nothing left for him in Finland. We tied up as many loose ends as we could over there. He wants to stay here, with me, with us." I give him a firm look, letting him know this isn't negotiable.

He sighs. "All right. I suppose this was going to happen no matter what I said."

I pull back and punch him on the shoulder. "You love my father, I know you do. You guys have had one hell of a bonding experience this last while." He mutters something unintelligible. "Besides," I go on, "he can go back and forth between our worlds with ease. Think of the movies he can smuggle in."

That does seem to lighten his disposition. "I suppose I'll allow my father-in-law to move in with us. Thank the

Creator it's a big enough castle. He can have the furthest wing."

"Deal," I tell him, letting him think he won. It's the little things in this marriage. I straighten up and smile. "I'm heading up to bed. Are you coming?"

He gives his head a shake. "No, I think I'll stay up a little while longer. I need time to be alone."

Sadness tugs at my heart. His voice sounds hollow now. The loss of Tuonen will be a mark on his soul until the end of time.

I swallow back the tears that threaten to flow as I make my way out of the dining room and up the many stairs to our chambers. It isn't fair that Gods can die. If you're supposed to be immortal, then you should be immortal. To have one live forever with the absence of another is cruel. This must be what all the vampires go through, assuming there are such things. Nothing surprises me anymore.

Once I'm in my chambers and getting ready for bed, my heart is too heavy for sleep. I keep seeing Tuonen sinking into the deep, keep hearing the sob that escaped Tuoni's lips and broke my heart in two. This is a castle of grief from which there is no escape.

I go to the glass doors of the balcony and look outside. It's snowing lightly, gathering on the stone railing and in the corners of the panes. It's beautiful in its own way—the great dark sea below, the jagged mountains in the distance. Somewhere, Kuutar's moon sits behind all those heavy clouds, but I don't expect to see fair weather for a long time. When I imagined us finally back at Shadow's End, I thought there would be sunshine and reason to celebrate. For some reason, I never imagined we would lose Tuonen in the process.

Was that naïve or just hopeful?

Is there even a difference?

I exhale heavily and stare at the flakes as they gather on

the window. At least the snow is pretty, though the more I stare at it, the lighter it becomes. I look up, and suddenly, I'm blinded, like a supernova is going off in front of me.

Instinctively, I block my eyes, though it takes me a moment to realize I'm part of the fucking sun and I don't need to do that. So, I lower my arms and watch as a bright ball of sunlight lands on the balcony.

I step out of the way just as the doors blow open. Snow fills the room, followed by the glowing figure of my mother, Päivätär, Goddess of the Sun.

"Mother?" I ask, immediately humbled by her blinding presence. "Why are you here?" I can't help but get a little nervous, like I'm in trouble for something.

She stares at me for a second, the solar flares around her body dimming before she says, "Do mothers not visit their children?" As if I dared to question her. Then, she says, "I have come to bear you a gift."

"Oh?" The last gift she gave me was the whole damn sun, so I'm a little wary about what this could be. "Wouldn't Kuutar be mad if you gave me the moon?"

"I'm not giving you the moon," she says in a huff, growing brighter, totally not understanding what sarcasm is.

"That's fine," I tell her quickly, not wanting to see her offended. She may be my true mother, but she scares the shit out of me. "So what is the gift?"

"The gift is sacrifice. Your sacrifice."

Oh, yeah, that's a *great* fucking present.

"Excuse me?" I exclaim. "A sacrifice?"

"You have the power of all life, Hanna. It is part of your bones, part of your blood. This power is stronger in you than it is in me because your humanity is strong enough to control it."

"And you think I should die because of that?"

What the fuck?

"Most of your power will die, yes, because you exhausted it first. But you are not dying, Hanna. You are saving the people you love. The people of the realm. The ones sent to Oblivion."

I shake my head. "I have no idea what you're saying."

"Your gift, Hanna, nurtured in sunlight, is that you can reverse Oblivion. Your gift of life can pull everyone out until Oblivion ceases to exist. The dead will return and walk again here."

I can hardly believe what I'm hearing, mostly because I don't understand it. "You're saying I can somehow, like, Uno Reverse Hell?"

She stares at me for a moment, and I can almost hear her brain trying to compute what *Uno* means. "You are light. Oblivion is dark. Your eternal sun and power of life will destroy it completely."

My heart starts to beat faster, hope rising in my chest. "So you're saying I have the power to bring everyone back to life? Tuonen? Bell? Rasmus? Vipunen?"

"Vipunen is not dead," she says to me, a hint of haughtiness in her tone. "He has been with me on the sun as punishment for getting involved with Tuonen's fate when he knows better. He has been watching you, though. He is proud."

Pick up the sword and try again.

I blink at that, my circuits overloading with too much information.

"I can bring back the dead. Like the *dead* dead?" I repeat.

"Every being who has been sent to Oblivion, yes," she says, patience waning. "And I do mean *every* being."

"Wait. So that means like Louhi and Rangaista and Salainen?"

"Yes."

My eyes widen in horror. "That's not fair."

"You are correct. It is not fair," she says stiffly. "If you want it to be fair, you would only bring some back, but not others."

"But...how?"

"Your power can only bring everyone back, but you do not possess the metaphysical ability to become a replacement for Oblivion and the great judge of humanity, only letting worthy souls in while keeping others out. That is not in your markup."

"If I may?" a voice says.

Startled, I whirl around to see the Magician standing in the doorway.

"What are *you* doing here?" I ask.

But his focus doesn't seem to be on me. It's hard to tell, since he doesn't have a proper face—he's like the superhero Rorschach but with stars and planets instead of ink blots. Still, I can feel he's staring at my mother.

I look back at her, and she nods.

"Yes, I knew you would come," she says. "Tell me your plans."

"Wait, what?" I stammer, watching as he glides across the room. He gives me a nod and then stops right in front of her.

"I am ready to evolve," he says to her. "I have done what I've needed to do."

"Uh, and what is that exactly?" I question. Because if you ask me, he seems to have done a whole lot of nothing.

His head swivels toward me, galaxies swirling across his façade, faster and faster. "I have done more than you know."

"Oh," I say. "So you read minds too? Not invasive or inappropriate at all." I jerk my chin at my mother. "I see why the two of you are friends."

"You wonder why I have let some people die while saving others," he says, his voice almost robotic. "You wonder why I saved Rasmus initially when he died later. You don't see the things put in motion. If I hadn't saved Rasmus, he wouldn't have been able to save Lovia, who has been instrumental to my evolution. She still is, right to the end."

"Okay..." I say, getting a little freaked out about how ominous he sounds. "So then what is your evolution? Why is it more important than peoples' lives?"

"For the very reason we have just discussed," my mother says in a patient voice. "Both of you are willing to be sacrifices for the greater good."

"Yeah, but..." I begin. "My sacrifice is stupid. I give up my powers, sure, Uno Reverse Oblivion, and then we'll have everyone back, but then all the shitty people will be back too, and round and round we go. We can't coexist here with Louhi and Rangaista."

"Oblivion was never necessary," the Magician says. "Not when I stood at the gates to the city and drew the cards. The bad went to Inmost. The mediocre went to the Golden Mean. The very good went to Amaranthus. Oblivion was something put in place as punishment beyond punishment long ago, and it should have never been for everyone."

I do a slow blink at him, trying to get him to catch me up to speed quicker.

He continues, "But if Oblivion is reversed, something has to take its place. Or someone, as it were."

I frown. "What are you talking about?"

"He is ready to become the void," my mother says. "He will replace Oblivion, holding the evil souls inside so the good souls can come back."

"I still have final judgment in the end," he adds.

I'm having a hard time getting my head around this. In some ways, I wish my Goddess self was coming through, because she seemed to have the mind of a computer.

"You become... I don't understand. How do you just become something like that?"

He places his hands together, and I notice how they look

like a velvet black sky pinpricked with stars. "The same way I became what you're looking at. I am a portion of the universe, as are you, in some ways. But my form is ever-changing. I exist in nothing. I am everywhere. I can reach out and touch you because I manipulate matter that way. I can also stop manipulating and just exist as stardust. If I become the void, I will cease to exist as you know it, but I will still exist."

"You would really do that?" I ask, touched by his dedication. "What about the city? Don't you need to draw cards and decide people's fate? Eventually, Tuoni will get that back up and running."

"All of Tuonela needs an overhaul," my mother says. "It has been a long time coming. It is why Kaaos had to happen in the first place." She pauses, tilting her head at me. "This is what occupies Tuoni's thoughts, as well as the loss of his son. But if you reverse Oblivion and the Universe becomes the void, letting only the good ones out and keeping the bad ones in, then Tuoni will have more time to think about what this realm really needs. He'll have his son back."

"When I tell Tuoni of the news, he will be relieved," the Magician says. "Of course, because it means Tuonen is back, and Tapio, Ahto, Kalma, the others who have been lost over the years, but also because there will be a new system. The newly dead won't be sorted into three layers of the afterlife. They will either be here, in Tuonela, or in the void, where I hold them prisoner."

I think about that for a moment. If there's no city, then everyone would just populate Tuonela like normal people would populate a land. They would live in the Frozen Void or the Hiisi Forest, build a houseboat community on the Great Inland Sea. Old people could turn the Liekkiö Plains into the next Palm Springs, complete with subdivisions and a golf course. Just give them all fire extinguishers for the occasional attack from flaming demon children.

It would take care of the problem that Lovia, and Tuonen, had before everything went to shit. They didn't want to spend their lives ferrying the dead. But if now all they have to do is cross the River of Shadows to the other side and drop them off to start a new life... They could even build a bridge. Tuonen would be so happy—

if he was alive.

"Tuonen will come back," the Magician says, reading me. "If you use up the rest of your power to turn the tide, I will become the eternal judgment of the void."

"I'm sorry it has to come to this, Hanna," my mother says. She sounds about as sorry as she ever will, but that's not saying a lot. "It is a loss."

"I don't mind giving up my power," I tell her honestly. "It's not a sacrifice. I'm not a warrior princess like Lovia. I don't see the need to have the ability to blast people and set them on fire in my day-to-day life."

Knock on wood.

"You might not lose all of it, either," she adds. "You might always have a touch of it embedded in you."

So I might end up being a glorified night light after all.

"Okay," I say, a wave of anxiety rushing over me. "So how do we do this? Is this going to hurt?"

"It won't hurt," she says.

I look at the Magician. "And it won't hurt you?"

He shakes his head. "This is my evolution. I am progressing to the next level."

And that's when I think of Lovia. Fuck, it's going to hurt the hell out of her, isn't it? From the downward tilt of a shooting star on his face, I know he's thinking about her too.

"None of us start out perfect," the Magician says. "We are all learning to become the things we need to become. This is our evolution, Hanna. This is the progression of the realm, of the afterlife. Sacrifice is often necessary when the change is for the best."

"Are you ready to become something again for the greater good?" my mother asks me.

I take in a deep breath and square my shoulders. "Absolutely." I pause. "Wait. What am I becoming?"

"You, Hanna," she says with a gentle smile. "You are becoming you."

CHAPTER FORTY-TWO

DEATH

The gardens of Shadow's End are a place of shattered grandeur—cracked stone paths winding between overgrown hedges and thorny roses as black as coal. The castle looms behind us, its spires like claws against the murky sky, while the dead ground beneath my boots hums faintly, as if holding its breath. I feel it waiting—something ancient and powerful, gathering just beyond the veil.

Hanna stands near the dry fountain at the center of it all, brow furrowed, looking beautifully deep in thought. The glow of her power is dim, flickering like the last light of a dying star. She's about to give everything she has left to "Uno Reverse" Oblivion and bring back the lost. To some, the cost would be too high. She will no longer be the powerful Goddess of the Sun—she is sacrificing that part of herself, and for what?

For us.

For love.

For her humanity.

Still, she remains the Queen of Tuonela, Goddess of the Dead, and if you ask me, that's pretty badass.

The Magician stands opposite her, cloaked in starlight, calm and unreadable as always. The air crackles faintly around him, a sense of inevitability hanging heavy. He has told us what must be done, that he will take Oblivion's place, that he alone can judge who returns and who remains behind. Without him, none of this works.

I don't want him to make this sacrifice. He essentially will cease to be as we know him now, but I know it is the only way.

"You don't have to do this," I say quietly, though the words feel hollow, even as they leave my mouth.

The Magician turns his head slightly, the galaxies in his eyes swirling as he meets my gaze. "I do," he replies simply, his voice calm. "You know I do. I know I do. The tapestry doesn't lie, and this isn't the end."

He steps toward Lovia, who stands at the edge of the group, arms tightly crossed, as though holding herself together by sheer will. Her face is a mask of pain, anger, disbelief at the idea of losing him.

"This just isn't fair," Lovia says suddenly, her voice cracking. "Why does it have to be this way?"

"Don't you want your brother back? Rasmus? Tapio?" he asks calmly.

"Yes but… Let Hanna do her thing and bring them back, and we'll figure out what to do with Louhi and—"

"That's not an option, Lovia," I say, raising my hand and cutting her off. "Defeating them took everything out of us. We can't go through that again, especially since there will be no real defeat. We'll never be rid of them."

She sighs, broken. She'll have to come to terms with it. If this works, if we can get everyone back, then it's worth everything, including the Magician. Besides, he is the one making this choice. It's his and his alone.

"You knew, didn't you?" she says, shaking her head at him.

"All along. Every damn thing you said, every riddle—this is what you were preparing for." She takes a step closer toward him, fists clenched. "And you didn't *tell* me."

The Magician's stars dim. "Would it have changed anything?"

She falters, her jaw working as tears spill down her face. "Yes. No—I don't know. You—" Her voice breaks, and she turns away.

The Magician reaches out, hesitant, as if he wants to touch her but doesn't dare. "It's because of you, Loviatar, that I can do this," he says gently. "You gave me a heart."

Her shoulders shake, but she doesn't respond.

Silence falls around us, the air tense with Lovia's heartbreak and the possibility of bringing our loved ones back. The idea of seeing Tuonen again nearly has me in pieces, but I try not to dwell on it, try not to get ahead of myself until I lay eyes on him and feel him in my arms.

Without much fanfare, the Magician turns to Hanna and says, "Do it," before stepping back into place.

Hanna looks at me briefly, her face lined with exhaustion, with fear, but also something else—a quiet, unshakable resolve. Hope. She nods once then turns toward the empty air before her. Golden light gathers at her fingertips, warm and fragile, as if she's holding the sunrise itself. It spreads outward slowly, waves of light rolling over the garden like a tide, chasing back the shadows. The Magician raises his arms as the glow washes over him. Starlight pours from him in answer, like a thousand embers scattering into the wind.

I watch as his form begins to unravel, the galaxies in his eyes spilling upward into the sky. His body disintegrates into a cascade of stars, glowing brighter and brighter as they rise, as though the heavens themselves are claiming him.

Lovia's anguished cry pierces the stillness, and she drops to her knees as he vanishes. I can't bear to look at her. It's a special thing to witness your child's first broken heart, and as trivial as it seems, I do feel her pain as my own and want to protect her from it.

But she will learn and grow in time.

The light that was the Magician grows brighter now, spreading across the garden, and then, just as suddenly as it began, it stops. For a moment, there's silence. The glow fades, leaving only the ruins of the garden and a cold, heavy stillness. My chest tightens.

Nothing happens.

I look around, the remaining Gods and troops who haven't gone home yet through the portal murmuring and whispering, fearing the sacrifice was made in vain.

Then, from beyond the garden wall, I hear it—footsteps.

Whispers.

I freeze, hardly daring to believe it as they come closer and closer, a murmuring crowd.

Slowly, I turn my head toward the gate, my heart thudding painfully in my chest, too afraid to hope.

Tuonen steps into view.

My son.

He walks toward me, his horns whole, his face young and alive again, his silver eyes wide with wonder. He looks at me, at the garden, and then his gaze locks onto mine. "Father?" he says softly.

The word shatters something inside me. I don't remember moving, but suddenly, I'm there, crushing him against my chest. My hands shake as I clutch him close, my breath ragged. He's real. He's warm. Alive.

"Tuonen," I choke out, my voice breaking. "Tuonen, my boy."

He clings to me just as tightly, murmuring words I can't hear over the sound of my own pounding heart. I don't care. I have him back. My son is back.

But it isn't just him.

From the garden gate, more figures emerge. Tapio steps forward, tall and strong, his antlered staff whole and gleaming. He walks arm-in-arm with Nyyrikki, his adult son, and Mielikki, his wife, their family of Forest Gods whole and complete again. Tapio nods toward me, his eyes filled with gratitude, and Tellervo cries out with unbridled joy as she runs across the garden right into their arms. Together, they topple into a patch of lemon balm and mint, laughing and crying, finally reunited.

Rasmus follows, his red hair bright as a flame. He gives Lovia a small, gentle smile as he passes. She's still kneeling, shaking, unable to look at him. He hesitates then kneels beside her, placing a hand on her shoulder. She doesn't resist —she just bows her head and weeps harder, her tears turning to ones of joy as they embrace. Torben joins them, pulling his estranged son into a hug and holding him tight.

General Pekka comes next, seemingly older now than when I first bestowed the title on him. He salutes me, a small, proud smile on his face while General Suvari and the rest of the army run toward him, hooting and hollering.

Then comes Ahto, my dear brother, a crown of coral and fishbone on his head, a trident in his hand. Vellamo yells for him and runs to his side, their reunion a little sadder when he realizes her injury. Still, they embrace, and he gives me a solemn wave. I wave back, eager to talk to him later.

After him comes Kalma, my old advisor, his wrinkled face smiling at me from under his hood. I didn't even know the guy had died, but that's probably a good thing. I'm happy he's back.

Behind him walks one of my Deadmaidens, veiled in black. For a moment, I think there has been a mistake, since they all turned against me in the end, but then Hanna runs toward her and pulls her into a hug. That's when I realize it's

Raila, Hanna's loyal servant, and the one who sacrificed her life for our escape when we were trying to get out of Inmost and into the Upper World. I'm briefly reminded that Raila is indeed an ugly as sin spider person underneath, one who ate her own children, but hey, she's one of us now.

More and more emerge—soldiers who fell in battle, allies we thought lost forever. They step into the garden like a tide of life rolling in, their faces shining with disbelief, relief, and joy. Even a unicorn steps out—Alku, I think its name is—and Sarvi immediately canters over to greet them.

But I'm back to watching Hanna as she pulls away from Raila and looks around. Tears streak Hanna's face as she watches the reunions, her hands trembling, the last remnants of her power flickering away like embers.

I look at her and finally see her for who she truly is—Hanna, the woman who saved us all; not just with her strength, but with her sacrifice. She gave up nearly everything she had left to bring them back, and though it cost her dearly, I can see the peace in her eyes.

"Are you all right?" I ask her softly as she comes over to me, Tuonen having gone to embrace Lovia.

She gives me a small, tired smile. "I will be."

"Do you feel anything? Other than all of this?" I gesture to the emotions flying around us.

"Maybe," she says, thinking it over. "A kernel of something, deep inside in my gut. I think I have some power left. Could be indigestion, though. It's hard to tell."

I can't help but laugh, the sound booming across the garden.

Fuck, that felt good.

From across the way, Tapio approaches me. He reaches out, clasping my arm in a warrior's grip.

"You brought us back," he says, voice thick with emotion. "Thank you."

"It wasn't me," I reply, glancing at Hanna, who now leans against Torben, utterly spent. "It was her."

Tapio bows his head toward her in silent respect before stepping back, his family gathering around him.

Rasmus and Tuonen are laughing with Lovia now. She still looks a little broken, but with them back, I think she'll manage.

The soldiers begin to mingle, laughter and tears mixing as they embrace, as they realize they have been given a second chance. Beyond the garden, the portal that Torben opened remains open for anyone who wants to return to their world.

And above us, even in the blue sky, you can see the stars. They burn brighter, shimmering like a thousand watchful eyes. I know the Magician is among them, guarding the void as he promised.

Hanna moves closer to me, her face soft, peaceful despite the tears still tracking her cheeks. "We're whole again," she says quietly.

I nod, glancing around the garden at all we had lost and all we gained. "We are."

CHAPTER FORTY-THREE

LOVIA

THE LIBRARY OF THE VEILS WAS ONCE A PLACE OF QUIET majesty, a sanctuary of knowledge, an encyclopedia of lives and souls. Now, it feels hollow, as though the air itself mourns its desecration. The stained glass windows still hold their vibrant colors—pale golds and violets, deep blues and greens—but the light they cast is dulled by dust and grime. Broken shelves and scattered books lie everywhere, some pages torn free and others soaked with dark stains. The lingering residue of Louhi's foul magic hangs in the corners, like cobwebs spun of shadow.

It has been a week since the final battle.

A week since we lost the Magician.

And we have so much cleaning up to do.

I kneel beside a heap of books, carefully sorting through them, running my fingers over frayed bindings as though they're fragile, living things. The act of rebuilding this place, of putting the pieces back together, gives me something to focus on, something to keep my hands busy while the weight in my chest festers quietly.

Rasmus works nearby, his voice a low hum as he mutters

shamanic incantations. He moves along the edges of the library, casting charms to cleanse the space of lingering corruption. Pale smoke drifts upward from his hands, curling through the air like silvered thread.

I watch him for a moment. He's focused, eyes narrowed, brow furrowed. The scars on his arms—old burns from Rangaista, etched like veins of memory—seem to gleam faintly under the light filtering through the windows. For all the sorrow I feel over the Magician, it can't compare with how happy I am that Tuonen is back—and Rasmus too.

The silence between us is comfortable, or at least, I want to think it is. I pick up another book and carefully wipe the dust from its cover.

"You're staring at me," Rasmus says suddenly, not looking up from his work.

I blink, startled. "I'm not."

He glances over his shoulder, one brow raised, the faintest ghost of a smirk on his lips. "You were. Am I not performing the magic to your satisfaction?"

"I'm sure it will do," I reply. "I was just…thinking."

Rasmus straightens, letting the spell settle into the air like a gentle exhale. "Dangerous habit, that, especially for you."

I glare at him, though there's no heat behind it. He teases me a lot, like the newfound brother he is. A real nuisance, if you ask me.

He walks toward me, brushing his hands clean on the edge of his cloak. For someone who has spent so much of his life walking the line between betrayal and redemption, Rasmus seems oddly steady now, as though he has finally found his place—or at least a purpose—in the aftermath of war. I envy that steadiness. I envy a lot of things these days.

"What are you thinking about?" he asks, crouching down across from me. His tone is light, casual, but I can see the careful way he watches me—like he already knows the answer.

I look away, focusing on a book in my lap. The leather is cracked, the lettering faded, but I trace it with my fingertips anyway. My throat feels tight.

"The Magician," I say quietly.

Rasmus doesn't respond right away. He waits, his gaze steady, letting the words settle in the space between us. Finally, he says, "You miss him."

The admission comes before I can stop it. "Of course, I miss him."

I swallow hard, frustrated at how weak I sound. I haven't allowed myself to say those words aloud until now. I haven't let myself speak of him at all. I thought holding it inside would make it easier—that if I ignored the hollow ache in my chest, it might go away.

It hasn't.

"I didn't even know what he meant to me until he was gone," I continue, my voice quiet. "He always knew. He *knew,* Rasmus. He acted like such an arrogant, maddening…oh, I don't know what the hell he was, but he was something all right. And all the while, he knew this was his fate. And I couldn't stop it. I couldn't change it."

Rasmus's expression softens, though he doesn't say anything. What could he say? There is nothing left. I grip the book in my hands tighter, feeling the edges bite into my palms.

"I keep expecting him to step out from the shadows," I go on, fully unloading now. "To smirk at me and say something cryptic. To ask if I'm still following the plan—his plan. Because he always had one, didn't he?" My voice shakes, and I hate myself for it. "He always knew what to do, and I'm left here, trying to make sense of it all."

I stop speaking, realizing my hands are trembling. I set

the book down carefully and press my palms flat against the floor, grounding myself. The Magician wouldn't want me like this. He wouldn't want me falling apart.

"He would say something infuriating, wouldn't he?" Rasmus says gently, and when I look up at him, his lips are curved into a sad smile. "Something about fate and consequences and how it had to be this way, how everything is one big fucking tapestry. He'd act like it didn't matter that he was gone, as if his own sacrifice was inconsequential. As if it didn't hurt you."

I nod, my throat tightening again. Rasmus understands more than I thought he would. He has been here before—been the one left behind, wrestling with grief and guilt. Maybe that's why it's easier to talk to him now, why I can say these things I've held onto for the past week.

"He was infuriating," I agree, forcing a weak laugh. "I hated how much he always seemed to know, how he never gave a straight answer. Made me want to scream sometimes."

"And yet you loved him for it," Rasmus says softly.

I freeze, my heart stuttering in my chest. The word hangs between us, sharp and undeniable. *Love.*

I want to deny it. I want to tell him he's wrong, that I didn't love the Magician—couldn't possibly love someone so enigmatic. He was the damn universe. He even knew I didn't love him, like he knew everything else.

But the words die in my throat; the truth is written all over my face, and Rasmus knows it.

"I don't know what I felt for him," I tell him. "Maybe it was love. Maybe it wasn't. But whatever it was, it's gone now, and it fucking hurts."

Rasmus leans back slightly, resting his arms on his knees. He doesn't push me to say more. Instead, he reaches for one of the books beside him and turns it over in his hands, as though inspecting it. His gaze remains thoughtful, distant.

"Grief isn't supposed to make sense," he says finally. "You can spend years trying to define it, trying to make it smaller, trying to understand why it hurts so much, but in the end, it's just...there, like a shadow that follows you no matter where you go."

"Great. That's comforting," I mutter.

He snorts softly. "I'm a shaman, not a poet. Forgive me if I don't have the right words."

I manage a small, tired smile. "No. You're doing good."

"He wouldn't want you to sit in this forever," he says after a moment.

I nod, though it doesn't make the ache lessen any. "I know. But it's still hard."

"Then let it be hard," Rasmus says simply. "Let yourself miss him. Let yourself hate him for leaving. And let yourself remember him. Because the alternative is forgetting, and we both know he deserves better than that."

His words hit harder than I expect. My chest tightens again, but this time, it doesn't feel like drowning. It feels like a release—like something inside me is finally breaking loose. I wipe my eyes quickly, pretending it's just dust, and thankfully, Rasmus doesn't comment. He just goes back to sorting books, his movements slow and deliberate.

The silence that follows is different. Lighter, somehow. The shadows in the corners of the library seem less oppressive, and the faint glow from the windows feels brighter, like the sun is reaching us for the first time.

I pick up another book, my hands steadier now. Rasmus works beside me, muttering incantations, his quiet presence a strange comfort. And for the first time since the Magician disappeared into the stars, I let myself hope that maybe, someday, this ache will be something I can carry—a shadow, yes, but one that doesn't swallow the light entirely.

For now, it's enough to keep rebuilding, to put the pieces back together, one fragile step at a time.

THAT NIGHT, I stand by my window, staring out into the inky darkness. The world beyond Shadow's End is quiet, cloaked in stillness, the sea crashing beneath us. For a long while, I see nothing but endless shadow and the faint outline of the distant mountains. My breath fogs the glass as I lean forward, my forehead resting against it.

Then, faintly, something catches my eye.

A shooting star.

Then another one, lighting up the sky before disappearing.

The stars are brighter tonight, as though the heavens themselves have been scrubbed clean. They glimmer like shards of silver, scattered across the black canvas. I stare at them, my chest tightening as I recall his voice—the Magician's steady words, his infuriating not-smile.

And for a heartbeat, I swear, the stars wink at me.

I stare, breath catching. My hands curl against the windowsill.

It's him. I don't know how or why, but I know it.

He's up there, watching.

He's all of it, everything.

"You always knew, didn't you?" I whisper to the night.

The stars don't answer. They just gleam, constant and eternal, but it's enough. A small smile tugs at my lips, the ache in my chest easing ever so slightly.

"I miss you," I say softly, the words carried away by the wind.

The stars shimmer once more—a silent acknowledgment, a promise that he's not truly gone.

And for the first time in days, I don't feel so alone.

CHAPTER FORTY-FOUR

HANNA

"My queen," Raila says, appearing in the doorway to the solar room where I'm sitting by the massive windows, savoring the last of my morning coffee in the sunlight. "There's someone approaching the castle."

I twist to face her, suddenly alert. The snowbird chirps in alarm from its perch in the corner of the room.

"Who? Where is Tuoni?"

"He's already gone to meet them. I came to inform you."

I slurp back the precious dregs and place the cup down before rising, a flutter of panic in my chest. It has been a few weeks now since we reclaimed Tuonela, and it has been quiet, if not busy, as we rebuild, all threats seemingly eradicated. And yet, I'm still as jumpy as ever.

"Well, do you know who it is?" I ask.

She dips her chin beneath her veil. "Your father said it's the disgraced shaman, Ilmarinen."

What the hell?

"Thank you, Raila."

I gather up the ends of my burgundy dress and hurry out of the room, the snowbird flying behind me. Ever since it returned to Shadow's End in the middle of the night, it has been following me and Tuoni everywhere. I don't really speak bird, despite my nickname, but I have the distinct impression that when my husband sent it to find his sister, Ilmatar, the bird ended up staying with her until the coast was clear and Tuonela was back in order. Can't say I blame it. At least it's not attacking Tuoni like it used to do, as funny as it was.

Damn, this castle is big, I think to myself, descending staircase after staircase as I race to the bottom. Sometimes, when I'm truly lazy, I find Sarvi and ask the unicorn to fly me down, broken horn and all. What good is being a queen if you can't have a flying unicorn transport you from time to time?

Finally, I burst out of the giant main doors and cross the drawbridge to see Tuoni, Sarvi, my father, and Rasmus gathered on the road around the other shaman. Ilmarinen looks worse for wear as he staggers toward the castle, my father and Rasmus holding him up.

"What's going on?" I ask as they approach. I peer curiously at Ilmarinen. "Where the hell did you go and what the hell are you doing here?"

"He was off being a coward," Rasmus says snidely. "He's been hiding all around Tuonela while the war raged on, too afraid to show himself."

"I'm sorry," Ilmarinen says weakly. "I just couldn't do it. I don't have your strength. She took it all from me."

I look over his head at my husband standing behind him. He's wearing one of his skull masks for the first time in ages, probably to intimidate the shaman. "He begged us for forgiveness," Tuoni says. "What do you think, my queen?"

I look into Ilmarinen's pleading eyes. They seem so broken by the world that I can't help but give in a little.

"Well, I think he was corrupted and tortured by Louhi for so long that perhaps we can be a little lenient?"

Rasmus scoffs, enough to draw a glare from me. "What? You're one to talk," I say to my half-brother. "You deserve forgiveness for being a rat bastard, and yet he doesn't? You were both corrupted by the same demon."

"Hey," my father chides, offended by my choice of words.

"Rat bastard is a figure of speech," I assure him—though, I mean, my father has been kind of a rat at times. Rasmus, me, and even Salainen are proof of that. He's a man with as many faults as me, but I love him anyway.

Rasmus grumbles but says nothing more. Ever since being brought back from the dead, he has found a way to annoy me at every turn. I suppose that's what brothers are good for. Since I grew up without any siblings, I can only guess, though I have to admit, I do like having him around. It makes our family seem bigger, and since he lives with my father in the farthest wing of Shadow's End, if either of them get on my nerves, they're easy to avoid.

I look at my husband. "I say we take Ilmarinen into the fold—but he can work for us and earn our trust."

Tuoni grins, always ready to dole out some form of punishment. He has been looking for new help ever since the troops went back to the Upper World through the portal. Only General Pekka stayed behind. The fact that he died and came back had broken through Tuoni's mental hold on him, and when he realized everything that had happened, the truth about us and the Underworld, he decided he wanted to stay. He now does odd jobs Tuoni sends him on, including going through the portal to procure the God's various addictions from the Upper World, though I think he'll eventually become an advisor, just like Kalma.

"The queen has spoken," my husband says, and I step out of the way as they lead Ilmarinen toward the moat.

"Hey!" I yell after them. "If you see Lovia, tell her I need a rematch!"

Will do, Sarvi says, hooves echoing on the drawbridge as they all disappear into the castle. *She'll be eager to watch you lose again.*

I can't help but laugh. Lovia and I have kept on our training. We might not have any enemies to fight anymore, but sparring is good exercise. Sometimes, Tuonen joins in, besting us both. The two of them have a lot of time to do what they want, now that the River of Shadows has an ice bridge across it, connecting Death's Landing to the Frozen Void. It's not the most welcoming spot for the newly dead, but the Keskelli trolls have taken it upon themselves to be something akin to both a toll booth operator (a *troll* booth operator?) and welcome wagon, the five of them taking shifts.

I know that both siblings have their sights set on going to the Upper World, though they promise to return to Tuonela one day. Lovia still wants to explore the world like a tourist and have various affairs (she says it will take a lot of guys to make her forget what sleeping with the universe was like, to which I say, good luck with that), and Tuonen has some mysterious rendezvous set with someone at some point in time. Whenever I ask, though, he never elaborates further. Fine, I've said, keep your secrets. The point is, the two of them are finally free of their roles in the Underworld, and it has been joyful to watch them rediscover themselves and find their agency.

I look over my shoulder at Tuonela, vast and macabre and wild, feeling the cool breeze blow back my hair and ruffle my dress. The surrounding sea is full of white caps, but I know somewhere beneath the surface, Bell swims again, along with Vellamo and Ahto. Vellamo's arm has even started to grow back, made of tiny coral that's slowly rebuilding.

It may have only been weeks since our lives returned to order, but I've never felt closer to the land.

Or to the heavens.

I glance up at the sun, which is unable to burn my eyes. I still have remnants of my power, able to create flames of my own doing. It's not much—like having lighters for fingers—but I still think it's cool, in an *Edward Scissorhands* kind of way.

Whether my mother is watching or not, I wave at her. She's somewhere up there in the blue sky, now with Vipunen, who has abandoned his cave to watch over things from a more distant position. Apparently, he chose the caves long ago to keep an eye on the God of Death and his family, but now that everything is in its right place, he has ascended to the next level of his Godliness.

Or my mother is holding the giant hostage. Though she seems to be an unfeeling entity, something tells me divine romance might be in the air. We'll see.

I continue to look around, my eyes scanning the snow-capped mountains. Somewhere beyond the ranges, the dead live. They aren't allowed to pass through Death's Passage—everything from there to here is off-limits—but the rest of Tuonela has been repopulated, eons worth of souls making new lives for themselves in every corner of the land. I've flown over the settlements a few times on Sarvi, watching as they build. It's like observing the dawn of civilization, and it's nothing if not humbling.

I might be a Goddess of Death and of Light, but I hope I never lose my sense of awe for humanity.

And that includes myself.

LATER THAT NIGHT, I lay curled in my husband's strong arms. We find solace in each other's company every chance we get. You'd think we're newlyweds, bonking away like bunnies, but it's pretty much true. This is the first time I have felt truly united with him, in our home, in our realm.

This is the first time I feel like I truly belong to him.

And he truly belongs to me.

That's what changed.

"I love you," Tuoni murmurs as he kisses me softly on my head. "I love you, Hanna, to the void and back."

My heart blooms within my chest, delight weaving through me. When I was in Goddess mode, in the hot springs with Tuoni, and he finally told me he loved me, I felt it. I didn't know it at the time, but it reached deep, breaking through my icy veneer. It found the heart and soul of me, and it planted itself, growing there. I think that's what got through to me in the end—the seeds of love he planted grew and blossomed until, finally, they were bigger than the whole sky, brighter than any sun.

I think that love saved me in the end. It gave me the courage I needed to become who I was meant to be, to embrace who I truly am: messy, complicated, and flawed.

And someone worth loving.

"I love you too," I say, gazing up at him, taking in the sight of his beautiful eyes, the silver bright against the black kohl. "Though I think you need to tell me that more often, to make up for all the times I told you and you didn't say anything. Talk about hanging me out to dry."

"You didn't say it *that* much," he says, grumbling. "How about I show you? You know me; I've never been very good with words."

So, I let him show me, since he *is* very good at that.

He takes me again, from behind this time, like the old days, both of us coming quickly, our bodies forever a hair trigger. I collapse into the bed once more, catching my breath before curling up beside him.

"I can call you Death," I whisper to him. "And now, I can call you mine."

Then, I reach up and tap him on the nose. "Boop."

He bursts out laughing and lets out a playful growl as he goes on the attack, smothering me with his body and tickling me all over.

Laughter and joy seizes me, burning impossibly bright, and we nestle back onto the covers, becoming one again.

ACKNOWLEDGMENTS

I'm keeping this short but sweet (for real this time), though I have an insurmountable amount of people to thank.

First of all, I want to say what a long, strange journey this series has been. I truly can't believe this is the last book and it is DONE. At times this series has really tested me, but it's these characters that held me together and kept me going. I truly love Death and Hanna Heikkinen, as well as Lovia, Tuonen, Sarvi, even that rat-bastard Rasmus. These characters are real to me and it's been a pleasure to channel their stories straight from Tuonela and into the pages.

I had the idea for River of Shadows back in 2018, maybe. Back then I thought it was going to be YA series, because back then adult romantasy was not the thing it was today. I ended up shelving the idea because I didn't know when I'd have time to write it, all I knew was that I wanted to write a series based loosely on the epic Kalevala, and Finnish mythology. Being a Finnish citizen myself, I was always drawn to the macabre world of my mother and my ancestors, and I wanted to bring it to life, showcasing a lesser known story of Gods and Goddesses.

But it wasn't until after my father had died that River of Shadows was born. Only then did I realize what true grief was, and I knew that if I were Hanna, I would travel to the ends of the world to bring him back. I still would.

So in January 2022, just months after my father and brother passed on, I brought Tuonela to life. I poured my heart and soul into the characters, and in a way it helped heal me in return. Though the road to series completion had many delays and ups and downs as I waited for my muse to come back, I'm glad I saw it all through to the end (though, just in case you're wondering, there is no novella called God of Death. That was an idea I had, a prequel to the series that I announced prematurely before I even wrote River of Shadows! But in the end I thought, you know what? I really don't care about how Tuoni and Louhi split up lol. So I abandoned it. That said, an epilogue featuring all four POVS is in the future. Follow me on IG or sign up for my newsletter via the link in my LinkTree, as I'll have more deets on how you can access the epilogue in the new year!).

Anyway, so much for keeping it short.

I'd like to thank so many people who helped bring this series to life over the years, and in no particular order: Laura Helseth, Stephanie Brown, Alexa Thomas, Lauren Cox, Rachel Whitehurst, Sandra Cortez, Jen Watson, Nina Grinstead, Kathleen Tucker, Catherine Glavin, Jessica Burke, Chanpreet Singh, Aubrey Vasquez, Justine Woods, Hang Le, plus my agent Taylor Haggerty, and my foreign agent Heather Shapiro. And the readers who have been so damn supportive of me and their passion for this series!

Last but not least, my wonderful husband Scott, my soul dog Bruce (may you forever live in Rauta), my very distracting puppy Perry, my Finnish mother Tuuli Halle and all her "sisu," and of course my brother and father, Sven and Kristian Halle. I'm sorry you never got to see this series publish, but I feel you in Tuonela anyway, watching it all unfold. I love you.

ABOUT THE AUTHOR

Karina Halle is a screenwriter, a former music & travel journalist, and the New York Times, Wall Street Journal, and USA Today bestselling author of River of Shadows, The Royals Next Door, and Black Sunshine, as well as 80 other wild and romantic reads, ranging from light & sexy rom coms to horror/paranormal romance and dark fantasy. Needless to say, whatever genre you're into, she has probably written a romance for it.

When she's not traveling, she, her husband Scott, and their pup Perry, split their time between a possibly haunted, 120-year-old house in Victoria, BC, their sailboat the Norfinn, and their condo in Los Angeles. For more information, visit www.authorkarinahalle.com

Find her on Facebook, Instagram, Pinterest, BookBub, Amazon, and Tik Tok.

ALSO BY KARINA HALLE

DARK FANTASY, GOTHIC & HORROR ROMANCE

River of Shadows (Underworld Gods #1)

Crown of Crimson (Underworld Gods #2)

City of Darkness (Underworld Gods #3)

Goddess of Light (Underworld Gods #4)

Black Sunshine (Dark Eyes Duet #1)

The Blood is Love (Dark Eyes Duet #2)

Nightwolf

Blood Orange (The Dracula Duet #1)

Black Rose (The Dracula Duet #2)

A Ship of Bones and Teeth

Ocean of Sin and Starlight

Hollow (A Gothic Shade of Romance #1)

Legend (A Gothic Shade of Romance #2)

Grave Matter

Darkhouse (EIT #1)

Red Fox (EIT #2)

The Benson (EIT #2.5)

Dead Sky Morning (EIT #3)

Lying Season (EIT #4)

On Demon Wings (EIT #5)

Old Blood (EIT #5.5)

The Dex-Files (EIT #5.7)

Into the Hollow (EIT #6)

And With Madness Comes the Light (EIT #6.5)

Come Alive (EIT #7)

Ashes to Ashes (EIT #8)

Dust to Dust (EIT #9)

Ghosted (EIT #9.5)

Came Back Haunted (EIT #10)

The Devil's Metal (The Devil's Duology #1)

The Devil's Reprise (The Devil's Duology #2)

Veiled (Ada Palomino #1)

Song For the Dead (Ada Palomino #2)

CONTEMPORARY ROMANCE

Love, in English/Love, in Spanish

Where Sea Meets Sky

Racing the Sun

The Pact

The Offer

The Play

Winter Wishes

The Lie

The Debt

Smut

Heat Wave

Before I Ever Met You

After All

Rocked Up

Wild Card

Maverick

Hot Shot

Bad at Love

The Swedish Prince

The Wild Heir

A Nordic King

The Royal Rogue

Nothing Personal

My Life in Shambles

The Royal Rogue

The Forbidden Man

The One That Got Away

Lovewrecked

One Hot Italian Summer

All the Love in the World (Anthology)

The Royals Next Door

The Royals Upstairs

ROMANTIC SUSPENSE

Sins and Needles (The Artists Trilogy #1)

On Every Street (An Artists Trilogy Novella #0.5)

Shooting Scars (The Artists Trilogy #2)

Bold Tricks (The Artists Trilogy #3)

Dirty Angels (Dirty Angels #1)

Dirty Deeds (Dirty Angels #2)

Dirty Promises (Dirty Angels #3)

Black Hearts (Sins Duet #1)

Dirty Souls (Sins Duet #2)

Discretion (Dumonts #1)

Disarm (Dumonts #2)

Disavow (Dumonts #3)

Made in the USA
Las Vegas, NV
28 December 2024

15493405R00256